The

FALLEN
MAN

The
FALLEN MAN

The Olympic Peninsula Series # 5

Cat Treadgold

The Fallen Man
ISBN: 979-8-9877363-5-7 (Trade Paperback)
ISBN: 979-8-9877363-6-4 (eBook)

Library of Congress Control Number: 2024906485

Any references to historical events, real people, or real places are used fictitiously. Names of restaurants and companies central to the plot are products of the author's imagination.

Cover design by Gemma Rakia @gemmarakia
Interior design by Cat Treadgold
Anacortes, Washington
Cat@CatTreadgold.com
www.CatTreadgold.com

Printed in the United States of America

To all the wonderful women in my life, starting with my sister Laura. My sisters-in-law Wanda and Cheryl and my daughters-in-law Laura and Marta. My sisters from another mother, Tina, Karin, Anna, Wendy, and Jill. And all the women who have provided love and support over the years. I don't get to see you in person nearly enough.

The Olympic Peninsula Series

The Silent Woodsman
The Guardsman
The Magic Man
The Changed Man
The Fallen Man

Beyond the Olympic

Peninsula series

Mister Movie Star

Coming Soon:
Miz Country Goddess

Mister Heartbreaker

CONTENTS

PART I

CHAPTER 1

TINKER, TAILOR, SOLDIER, SAILOR; RICH man, poor man, beggar man, priest ….

No, that wasn't right. No priest in that nursery rhyme. Who will I marry, the girls asked themselves. "Priest" wasn't an option, though "thief" was. Go figure. Edward was—officially—still a priest. The Church held you in its talons with the strength and tenacity of a harpy eagle. The wheels of laicization turned ever so slowly. Only the pope himself could release you from the vow of celibacy. Someday Edward would be free, but he would never marry. He was still a rich man, thank ⁚… Who to thank now? Not God.

A poem came to mind: "A book of verses beneath the bough; a jug of wine, a loaf of bread, and Thou." "The Rubaiyat," by Omar Khayaam, all the rage in Edward's day. His day. His youth, that is. "Every dog has its day." "Day is done, gone the sun." He looked down at his book. Not a book of verses, but his brother's thriller, *Kapow*, the series opener. Good stuff, hardly poetry. A gripping thriller in a cozy café; a stein of Guinness, a bowl of gumbo, and …." What rhymed with café? He had no "Thou." "A roll in the hay." Or maybe, "a great lay."

"Hello."

He looked up at the woman, feigning surprise, as if he hadn't been drooling over her for the last hour. She pranced around the café on her stacked sandals like a beautiful wild mare, her impossibly long, firm legs peeking through the slit in her pencil skirt. A long plait of shiny black hair hung halfway down her back. Her eyes were … green. A deep, complex range of greens and golds—all the colors of the rain forest. Her complexion was creamy and sun-kissed. She had to be sick to death of oglers like him.

"Would you like anything else?" she asked in her low, sultry voice. She pointed at his empty stein. "The kitchen is closed until dinner, but I can bring you another beer. Guinness?"

How did she know? She hadn't taken his order. He looked at his watch. Two thirty. "I should clear out so you can prep for dinner," he said uncertainly.

"Nonsense. Hang on."

She was back in a flash with a Guinness for him and a glass of water for herself. "On the house." She slid into the chair across from him, crossing her long legs. "You're turning into a regular. I know the gumbo is good, but you should give something else a try. The shrimp étouffée, for instance."

Ah, she'd been watching him too. This was his third visit.

"Lisette Manegold." She extended her graceful hand with its manicured, short red nails. Then retracted the offer as if fearing he might not consider her a social equal.

He'd been too slow to react. Folding his hands on the table, he said, "*Your* café, then. Why Cajun? Are you French?"

"Not that I know of. Mostly Polish on my Dad's side. Irish on my mother's. I was born and raised in New Jersey. A tourist town. Cape May."

"You have a French mouth." She blushed, and he winced. The observation had been insanely personal. He was woefully out of practice in polite society. He'd meant that her lips were full, luscious, and drooped sensually at the corners. Until she smiled, which she did now.

"If I'm not mistaken, you're an O'Connell brother. Edward? The *priest*."

The word was loaded enough to flatten him.

"Oi, that sounded bad," she added quickly. "Not a criticism. Like Father Ralph de Bricassart. Handsome, like him." She wiped her brow. "Phew. Can we start over?"

"Never read it," Edward said, acknowledging the reference to *The Thorn Birds*. It wasn't the first time he'd been compared to Father Ralph. Had the fictional priest ended up leaving the church for the sake of love? He thought not. Probably came to a bad end. "*Former* priest," he clarified. "I had a parish in Philadelphia. A hop, skip, and a jump away from Cape May."

"Ah." A more vehement shake of the head. "Haven't been home since I graduated high school. My restaurant's first location was in Port Angeles." She sounded wistful. "Probably should have stayed put."

"Why the move?"

Her smile didn't reach her eyes this time. The pause might mean she was inventing a lie. "It seemed time for a change. I still own the building. Here I only rent. Port Townsend generally has a more sophisticated clientele." She grinned. "Doesn't mean they don't enjoy karaoke. I limit that to one night a week."

The silence lingered.

"My real name isn't Lisette," she confessed. "It's Leslie. But I hate that name. I wasn't too fond of Leslie the woman, either. That phase in my life. So now it's Lisette."

Ah, interesting. Edward had a talent for eliciting confessions. Her blush told him she wished she could take it back. Most Leslies reinvented as Lisettes would feel the same.

She stood and said in a more formal tone, "If you'll excuse me, I have work to do before we open for dinner."

"Of course." Before she could anticipate him, he reached for her hand and felt a jolt of connection. Nothing more, he was relieved to note. That is, no messages from beyond. He did enjoy the feel of her slim, cool fingers. He gave the hand a little shake before releasing it. Seeing how the gesture unbalanced her, he regretted the impulse. Now he was just another handsy man wanting a piece of her. But that wasn't the vibe he got from her. Regaining her composure, she gave him a friendly nod before disappearing into the kitchen. If only he could invite her back to his hotel.

He left a twenty-dollar bill on the table and headed out onto Water Street, festooned for Christmas with reams of colored lights like the Victorian town it was, eager to bank on the season. Lisette's home town of Cape May was another Victorian seaside village, only with white-sand beaches and water warm enough for swimming, at least in the summer.

Edward vastly preferred this version of Christmas—a fantastical season of goodwill and largesse presided over by a jolly old elf—to the solemn celebration of Christ's birth chosen by the Church to coincide with Winter Solstice. He no longer resented the Church, just wanted nothing more to do with it. All of it: the baby Jesus, the suffering and bloody Christ on the cross, the blessed Virgin Mary, the Holy Trinity. He thought of the deacon who had tried to frame him and sought once again to banish the lowdown skunk from his mind. If not for his special abilities, Edward would still be mired in that mess. Instead he was free. "Free to be you and me," someone had said. Marlo Thomas. Snippets like that, a jumble of thoughts from his secular past, kept popping into his head. What did it mean to be free to be … him? Shouldn't it be "he"? Technically.

The air was crisp, cool, and briny, and he pulled up the collar of his cashmere peacoat and adjusted his scarf, taking a moment to observe a freighter far out in the bay. The old children's song, "Barges," came to mind.

Barges, I would like to go with you,
I would like to sail the ocean blue.
Barges, is there treasure in your hold?
Do you fight with pirates, brave and bold.

Nope, no more sailing off into adventure. Not for him. He thought he understood why his restless family had resettled here, leaving the cruel world behind. They wanted—and deserved—an explanation for his self-imposed exile. All in good time. Unlike him, they were fundamentally nice people.

He climbed the Terrace Steps, the long staircase that began at Haller Fountain and was presided over by a lovely naked nymph. He could use a tumble with someone like that. He wondered if Lisette was dating anyone. She seemed interested. Or maybe, being in the hospitality industry, she treated everyone like that. He'd gone a little wild since leaving the priesthood. It was a short leap from total celibacy back to sexual profligacy. Not much in between for a guy like him. *You can't continue on the road to ruin in Port Townsend*, he reminded himself. *This town is too small.* Perhaps that was why he'd chosen this destination after the debauched sojourn in Paris. For some reason, he'd been drawn to the idea of a family Thanksgiving, and his mother had convinced him that his return to the fold would be celebrated with a fatted lamb. Or in this case, a not-so-fatted wild turkey. Not that he'd been prodigal. He *had* been judgmental, but the reason wasn't simple. "Lead us not into temptation," the Lord's Prayer said. Not, "Keep us from sinning."

Edward had toyed with the idea of visiting the O'Connell Compound ever since he first began tracking his family's life events and scandals in the press—tabloid and otherwise. First Joe's career as a country music idol had been stalled by vocal nodules; then he'd married a normal woman he'd rescued in the woods. As normal as a blazingly blue-eyed, golden-skinned goddess could be. A man would give up a lot for a woman like that. The requiem for Joe's career had been premature. Fickle as his vocal cords remained, he still pulled off the occasional tour.

Their sister Teresa's run-in with some local thug had led to her marrying Liam—the twin brother of Ali, Joe's wife. Liam might be even more beautiful than his sister, despite the shrapnel scars. Those otherworldly blue eyes had been passed on to Joe and Ali's identical twin girls.

David had returned from practicing medicine in Africa and was now a script doctor. His nubile actress wife had done exactly one movie, where her bountiful charms were on full display, and it was unclear if she intended to keep her Screen Actors Guild membership current. Edward had seen that movie, titled *Insanity*, at the Rose, Port Townsend's historic theater, now a movie house. David was a lucky man.

Jake was shacking up with a married woman in a rented Victorian B&B, having abandoned his position as CEO of the family business to write bestselling novels.

In short, while Edward lost ten years caught up in a series of, in retrospect, meaningless rituals, his siblings had been busy. They were all here now. He'd tried a little familial bonding on Thanksgiving, but his mother kept pulling him back to her side as if he were six years old and liable to wander off and be devoured by a cougar or a grizzly bear. Or was she afraid he'd leave her to the mercy of the savages? She'd been surprisingly upset when he'd chosen to stay behind while she and Rostand returned to Seattle. Enough to rend her garments, had they lived in biblical times. Or maybe not. Her garments were far too expensive and well-tailored. Jake and Teresa had submitted to her formidable will for years. Had she believed that Edward would take their place?

He was staying in a suite at the Bishop Hotel on Washington Street, even though Joe and Ali had offered one of their guest cabins. He'd go it alone for now. Baby steps.

He didn't know the address but had been told that Teresa's office was located on the edges of the business district on Lawrence Street. *Ah*, there it was, a Victorian sorely in need of TLC. The sign read,

TERESA O'CONNELL RYAN, INTERIOR DESIGN
OFFICE HOURS 9-11 & 1-3—OR BY APPOINTMENT

It was almost three. Should Edward have made an appointment? He rang the doorbell. If no one answered, he'd call Teresa on her cell.

The door was opened by a young woman. *Cleopatra*, he thought. Tilted eyes, a full red mouth, fine, dusky skin, and a long, aquiline nose. Average height, something like five-five. Voluptuous but slim. *Wow.* Young. *Too young for you, old man.*

"I'm—"

"Edward," she broke in. "Can I call you Eddy?" She grinned. Her voice was … tart. Acidic. But also teasing. To him, "Eddy" was a small whirlpool.

"No." He grew flustered.

"Ed?" She tilted her head.

"Eddy sounds like the neighborhood cutup and Ed could be a killer for hire. I've never been particularly fond of 'Edward,' but it's the best of the alternatives and I'm stuck with it." His middle name was "Pilkington." She'd have a field day with that. She was too cheeky by half. Physically, undeniably gorgeous. But too "cute" and not in a positive sense. Immature. Just as well. He didn't want to be attracted to Teresa's … whatever.

"I'm your sister's apprentice," the woman explained. "Xenia Britt."

"Interesting name. Celtic?"

She shrugged. "With a name like Xenia, I would assume Greek or Russian, wouldn't you? I never knew my mother. She gave me up, left me on the steps of some church in Seattle with a card that read, 'This is Xenia. Please take care of her.' I chose 'Britt' at random when no one adopted me. I was raised by foster parents. You know, a FOSSP kid."

He waited for more information.

"Foster Splash Pad, Ali and Joe's non-profit? They help foster children who've aged out of the system get on their feet." He must have still appeared puzzled because she added, "Ali and Liam were foster children. Come on, you knew that, right?"

He didn't know much, and that was a fact, as her condescending tone reminded him. "Sure," he said. Someone, namely Teresa, needed to bring him up to speed. "Where is Teresa, by the way?"

Xenia pouted. "I'm boring you."

"Not at all. I'm highly entertained." Had that sounded sarcastic? He didn't enjoy being teased. Xenia was making him feel like the nerdy kid in junior high you could mock to his face. He'd never been *that* kid. "I'll catch up with her later." As he turned to leave, his delighted sister walked into the room.

"Eddy!" she cried and gave him a giant hug. He grimaced, kept his hands in the air. Now Xenia would never call him anything else. Not that he planned to seek out her company in the future.

"Hey, Teresa," he said, not using his nickname for her, Ter-Ter. He hoped she'd catch on and call him by his adult name too.

"Come with me," she said, dragging him into the kitchen. "I'll make us tea."

"Why don't we go out?" The last thing he wanted was for Xenia to overhear their conversation.

"Okay, sure. There's a café a few doors away. They have these little butter cookies I adore. Xenia, I'm going out again."

Once they were seated in the coffee shop, Edward asked, "How long have you been … mentoring Xenia?"

"I dunno, a few months? I'm teaching her all the stuff Mom passed on to Jake and me about antiques, furniture styles, rugs, whatever. She's a quick study. We all help out with the FOSSP kids in any way we can. Sharing our talents, such as they are. Liam teaches them 'shop' skills like woodworking. Jean-Louis has discovered some gifted chefs and hired others—the best-looking men of the bunch, mostly—as waiters. Others help out with clean-up and child care at the compound for overly generous hourly rates and a leg-up on their college careers. The majority live in FOSSP housing in town, but Joe and Ali bought the house just down the road so the ones who work at the compound don't need to own cars or travel late at night. Jake does some grammar tutoring, Chiara some informal counseling. Like that. Don't priests do counseling? You speak fluent French and Italian. You could get involved."

He shook his head. "I won't be here that long."

Her chuckle was half-hearted. "We all say that."

"How far along are you?" he asked. "May I?"

"Of course." She held his hand to her baby bump. "Just over seven months."

A girl, he thought. *She'll be born too quickly. Someone needs to know that's going to happen and prepare.*

"What?!" From her look of alarm, his dismay must have been transparent.

"Nothing. Just wondering at the miracle of, uh, procreation. Are you happy?" *She is now*, he thought. *The marriage was shaky for a while.*

"Of course!" she said. "I'm having a girl. You know me. I will adore dressing her."

Her husband is afraid she'll spoil her, Edward thought. *Damn*. He shouldn't have touched her. He willed the messages to stop, and strangely enough, they did.

"Are you still at the Bishop? You should stay with us. Liam's house"—she caught herself—"*our* house is only a few blocks away. Or stay at my office. There are bedrooms upstairs."

"Bedrooms, plural?"

"Xenia is staying in one of them, but they have ensuite bathrooms."

No way, he thought with an inward shudder. "I'm fine for now," he told her.

"Come to dinner this evening. Liam is cooking spaghetti and meatballs. He always makes enough for an army."

"Thanks, that sounds good. I'm looking forward to getting to know your husband." *And figuring out why you refer to your shared home as his,* he added silently.

Her clear sky-blue eyes were troubled. "You're not going to disapprove of us, are you? Mom does. She thinks Liam is a handsomer incredible hulk. So what if he only has a degree from junior college? He's super smart and has more ingenuity than anyone I've ever met. He can hit the bullseye on a target with a hunting knife first try. He can fix or build anything."

"Impressive," Edward said evenly, endeavoring not to sound ironic. His sister of yesteryear would have turned up her nose at such hands-on skills. She obviously worshipped her husband. That might be part of the problem. "I hear he's going to be an actor now, too."

She nodded, less pleased with this development. "He's been cast as Damon Morehouse in Jake and David's movie. Maddie's going to be the villainess. George Reed Masters will be Damon's best friend."

His eyebrows shot up. He was surprised no one had filled him in about the movie casting at Thanksgiving dinner. Although … his mother had been glued to his side, and that movie was her least favorite subject. "The guy she was humping in that movie *Insanity*?"

"Well, yes," Teresa admitted, biting her lip.

"That sounds awkward. Damon must buy condoms by the case in that book."

Teresa avoided his eyes. "Jake and David reworked the story when they wrote the script. It doesn't much resemble the source material. Besides, there's safety in numbers. As long as he's not pursuing one particular woman …."

"Yes, of course. Though fans of the book might be disappointed. Are you and Liam all right?"

Now she did look at him—with narrowed eyes. "Did someone tell you about Kilo?"

"Kilo?" At first Edward couldn't place the name. "You don't mean the boy you eloped with way back when?" The memory shamed him. Egged on by their mother, he'd pulled a Mr. Darcy and dragged them back from "ruin," only no one had paid Kilo to make an honest woman of Teresa. The marriage had been annulled, Kilo roughed up and humiliated, and Teresa had been whisked off to Cape Cod and told to behave or be disinherited. Not long after, each of them inherited a separate fortune from their grandmother. Too late for Teresa and Kilo. The "boy" had gone on to join a prestigious modern dance company. Last Edward had heard, that was the end of his association with Teresa.

Teresa's cheeks were on fire. She covered them with her hands. "The very one. When I first arrived here, I discovered Kilo had opened a yoga studio on Lawrence Street, and we flirted a bit. Nothing more. He and Maddie … Oh, for Pete's sake. It's hardly a secret. They were in a play together and, uh, dated for a while. Shakespeare's *A Midsummer Night's Dream*. Her agent saw a performance and got him cast in a pilot—the reboot of that old TV show *Hawaiian Eye*. After he and Maddie broke up, he asked me to go to Maui with him for the filming."

Edward was confused. "Was this *after* you married Liam?"

"Yes. The invitation was a total surprise. I wasn't tempted, but Liam didn't believe me. He keeps thinking I want to be with someone more creative or educated. It's so stupid. I only want to be with him." She heaved a heavy sigh.

Now Edward recalled more about Kilo, how they'd met when he was a dance scholarship student at Cornish College of the Arts. Teresa had been studying private piano with a teacher there. She, the model student at the all-girls' Catholic high school. He, the exotic, sexy part-Hawaiian son of a struggling single mother. Of course those two beautiful kids from opposite sides of the tracks would fall in love.

Teresa had dreamed of becoming a concert pianist, but their mother had put the kibosh on that lofty calling. Teresa had been raised to think creativity and education were everything. Maybe that was why Liam had decided to give acting a try. Although what Liam would be doing in Jake's movie might not fit Teresa's idea of "acting."

What a mess.

CHAPTER 2

——◦——

AFTER KNOCKING AND RINGING THE doorbell a few times to ensure Reynard wasn't home, Lisette used her key to let herself into her boyfriend's showplace Victorian. She'd left him a voicemail message warning that she'd be home early, having learned the hard way not to surprise him.

As a pianist and composer with his own recording studio in the basement, Reynard was here most of the time. Unless he was in Los Angeles, collaborating on a film score. Lisette still marveled at the expense and care that had gone into restoring and decorating this place. They basically lived on the set of *Upstairs, Downstairs*. All new and pristine yet historically accurate. *New* Victoriana—expensive reproductions. What a concept. Reynard saw used and antique items as germy. What did that make her? Did her sexual past bother Reynard? She'd never raised the subject, and he'd probably freak if he knew the half of it. Or did he know already? One could never tell with Reynard. He'd probably had her investigated.

He *did* have impeccable taste. She sat primly on the burgundy velvet couch as if waiting for Hudson the Butler to come in and offer her a glass of sherry. *Oh*, she was tired. Normally she stayed at Café Lisette until the end of the dinner shift, which was why Reynard wouldn't expect her.

Through one of the many narrow sash windows positioned in a row, she stared out at the bay. You couldn't see much this time of night. Like most of the larger Victorians, the mansion was a former bed and breakfast. It was located close to the Terrace Steps that led to the tourist area. She wasn't sorry Reynard had convinced her to move to Port Townsend, but she did regret giving in to the pressure to move in with him. How could he truly "acquire" her otherwise? He needed to keep tabs on his possessions.

She thought of Edward. A lost soul, she'd concluded. Reynard was good-looking enough to be a hero in an Alexandre Dumas historical romance, but Edward was in a class of his own. He was a hero out of a fantasy novel—otherworldly handsome, like an angel fallen to earth. And yet, he seemed surprised that she'd noted his other visits to her restaurant. If not for Reynard …. Her sigh was amplified in the ridiculously clean and uncluttered room.

She'd met Reynard over a year ago, in September of 1998, when he'd had lunch at her café in Port Angeles. He'd bowled her over, scooped her up as if she were a fortune in bullion washed ashore after a storm. She'd been close to thirty-two then. He was older, but a man's age didn't matter. Now she was thirty-three and he was forty. She had no starry-eyed fantasies of long-term commitment. Soon he'd seek out someone younger and blinder to his faults. He'd already decided her treasure was too tarnished for him. She wasn't quite *comme il faut*, not as polished as she appeared. Creative, but lacking. An *artiste manquée*. He was a man who mastered his skills, and she was a dabbler. A little of this, a little of that. Once she realized she could achieve excellence at something, she lost interest. Unless there was a truly valid reason to persist. Her ability to cook, run a business, and make smart investments didn't count. That was probably why she stayed with Reynard—he was unobtainable. She'd never married and had no desire to do so. He thought he owned her, but she'd always assumed he would put her out to pasture before the relationship had run its course. For her, that is. Whoever said, "No man is an island" had never met Reynard.

Now she was rethinking that assumption. What if *she* broke free before he was ready to let her go?

Reynard didn't want children. He'd even had a vasectomy. No need for condoms.

She heard Reynard's Mercedes purr into the driveway and stayed seated as the key turned in the latch and he let himself in. When he walked into the living room, she gave him her most brilliant smile. He smiled back, automatically. Funny how his smiles always struck her as predatory.

"You're home early." He sounded annoyed.

Home sweet home, she thought. *Hah.*

"My feet were tired," she said, wiggling her toes at him. She'd kept her stockings and garter belt on because he liked taking them off for her. She picked up her shoes and stood to greet him. In heels or stacked sandals, she was almost as tall as he was. She kissed his pursed lips. *Ah*, he was in a mood. She didn't bother to ask him where he'd been. If he wanted to tell her, he would; otherwise he'd resent her nosiness. He had an unerring instinct for any new "talent" in town—that is, beautiful women. He would be scouting for her replacement.

"I'm going to shower," she said, "if that's okay with you." Still standing in front of him, she unbuttoned her blouse so he could see her breasts, nipples visible through the sheer fabric of the bra. "Join me?" She detected a spark of interest in his eyes, a remnant of his former desire. Usually a shower was her first priority upon coming home. Reynard didn't like the restaurant smells she carried around with her, especially in her long hair. She washed it so often that she must have spent a fortune on conditioner. The words, *"Donc, c'est ainsi"* were on her lips. French for, *So that's the way it is*. But why start a fight? Much as her imperfect French annoyed him, it got the job done. She'd hoped that living with him would improve it, but Reynard had no wish to hear her butcher his mother tongue.

Without waiting for a reply, she went upstairs. He would get over his mood … or not.

She showered and got into bed. Usually she slept in the nude, but tonight she put on a flannel nightgown. She was cold and didn't think Reynard would be open to sharing body heat. As she burrowed under the covers, she heard piano music. A man concerned for her comfort would have gone down to his studio and used the digital piano and headphones. At least he'd chosen something calming, a Debussy prelude.

Sometime later, she surfaced enough from sleep to feel him slide in beside her. He reached for her, and tired as she was, she let him. She never told him no. He would throw it back at her in future arguments. Besides, Reynard was too proud of his lovemaking skills to ignore her needs. He never did anything half assed.

Annoyed to find her in a nightgown, he pulled it impatiently over her head. He spooned against her, running his fingers lazily along her breasts and belly, tracing small circles until he reached her narrow strip of pubic hair. She was ready for him. He pulled her to her knees and entered her from behind, kissing her back and massaging her breasts. It was his favorite position, perhaps because he didn't have to look her in the eye. That was all right; it was good for her too. As he moved in a steady rhythm, one hand skittered down to play with her sex. All rational thought ceased as she gave in to the moment. When it was over, she sighed, partly in satisfaction but also in resignation.

Now she was fully awake. In those first few months, she'd imagined herself in love. On the surface, Reynard was quite a catch, with fine features, long-lashed bedroom eyes, thin but well-defined lips, luxuriant brown hair, and a soft short beard. For such a dapper man, he had a deceptively strong physique. He worked out religiously in the small basement gym next to the home studio. And he was freakishly flexible. Once, early in their relationship and out of the blue, he'd walked on his knees across the floor then performed a walkover. He had the grace and coordination to dance flamenco. He could have done so many things. It was unfair for one man to have so much beauty and talent and so little compassion.

In the beginning, he'd taken her hiking, biking, and kayaking, bought her extravagant gifts of jewelry—a tennis bracelet, diamond studs—and clothing. A cashmere sweater, a mink-lined leather car coat. He'd even taken her to Paris for ten days, dining at nothing but Michelin-starred restaurants and staying at the Prince de Galles, a 5-star Art Deco hotel located near the Champs-Elysées.

With regard to his profession, he was rigidly disciplined. He played piano a minimum of four hours a day, sometimes much longer. The rest of the time was spent in his studio, working on film scores. Other than an insatiable appetite for sex, he had no vices. He even drank wine in moderation—unlike anyone she'd ever known, including herself. If she had more than two glasses, he made his disapproval known. She'd pour a third glass just to goad him.

Two months into their relationship, he'd said, "Let's always be like this." They'd just made love three times and had basically tried to climb inside each other's skins. Her euphoria didn't die, exactly, but those words eroded its edges. No mature adult had such unrealistic expectations for a long-term relationship. No wonder he'd been divorced twice—experiences mentioned only in passing. Who knew how many other women? She'd been tempted to ask him about the duration of his longest relationship. Her best guess was two years, with the final six months spent on the lookout for his next lover.

After the "Let's always be like this" comment, she'd known they were on borrowed time. *Enjoy it while it lasts*, she told herself.

Soon after, the jealousy began. At Matthew's soiree, she could tell he wanted to murder Liam. She'd been mortified to confront the man she'd basically propositioned in Port Angeles. Who knew he was married to the society princess Teresa O'Connell? She'd wanted to sink into the floor. Having noted her reaction, Reynard assumed she and Liam had slept together. She was reluctant to admit he'd rejected her. Her official story was that they'd met in Port Angeles at her restaurant there and exchanged friendly small talk, nothing more. He didn't buy it. No wonder. Liam had been kind of a jerk at the party, implying a connection longer than one short but intense conversation in a notorious pickup bar.

Lisette suspected Reynard was too damaged for any real, lasting relationship. Any talk of his parents was devoid of fondness. His mother was one of those women they called "delicate," when she was really a garden-variety alcoholic. His father was a locomotive engineer who stayed away so much Reynard believed he had another family somewhere. As soon as he could manage it, Reynard became the provider, at first earning a living through teaching, an occupation he clearly loathed. His musical brilliance earned him a free ride in the French educational system. After his mother died in Reynard's seventeenth year, he moved out and never contacted his father again. How did you thrive after a childhood like that?

Lisette's own parents were typical middle-class WASPs. Though chilly, they clearly cared about her and her brother Steve. They ran a restaurant in Cape May—American food all the way—where she'd learned about the business from the ground up. By the time she was eighteen, she could cook, wait tables, balance books, even break up fights. Her mom and dad still ran the restaurant in Cape May, but Lisette rarely went home, and their phone conversations were brief. Steve lived in Bucerias, a beach town near Puerto Vallarta, with his wife and two children. After they'd married, he taken to describing her family as "Spanish" rather than "Mexican" to drive home their pure bloodline. Lisette wasn't sure how he earned a living. This and that. She suspected his wife's family money supported them while he hung out at the local bar and surfed. They exchanged one-sentence Christmas cards.

It would be so simple to pack her two bags and leave. None of the décor or books were hers. She kept her few non-clothing-related possessions in a small apartment above the restaurant next to her office. It was a drag to leave at Christmas time, but she wasn't going to ruin the holiday for herself by spending it with a man who barely tolerated her. That would be lonelier than being alone.

Finally she fell into a fitful sleep, and when she awoke, it was already nine. Reynard usually rose at six and breakfasted alone before shutting himself in his studio. He wasn't using the headphones. She listened. She did like his compositions, which owed a lot to Debussy's and Ravel's later, more adventurous work.

She headed upstairs to the attic and pulled out her large suitcase and her carry-on bag. After her scant possessions were packed and hauled to the front door, she left her key on the kitchen table along with a note that said simply, "*Adieu.*" Then she tore it up and wrote, from memory,

> *Comme tout meurt vite, la rose déclose,*
> *Et les frais manteaux diaprés des prés;*
> *Les longs soupirs, les bien-aimées, fumées!*

Loosely translated, it meant *Everything dies quickly, the rose withers, the fresh grass turns brown. Long sighs, lovers ... up in smoke!* Reynard would recognize the words—from a poem by Charles Grandmougin set to music by Gabriel Fauré. The title: "*Adieu.*" Farewell, see you never. Not *au revoir, see you again.* Unfortunately she would see him again. It was a small town.

The diamond earrings and tennis bracelet sat on the nightstand in the bedroom. It would be just like Reynard to pass on the expensive clothing gifts to her successor. Those she kept. Otherwise she might have to observe them parading around town without her.

She rolled the suitcases out the door and hefted them into the back seat of her black Mazda Miata convertible. The trunk was too small. She was only driving a few blocks. *Stupid, impractical car.* Her next one would be a rugged Subaru Outback.

* * *

Dinner with Teresa and Liam had been a surprisingly entertaining affair. Edward had learned several useful tidbits:

One, according to Liam, Lisette was a former call girl.

Two, Lisette was currently dating the town's celebrity composer, pianist, and wannabe rapist—if you believed Teresa.

Three, Edward really wanted to dislike Liam.

Four, Liam was a hard man to dislike.

Five, Liam made a mean spaghetti and meatballs.

Six, Teresa thought Xenia was the next Martha Stewart.

Give me a break, he thought. Liam's negative opinion of Lisette was based on one encounter in Port Angeles, when she had come on to him like Stupifyin' Jones on Sadie Hawkins Day. Not his words, Edward's interpretation. Edward had a soft spot for Stupifyin', especially as played by Julie Newmar in the movie. Come to think of it, Liam did look a bit like L'il Abner, only with brains. Black hair, blazing blue eyes, muscles earned through manual labor, honey-colored skin. Side by side, Liam and Ali were obviously siblings, given the unusual coloring and arresting blue eyes—both gorgeous but otherwise quite different. Liam resembled their father Duncan, who claimed Ali was a dead ringer for their mother. Duncan and their birth mother had spent exactly one evening and night together. No photographs existed to prove his claim. The mother had recently surfaced in Port Townsend, a wreck of her former self, then skipped town after Liam gave her enough money to keep her in drugs for a while.

Liam's contention that Reynard was an aspiring rapist was based on the time he'd invited Teresa in for a nightcap and hadn't seemed inclined to take no for an answer. They'd been sitting in his car. No clothing had been torn or body parts groped. Edward was on Team Teresa, definitely, but he couldn't help but wonder if Reynard had simply misread his sister, who had obviously been using him to try to get over Liam.

He wanted to dislike Liam because the man was too arrogant by half. He had way too much power over his sister, power derived from his sexual prowess. Because really, what did Teresa and Liam have in common? Teresa the society princess, interior designer, accomplished pianist, fashionista, with a BA in creative writing from a Seven Sisters' college. Liam the foster kid, former machinist, handyman, woodworker, knife-thrower, future action star with an associate degree in … what, machine tool technology?

And yet … the guy was irresistible. His self-deprecating humor and soupçon of vulnerability made his cockiness bearable and him endearing.

Finally, the guy was a hell of a cook. He made spaghetti and meatballs that tasted like osso buco. Good thing, too, because Teresa could probably turn that same dish into something soldiers in trenches wouldn't touch.

Lastly, Xenia. Really? His first impression was that she would make a highly effective vampire, no personality change required. Teresa saw her as a Greek—or was it Russian?—Anne of Green Gables. She was older than he'd assumed, had just celebrated her twenty-sixth birthday. They seemed to think she'd make someone a good wife. Who, him? They had to be kidding. When he'd raised the subject of Lisette, they'd both gasped in horror as if he were a dalmatian puppy smitten with Cruella de Vil.

Their disapproval didn't discourage him one bit. In fact, he was on his way now to Karaoke Night at Café Lisette.

At some point he really had to figure out his wardrobe. He was wearing a button-down shirt and jacket with black jeans and dress boots. Was that too fancy for Port Townsend? David and Joe—when he wasn't inhabiting his alter ego, country music star Joe Bob Blade—dressed BPO all the way. Jeans, T-shirt, flannel shirt, parka. The occasional sweatshirt. Liam bucked the trend with his gazillion-dollar leather jacket. Edward wanted one too.

Jake had lost his buttoned-up quality, but even in flannels, he looked expensive. He'd clearly experienced a damascene moment. Edward couldn't wait to hear *that* story.

CHAPTER 3

JOE AND MATTHEW HAD SPENT the morning improvising in the recording studio. The session guitarist and bassist who had moved to Port Townsend after touring with Joe as a sideman was now a collaborator and close friend.

While waiting for Ali to join them for lunch, they reclined in companionable silence in the living room of the Log Palace, ostensibly reading the *New York Times*. The leather couch they shared might have accommodated Bigfoot, Smokey the Bear, and their significant others. Joe's brain was traveling down unproductive paths of darkness. Matthew was, apparently, occupied more fruitfully, humming to himself as he tended to do when mulling over a musical passage that didn't quite work. Joe recognized the bridge of the song they'd been writing together.

The long newspaper article Joe was skimming concerned the chaotic protests that had shut down the opening ceremonies of the World Trade Organization conference in Seattle. Enough of that. Having studied both sides of the issue, he couldn't declare for one side or the other. And he wasn't in the mood to ponder the world's struggles.

Instead he pondered the cavernous living room. At the moment, the couch was the only piece of furniture. The place they'd dubbed the Log Palace was just that—a mansion made of whole logs, a nod to the tiny cabin where he and Ali had first met under dire circumstances. It stood majestically—one might say, inharmoniously—alongside the so-called Sea Captain's House. The original dwelling, now owned by David and Maddie, was still the heart of the compound. Though only ten years old, that building had been designed to fit in with the town's American colonial structures. Port Townsend's main attractions were its grand old Victorians, mostly Queen Anne style like Liam's fixer upper and Reynard's and Matthew's lovingly restored mansions. As far as Joe knew, the former B&B Jake was in the process of buying was the only Italianate-style Victorian in town. Its ornate splendor drew the eye like an emerald-cut blue sapphire among rough diamonds.

Like the officers' quarters at Fort Worden, the Sea Captain's House featured cedar siding, rows of sash windows rather than a few large ones, and other retro touches.

How the hell should we finish this room? Joe thought, an ongoing quandary. The black leather couch faced a gas fireplace made of river rocks. Should they have chosen fieldstone or ledgestone instead? Recliners to match the couch … that was a no-brainer. A coffee table …. What kind? Farmhouse style, rustic? A huge mural of Paul Bunyan and his blue ox? They could recreate the one that had decorated the walls of the Paul Bunyan Room at the now defunct Frederick & Nelson department store in Seattle. The children would love it. A mural that was essentially a primitive graphic might be a step too far. Folk art was one thing …. If they weren't careful, the compound would soon resemble a novelty motel. Perhaps it did already.

Teresa had found the Sea Captain's House for Joe and Ali. Its main attraction for Joe was the separate recording studio, built by an independently wealthy amateur musician who lived there only a few years. Then there was the isolated location, extensive grounds, beach access, and a massive flagstone terrace with a sweeping view of the Strait of Juan de Fuca. They had erected two new guest cabins for a total of five and expanded the entertainment area by adding a safari tent. The tent was a nod to David's nostalgia for a romanticized British colonial Africa that had probably only existed in the movies.

Hoping to spend more time in his new home, Matthew had been learning the recording-engineer trade from self-taught Joe. The future of Joe's alter ego, Joe Bob Blade, was up in the air. Now that his voice was clear, Joe should be planning another tour. They were all a little too comfortable now, like the supposed guard dogs, best friends Harry—a German Shepherd mastiff mix— and Coogan—part Jack Russell and part chihuahua.

Matthew was absentmindedly petting Harry while Coogan snoozed with his tiny head in Joe's lap. Liam, their self-appointed security expert, had intended that the dogs remain outside and sleep in the garage. Now that he and Teresa lived in town, neither Joe, Ali, David, nor Maddie had the heart to keep them outside. Matthew's golden retriever, Charlie Pride, was on a walk with Liam, who'd volunteered for the thankless job of training the goofy puppy. As canine lords of the manor, Harry and Coogan were not amused by the naughty antics of Charlie, who had earned his share of nips and growls. When the older dogs had pointedly stared at Joe and Matthew, as if to say, "How is he *our* responsibility?" Joe had suggested that Liam teach the puppy some manners.

Matthew had stopped humming.

"Did you figure it out?" Joe asked.

"Maybe. I'll run it past you after lunch."

"How did the photo session go?" Joe asked. Yesterday Xenia had photographed the Art Deco living room Teresa had designed for Matthew. They'd be featuring it on the website.

"Oh, yeah. Fine."

Matthew, who kept his cards close to his chest, made Liam look like a chatterbox. Ali believed he and Jeremy were seeing each other—whatever that meant—but no one knew for sure. Not even Maddie, who was fast friends with the charismatic actor. Matthew's energy was way mellower than Jeremy's. He had an ageless boy-next-door appeal and no wish to take center stage. That was just as well; the Adonis-lookalike Jeremy had center stage permanently staked out. Joe imagined that Jeremy literally ran circles around Matthew, just as the more energetic Coogan sometimes ran circles around laid-back Harry.

The tiny whirling dervish and his hulking gentle-giant friend looked up and wagged their tales. Joe stood to give them each a proper rubdown. "*Fine*," he said, repeating Matthew's one-word answer. "Care to elaborate?"

Head cocked, Matthew gave the question some thought. "Xenia and I had an odd conversation. Apparently she goes for a run every morning at eleven, like clockwork. Her routine ends with going up and down the Terrace Steps as many times as she can stand. A few days ago, Reynard was there, sitting on one of the stone benches that curve around Haller Fountain. They got to talking, and Xenia told him how Teresa was helping her to become an interior designer. Reynard mentioned having a guest room that needed 'refreshing.' " Matthew formed finger quotes. "She was excited, naturally. Reynard confessed that Teresa wasn't a fan of his and that if Xenia was interested, they should proceed in secret."

"Did you tell her that was a terrible idea?" Joe asked.

Matthew gave a helpless shrug, his distaste for the offer clear. "She's an adult. And as a former foster child, chances are good she's been around the block more than most twenty-six-year-olds. I'm friendly enough with Reynard. He can be entertaining company if you're not a rival or prey. I tried to tread carefully with Xenia. I told her Reynard has a live-in girlfriend. He doesn't hide the fact that most of his relationships have the lifespan of a butterfly. I didn't mention Lisette by name. Or that he's been hinting that it's run its course."

"Did you tell her what went down with Teresa?" Joe asked.

"Truth is, I can't say for sure, can I?" Matthew raked his fingers through his unruly mop of brown curls. "Anyway, Xenia insists he's too old for her. She just wants the work experience."

Joe smiled wickedly as he imagined how Reynard might react to being called "too old." "What do you think of Xenia?"

"Nice girl. A little… hungry, perhaps. That's what comes of being starved as a kid, even if it's only for affection." His brow furrowed. "You think she'll fall for Reynard, despite the age gap? Oh. You've chosen her for *Edward*." A wag of his finger. "You're playing matchmaker again."

"Not me," Joe rushed to say.

Matthew blew out an exasperated puff of air. "Listen … if Xenia thinks Reynard has one foot in the grave, she won't go for Edward either. He's only two years younger."

Joe nodded. "If asked for my two cents, I'd say, stay the hell out of Edward's private business. He's obviously been through some serious shit."

Matthew raised his eyebrows. "I wouldn't know—I only met him that one time, at Thanksgiving. The Catholic Church sure is embroiled in a buttload of scandals these days, though. And Edward …. He's *way* too good-looking to be renouncing worldly pleasures. Are you sure he's not gay?"

Joe laughed. "Interested?"

Matthew also laughed in that hearty, good-natured way of his. "I have my hands full."

Joe nodded as if he understood. He didn't. Did Matthew mean he was fully immersed in the new relationship with Jeremy or that he was too busy with musical projects? "Edward isn't gay," he said. "He could be bi, I suppose. I only ever saw him with girls—women, rather, because he wasn't into girls his own age. Not that I witnessed much firsthand. He was four years my senior. I heard from my friends with older brothers that he was a legend with the *ladies*." He gave the word an ironic twist. "An all or nothing kind of guy, I guess. Could be bipolar."

"He seems cool to me," Matthew said. "More light-hearted than the rest of you, in fact."

No kidding, Joe thought. He himself had an entire list of things that were bothering him. Ali's first pregnancy had been difficult enough. This time around she'd started with severe morning sickness and was now coping with gestational diabetes. Then there was the twins' daunting energy and all the run-up to *Kapow*, the movie based on Jake's book that could well destroy both David's and Teresa's marriages. Maddie and Liam would be away filming for months while Teresa nursed a newborn and David stewed over whether the actor George Reed Masters was still lusting after Maddie.

Joe's détente with his twin Jake was one bright spot. Ever since they'd fixed the fence together. They'd been close once ... before all the weirdness. First a scuffle over a girl in high school, later over a woman in college. Then Jake had plotted to take Ali away. Ancient history now. His brother had a new love, Chiara, who'd come to Port Townsend as Lorenzo's guardian. Her divorce from Arnold was nearly final. Lor was David's son by Chiara's sister Sylvia.

He looked up to find Matthew eyeing him speculatively. "Maddie and Teresa prefer to focus on getting others to hook up rather than working on their own relationships. You and Ali are solid, obviously."

Matthew had a point about their meddling in other people's affairs. *It's a regular Peyton Place*, he thought. The "Hotel California," where you could "check out but never leave."

Ali shuffled in, one hand spanning her belly, the other holding her back, her smile strained. He tried not to wince. She was seven months along, but she looked ready to pop. His darling wife was usually a champ at keeping her spirits up—at keeping everyone's spirits up. Not so much lately. She'd simply run out of steam. Once, when they'd discussed backpacking, she'd told him she wasn't "a pack animal." He wished he could carry the burden for her. Oh well, it would be over soon enough. He was seriously considering a vasectomy. They'd discussed adopting or taking in young foster children.

"Lunch is ready," his wife chirped with effortful cheeriness. "You guys hungry?"

They settled in at the kitchen counter, a butcher's block large enough for five beefy butchers to go about their business with room to spare. Ali had prepared tuna melt sandwiches. They relied on FOSSP kids for dinner prep. Sandwiches and salads they could manage themselves. Group events centered around the Sea Captain's House. Force of habit, perhaps. The parlor and dining room were cozier now that Maddie and David had dismantled Teresa's starkly beautiful Art Deco parlor—the kind of room where putting your feet up, even shoeless, might get you banished to the basement. Not that any of the furniture had invited lounging. It *had* provided the perfect backdrop for family Christmas photos.

"How are the twins?" Matthew asked as Ali placed their napkins.

"Calmer today. Did Joe tell you about the dancing?"

Joe couldn't help but grin. "You tell him."

"I was playing a CD of the opera *Carmen*, and Josie started swaying her hips. Caryn joined in, and they both started doing this sway/sidestep thing, only in one direction. When they butted into the couch, they didn't reverse, just kept going like wind-up toys that had hit a barrier. It was hilarious. Who knew dancing was so instinctive?"

"We got most of it on video," Joe said, knowing Matthew wouldn't ask to see it. He'd privately told Joe that children weren't for him. Would that change if he found the right partner? With his patience and thoughtfulness, Matthew would make a great father.

"Which part of *Carmen*?" Matthew asked. "The 'Habanera'?"

Ali smiled. "Good guess."

"It *is* one of the dancier tunes. How long does Edward plan to stay in town?"

"No plans, I think," Joe replied. "I haven't had a chance to sit down with him. With a four-year age gap, it's not like we've ever been close. But the definitive break seems tied to Da's death. At the wake, Teresa and I drank ourselves blind, hugged, cried, and generally fell apart. Jake managed a show of dignity but passed out on the couch. Then there was Edward. A zombie. He sat in the corner with Mom, who also appeared to be lobotomized, to receive guests. He *seemed* to have his shit together. I figured he had better inner resources than the rest of us—all those philosophy degrees, you know. A bachelor's and master's from Harvard. Well, technically, he had two months to go on the master's."

"I was a comparative religion major," Ali broke in. "It's a little like people with problems becoming therapists. You study those subjects because you have questions most people don't bother to ask themselves. They're content with relying on blind faith, I suppose. The 'answers' I found were cold comfort."

Joe squeezed her hand, knowing how the news that Liam had been declared "missing presumed dead" had almost killed her.

She squeezed back. "Sorry, sweetie, I didn't mean to interrupt. You were telling us about your dad's wake."

"I've got nothing more to add about that. You'd have to ask someone who stayed more or less sober, like Edward. Afterward, when he spoke at the funeral, which was open casket"—Joe grimaced—"he was so emotionally detached, he might have been a distant relative. Very professorial. His so-called eulogy was a rambling lecture on the great philosophers' views of death. Then, like an actor combining monologues from different plays, he segued into the meaning of Psalm Twenty-Three—you know, 'The Lord is my Shepherd.' Some of it made sense, and some of it was even comforting … or maybe that just his sonorous voice and angelic appearance. Later I concluded he was simply rambling with half his brain turned off. That summer, he took off for Europe and spent a year in Rome. He was almost twenty-five when he returned to the States."

"When was the last time you saw him?" Matthew asked, his wide brown eyes shining with sympathy.

Joe felt his own eyes brim with tears. He took a moment to get a grip on himself before replying. "That Christmas he came home for a visit. I remember thinking there was something off about him then, like he was heavily medicated. Obviously not, because the next thing we knew, he was pursuing his Doctor of Divinity at the Catholic University of America in DC. Then he became a priest in Philadelphia. With credentials like that, combined with brains and elegance, we all figured he was destined to be a bishop or even a cardinal. We never thought he'd throw in the towel after less than ten years."

Matthew raised his eyebrows. "That's quite a story. I hear it's the celibacy that's gets 'em."

Joe nodded. "I'm surprised Edward's not the one with the natural child."

"One could still surface," Ali said.

"Was Edward molested, do you think?" Matthew asked as though curious where Edward went to high school.

The question caught Joe off guard. "Huh?"

"Edward's the best-looking of you all," Matthew replied matter-of-factly, "and that's saying something. If he was sexualized early, compulsive behavior like that makes more sense." As Joe sat there, mouth agape, Matthew finished the last bite of his sandwich and took the plate over to the sink. "When do they start filming *Kapow*?"

Bless him, Joe thought. He was done with that subject. "Uncertain," he said aloud. "Liam and Maddie will report to L.A. in early February for martial arts training. Costume fittings, makeup tests. Filming starts in mid-April. Or so Teresa tells me. She can't wrap her brain around being on the road while nursing." He rubbed his forehead. "If she stays here, Liam will miss those early months of development. Of course he'll come back when he can, and I'm sure she'll miss him enough to make the effort to visit the set for at least a weekend or two."

"Get her a camcorder like yours," Matthew said, helping himself to a cup of tea. "Video cameras are so user friendly now. Better than nothing."

"I wish the picture quality was better," Ali said. "As for the movie, the timing does stink. I'll ask Teresa to move in with us while Liam's away. Xenia's great with kids, but she's learning the interior design business. Teresa won't want to saddle her with caring for an infant."

"What's up with your children's book?" Matthew asked. "*The Minions of Moss Manor* or something like that. Is it selling?"

"*The Way to Moss Manor*," Ali corrected him with a laugh. "It's early days. The stores in town can't keep it in stock, but it hasn't shown up on any best-seller lists."

"Yet." Joe gave her hand a smacking kiss. "Give it time."

"The pillow shams and children's pajamas are flying off the shelves. Also sheets, duvet covers, and dish towels. Chiara and I are collaborating on another book now, by special request of Lorenzo. *Salish Sea Stories*."

Matthew scratched his head. "Will readers know what you mean by Salish Sea, do you think? I know an official name change is in the pipeline. My new friends tell me it's meant to honor the Salish tribes and get people more interested in protecting those waters. I gather 'The Strait of Juan de Fuca Stories' was too much of a mouthful?"

"Not to mention that 'Juan de *Fuca*' is easily mispronounced in a way parents might not appreciate," Ali said. "I was told a lot of people around here already refer to those inland waters as the Salish Sea, which includes Puget Sound and the Strait of Georgia. Given a choice, I'd have written *Return to Moss Manor*. But low tide is Lorenzo's new obsession. He can't stop talking about Sammy the Sea Star and Duncan the Dungeness Crab."

Matthew wrinkled his nose. "Don't crabs *eat* sea stars?"

Ali lashed the counter with her napkin as if throwing down the gauntlet. "Not in our book, by gum." She smiled. "I knew that, actually. I do my research, even if I don't always stay true to it. I have no idea how to handle their shared meals. They could be vegans. Or we don't mention eating at all."

Matthew still appeared skeptical. Joe adored Ali's drawings and watercolors. However, sea creatures weren't warm and fuzzy like Ali's cuddly rain-forest dwellers. But then, his favorite character in *The Way to Moss Manor* had been a banana slug named Bunty.

"Duncan the Dungeness Crab," Matthew repeated. "After your dad?"

Ali's birth father had reappeared in her life only a few years ago, having discovered her existence through a newspaper photo in which she was a dead ringer for her birth mother. Meeting her had confirmed his suspicions that she was the result of a rare one-night stand. The rapport between them had been instantaneous.

Ali grinned. "I don't think he'll mind, do you?"

CHAPTER 4

CAFÉ LISETTE WAS SO CROWDED it resembled an anthill. Though the start time for Karaoke Night was nine, by eight forty-five the already claustrophobic space was packed enough to be shut down by the fire department. With no free tables, Edward leaned against the bar, jostled on all sides. He'd only ever been here for lunch, and always on the late side. At six feet three, he stood a head above the other patrons—mostly younger singles looking for love. Gin and tonic in hand, he moved over by the wall in hopes of blending in with the woodwork. The perpetual scowl he wore deterred no one. He responded to the "hi's" and "hello there's" with a vague air of hostility. That kept the women at bay, but not the men.

He was just about to bolt when Lisette appeared, holding a microphone and waving at the crowd. "Hello, divas, divos, and deviants! I hope you brought your chops with you. And I ain't talkin' about lamb chops." Wild cheering. "I guess that means yes. I'm going to start us off with a song that fits my mood about now. Don't ask me who it's about because I'm not telling. One hint: it's not about Mick Jagger or James Taylor." Loud hooting. "Hit it, Bobby."

The headwaiter/disc jockey, a fiftyish man in a rugby shirt and jeans with a baldness pattern similar to a monk's tonsure, pushed a button on the karaoke machine. Edward recognized the introduction to Carly Simon's "You're So Vain."

Edward was grinning like a fool. Lisette was phenomenal. *Eat your heart out, Carly.* At the second chorus, she yelled, "Everybody!" and the crowd enthusiastically joined in. Handing the microphone to Bobby, she strutted around like Mick. Her outfit was a variation on her usual uniform, a low-cut silk blouse and knee-length pencil skirt, but this one had a deeper slit, providing tantalizing flashes of firm, shapely legs and—Lord help him—garters. He swallowed hard.

He scanned the crowd. Wouldn't Reynard want to see her strut her stuff? Would she have chosen a song like this if he were here? Doubtful. When she took a bow, Edward applauded louder than anyone, adding a wolf whistle for good measure. *Whoops*, that drew everyone's attention to him again. "Mr. O'Connell," she said in her master of ceremony's voice, "what will you be singing?" She held out the microphone, putting him on the spot. Downing the rest of his gin and tonic, he put the glass aside. What should he sing? Something easy and obvious. " 'I Walk the Line,' Johnny Cash," he told Bobby as he took the microphone.

If only he'd had one more drink …. *Oh well, here goes*. He shuffled his feet as Bobby queued up the music. Then he thought, *To hell with it*. He went the silly route, as she had, directing the lines to different people, both men and women. The crowd ate it up. The song suited his deep voice and limited range.

Lisette made him take several bows before handing the microphone to a frantically waving customer who was yelling, " 'Free Bird,' Lynyrd Skynyrd!"

"Shouldn't you do that one at the end?" she joked. The scrawny lad, who probably had a fake ID, shot her a puzzled look.

As the opening played, she came to Edward's side and said in his ear, "I thought 'Free Bird' was for encores."

He leaned in to hear her better. *God*, she smelled wonderful. Like orange blossoms and fresh bread. "Are you sure that guy is drinking age?" he asked.

"I've carded him before. Believe it or not, he's twenty-three. We've reached that age when everyone under twenty-five looks like a child."

"What … you're older than twenty-five?" he said. Up close, she did have the supple skin of a teenager.

Her smile was distinctly flirty. "You're nice."

"You're terrific, you know," he treaid.

Her smile broadened. "Ah, I bet you say that to all the girls." After the verse, she jutted her thumb at the young Lynyrd Skynyrd wannabe. "Maynard G. Krebs isn't too bad."

Edward nodded. "All he needs is the goatee."

She wrinkled her nose adorably. "I doubt he could grow one."

Edward had to resist the urge to bury his nose in her shiny black hair as he whispered, "Do you think anyone this age knows about Dobie Gillis anymore?"

He was so close when she turned to reply that their lips almost touched. She didn't shy away. Had he imagined the flare of desire in those mesmerizing green eyes? Finally she said, "They'd have seen it in reruns, like we did."

For the rest of the evening, she kept him at her side as if he were her cohost. After the crowd had mostly dispersed, she patted his arm. "I thought you needed protection. I saw how they all gravitated to you, like they were bears and you were a great big honeycomb."

"Can I buy you a drink?"

She batted her lashes. "Only if you let me charge you double."

"Make it triple and you've got a deal."

Her laugh was dark honey. "Whatever you say. Just let me lock up first."

As she walked over to the main door, a man burst in. A snarling man. Sharp teeth. Handsome too, Edward had to admit, and nattily dressed in black jeans, a linen shirt, and an open, buttery-leather jacket. It had to be Reynard. He'd seen no one else in Port Townsend remotely worthy of Lisette in looks and bearing.

"How *dare* you?" He brandished a piece of paper so that it flapped like a panicked pigeon. "A *poem*? You are *not* the poetic type. I don't deserve a face-to-face explanation?"

" 'Deserve,' " she repeated. "It's not about 'deserving.' I'm acknowledging our basic incompatibility. And your obvious loss of interest. It's clear to me that it's over. Am I wrong?"

His mouth worked, as if forming and discarding words. Or was he swearing under his breath? That's when he caught sight of Edward, who'd retreated into an unlit part of the room in hopes of staying out of the discussion. "Who is this man skulking about?"

Edward stepped forward. "I'm hardly *skulking*." *Don't laugh*, he told himself. *This guy could punch you. Then you'd have to flatten him, and that would probably land you in jail.*

"He means nothing to me," Lisette said in French. "He was here for karaoke. He lost his car keys and we were looking for them."

Edward, who spoke French, thought, *I hope he doesn't offer me a ride. The hotel is one block away.* Clearing his throat, he said in English, "They aren't my car keys, they're my house keys." Why had he said that? He had only one key. "I mean my hotel room key." *Damn.* Worse and worse.

Reynard's lips twitched. Was he really going to laugh? "Who is this clown?" he asked Lisette in English, jabbing a dismissive finger at Edward as if he were Bozo himself. A spark of recognition. "You look like a combination of David O'Connell and his brother Jake. So you are obviously an O'Connell. *Merde*, how many of you are there?"

"Four brothers, one sister," Edward said helpfully.

"You must be the priest." Reynard blew out his cheeks, and the situation deescalated. "Where's your clerical collar?"

"In the wash?" Edward suggested. "If I wore it to karaoke, it might put a damper on the general mood." He wondered how religious Reynard was, if at all. If still a practicing priest, Edward would have been compelled to the wear the collar everywhere.

Catholic or not, Reynard seemed to understand that Edward was pulling his leg. He blew out another puff of air, a disgusted one, and turned back to Lisette. "We will continue this discussion tomorrow, when you have had time to calm down."

She spread her arms and did a little shimmy. "I'm perfectly calm."

Not appreciating her flippancy, he ground out, "When you've had time to come to your senses then."

"There's nothing more to say," she insisted. "I've already told you my reasoning."

"We will talk tomorrow," he insisted. He might as well have added, *And that's an order*. He turned tail and stormed out without waiting for an answer.

"No, we won't," she called after him, but he was already gone.

"Is he dangerous, do you suppose?" Edward asked, breaking the silence that followed Reynard's dramatic exit.

Lisette shook her head. "He's not going to beat me up—if that's what worries you. He is done with me. I just got tired of waiting for him to call it."

"Call it?"

"Call the game. Call it a day. Whatever."

"Was it a game?

"Maybe. I didn't think so in the beginning. The more fool I."

She went over to the bar and picked up a bottle of white wine. "I'm having a drink." She looked at the label. "It's nothing special, but it's open, and it's either drink it or dump it." She poured two glasses and handed one to him.

They sat at a round table, as if waiting for Bobby to take their orders.

"You broke up with him via poem?" Edward asked.

"A note wouldn't have the same annoyance value."

He laughed. "Which one? The poem, I mean."

"The first few lines of '*Adieu,*' by Charles Grandmougin, set to music by Gabriel Fauré."

Edward was delighted by such a grand gesture. "Isn't that kind of obscure?"

Her eyes twinkled with mischief. "Not to Reynard. He used to coach classical singers. He knows the art song repertoire. It had the added advantage of being in French. He thinks my French is less than adequate, that I speak it like '*une vache espagnole.*' A Spanish cow. That I lack class overall."

"Ridiculous," Edward said. "How do *you* know the repertoire?"

She drank half her glass and refilled it. "I took singing lessons in Paris. While I was getting my *Diplome de Cuisine* at Le Cordon Bleu."

That had to be one of the best cooking schools in the world. "He wasn't impressed with your culinary education?"

In a French accent close to Reynard's, she said, " 'Cooking iz not an art.' He nearly qualifies as a professional-level chef himself. It was his backup career in case composing didn't pan out."

"You studied to be a chef. But you aren't the chef here."

"When I opened Café Lisette in Port Angeles, I was. But I got tired of the lifestyle and the hours. Then my other investments started to pay off, and I hired someone else to do it."

Investments. No wonder she dressed so nicely. So … Reynard *wasn't* supporting her. "Keeping" her, as some put it. He'd heard that Le Cordon Bleu's tuition was expensive. Did they offer scholarships, and if so, to women? He'd guess male chefs were still overwhelmingly preferred, especially in defiantly sexist France.

"Back to the lines you chose for your kiss-off poem … could you sing them for me?"

In a soft voice, she sang, "*Comme tout meurt vite, la rose déclose, et les frais manteaux diaprés des prés; Les longs soupirs, les bien-aimées, fumées!*"

He sighed with pleasure. "Lovely. You could have been a classical singer."

"Hardly," she scoffed. "My voice is tiny. Well, obviously I can sing louder than that, but I can't project very far without a microphone. It's just another of my dabblings."

"Dabblings," he repeated. "You are far too hard on yourself." He glanced around the room. "You don't need to clean up?"

She took a closer look at their table, then fetched a bar towel and wiped it down. "That'll do for now. A janitor comes in every morning to clean and put everything to rights. My bartender Sid cleans as he goes."

They sat down again, suddenly awkward. "So, you understand French." She chuckled, recalling the exchange. "House key? Hotel room key?"

He started laughing too. "I felt compelled to clarify. Otherwise, if he'd insisted on giving me a ride, the jig would have been up."

After they'd dried their eyes, she said more seriously, "Liam is your brother-in-law."

"Yes."

She looked up at him through her lashes as if to say, *How much do you know?*

"Not much," he replied to her unspoken question.

"What?"

"I don't know much. Only that you … and he …."

"What?!" She bristled like a cornered cat. "*Nothing* happened between us."

He waved his hands to calm her down. "I didn't mean to imply that. Liam was impressed with, uh, the intensity of your, hm, approach."

She cradled her forehead as if at her wits' end.

"I don't care," he said.

"Don't care about what?"

"Don't care that he has the impression that you're—"

"A slut?" Her tone was deceptively casual.

"Harsh word, and not one that I'd ever use to describe you." He finished off his wine.

She shook the bottle and found it empty. "Now for the red." She fetched another. "Do you need a fresh glass?"

"Is it something special?"

She made a show of examining the label and shook her head with mock gravity.

"Then, no." He held out his glass for her to fill. "Liam is under the impression that you used to be a call girl."

She was taken aback. "*What*? Oh, good Lord, what gave him that idea?"

"You must have been quite … tempting."

She looked pained. "Not tempting enough. And I wasn't with Reynard then. Liam is …."

She seemed at a loss for words, so Edward said, "If I were gay and not his brother-in-law, I'd do him."

She let out a little yelp of laughter. "How could you have *ever* been a priest?"

"A question I often ask myself," he said, in all seriousness.

"What will you do now?"

He considered how to reply. "Another frequently asked question. Jake has had some luck with his thrillers. Maybe I'll write a memoir. Or erotica. Or both. I'll combine them. *Confessions of a Randy Priest.*" He shook his head. "I wasn't a randy priest. I was a devout priest, never strayed. You would have hated me. I was not warm and fuzzy. I had to maintain a certain … uh, hauteur. Otherwise every unmarried and unhappily married woman in the parish would have been scratching at my door like cats in heat." *Damn,* that had come out wrong. Not only was it crude, but it sounded boastful. Embarrassed, he checked for her reaction. She stared at him intently, and he was struck with the certainty that she preferred honesty to his usual self-deprecating BS. She was a stunningly beautiful woman. He wanted to push her up against the wall, reach under that slit skirt past her garters and do all manner of randy things to her. But of course that was out of the question. She would assume he just wanted her body. Maybe that *was* all he wanted. Was that so bad? *Yes. Leave her alone. She just broke up with her boyfriend. She deserves better than what* you *have to offer.*

"Was it the celibacy?" she asked quietly. "Is that why you left?"

"No." He really didn't want to get into the intricacies of his decision not only to break his vows but leave the Church entirely.

Summoning all his willpower, he stood to go. "Can I drop you somewhere? Oh, that's right, I don't have a car. Do you have a place to stay?" Was he inviting her to his hotel room? Yes, he was. So much for *that* resolve.

Her smile had an ironic edge. "Where are you staying?"

"The Bishop."

She grinned. "Nice. I'd love to see your room. Another time, perhaps." She pointed at the ceiling. "There's a room with a bed next to my office upstairs."

Was she inviting him up to her bedroom? He stood very still. *Yes, please ….*

"It's been a fun evening, Edward O'Connell. I loved your Johnny Cash." She reached out to shake his hand. "I hope you'll come again for karaoke next Wednesday. We could do some Christmas songs. Nothing religious, though. Hey! How about a duet of 'Baby it's Cold Outside.' " They fell into uncomfortable silence as those suggestive lyrics came to mind.

His laugh sounded stagy. "Uh, yeah. That would be fun."

No invitation, then. He took her hand but didn't shake it, just savored the feel of her long, cool fingers. The light contact delivered, thankfully, no glimpses into her future. "Can I see you before that?"

"You'll come for lunch, right? You're almost a regular."

"Of course," he said, holding her gaze. However, the last thing he wanted was to act like some lovesick calf and turn her off entirely. She obviously wasn't that into him, a realization that was totally intriguing.

Back in his hotel suite, Edward could think of nothing but Lisette. Needing distraction, he reached for one of the books shelved in the nightstand, an antique, leather-bound gold leaf hardcover edition that served more as a decoration than reading material. Willa Cather's novel, *Death Comes to the Archbishop*. He made a disgusted sound. He recalled the story only vaguely, except that the priest at its center, who ultimately becomes an archbishop, witnesses rampant corruption among the priests of the New World. The Catholic Church: so well intentioned and yet so destructive. He should have become an Episcopalian. Maybe then he'd still be a priest. But no. The circumstances that had ended his career were hardly peculiar to the Catholic Church. And his unusual—for all he knew, unique—*gifts* were dismissed not only by the Church, but the world at large.

* * *

Lisette locked the door the instant Edward left. She was worried Reynard might still be lurking about but also afraid she might give into temptation and go chasing after Edward. How lovely it would be to fall into his arms …. But what then? He might even be a virgin. They barely knew each other. The man she'd spent such a carefree evening with simply could not be the devout celibate he'd described. In her mind, religion was a form of brainwashing. She'd wasted over a year with Reynard, who she now believed was a sociopath. This wasn't the time for another ill-advised leap of faith.

Like most other structures on Water Street, the building that housed Café Lisette was over a hundred years old. The stairs creaked loudly as she climbed to the second floor. She'd never actually slept in the bedroom adjoining her office. The sofa bed was not a good one. Bobby had slept here a few nights while his plumbing was being fixed and never complained, so it couldn't be *that* bad.

She paused to appreciate the pier outside her window, decorated, like everything else in the downtown tourist area, with a myriad of colored lights. The dark season was bearable during the holidays, but after …. *Ugh.* January and February. Not that Reynard's house was so comfy. But being with him had its compensations. He could be charming, and to begin with, he had adored her. What a novelty that had been. *Adored.* She blew out a raspberry. *Who* had he adored? Some fantasy version of her. As her flaws and shortcomings had inevitably been revealed—the half-assed way she approached her various creative talents, her messiness, her tendency to blurt out the truth—she had watched that adorable version of herself he envisioned in her stead chipped away at, little by little, until it crumbled completely. Why hadn't she noticed sooner? Because Reynard had still cast enough smoldering looks her way that—foolish girl—she'd imagined it might be possible to salvage what they'd once had.

She hardly slept, tossing and turning in a fruitless search for a comfortable position. She could feel every damn spring in that poor excuse for a sofa bed. In fact, she could have described the mechanism from feel alone. She thought of the fairytale "The Princess and the Pea," where the princess could sense the presence of the pea no matter how many mattresses they piled on. Even the best-looking girl had only a few years of being a metaphorical princess, where such qualities were prized. In today's world, extreme sensitivity would just annoy the hell out of the prince, who would go in search of a more durable—and younger—replacement. Strands of gray threaded Lisette's long black hair and laugh lines framed her green eyes. How old was Edward? Late thirties, she guessed. He had years left to attract young females. Like Cary Grant, he'd be handsome into his sixties and beyond.

The next day, Lisette kept one eye on the door of the café, expecting Reynard to storm in and demand an explanation. He never did. Lunch came and went with no sign of Edward. Even after the kitchen closed, she willed him to stop by for a nightcap. *Nope.*

That's when it dawned on her: she was going to spend Christmas alone. Even her headwaiter Bobby and bartender Sid had private lives outside the restaurant. She'd lost touch with her friends in Port Angeles. Between Reynard and the restaurant, she had almost no leisure time, and nurturing close friendships wasn't her strong suit anyway. People did like her, though, once they realized her glossy exterior wasn't who she really was. She could phone those friends in Port Angeles …. But how would one or two nights of socializing change anything? The men in this town, other than Reynard, were thirty years her senior or more. The karaoke crowd were mostly too young for her, and many of them hailed from towns nearby such as Chimacum or Sequim. Edward was a temporary visitor, living in a hotel.

Was it time to move again? How about Arizona? Sun and heat in the winter—what a concept. But the Olympic Peninsula was in her bones. Her lungs would shrivel without sea air. Her soul needed snowy mountain peaks, crashing waves, and moss-and-lichen-draped primeval forests.

If possible, the sofa bed was even more torturous the second night, like the thinnest air mattress atop a mass of tree roots. As she propped herself up with pillows, she toyed with the idea of moving into the Bishop for a few days. *As if.* She was financially comfortable at the moment, but if drastic change lay ahead, she couldn't afford to stay in a nice hotel. She wished she were better friends with Matthew. The affable gay musician had lots of room in his Victorian, and he was generous to a fault. She had no doubt that if he stopped by Café Lisette and discovered her predicament, he'd offer her his hospitality. But Matthew, like Liam and all those O'Connells, frequented Kelpies, the gastropub on the third floor of the Joyce & Kesselman Building where the cool kids hung out.

She plumped her pillow with enough force to send feathers flying. Dispirited, she lay back and stared at the ceiling, where a crack was forming. Thank God she didn't own *this* building. When she finally slept, she dreamed of being lost in the forest with no hope of rescue.

CHAPTER 5

ONCE AGAIN JAKE WAS DRIVING his BMW to a Saturday night to-do at the O'Connell Compound. With new guests and FOSSP helpers, these events grew ever more elaborate. Tonight some of Jean-Louis's apprentice chefs were vying to outdo each other in the kitchen. It was only December fourth, so what were they celebrating? Advent? Being alive? Considering how David had brought Chiara back from the brink of death after that terrifying accident, Jake did see being alive as worth celebrating. He could hardly wait until her divorce was final. He already had a ring picked out—a brilliant ruby surrounded by small diamonds. He wanted to shower her with gifts. So far she'd only let him pick out a few outfits and a drawer full of sexy lingerie. He smiled, recalling how she'd chided him for their impracticality. "Those are for you," she'd said. How right she was.

His love had insisted on sitting in the back seat so Edward could ride upfront. Jake stole a glance at his older brother, who seemed wholly absorbed in the scenery, though there was nothing to see in the darkness. Even in daylight, Hastings Avenue was just another paved, tree-lined road, one of the least scenic parts of Port Townsend. This was the first time Jake had spent time with Edward since Thanksgiving, and he wasn't sure how to break the ice.

Say anything, he told himself. "What have you been up to?"

Edward had a gleam in his eye when he turned to face him. "Oh, this and that. A lot of walking and exploring. I've discovered a delightful little café that serves Cajun and creole cuisine."

"Café Lisette," Jake said, instantly understanding the appeal of the place for Edward. Lisette, of course. Didn't she live with Reynard? "Good, uh, food?"

Edward's chuckle was decidedly un-priestlike. "Entertainment too. Wednesday is Karaoke Night."

Jake was amazed. "*You* sang karaoke?"

"I did. Lisette is also quite the entertainer." Jake could just imagine. "Get your mind out of the gutter," his brother added. "Nothing like that. She has a beautiful singing voice, very versatile."

"Funny," Jake said, "she and Reynard were at a party we attended. Reynard played piano—the man's a phenomenon—but Lisette didn't sing."

Edward didn't reply immediately. "That makes perfect sense."

Jake tried being blunt. "Is she still with Reynard?"

"No."

Just what he deserved: a blunter answer. "You do know she and Liam—"

"Nothing happened," Edward interrupted him. "She told me they met in Port Angeles at a pub. She came on strong, but he wasn't having any. That was before Reynard. She has no history as a call girl."

Judging by the degree of his irritation, Edward was a goner. Jake hoped Lisette wasn't the maneater Liam had made her out to be. If Edward remained in Port Townsend and championed Lisette, family get-togethers were about to get even more interesting.

"What brought *you* back to Port Townsend?" Edward asked, giving him a taste of his own medicine. "I know about the change of professions, though I'm guessing there's more to it. I remember all those short stories that were accepted for publication in high school. Everyone was impressed but Mom and Da. Joe and Ali seem to be running a retreat for the very, *very* nervous."

Jake grinned, appreciating the reference to Mel Brooks' movie, *High Anxiety*. "More like a retreat for lost souls," he said. "Liam was decompressing after his rather intense experiences in Jerusalem following the terrorist attack that almost killed him. He was presumed dead."

"That's where he got the scars," Edward said. "He wears them well."

"Teresa was fleeing Mom and her charities as well as an unfortunate engagement to a manipulative bastard."

"Are you talking about Paul Andrews?" Edward asked. "I met him once. He seemed innocuous enough."

"That's a story for another time," Jake said. "Jealousy led him to do something phenomenally stupid. It just pushed Liam and Teresa together sooner."

"Mom must have been bummed," Edward said. "He's Catholic, successful, educated in the 'right' schools, and almost as rich as us."

"Along with being a hopeless lush," Jake said.

Edward shook his head. "Ah, too bad. The downfall of many an Irish lad. Tell me more."

"As I said, a story for another time. David was burned out from being a charity doctor in Africa."

"There was more to it than that," Chiara said from the back seat. "You might as well tell him, Jake. Haven't we learned the hard way that families shouldn't keep secrets?"

"Much as I'd like to enlighten you on that score," Jake said, "it would require more time than we have now." He punched in the code for the gate and proceeded down the gravel road leading to the compound. "Besides, it's best that David tell you his own story." They drove the mile of gravel road in silence.

Jake was vastly relieved not to be the one to break the news to Edward about David's ability to heal and his own "gift" of communing with ghosts. Even an ex-priest was bound to believe healing was the exclusive province of Our Lord and Savior and martyred saints. And the concept of ghosts had to violate some Church doctrine.

The scene that greeted them was considerably more sedate than Jake had anticipated. Just an intimate dinner for eleven—core family, with the addition of Xenia and Matthew. Usually they did buffet style and sat in the Sea Captain's House dining room. Ali had put two leaves in the custom-made maple Amish trestle table in the dining room of the Log Palace. The interior of their new home still had a bare-bones appearance that mystified Jake, given Ali's artistic eye and Teresa's talent for interior design. In his opinion, what it needed was a large nineteenth-century landscape like the ones that hung in the attic room of his rental Victorian, painted by his resident ghost—when he'd been alive, of course. Far be it from Jake to advise Joe and Ali how to decorate their home.

The three of them were the last to arrive, and most of the guests were already seated and drinking cocktails. After Jake and Chiara were seated, Jake noticed that the only spot open for Edward was between Xenia and Ali. By design, of course. The sneaks. Edward was too old for Xenia, and besides, he was hung up on Lisette. Too bad no one knew that except Chiara and Jake.

* * *

Edward helped himself to a cocktail before taking his seat at the impossibly long, exquisitely crafted table, wishing he'd made himself a double.

Sir Robin, pass me the mutton leg, he thought.

"Hi, Eddy."

Hell's bells, they'd seated him next to Xenia, Teresa's easy-on-the-eyes but annoying intern. He'd have to make the best of it. Her low-cut blouse left nothing to the imagination, showcasing two perfect breasts in a lacy bra. Like truffles wrapped in frilly paper, tasty but liable to make your teeth hurt. "Hullo, Xenia," he said, assuming an avuncular air. "Perhaps you would be so kind as to call me Edward."

She looked abashed. "But Teresa ...." She stopped herself. "I'm sorry. Of course. Ed-ward." The way she said his name, splitting it into two distinct syllables, proved she wasn't done ribbing him. *Lord, give me strength.*

A pretty, round-faced intern filled his glass and Xenia's with white wine and set the bottle in front of them. He sipped. *Excellent.* A big California chardonnay. His siblings certainly knew their wines. He looked around to see who else he might converse with. Ali had disappeared into the kitchen. He'd hardly made a dent in his cocktail. He finished it off before returning to his wine. After all, *he* wasn't driving.

"So, Xenia, how's business? Any interesting projects on the horizon?" His tone was so formal, he might have been interviewing her for some obscure periodical.

"Do you know Reynard Silvestre?"

"I've had the pleasure," he said with subtle irony. Not like a journalist— like a bad actor playing a guest at a duke's wedding breakfast.

"He asked me to decorate his guest room." She preened a little, as if Reynard had sought her out specifically for her brilliant designs.

"Oh?" This he wanted to hear. "How did you meet?"

"I jog most days around eleven, and he lives near the top of the Terrace Steps—above Haller Fountain. Part of my workout involves going up and down those stairs."

That sly fox, Edward thought. He'd arranged a "chance" meeting. *Good.* Now Edward could avoid that area between eleven and noon. He kept his smile friendly but bland. "How does Teresa feel about this?" His baby sister was sitting at the opposite end of the table, carrying on a spirited exchange with Maddie. "You may not know this, but she has a poor opinion of Reynard." *To say the least,* he thought.

Xenia shrugged with enough force that he caught a glimpse of rosy nipple. Intentional? Women *did* like to flash him. She was quite attractive, objectively speaking, but she didn't improve upon acquaintance. "I'm not worried," Xenia was saying. "Teresa wouldn't love the idea, but really, it's just a guest room. This is a small town. He wouldn't try anything funny. He's not going to rape me."

Maybe not, but he might seduce you, Edward thought. "Don't you think you should at least discuss the, uh, job prospect with Teresa?" It was a safe bet that Reynard's guest room was already exactly as he wanted it to be. He was, however, in the market for a decorative woman.

The girl's plump red lips were pursed in a mutinous expression. Noting her empty glass, Edward made like a dutiful host and filled it. *Moving right along* …. It shouldn't surprise Edward that Reynard would set his sights on Xenia. Now that Lisette had left rather than waiting for the musician to dump her, his pride was wounded. He'd need a girlfriend who could really get under his ex's skin. A beautiful young O'Connell protégée. *Perfect.* No point in drawing Xenia's attention to this inconvenient fact. She was a consenting adult. He wished she'd stop making goo-goo eyes at him.

Ali took her seat again, and while they ate their crab-cake appetizers, he got her talking about the children's books she was illustrating and co-writing with Chiara. He privately questioned the idea of a children's book about starfish and crabs, but their first book was doing well, so she and Chiara must have some special magic. He was enchanted by Ali's kindness and humility. If anyone could make a fun children's book about ugly sea creatures, it was she.

Speaking of crabs.... "This is excellent." He pointed his fork at the remaining bite of crab cake. "Did you make it?"

Ali's deep blue eyes sparkled delightfully. "My cooking skills are rudimentary. During my first pregnancy, I killed some time and wasted many perfectly good ingredients trying to channel Julia Child."

"This was while you and Joe were living in Paris?"

"Yes. I was pregnant with twins and even more … ungainly than I am now. Being pregnant in Paris in the winter was no *pique-nique*. Especially with Joe gone most days. He was renting a basement recording studio on the Rue de Rochechouart in the ninth arrondissement." Her eyes darted around the room, as if she realized the remark might be interpreted as critical of her husband. It was not as if Joe had heard or was even paying attention. He was deep in discussion with David, who was describing the intricacies of a screenplay he was working on. Ali tried to backpedal. "The studio wasn't far away. Our apartment was in St-Germain-des-Prés."

"It's okay," Edward reassured her. "The best men can be clueless when it comes to their wives' needs." He should know. He'd heard far too many confessions from wives whose complaints of neglect would have been news to their husbands. And were often coded invitations to Edward. He patted her hand sympathetically.

He instantly regretted touching her. Now he saw that this pregnancy was going to have complications too. The term "mild placental abruption" echoed in his head. Something about the placenta tearing? "Mild" didn't sound *too* bad.

He hoped his consternation didn't register on his face. "Will you return to Seattle for the birth?"

"My due date is February second. So … at the end of January."

Too late, he thought.

"When is Teresa's due date?"

"January twenty-sixth."

He hoped Teresa planned to give herself an extra week, although his premonition didn't indicate a premature birth. He wanted to tell Ali, "She should really go back soon after New Year's." Instead he said, "Ah, how great is that? The children can celebrate their birthdays together." Time enough for him to figure out how to convey the message without revealing his secret.

The next course was a beef dish. Along with another excellent bottle of wine, Burgundy this time. "Beef bourguignon?" he asked Ali.

A self-deprecating smile. "We're *oh* so classy here. I'm not sure if you realize we are being treated to a special multicourse meal prepared by one of Jean-Louis's protégés. It's a lot of food. Feel free not to clean your plate. The dogs will be eternally grateful."

"I'm a large man," he said, patting his flat stomach. "I can handle it."

"We noticed," Xenia said, admiring his broad shoulders and batting her eyes.

Ignoring his silent plea for help, Ali batted her eyes in imitation of Xenia.

Throughout the salad course, Edward peppered Ali with questions about their stay in Paris. Until she stood up to check on dessert.

"It's all fantastic," Joe told Tiger, the chef in training, a small, dark man of East Indian descent. "But with so many courses, you need to serve smaller plates. We're trying to keep our girlish figures."

Tiger hung onto the compliment, ignoring the advice. "Wait till you see dessert. It's Baked Alaska."

A collective groan rose up, followed by laughter and reassurances that Tiger was a superb chef.

Ali waved her napkin in surrender. "Not me. I'm having enough trouble with my blood sugar. I'm going to check on the twins."

That left Edward alone with Xenia again. She asked him about Paris, saying Teresa had dangled the possibility of taking her on a buying trip. He didn't bother to point out that Teresa wasn't going anywhere without Liam and the baby for a long, long time. She was about to be a new mother with an actor husband galivanting around any number of exotic locations. He helped himself to more Burgundy.

Dessert was a long time coming. Edward had no choice but to engage Xenia in further conversation. He began to regale her with stories about his favorite Parisian parks and cafés while reminiscing in his head about the women he'd met in those parks and cafés. Aimée in the Parc des Buttes Chaumont. Brigitte at les deux Magots. He'd probably gone through the entire alphabet. No "X" of course. It was a good thing that making it to the end of the alphabet wasn't on his bucket list. The intrusive memories made for choppy conversation as he sought to censure the inappropriate details.

He soon regretted his enthusiasm. Xenia was more interested in him than ever. How would he manage to put her off? Better if she *did* go for Reynard. If any woman could handle that slippery Frenchman, it was Xenia. He'd take her to Paris for sure. Edward's wanderlust had exhausted itself. Nothing left but the "lust," and it wasn't for Xenia. He conjured an enticing image of Lisette, sleeping alone in her upstairs apartment, her curly black hair loose and spilling over her full breasts, her long legs stretched across the bed, parting for him ….

Interrupting his wicked thoughts, Tiger marched in, hefting the flaming Baked Alaska with such ceremonial solemnity that it might have been the head of John The Baptist. It was an enormous lump of browned meringue that came to a peak—like Mount Rainer with dirty snow set afire.

"Such a pity Becca and Jean-Louis couldn't be here," Joe told a beaming Tiger. "They would be so proud." To the others, he explained, "They had an important event at the Bellevue location of La Fête Sauvage—a corporate Christmas party."

Ali rushed back in as fast as her burden would allow, expression apologetic. "Has anyone looked outside lately?"

"Sure," Tiger said, unconcerned. "It's snowing, but it's not supposed to stick to the roads."

Ali grabbed Joe's arm. "Sweetie, let's have a look. The thermometer says thirty-one, and it's snowing *hard*."

While they were gone, hunks of Baked Alaska were distributed, along with an excellent Sauterne. Joe's wine cellar alone made Edward look forward to future events. Normally he limited his consumption to two glasses. Tonight he'd lost count. He'd feel it in the morning.

The news from outside was bad. "It's sticking," Joe said. "You should all stay the night. We can accommodate everyone, no problem. And we have extra winter gear, courtesy of Big Paul's." To Edward, he said, "Whenever Mom visits, she brings along samples from the latest line of gear and clothing."

They assigned Edward to the cabin on the far end, one of the originals that came with the Sea Captain's House. Again, he chastised himself for overdosing on vino. He'd been nervous about attending a "family" event and thrown off kilter by forced proximity to the kittenish Xenia. The cabin had knotty-pine paneling, a crazy-quilt comforter, and what looked like the original wall-to-wall carpeting. A far cry from his room at the Bishop, but the mattress was decent.

He showered to clear his head, wishing he'd also gone easier on the rich food. He longed for some kind of digestive remedy, even plain old baking soda in water, so he was delighted to find Tums in the medicine cabinet along with a bottle of ibuprofen. So thoughtful of Ali and Joe.

Still wearing the terry cloth guest robe, he lay down on the bed and closed his eyes. *Oh, wait*, he needed to lock the door. It was a safe bet that Xenia would come sniffing around.

The lock was stuck in an open position, and the chain was one small tug away from detaching from the wall. In fact, it came off in his hand. *Damn.* He was too tired and tipsy to do anything about it. Even with a screwdriver, the wall was crumbling around the screw that held the chain on one side. He'd have to hope Xenia had more common sense than he gave her credit for.

The space heater was too loud, and he turned it off. Then he was cold, despite the robe. Wishing for flannel pajamas, he finally drifted off.

He was woken by the squeaking hinges of the door. *Surprise, surprise.* Wearily, he tightened the sash of the robe and swung his legs over the side of the bed. Xenia was shrugging out of her parka and boots and stood there in what had to be one of Teresa's silk robes. It was far too fine for a girl in her position to afford. The hot pink complemented the warm tones of her skin.

"You don't look very surprised to see me," she purred. The robe slithered to the floor, and he gulped, his cock instantly jumping to attention. It had been a long time since Paris.

He could definitely see where her confidence came from. Her body was spectacular. Though her legs weren't long, they were nicely muscled from all the jogging. Her belly was flat, her hips wide, and her breasts impossibly perky. He squeezed his eyes shut. "Xenia, I didn't invite you here, and you need to leave … *now. Immediately.*"

He felt her sit down next to him on the bed and reach inside his robe. He pulled away, but not before she'd discovered his enthusiastic cock. "I have condoms," she whispered. He could smell the cloyingly sweet scent of coconut lotion.

"Yes, I'm a normal man, and the flesh is weak. But it wouldn't be fair. I'm *much* older than you, and I have no interest in pursuing a relationship with… with anyone."

"Was I proposing a relationship?" she asked reasonably.

She plopped into his lap, her arms locked around his neck, and he growled in frustration. Was she going to rape him? Even if he weren't fixated on Lisette, he would *not* have gone for Xenia. Physically, she was his type, anyone's type, but emotionally there was something off about her. No doubt she had more than a few hair-raising stories from her history as a foster child.

He pushed her off his lap and held her at arm's length. "No," he said firmly. "This isn't going to happen. The sooner you realize it, the less frustrated you will be. I'm sorry, truly."

She struggled, but only a little, then heaved a mournful sigh. He could well imagine that she wasn't used to rejection. He half expected a slap when he let her go. He let her go anyway, but the blow never came. Instead, she retrieved her robe, taking much longer than necessary to put it back on, staging a little show for his benefit. He turned away. Was this an acknowledgment that the battle was lost or merely a retreat? She clearly still believed in her powers of seduction.

"I'm going now," she said, to call his attention back to her. "Sleep well." At the door, she peered over her shoulder with one last sultry look.

Alone again, Edward fell back on the bed, breathing hard. *Damn, damn, damn.*

When he finally drifted off, his sleep was so light that he wasn't entirely sure it was sleep. Other than the visit from Beverly Bigfoot, a character in Ali and Chiara's children's book. A fairly compelling bit of evidence. Finally he gave up and pulled back the curtains. Outside, the driven snow glowed in the darkness. His watch said ten after six. If he'd had proper boots and warmer clothing, he would have loved to take a walk. He should have accepted Joe's offer of Big Paul's gear. His calfskin dress boots were little better than slippers.

Where were his boxer briefs? He'd left them on the chair, along with his other clothes. *Damn.* Xenia had taken a souvenir. He threw on his cashmere peacoat and trudged down to the Sea Captain's House, where a light in the kitchen indicated another early riser. It was David, who found him a pair of snow boots and agreed to join him on a walk around the grounds after they'd shoveled the path. There was maybe six inches of snow.

The lights were coming on in the cabins as they trudged away from the house and proceeded down the snow-covered road. "How did you sleep?" David asked.

"Lousy," Edward said with good humor. "I had a visitor."

"Oh?" David said, unsurprised. "Xenia, huh? Lucky you."

Edward gave him a baleful look. "*Not* lucky. I did *not* want to get lucky, and certainly not with her. She's a child emotionally, or maybe just warped. The lock on my door is broken, so she let herself in. She probably thought the unlocked door was an invitation."

"Good Lord," David said, shaking his head. "Listen, man, I am so sorry. When Liam was living here, nothing was ever broken or malfunctioning. He was always on the lookout for projects. Joe and I can fix things too, of course, but we don't have the same enthusiasm for it." He groaned. "You were a sitting duck."

"Listen," Edward said, "it's not the first time women have done stuff like that—tried to trick me into bed, I mean—but this situation is stickier because you are all so protective of her. What's worse is that she's Teresa's pet project, and everyone seems to think we'd make a dandy couple. I'm not interested, and I don't want her thinking that if she persists, her efforts will pay off." He paused. "The damned imp took my boxer briefs."

David seemed to find this hilarious, so Edward went on, "I also don't want her to lie about what happened, so I'm counting on you to back me up if it ends up being her word against mine."

"I don't think she'll do that," David said. "She owes this family a lot. It's not in her best interests to make trouble. We'll ensure you're never put in that position again. Should I tell Teresa?"

"I don't know," Edward said, throwing up his hands in frustration. "I don't want to turn Teresa against her. I'm sure she's had a tough life."

They were standing at the end of the road now, next to the first code-activated gate, staring out at Hastings Avenue, thick with snow. "No snowplow yet," David said, "and I wouldn't hold my breath. You'll be stuck here a while longer, I'm afraid."

"That's okay," Edward said, "I drove with Jake and Chiara, and I wouldn't want to rush them or embarrass Xenia by scurrying off like a panicked rabbit. For now, let's not blab about her ill-conceived bootie call. Exposing her should be a last-ditch solution."

David looked both ways, up and down Hastings. "No cars, not even four-wheel-drive vehicles. We should take advantage of this rare opportunity." As they continued onward, he added, "You know, you are too charming for your own good. I'm sure you didn't intend to lead Xenia on, but I can see how she might have misinterpreted your behavior."

Edward dragged a hand through his hair. "Yeah. I had too much wine. Damn Joe and his wine cellar."

David burst into full-throated bass-baritone laughter. "You *are* harsh. Damnation should require a greater sin than that. Although I agree, it's a mighty temptation."

CHAPTER 6

———◆———

AT NOON ON TUESDAY, CAFÉ Lisette bustled with a larger than average crowd. Snow and icy roads had effectively shut down the town for two days. After her chef's car slid into a ditch, Lisette had been forced to close for the weekend. All that was left of the storm were some piles of dirty snow—the remains of snow sculptures or mounds created by shoveling. Otherwise, it was a typical winter day with blue skies, a few puffy clouds, a stiff sea breeze, and temperatures in the low forties.

No sign of Edward since Karaoke Night. The slick sidewalks had kept Lisette from her daily six-mile run, essential to her mental and physical health. With a sigh, she headed to the gym, where most of the men who ogled her were retirement age. *Someday soon that will be your dating pool*, an evil little voice in her head whispered.

Though she'd pasted on a smile, boredom and lack of sleep had left her restless and irritable. The rooms above the restaurant were dingy and drafty, and there was no TV. She could have done with a roaring fire and a decent novel, neither of which was an option. She read mostly popular fiction borrowed from the library, closed by the snow. At Reynard's, she'd had his extensive collection of books at her disposal. Some novels, such as Stendhal's *The Red and the Black* and *The Charterhouse of Parma*, were basically romances so good they were considered classics.

Lisette now had a better appreciation for how pleasant life had been at Reynard's—when he wasn't around, that is. She'd thought Edward was a possibility, but apparently she'd overestimated her charms. Today she was acting as hostess, and in between, approving Chef Marky's weekly specials,

48

which lacked his usual creative flair. He was preoccupied with his own woes—two young children recovering from the flu. She wasn't sure how he managed, in that his job occupied most of his waking hours. The one day he stayed home, she filled in and enjoyed the distraction. He wouldn't appreciate her dictating the specials. No matter what was featured, customers usually ordered the gumbo or Shrimp Étouffée.

As if alerted by some sixth sense, she looked up to find herself face-to-face with Edward, so handsome that she almost forgot to breathe. She smiled in spite of herself. "Mr. O'Connell," she said, as if he were any other regular, "I was beginning to think you'd found a new hangout."

He gave her that signature O'Connell grin that could melt you on the spot. "Heaven forbid," he said. He looked around. "You're busy today." He eyed the second chair at the small round table. "Can I join you?"

"Be my guest." Her headwaiter responded to her signal. "Bobby, can you get Mr. O'Connell a Guinness and… how about jambalaya? We're doing it Creole style today. In other words, with tomatoes."

"Sounds great."

"I see you survived our blizzard."

He laughed, as he was meant to. "It's hilarious the way this area is paralyzed by a few inches of snow. You get it, coming from the East Coast." Bobby set the Guinness in front of him. "Can I buy you a glass of wine?"

"Not while I'm working." She stifled a weird urge to lead him up the stairs right now, even though making love on that horrid sofa bed would either break the sorry piece of furniture or their backs. "Normally I like the snow. Here it's a rare treat. People are afraid to drive, so it stays beautiful longer."

"Normally?"

She blinked back tears, but one escaped, and she quickly wiped it away with her knuckle. "That was silly," she said with an embarrassed laugh. "Maybe it's this season of enforced jolliness … or having to adjust to new circumstances. It's been a strange few days. Uncomfortable."

He assumed she was being literal. "Lumpy bed? Drafty window?"

"Check, and check." She marked the air. "The mattress on the sofa bed is most definitely not Posturepedic. The single-pane window is at least fifty years old. The library was closed so I had nothing to read, just some old magazines. No TV, not to mention cable or a VCR. Just my own lurid imagination for company." *There you go, blurting out your uncensored thoughts again.*

"Ouch, that does sound awful." His tone was warm and sympathetic. "I was stranded at the family compound until Sunday afternoon."

"Terrible," she said, not meaning it. What better place to be stuck? She did breathe easier, knowing the reason for his absence. "They must live in the lap of luxury."

"The accommodations are first rate," he said, carefully.

She tried to read the subtext. "And yet…" she prompted.

He didn't elaborate.

The jambalaya arrived, and Edward dug in with gusto.

"Old family recipe," she said, lapsing into her usual flippancy.

"Is that so?"

"No. My family's restaurant was all-American. Fried chicken, prime rib on Saturdays. Hamburgers, French fries, apple pie."

"Ah-ha," he said. "Your family had a restaurant."

"More like a diner."

"This is your recipe?"

"My take on it."

"So … Reynard."

She gave a little start. Weren't they done with that subject? "What about him?"

"Does he still want to talk?"

She'd known Reynard would let it go. She wasn't worth fighting for. "No. Not that I'm surprised."

"Would it disappoint you to learn that he has his eye on a new candidate?"

He watched her carefully. How could he possibly be privy to such information? Did he think she was still hung up on Reynard? She gave a careless shrug. "No … but it might wound my vanity."

He nodded. "At dinner Saturday night, they put me next to Xenia, Teresa's assistant. She told me Reynard had asked her to redecorate his guest room."

Lisette tried to recall a room officially designated for guests. In their year together, Reynard had never had houseguests, and she couldn't imagine that happening.

"His house used to be a B and B called 'The Captain's Retreat.' There are many guest rooms, none of them unfinished. Reynard doesn't do 'guests.' He has few friends, and he isn't generous with those he has. He was raised by a single mother who died soon after he left home. But if he did invite, say, some business associate from L.A. to stay, he would hardly be concerned for their comfort or their décor. In fact, he'd probably pay to put them up at a hotel. What does Xenia look like?"

"A drunkard's dream …" Edward began.

"What?"

"I was thinking of the old song by The Band, 'Up on Cripple Creek.' I imagine that if you were drunk enough, Xenia would be your dream girl. Not that it takes being literally drunk. Drunk with lust works. She is quite beautiful by any standard. Exotic. She's a former foster child, so all she knows of her background is her first name. With that spelling—it starts with an X—she might be Greek or Russian."

"Drunkard's dream," Lisette repeated. She could do without listening to Edward wax poetic about Xenia.

"What I meant to say is, there's something off about her. For me to respond to her would require a major lapse of judgment, an altered state. Even then …. I'm in the minority. The others in my family all seem to think she's …."

Lisette leapt into the pause. "Perfect for you? How old?"

"Twenty-six."

"And you are… thirty-eight?" He nodded. It was the silver sideburns, she thought; otherwise, she'd have guessed much younger. "Twelve years apart. Perfectly respectable. Reynard is forty. Fourteen years difference. He'd be a peacock with his train on full display."

Edward laughed. "That's what they call the spreading tail feathers, a train?"

"Yes."

She knew Edward wanted something from her. At the very least, sex. The way she'd been feeling lately, she was sorely tempted to let that happen sooner rather than later, even if it lasted only a fortnight. But then where would she be? More depressed than ever and still up shit's creek. Living in a crappy apartment above a restaurant. And what if he really was a virgin? *Awkward.* "I'm thirty-three," she responded to the question hanging in the air. "My birthday was two weeks ago." At the moment, weeks seemed to matter.

Edward grinned. "Prime of life."

The warmth of his gaze made her cheeks heat up. "Did Xenia tell you how she and Reynard met?"

"She jogs every day around eleven, using the Terrace Steps for conditioning."

Sneaky bastard, she thought. "He laid a trap for her, then. That explains why *I* never see her. I use those stairs for conditioning too. I jog in the morning before the lunch shift or between lunch and dinner."

There was an awkward pause. His plate was clean and his glass empty. A party of five waited to be seated. When Lisette tried to insist his meal was on the house, he acted as if she'd wounded his masculine pride. So she signaled for Bobby to bring him the check. By the time she'd finished attending to the customers, Edward was gone.

* * *

Edward waited until Thursday to "run into" Lisette. Why not take a page out of the crafty Reynard's book? It was a beautiful day, and she was bound to go jogging at some point. His knees weren't what they used to be, and normally he limited his runs to six miles. He didn't want to alert the neighborhood crime watch, so he tried not to loiter too conspicuously. She was a no-show.

On Friday, he got lucky. Running up and down the Terrace Steps was a tedious business, harder than it looked, and he was just about to call it a day. His sweatshirt was soaked through, and when he sat on the bench to cool off, he quickly felt chilled.

Just as he'd decided that he didn't want to "run into" Lisette looking and feeling like a wrung-out dishtowel, his quarry emerged from her café. She wore Lycra shorts that showed off her firm thighs, a thick black fleece jacket and gloves, a bright yellow woolen cap, and a matching puffy vest. Her long black braid bounced behind her. Seeing her like this, Ali might draw her as an adorable bumble bee. Lisette was just setting out, and the sun was about to go down. She switched on a headlamp. *Damn*, he hadn't expected her to run in the dark. Now what?

Seeing him on the bench, she sprinted over, graceful as a gazelle. "Edward! Fancy meeting you here." Laughter sparkled in her bright green eyes. All that subterfuge for nothing.

Feeling like an idiot, he stood up. "Those stairs kicked my ass. I need to go soak in a hot bath."

She was jogging in place. "Oh, that sounds lovely. All I've got is a shower with poor water pressure. Well, see you around! The restaurant opens at five thirty. That means I have only an hour before I need to start getting ready."

"You want to run with me back to the hotel? Uh … I meant as far as the hotel. You could continue on from there."

"Okay! Let's go." She took off, and he reluctantly picked up his pace. "You missed Karaoke Night," she said. "A guy did a dead-on version of 'Don't Stop Believin'.' He had a fantastic set of pipes."

"By that band Journey, right? Not my favorite. Not my range, either. Good turnout?"

Keeping her eyes on the sidewalk, she said, "You spoiled me. It was way more fun with you there. I thought we were going to do 'Baby it's Cold Outside.' "

"Rain check? Or should I say snow check."

"The snow was gone." Had he imagined the reproach in her voice? He hadn't meant to play games, or maybe he had. He'd been afraid to come off as too eager. When he didn't offer an explanation, she asked, "What have you been up to?"

Dreaming of you, he thought. What he said was, "There was a Christmas-light decorating party at the compound last night. Our childhood tradition was to cram as many lights as possible on every available surface. It isn't Christmas at the O'Connells unless the power company issues a citation."

"They do that?" She wrinkled her nose at him.

They had already jogged several blocks past the hotel. She set a punishing pace, making talking difficult. "I imagine they just send you one of those charts showing that your usage is way up to shame you into behaving."

"Didn't they tell us not to use Christmas lights one year?" Lisette asked.

"I believe that was 1973. The energy crisis. Very disappointing for the O'Connells. I was twelve. Teresa wouldn't remember. She was only two and a half."

"It's a vague memory for me. I was seven. We spent a lot of time waiting in line at the gas station with my mom to top off the tank of our Chevvy Impala. Our diner was the height of cozy Americana. Without the festive lights and the Christmas trees, we lost some business. It was a real drag for my brother and me."

"What were you like then?"

"You wouldn't believe it. A daredevil. I could throw a football as well as the boys, but they wouldn't let me play. One of them told me I was a 'lesbo.' So I slugged him." She smiled. "Gave him a shiner. Never even got punished for it. He didn't want to admit he'd been bested by a girl."

Edward had a hard time imagining this elegant creature as the neighborhood hellion in pigtails with middle-class parents and a mean right hook.

He slowed to a stop, realizing how dark it was. "I should turn back. I don't have brightly colored clothing or a headlamp."

She kept jogging in place but didn't speak. Dare he hope she didn't want to let him go?

As he began to stretch, he said impulsively, "I wish you could see it."

"What?"

"The O'Connell Compound. I could invite you. Monday night."

Her expression grew guarded. "Are you kidding? I'd be about as welcome as Delilah at Samson's funeral."

He chuckled under his breath. "They were both crushed to death after she cut his hair and he brought the temple down on their heads."

Her sultry laugh sent a thrill through him. She shook her head. "I should avoid biblical references. The only Bible stories I know I learned in Sunday school, and I stopped attending church at an early age. Sorry, we weren't Catholics."

"Denomination?" he asked.

Now she was stretching too. "Lutheran. My parents weren't that into it, but they didn't want to raise heathens, so they went to church for the sake of my brother and me. They raised heathens anyway. Too bad for them. Come on, I'll escort you to your hotel. I should be getting back in any case. We can walk. Cool down."

"I didn't mean to cut your run short."

"A *fast* walk." She picked up the pace.

"Seriously," he said, "be my date on Monday night."

She regarded him bleakly. "Let's see… Liam thinks I'm a former prostitute and Teresa is convinced my ex-boyfriend is a rapist. They *all* think I'm up to no good. I'd be *real* popular. I can assure you that Reynard is no rapist, whatever his failings. He told me what happened. He tried to get Teresa to come in for a nightcap, and she fled. Before he knew it, Liam had whooshed up on his Harley and whisked her away. Reynard is convinced that Liam was tailing her. How else could he have appeared out of nowhere?"

Edward nodded sagely. "I figured it was something like that." Trying a different tack, he asked, "Where's that vaunted moxie? The little girl who wanted to play football so much that she was willing to stand up to the town bullies? Besides, they're nice people, really. I'm confident you can win them over. Jake was *persona non grata* until recently. And I didn't talk to them for years. They got over it."

She came to a halt and turned to face him. "Why is that? It makes no sense. You are the nicest guy I've ever met."

Nice, he thought. *Just shoot me now.*

"I meant that as a compliment. Do you think I don't appreciate *nice* after all the bad boys I've known?" She directed her gaze down the decked-out street as she added, "Nice *and* gorgeous. What woman could resist that?"

That's when he noticed that they stood in front of his hotel.

"Okay," she said, "let's do it. No one calls Lisette a coward."

He watched her sprint off toward her café. Then he looked down and saw that she'd dropped a glove. Intentional? Yes! Here was an excuse to see her again before Monday.

After reverently picking it up, he climbed the long staircase to his suite, where he drew a hot bath. The setup included a kitchenette, so he warmed up leftovers from the refrigerator for dinner, then sat down to watch the news. He was channel surfing when he picked up the glove again.

And reeled. He hoped it wasn't too late.

CHAPTER 7

———•———

LISETTE FLOATED INTO HER CAFÉ. She couldn't believe Edward had asked her on an actual date. Then, as the evening wore on, the doubts crept in. She hated having to prove herself, especially having to prove that she was *nice* enough. She wasn't nice. She didn't do volunteer work or donate to worthy causes. She didn't go out of her way to help little old ladies cross the street. She had a smart mouth, an expensive wardrobe, and no higher education other than a culinary arts degree. Nothing to respect here, not for a family of their ilk. Like Reynard, they had fancy degrees that allowed them to perfect their skills until they achieved excellence. She'd lost interest in her one bona fide skill—the art of *haute cuisine*. When she'd decided to open a restaurant in Port Angeles, she'd researched which cuisine wasn't available on the Peninsula and come up with the concept for Café Lisette, even though she'd never been to New Orleans. After a rave review in the *Peninsula Daily News*, her bistro had packed them in during lunch and dinner, especially on weekends. The concept had been less successful in Port Townsend, but she wasn't losing money. Karaoke Night had attracted new customers, though they were less interested in the food than the mixed drinks.

The faculty and students at Le Cordon Bleu would look down their noses at Café Lisette. Creole and Cajun "cuisine" was just country cooking.

Lisette had no clue how to go about convincing the O'Connells she didn't deserve the label they'd stamped on her, thanks to the run-in with Liam at the pickup bar in Port Angeles and her relationship with Reynard—*conniving vamp*.

"Lisette?" It was her bartender.

She started at the sound of his voice. She was supposed to be going through the credit card receipts.

"Sorry. Didn't mean to interrupt. I'm toast. Okay if I take off?"

"Of course. Thanks, Sid. Can you lock the door behind you?"

"Yeah, sure. Later, 'gator." He doffed his hat and she grinned. The "gator" thing came from jokes about their style of cuisine, which hailed from the land of alligators, Louisiana. She really should travel there one day.

After he was on the other side of the door, she waited for the key to turn in the lock. Instead, she heard an *oof* and a dull thud. Her blood ran cold. Putting the metal box containing the credit card receipts and cash on the chair beside her where they couldn't be seen from the door, she scuttled toward the bar. They kept a loaded gun hidden on the lowest shelf. Was there time to retrieve it? She needed a weapon *now*.

She cast about for an object suitable for bludgeoning.

Too late.

A man burst in, brandishing a gun and shaking like an overtaxed engine. Good Lord, what had he done to Sid? Some weird instinct of calm claimed her body. *Don't panic and he won't kill you. It's money he wants. If he were a professional killer demanding some retribution for the past, he'd have shot you by now. He's just a run-of-the-mill drug addict needing a fix.*

Holding up her hands to show she didn't have a weapon, she sidestepped toward the bar. What would he do when he discovered the cash register was empty? Could she lie and say the cash box was already in her safe? He'd just make her open the safe. Better to give him the cash box. *Stall,* said a little voice in her head. Maybe Sid would regain consciousness—if he wasn't dead. *Jesus, poor Sid.*

Her brain was a jumble of random thoughts. Quotes from poetry and songs. "The past isn't past." "The past is too much with us." No, neither of those were correct. *Sorry, Faulkner and Wordsworth.* "What I did for love." More like, "What I did for money." Perhaps her life was flashing before her eyes. Her life. If it ended now, what had it all been for? *What a joke.*

Another man burst in. In a blur of motion, the would-be thief crumpled to the floor. His gun skidded toward the bar.

"Lisette, are you all right?" Edward helped her into a chair and draped his cashmere peacoat over her shoulders. The heat of the soft wool and the clean, spicy scent of his aftershave imbued her with warmth and comfort.

"Sid ..." she began.

"He'll be okay. He was coming to when I arrived. I didn't have time to check, but I'd say our friend here pistol-whipped him. Probably just has a knot on the back of his head."

She was trembling. He knelt down and wrapped her in his arms. "Shh. I've got you."

Sid staggered in and sat on a stool at the bar, rubbing the back of his head.

One arm circling Lisette, Edward drew his cell phone from his coat pocket and called 911.

"What if he wakes up?" Lisette's gaze was fixed on the prone figure of the thief.

"I hope he does, eventually," Edward said. "That blow can be fatal. I don't use it lightly." He went over to check on the man. "He's awake, just disoriented. If he tries to get up, I'll flatten him again."

The man groaned.

There was no need for flattening. The police arrived in ten minutes, and after briefly assessing the situation, cuffed the intruder and read him the Miranda warning. By then Lisette had found a cold gel pack for Sid's head. When the two officers finally got a good look at Lisette, their eyes widened with interest. She was used to this sort of reaction, which normally amused her. They were young guys, one of them scrawny, the other big as a tank, like he took steroids. Their manner was overly solicitous, but she supposed that was better than suspicious or disrespectful. *Ah, the perks of beauty*, she thought. *You'll miss them when they're gone.*

After inquiring about everyone's welfare, the beefy officer said to Sid, "Sir, you should go to the ER. That's a nasty bump." He cast his hot gaze on Lisette, and she pulled the coat tighter around her shoulders to shift his focus to her face. "He meant to rob you?"

"Yes. He came in carrying a gun and shaking like he was about to explode. I tried to stay calm."

"Well, now you're in shock," he said in a gentle voice, "so it's a good thing you have that coat. Where did the gun go?"

She pointed to the floor next to the bar, which had halted the weapon's skid.

"You're lucky it didn't go off." Slipping on gloves, the policeman gingerly picked up the gun and examined it. "Like I thought—not loaded. Jeez, this thing's an antique. Probably belongs to his father or grandfather. He looks about eighteen."

The intruder lay still now, staring bleakly into space.

The officer turned to Edward. "How did you, uh, incapacitate him? Do you work here?"

"I'm a friend," Edward said too quickly. "I was helping Lisette put things in order when this guy burst in. He didn't know I was there. That's why I could sneak up on him. I, uh, hit him in the neck."

"Jesus," the big officer said and gave a low whistle. "Like Captain Kirk in *Star Trek*? You knocked him out with a karate chop?"

The assumption seemed to annoy Edward. "I didn't knock him out. When you hit the vagus nerve, you stun them. I'm a twelfth-degree black belt. Judo. Actually, now I'm a white belt—that means 'purity.' It's what happens when you've …. Never mind."

Lisette wanted to laugh. Sid was staring at Edward as if he were a space alien, knowing as he did that the part about "helping out" was total BS. Far be it from her to contradict Edward's story.

The policeman was busy filling out his report. "It's pretty clear what happened here. The guy obviously needs a fix. Attempted burglary, assault with a deadly weapon."

He took down all their personal information, gave Lisette one last soulful look, and wished them all a nice evening. "If we need you to testify, you'll hear from us. The guy might just plead guilty and save us all time and money." He turned to Sid. "Can you drive?"

Sid shook his head and winced. "I called my girlfriend, Margie. She's on her way. Shouldn't be long."

"Good. We'd give you a lift, but this lowlife will be in the back seat." They hauled the cuffed man to his feet.

Margie arrived. It was a short car trip, Lisette knew, in that the two of them rented the basement of a Victorian a few blocks away. Still holding the gel pack to his head, Sid said, "Uh, Lisette, Edward, it's been real." Thank God Edward had identified himself so that Sid had a name for this man who had supposedly been helping her close up. "Lisette, I'll give you a call in the morning. You gonna be okay?"

"I'll stay with her for a bit," Edward said.

Lisette gave her bartender a hug. "Thanks, Sid. The question is, will *you* be okay?"

"Yeah, sure. It could have been worse."

"You take care. I'm so sorry."

"I thought stuff like this didn't happen in Port Townsend," he admitted.

"We've got drugs and homelessness like anywhere else," the beefy officer said in a self-important voice.

After they were alone again, Edward fetched the open bottle of white wine from the bar and poured them each a glass.

She took a long sip. "Are you going to tell me how you knew I needed help?"

"You dropped your glove."

She had no idea what he was getting at.

"After you left me earlier today, I saw that you'd dropped a glove. When I first picked it up, I got nothing. But later, I touched it and … I saw the man with the gun coming into your place. I got here as soon as I could."

"You *saw* him?"

"In my head."

"You're clairvoyant." She couldn't believe her ears. *A clairvoyant priest?*

"Sometimes," he admitted.

They were both silent as his revelation sunk in.

"You know this is going to be in the newspaper," he added.

She rubbed her aching temples. "Not the kind of publicity I need."

He smiled and touched her arm. "Yeah, but the story might make for a dandy icebreaker Monday night. The family will have no choice but to be nice to you."

She laughed at the silly expression on his face. Immediately afterward came the thought: *another man putting you on a pedestal.* Didn't they get that no one could live up to those kinds of expectations? If he knew the whole truth about her past … what then?

She sighed. "I already said I'd come, didn't I? But don't blame me if they have the stocks set up for me."

"No stocks, I promise. Just a nice old-fashioned rack."

"You joke about this now …." She took his hand and laid it on her arm. "Tell me what will happen tomorrow."

He moved her hand to his cheek. "It doesn't work like that. Most of the time when I touch a person or object, I get nothing." Releasing her, he held up his right hand, the fingers of the other splayed on the table. "I swear on this holy table to remain by your side and keep you safe from my family's torture devices, both real and metaphorical."

Shaking her head as if he were hopeless, she reluctantly handed over his coat. "You're goofy, you know."

"But lovable." He took the coat. "Does this mean I'm dismissed?"

She smiled. "For now."

He obviously wanted a kiss. But she knew it wouldn't stop there, and this godawful night, on her shitty sofa bed, was not the right time or place to start a love affair with a thirty-eight-year-old who might possibly be a virgin.

CHAPTER 8

FIVE O'CLOCK ON A SATURDAY. Jake had been working for several hours in his second-floor study on the rewrites of *Zwap*, the third Damon Morehouse thriller. The problem with using *Batman* action words as titles was that there weren't many good ones left. He'd originally ruled out *Bonk* because of the sexual connotation. But it might just work. *Bonk* was tame compared to *Octopussy*. His thoughts drifted to the beautiful woman hard at work in the attic bedroom. She preferred to write at a desk next to the window overlooking the bay.

Chiara was stewing over another chapter of *Salish Sea Stories*. Some of the sketches Ali had given her had her scratching her head, wondering what kind of story could bring together starfish—make that "sea stars"—crabs, and the kind of fish that hung out in the Salish Sea. The most likely candidates weren't colorful, not like tropical fish, and the water was cold and murky. Ali and Chiara had started the book at the request of David's son, four-and-a-half-year-old Lorenzo, who'd fallen in love with sea stars while exploring the wonders of low tide. Chiara had been the one to raise Lorenzo for his first four years of life. His birth mother, her sister Sylvia, was an ER doctor in Chicago and had no maternal instincts. Lorenzo's unintentionally funny questions and comments were sprinkled throughout their first book, *The Way to Moss Manor*, giving it adult appeal as well.

Now that Chiara no longer lived at the compound, she didn't see as much of Lorenzo. Jake hoped she didn't regret moving in with him. The stately, shockingly blue Italianate Victorian was a far cry from anything his former CEO self would have chosen to inhabit. He'd put his fancy modern digs in North Bend on the market. He wouldn't be caught dead there now—too austere and uninviting. He chuckled to himself over the expression, "caught dead." Someone *had* been caught dead in *this* crazy old place. Simon Elliot, a late-nineteenth-century landscape painter who had died young of a wasting disease, had once occupied the attic room. For all Jake knew, Simon's ghost had moved on. Only once had he appeared to Jake—in a dream. Jake's prior experience with specters, along with what the dead artist had told him, led him to believe the visitation was genuine. Jake's other ghostly encounter, more like a possession, had been with his friend Rory. Neither Rory nor gentlemanly Simon had any interest in scaring anyone. Well, there had been that time Simon scared the pants off George Reed Masters, Hollywood heartthrob ....

Jake just shook his head. For a big action star, George was kind of a wuss. Better that he should play Troy Benz, the character inspired by Rory, than Damon himself. Somehow Rory had arranged that, and George implied that his dead friend now resided in *his* head. The honor of portraying Damon had gone to his supremely macho brother-in-law Liam. David's wife Maddie would make a wonderful villainess because she was the last person you'd suspect of being evil. That was the whole point of Lorelei. She threw people— namely, men—off balance with her pretty-pretty face and va-va-voom body.

A knock on the door, and Chiara stuck her head in. "*Caro*, will you save me from myself and join me for a glass of wine?" The corners of her mouth turned downward in a clownish expression of despair. "I am at my wits' end." She paused. "Did I use that right? I may mean it literally. I have no more wits left, not that I am at the end of my rope."

Adorable, he thought. A native Italian who had moved to the States as a teenager, Chiara often puzzled over American idioms.

"I get your drift," he said.

"You get my drift? You understand my intention?"

"*Esatto*. Well, not quite 'exactly.' More like I get the general sense of what you mean."

She repeated the phrase quietly to herself a few times to make it stick. "Are you ready to 'call it quits' for the day?" Another newish idiom.

"Most definitely." He pulled her into the room and enfolded her in his arms, rocking back and forth. "But first, a sip from the nectar of your lips."

She giggled as he kissed her lips, then her neck, where she was ticklish. The kiss quickly grew serious. "Oh, my," she said as he pulled up her skirt and hoisted her onto his desk. "You're making my head spin. It's a big leap to go from Oxana the Octopus to Damon Morehouse."

He reluctantly pulled away. "I can't help it if the sight of you instantly puts my mind in the gutter."

His answer elicited more giggles as she repeated softly, "Mind in the gutter!"

He purposely employed as many idioms, or should he say clichés, as he could just to delight her. Over her merino wool A-line skirt, she was wearing a fitted cashmere sweater with a plunging neckline—the kind of "immodest" outfit she'd never have dared to wear in her former life as the neglected wife of a clueless software engineer who cheated on her. Jake and Chiara had both turned their lives upside down, and so far their new circumstances suited them perfectly. He couldn't wait until her divorce was final so they could marry.

They descended the winding staircase to the parlor, where a fire crackled in the hearth, and he uncorked a bottle of white wine. This tradition of them sharing a cocktail hour to decompress and talk about their work had become necessary to his creative process. He chuckled at the term "creative process." Could a thriller involve a creative process? What he did was better described as piling on absurdities.

"*Salute!*" she said as they clicked glasses.

After a few sips of wine, he said, "You first. Oxana the Octopus doesn't ring a bell."

She heaved an exasperated sigh. "She's one of the new characters Ali sent over. Here, I'll fetch the sketch book." While she was upstairs, he took a moment to appreciate the stately parlor with its ornate scrollwork and multitude of naked and semi-naked figurines, some of them incorporated into useful objects such as clocks or lamps. He was particularly fond of the occupant of one lamp, a dead ringer for Chiara. When he'd first moved in, he'd packed up most of the clutter but kept the erotic objects that called to him. There were a surprising number of them. Had they belonged to Simon? Perhaps the artist would tell him one day. In a dream, like last time.

Chiara plopped back down on the couch and handed him the sketchpad.

He flipped to the first page, clearly labeled "Oxana." The octopus's sex was indicated with graceful limbs Tread long eyelashes. No visible mouth. Ali did try to give her anthropomorphized creatures some anatomical integrity, though he doubted octopuses had eyelashes. She had scribbled helpful notes. He read aloud, " 'Squirts ink to hide herself and hurt her enemies.' Does she have enemies in this book? I thought all these creatures were benign."

Chiara wiped her glasses with her napkin, allowing him to better admire her wide brown eyes. "Perhaps she believes a creature is her enemy because he is different but then discovers otherwise. She releases the ink, and the creature complains that it hurts his eyes.”

“Ah, a subtle message.” He read again from the list, “ ‘She has three hearts.’ ”

Chiara grinned. “What better metaphor for love than three hearts?”

He kept reading, “ ‘Octopuses have nine brains. Each of its eight arms has one.’ ”

Chiara shook her head. “I’ll have to think on that one.”

“Perhaps she solves everyone’s problems,” Jake said. “The others resent her interference until they come to realize how wise she is. You know, ‘Mother Knows Best.’ ”

“I thought it was father who knew best.”

“In the old fifties TV show, yes, but the mother was pretty smart too.” He flipped the page. “ ‘Silas the Spotted Ratfish.’ ” He pointed. “I totally get the appeal of this one. Cute as a button.”

Her brow furrowed. “What’s so cute about a button?”

He grinned. “Beats me.” Ali had included a photo of an actual ratfish. He held it up. Ali’s sketch made it look even more like a mouse with fins. “It’s the eyes,” he said. “Eyes and a tail like rattus rattus. A snout like a duck.”

“Rattus rattus?”

“A roof rat. Cute as heck but very destructive.” He read further. “ ‘They eat small crabs, clams, shrimp, and sea stars.’ Ali has included a note here: ‘Not in our book!’ ”

Chiara chortled and snatched the sketchpad away. “*Basta*. My head hurts. Silas will have to figure out an alternative diet. If humans can survive on a diet of vegetables, Silas can adjust too.”

Jake waggled his brows. “Cue the remark from Lorenzo.” In a small child’s voice, he said, “ ‘I feel sad for Silas. I don’t want to eat only vegetables. And *Zia* Chiara, you eat lots of meat.’ ”

She rolled her eyes. “How is your work going?”

“Fine. Only, I got to thinking about Book Four.”

“What will happen in Book Four?”

He blew out a long stream of air. “Lorelei falls in love and abandons her evil ways?” It was a question.

“All right. Who does she fall in love with? And what if they incorporate that into the next movie?”

He pulled her into his lap. “If Maddie is going to have a real career, sooner or later she’s going to be called on to have a love scene with another character. No one's going to cast her as the best friend or sexless sidekick for another ten or fifteen years."

Removing her glasses, Chiara laid them on a side table and gave him a soft kiss. "Not if David has anything to do with it." As his fingers danced under her sweater, she said in a breathless voice, "How do other actors cope with such issues?"

"Badly," he said, his own voice strained as he kneaded her breast. "Lots of broken marriages."

"I'm glad you're a writer," she whispered.

"That's because you know that every female love interest I write is you," he whispered back as he pulled off her sweater.

All talking ceased as he concentrated on her breasts. He could think of no words that could do justice to them, nothing that wasn't a dime-store-novel cliché. Pillowy, perfect orbs. A rack to die for. They'd been hidden under baggy clothing for so long. A crime, that was.

This was usually how their cocktail hour ended. It was true what he'd told her: Chiara had erased the memory of all his former lovers.

Later that night, after they made love yet again, he drifted into a deep, blissful sleep.

Something was pulling Jake to the surface, as if through thick paste. His limbs were paralyzed, giving him no choice but to go along with it. Even in his immobile stupor, he knew not to be afraid. No ghost had ever tried to harm him.

Where was he? He'd emerged into zero gravity. He might have been floating inside a cloud. A figure materialized from the haze—a young woman with long black hair, dark eyes, olive skin, and classic features. She wore a '60s "mod"-style red-and-blue-striped party dress with a short skirt and shimmery pink stockings. Her image came in and out of focus as if someone were adjusting a knob. The resemblance to Ali was striking. This had to be Nancy as a young woman. Which meant she was dead. Though her lips didn't move, a female voice in his head said, "My mother still lives. In Yakima. Fitzpatrick. S—." An S. Or an Sh? The first letter of her mother's name? Then the image vanished as if the film projector responsible for it had been abruptly switched off.

He was back in his bed, staring at the ceiling, starkly awake. S Fitzpatrick, Yakima. It was something. How many Fitzpatricks were there in Yakima? Probably hundreds. Sarah, Sandra, Sally? Shelly? What if he'd misheard? No harm in giving the information to Liam. Thanks to the strangeness of the past year, his brother-in-law wouldn't write him off as a kook. He didn't want to upset Ali when her pregnancy was already so difficult.

"*Caro*?" Chiara was awake, watching him. He looked at the bedside clock: eleven past two.

"I think Nancy just died."

"Liam and Ali's birth mother? Oh, that's sad. You saw her?"

"Yes. She told me her mother is alive and living in Yakima. I got a last name: Fitzpatrick. But she blipped out before I could get the first name. I'm fairly certain it started with an S or an SH."

"This is good news," Chiara said, sitting up.

He blinked. "How is that?"

"Because she was already too far gone by the time she reappeared in Liam and Ali's life. Too addicted and unwilling to fight that addiction. You told me her mind wandered. If they locate her mother, they might learn something positive they can convey to their children. Some small comfort. How old is … *was* Nancy?"

Jake loved that she didn't doubt his improbable story for a second. "Duncan told Liam she was almost twenty-one when they met at that party and had a one-night stand. That would make her somewhere around fifty now. Her mother could be as young as late sixties."

Chiara fell back asleep in Jake's arms. His brain continued to whir. Liam would have already braced himself for Nancy to come to a bad end. He'd done what he could for this sad, selfish wreck of a woman, treating her with all the care and respect one might give a loving parent—the kind who didn't leave you in a hot car while searching for a fix. Ali had kept her distance, which meant she might be racked with guilt, might wish she'd tried harder to reach the remnants of their once vibrant mother.

How and where had Nancy died? Had she OD'd alone in a flophouse or worse, a crack house? Should Jake wait till her body was found? It wasn't as if Nancy would be carrying ID to connect her to them. She'd be stashed in a morgue drawer somewhere until buried in a pauper's grave. If indeed she was ever found and not lying entangled in seaweed at the bottom of the ocean. If only her departing spirit could have hinted at how to find her remains ….

Perhaps she'd contact him again.

He hoped the end hadn't been too horrible. It could be that Ali and Liam would find closure at last.

CHAPTER 9

A BRIEF AND VAGUE ITEM about the Café Lisette incident appeared in the Police Log of the Port Townsend *Leader* Monday morning:

> **At 11:16 p.m. on Dec. 10,** police responded to a caller reporting an after-hours attempted robbery at a café on Water Street. Police reporting to the scene found four individuals: an employee with a minor head injury, the owner and her friend (both uninjured), and the suspect, an incapacitated man who appeared to be under the influence. The suspect had confronted the owner with a gun and demanded the contents of the cash register. A friend helping the owner at closing time felled the man with a well-aimed blow to the neck. Charges have not yet been filed.

The brief report didn't include names, which was just as well. Edward figured the tabloids were always on the lookout for sensational stories featuring any O'Connell family member or friend. Their attention had been diverted from Joe to Maddie after her sensational movie debut, and now to the family joint venture that was the screen adaptation of *Kapow*. Edward's own messy fall from grace had been kept from the press. True, his deacon's plot to drag him through the mud had come to nothing. But not for lack of trying.

If anyone at the compound had read the short paragraph in the *Leader*, they were unlikely to connect the dots. So Edward left a message on Joe's cell phone: "Hi Joe, Edward here. I'm looking forward to tonight. Just a heads up that I'm bringing a guest—Lisette Manegold. Hope that's okay. There was an attempted robbery at Café Lisette Friday night, and she's still rattled. See you at six thirty."

He'd been tempted to add, "Please keep an open mind," but acknowledging their objections to Lisette wouldn't help. He was counting on their impeccable manners and distaste for confrontation. They couldn't admit she was unwelcome without jeopardizing their fragile relationship with him.

At 6:15, he parked in front of Café Lisette. There was an open spot because the restaurant was closed on Mondays. Lisette appeared, searching for his car, and he gave a jaunty honk to alert her to his presence. She was dressed in black jeans, low-heeled boots, and a wool car coat, cap, and scarf. Her hair was tied back in one long braid, and her eyes were concealed behind round, rimless, tinted eyeglasses. She reminded him of a young Anne Bancroft in *The Miracle Worker*.

Wipe that grin off your face, he told himself. Her attempt at dialing down her appeal had failed miserably. The effect was more, "model hoping to remain incognito on the way to a photo shoot."

Lisette must not have realized the polite honk was for her. He opened the car door, leaned out, and waved. He had to yell, "Lisette … here!" before she saw him. He hoped she wouldn't be put off by the car—a new, black Audi A6 he'd picked up in Port Angeles. For a man of *his* means, it wasn't an ostentatious choice, was it? A comfortable, reasonably priced luxury vehicle, 4-wheel drive to handle crummy weather.

He ran around to the passenger side to open the door for her.

"New?" she said before sliding in.

"Yes." Was she laughing at him? "I needed a car." He sounded defensive.

"It's nice."

"It amuses you?"

She didn't answer, so he shut the door.

"Very practical," she said as they fastened their seatbelts. There was still laughter in her voice.

Now he was smiling too. "You were expecting, maybe, a Ferrari?"

"At the very least a Porsche."

"I'm not exciting enough for you." Part of him suspected it was true. Compared to Reynard, he lacked panache. Maybe he should have bought a Ferrari. He pulled away from the curb. "What does Reynard drive?"

Now she was grinning. "A Mercedes C-forty-three 1998."

"It figures."

"You put Reynard to shame." He could feel her eyes on him, but he kept his on the road. He knew what she meant, but the idiom called to mind the very real shame he had felt when his career in the Church had gone to the dogs.

After a moment of silence, he sent a mischievous glance her way.

"What?" Now *she* sounded defensive.

"I wasn't expecting ..." he began.

"You were expecting Lisette of Café Lisette fame," she said in her usual flippant tone. "Her image lures in customers. That's not who I am."

"I like that Lisette a lot. I like this one even better."

"I thought you might," she said with a shy smile. He was totally intrigued.

"Prescription glasses?" he asked.

"I usually wear contacts. These adapt to the changing light." After a brief silence, she went on, "So, tell me the secret."

His stomach lurched. Was she referring to his break with the Church? "The secret?" he repeated.

"How to win them over. Your family."

"Oh." He exhaled noisily. "They're a mystery to me too. Whenever *I'm* in possibly hostile territory, I ask a lot of questions and keep on smiling. While trying hard not to appear too predatory."

She bared her teeth and growled. "Grr. Do my smiles strike you that way?"

He chuckled. "That's more Reynard's thing. What I noticed about him first. Very sharp teeth."

The laugh, so genuine and merry, didn't belong to a cynical woman. "I'll be meek as a lamb."

"If you try too hard, they'll know. They have excellent bullshit detectors, unfortunately. Quiz them about the movie. That will keep them talking for a good twenty minutes. Jake wrote the book, David the screenplay, and Maddie and Liam are the stars. David's a script doctor now. In his revised version, George Reed Master's role is on a par with Liam's. And George doesn't share screen time with Maddie."

"Why *is* that?"

"She and George had some steamy scenes in Maddie's debut movie, *Insanity*. I was told that during filming he suggested they rehearse in private."

"Ah. One always assumes that happens on movie shoots. I saw *Insanity* at the Rose. They had some nice, er, *chemistry*."

"Stay by my side, fair maiden, and no harm will come to thee."

She laughed, as she was meant to. "How much do they know about you?" she asked, making him queasy again.

"No more than you do, I'd imagine."

"Care to remedy that?"

"We're out of time," he said as he punched in the code and turned onto the gravel road leading to the compound.

"Will there ever be a right time, I wonder," she said, not in the form of a question.

"If I have my way, then certainly. A right time for you to share your story too."

"Oh, *my* story. Not for public—or private—consumption." She frowned. He'd suspected as much. "I'll tell you what…." Her smile was unconvincing—tight-lipped. "We'll save it for a more appropriate occasion, say, Halloween."

That bad, he thought. "I'm incapable of being shocked, you know."

"Of course." Her tone was deceptively light. "You assign me some 'Hail Marys' and presto! Clean slate."

Damn. Had she killed someone and hidden the body? He was so taken with her, not even that would matter at this point.

The unsavory possibilities crowded Edward's thoughts to the point where he didn't dare speak at all. Fortunately, they'd arrived at the compound.

* * *

"Edward and Lisette just drove up," Teresa said in a voice full of dread.

You'd think she'd just spotted the Grim Reaper, Ali thought. She wanted to say, "No matter what you think of Reynard, Lisette isn't guilty by association." Also, "You of all people can't blame Lisette for being attracted to Liam." She hoped her sister-in-law wouldn't let her bad attitude ruin the evening.

Watching Edward and Lisette walk down the hill, Ali had to laugh. Was this really how Lisette looked when she wasn't working or accompanying Reynard to a cocktail party? Doubtful. But she applauded the woman, whose toned-down appearance was obviously meant to put them at ease. The couple's body language was telling—the way Edward was quick to reach out and steady her, surefooted as she was, and the way she seemed to welcome his fussing. They hadn't slept together yet, but it would happen soon. Good for Edward. He wasn't rushing her, as Reynard no doubt had.

How old was Lisette? In this outfit, she looked like a co-ed at a snooty college. On weekends, this woman would compete in dressage with her thoroughbred stallion, "Gawain." Did she come from a fancy family? She must have inherited her excellent genes from someone impressive. Ever since Jake had warned them of Edward's interest, she and Joe had privately looked forward to observing Lisette outside her comfort zone.

The path from the carport led directly to the door of the Sea Captain's House kitchen, where Teresa, Liam, Ali, Joe, and Jake had been sitting around the granite island. Dinner preparations were underway at the Log Palace, which could accommodate larger parties. After Edward introduced her, Lisette shook hands all around. Not even Teresa—laughably stiff and resistant—escaped her outpouring of warmth, but when Lisette got to Liam, she kept the handshake noticeably brief and couldn't meet his eyes. Liam, overcompensating, out-jollied Santa Claus himself. Without the high heels, Lisette wasn't as daunting as Ali remembered from Matthew's cocktail party. She was slightly taller than Ali's five-nine, with unusual eyes that tilted downward at the corners and sparkled green and gold. Ali caught a quick glimpse when Lisette removed her glasses to clean them.

She saw how Edward's eyes skittered around the room. "Just immediate family tonight," Ali reassured him as she moved in for a hug and felt him relax. "Maddie and David went into town, but they'll be back soon." *He really dislikes Xenia*, she thought, *or at least mistrusts her*. Had Teresa's protégée come on too strong at dinner last weekend?

"I love all the outdoor lights," Lisette gushed. "The North Pole itself couldn't be more festive."

Joe uttered a dry laugh. "You don't think it's too much?"

"You must mean all the red," Ali said. "My mother-in-law thinks it's less Christmas than fire and brimstone."

"Don't worry about fire and brimstone," Edward said lightly. "None of us have behaved *that* badly."

Ali caught the dismayed glance Lisette cast in Edward's direction. *Interesting*, she thought. What was she hiding?

"Are the children downstairs?" Edward asked.

"The children, along with Chiara and the nannies," Ali said. "Well, technically, May Allen is the only nanny. Susan came to stay and never left. She's not official, but she helps out wherever she can, and we love her. She still competes as a weightlifter. Lisette, would you like to meet Lorenzo and the twins?"

Joe, Ali, Lisette, and Edward followed the sounds of childish glee down the stairs to the rec room, which was dominated by a large noble fir tree. Of the three Christmas trees they'd decorated—one in the living room of each house—it was Ali's favorite because she'd created many of its ornaments based on characters from *The Way to Moss Manor*. It was crammed with cookies, tinsel, candy canes, and other handmade touches. The upstairs trees were festooned more elegantly with O'Connell family heirlooms. Mostly to make her mother-in-law Carrie feel more at ease.

Lisette gasped when she saw the twins. "They are so like you!"

"Except for the curls," Ali said, smoothing back her own straight, chin-length bob. "Their hair is more like yours." Tonight the woman's enviably long, thick, and wavy locks were bound in a braid, a few stray ringlets framing her heart-shaped face.

"But those eyes …. The only time I've ever seen blue like that …" Lisette trailed off, blushing.

"Liam and me," Ali said. "Inherited from our Irish father."

Lisette, needing to veer off that subject, was staring at the tree with naked admiration. "Where did you get those ornaments?" she asked. "Is that Bigfoot in a dress and apron? Crossdressing Bigfoot?"

Everyone except Lorenzo laughed. "That's *Beverly* Bigfoot," he replied solemnly.

"I'm sorry," a contrite Lisette said. "I didn't mean to make fun of her, honest. Do you know the names of the other animals?"

Lorenzo nodded vigorously. As Lisette pointed out each ornament in turn, he identified them with hilarious gravity, as if naming suspects in a lineup. Lisette's deadpan expression never wavered.

"Ali designed them," Joe explained. "They're from the children's book she wrote with Chiara, *The Way to Moss Manor*. Every last one is a creature who is found in the Hoh Rain Forest."

"I had no idea you were such a skilled artist," Lisette marveled.

"Mostly I draw pencil sketches," Ali admitted, gratified by the praise but also ready to move out of the spotlight.

"She's crazy talented," Joe said, drawing her to his side.

Josie, who was bouncing on a rocking horse, rent the air with a shrill scream of joy. Joy quickly became outrage when Caryn, face scrunched up in frustration, tried to push her off. Ali crouched down to Caryn's level and caressed her cheek. "Sweetie," she said in a soothing voice, "let's find something else for you to play with."

"Horsie *mine!*" the child yelled. *Mine*: her favorite word.

"Caryn, do you see this ball?" Lisette asked, making a goofy face. Kneeling down, she bounced the nerf ball against the wall. "Wanna play with me?"

Caryn toddled, arms flailing, toward Lisette. Ignoring the ball, she grabbed the long braid that fell across her shoulder and tugged. "Horsie!" she cried out, referencing the rocking horse's braided tail. Gently extracting her braid from Caryn's fist, Lisette got down on her hands and knees and whinnied softly.

Caryn was delighted. "Ride horsie!" she demanded.

At Lisette's silent request for permission, Ali nodded, smiling. Then worried that Lisette's look had been a veiled plea for intervention. Lisette helped Caryn to climb onto her back. Crawling in a circle, she showed off her surprisingly rich repertoire of "horsie" sounds—neighs, nickers, whinnies, and snorts. She kept her braid dangling in front, out of reach.

When Caryn's interest in horsie riding showed no signs of waning, Ali told her daughter, "That's enough for now, sweetie. Horsies get tired too."

Caryn fussed but was easily distracted by Susan, who had started a nonsensical dialogue between two toy animals, a stuffed elephant and a dragon made of yarn.

"Dragonetta!" Caryn cried out in delight.

"Lisette," Ali said, "you look as if you could use a drink. What can I get you?"

Lisette sat on the loveseat behind Lorenzo. The boy was sprawled on the floor, drawing in an oversized sketchbook. He gave the newcomer a shy but admiring look.

"I'd love a glass of white wine," Lisette said. "Whatever's open."

"Whatever's open is sure to be excellent," Edward said as he sat beside her on the loveseat.

When Ali came back downstairs, Lisette was using Lorenzo's crayons to draw a picture for the boy, who couldn't stop staring. *Lor certainly appreciates beautiful women*, she thought, recalling his first meeting with Maddie.

Lisette concentrated on her picture for several minutes, working quickly. Then she showed it to Lorenzo. "See? You're Superman."

It was a clever but flattering caricature, with Lorenzo's somewhat prominent ears, wide green eyes, and shock of red hair. Recognizable but also cute as heck. He was standing in a Superman pose in the proper costume, a big "S" on his chest and a cape sailing behind him.

"Where did you learn to do that?" Ali said, a bit awestruck. "It's brilliant."

"No," Lisette scoffed. "It's a parlor trick. I lived in Paris for a year while I was going to cooking school. A caricaturist at the Place du Tertre gave me a few lessons."

Joe pointed emphatically at the drawing. "You learned to do *that* in a few lessons?"

Lisette was already fully absorbed in creating another caricature.

Ali went over to where Caryn was using a toy phone to bash a stuffed rabbit. "Sweetie, be kind to Sunny Bunny," she cooed to the energetic child. With a squeal of delight, Caryn continued the assault. The bunny was holding its own. Ali considered sending a note of appreciation to the toymaker praising its sturdy construction. She fervently hoped she wasn't raising twin sociopaths.

She heard a "Wow! Would you look at that?" from Edward and turned to see him staring at the newest drawing. It was clearly Edward as Dudley Do-right, his main feature a prominent cleft chin. Unlike Dudley's, the hair in the caricature was auburn and the blue eyes shone with intelligence and a hint of arrogance. Ali covered her mouth to stifle a snort of laughter.

"So … *this* is what you think of me," Edward said, hands raised in mock despair.

"Not anymore," she said, "but when I first saw you at the restaurant, you did remind me—just a bit—of him. The three of you—Joe and David included—all have that classic dimpled chin." She tried to snatch the drawing away from him.

"Nope." Edward held it out of reach. "I'm having this framed."

None of them had seen Teresa come in. Clearly taken aback by the general levity, she announced in a huffy voice that dinner was ready and went back upstairs.

Lisette, biting her lower lip, watched her leave.

"Don't mind her," Ali said. "It's the hormones."

"If you draw her," Edward said in a low voice, "please, just make her really pretty."

Lisette shook her head. "I wouldn't dare draw her. A caricature is only fun if the model has a sense of humor about herself … or at least understands that the aim isn't to mock her."

"No worries," Ali said, touching her shoulder, "she'll come around."

As they all climbed the stairs, she heard Lisette whisper, "I'm sorry, Edward. I didn't mean to call attention to myself. You warned me not to try too hard."

She didn't hear his reply. Thank God Ali had excluded Xenia. It was unusual for them to gather on a Monday. She hoped Teresa wouldn't tell her intern about the dinner. Her sister-in-law seemed to regard the young woman almost as a sister. Ali had her doubts. Something about Xenia's behavior was eroding her trust. She just couldn't put her finger on what it was.

CHAPTER 10

———✦———

Being whisked along in Edward's car was like flying in a private jet, or so Lisette imagined. Such a smooth, quiet ride. The road noise in her Miata was so bad she feared for her hearing, especially with the radio on and the top down. Once she'd fancied herself the epitome of cool in that car. Her arm candy days behind her, Lisette was stuck with an impractical, uncomfortable sports car.

"I thought that went well," Edward said with a self-satisfied smile.

He missed her incredulous look, his eyes being on the road. "I'm glad *you* think so. Ali and Joe are happy to give me the benefit of the doubt—"

"Are you kidding?" he interrupted her. "You totally won them over by enchanting their children."

"I hope Ali didn't think I was impinging on her territory with the caricatures."

"Not at all," Edward scoffed. "It's obvious that she likes you."

"The way Teresa looked at me, the drawing I gave Lorenzo could have been a poison apple."

"Maddie and David liked you."

She shrugged. "Maybe. Maddie comes from a middle-class background like mine, so we'd be more likely to find common ground."

"So it's only Teresa and Liam who are the problem. Liam was perfectly nice."

Lisette grunted. "His attitude toward me is not encouraging. A little supercilious. Like I'm a con artist, and he hasn't figured out my angle."

"I think you're reading too much into it. Anyway, they'll have to accept you."

"Oh? Why is that?"

Did he really mean to imply she wasn't just a passing fancy? He just kept driving, that goofy smile glued on his face.

Lisette couldn't stand the awkward silence. "That is some screwed-up situation with the movie," she said. "Liam will be off on some distant set when their child is a newborn."

Edward's smile vanished. "It's worse than that," he said.

She waited.

"Ali and Teresa are both going to have complications in their pregnancies. Neither situation will be serious if they know what's coming."

"One of your premonitions?"

"Yes."

"Why not tell them?"

"I'm waiting for the right time. They need to trust me first. Know for sure I'm not a nutcase."

"Point taken."

He tapped her knee, a touch so light it might not have happened, yet it shot a zing of desire straight to her core. She took a deep breath to calm herself down.

"Don't worry," Edward continued, "there's time. The births won't be premature, although Ali will need to take it easy for at least three weeks before she delivers. If she goes to Seattle right after New Year's Day, she should be fine. Teresa's due date is the week after. That birth will happen too quickly. As long as the doctors are on the alert, they can keep her and the baby safe. I'll figure it out. In the meantime, I intend to enjoy the holidays. It's been a long time since I've been able to celebrate a secular Christmas. Advent for me has always been devoted to laboring over my sermon. It needed to be powerful enough to convince all the Cultural Catholics to mend their errant ways. So of course I always fell short. Historically, Christmas is just the Church co-opting Winter Solstice." He capped off that possibly blasphemous remark with a signature O'Connell grin.

Lisette was not a particular fan of Christmas, having no family tradition of joyous rituals and a lot of memories of tired parents, a grumpy brother, and a no-show Santa. Her parents went all out with decorations at the restaurant— but not at home. The Smiling Dolphin Diner didn't close on Christmas Day, its aim to take business away from the Chinese restaurants, normally the only establishments open because the owners weren't Christians. Even after she left home, Lisette had not found the kind of close friends or sentimental lovers who could reframe the holiday for her. For a brief moment, she allowed herself to imagine spending Christmas with Edward. *Don't get your hopes up,* she admonished herself.

The evening with his family had been unexpectedly fun despite Teresa's cold shoulder and Liam's supercilious looks. She wondered what she'd seen in the guy, other than his handsome surface.

Time to veer away from the subject of family holidays. "About that movie, *Kapow*…. They aren't the producers. How much you wanna bet Maddie will ultimately be called upon to take off her clothes and make love to both Damon and Mickey? That's what the audience will want… and expect. The movie has the same title as the book, so won't fans be disappointed if it isn't marginally faithful to its source material? There's no guarantee the producers won't bring in other experts if they feel the screenplay needs improvement."

"You'll get no argument from me," Edward said. "You can't blame my family for hoping otherwise."

He pulled up in front of the hotel.

"I thought you might want to see my suite. It's one short block from the café. If you need to call it a night, no problem. I could walk you home. It's a beautiful evening, and the entire street is festooned with colored lights, wreaths, and garlands. And—"

If Lisette didn't stop him, he'd talk himself out of the invitation. She tugged on the sleeve of his coat. "I'd love to see your suite."

He parked in the side lot reserved for guests, and they climbed the long staircase to where the suites were located. Edward's offered the same quasi-Victorian trappings as the hallways—period-appropriate portraits and rural scenes, ornate silk wallpaper in vibrant colors, and rich blue carpeting. She gave an involuntary sigh of pleasure. So nice not to breathe air saturated with an unappetizing mix of cooked fish and hot peppers.

Through the open door, you could see right into the smallish bedroom, overwhelmed by its king-size bed. She asked to use the bathroom and tried to ignore the inviting tub and matching guest robes. The bedroom was mirrored on three walls. *A veritable adult playroom,* she thought, seeing her pale image from several angles and imagining both of them reflected in a tangle of naked limbs.

Back in the living area, Edward sat on the couch, holding a book. "Be my guest," he told her.

She blinked rapidly. "What?"

"Take a bath. I know your current accommodations are… spartan.

I'll keep myself occupied." He showed her the cover of the book, a simple graphic of a hammy fist slamming into the side of a handsome male jaw. The word "Thwack" was framed in a jagged cartoon bubble. "Jake gave me an advance copy of his latest thriller."

"The cover model has the famous O'Connell chin," she observed with a laugh.

Cocking his head to one side, Edward gave the design a long look. "Joe will get a kick out of that. A private joke, in that Jake is the only son who didn't inherit Da's cleft chin."

As Lisette stood frozen in place, trying to shut out the insistent voice telling her to resist Edward until she knew him better, he was already running her a bath.

"There. I made up your mind for you." He yanked both robes off their hangers and handed one to her. He kicked off his shoes. "Go." He made a show of piling the multitude of pillows into a nest, putting on his reading glasses, and getting settled on the bed, fully clothed. "Don't mind me. Pretend I'm not here." His sly smile was absolutely devastating. *Damn him*. Was something going to happen? They hadn't even kissed.

* * *

On the silent drive home, Teresa struggled with her conflicting emotions. What did she have against Lisette, anyway, other than the fact that all her insecurity about Liam had manifested itself in her person? The woman seemed nice enough, and Edward was obviously a goner. She couldn't imagine a worse trial by fire than a priest leaving the Catholic Church. Why had he left? It might have been as simple as not wanting to remain celibate or as complicated as a sexual scandal. She didn't want to contemplate *that* possibility. Their mother would be mortified.

"What do you think happened to Edward?" Teresa finally said into the darkness of the car. "A scandal?"

"Yes," Liam said. "The Church is extremely efficient at shoving shit like that under their silk Persian prayer rugs. I just hope it didn't involve altar boys."

Teresa gasped. "Altar boys and Edward?"

"Altar boys and someone else. Edward couldn't witness something like that without reporting it, and if the culprit outranked him, that might have signed his career's death warrant right there."

"Or, he could have gotten tired of celibacy."

"Or that." Liam frowned. "But that's not all of it."

"What do you think of Lisette now?" Teresa asked.

"I still think she has a questionable past. Maybe as a high-end call girl. Or an expensive escort."

Teresa felt unaccountably offended on Lisette's behalf. "Why would you think that? I know you have a sixth sense about the women you're close to, but surely that wouldn't include Lisette."

"If that's even her name," he said, maddeningly.

"She didn't try to sell you her services the one time you met, did she?"

"Nope." His white teeth flashed in the darkness. "You're defending her now? The way you were acting, you'd think she was about to pop up and treat us all to a performance of 'Put the Blame on Mame.' "

"What?" Teresa had no idea what he was talking about.

He quoted, " 'One night she started to shim and shake; that brought on the Frisco quake.' You've never seen *Gilda*? Great Rita Hayworth movie. One of the sexiest film performances, ever—"

"All right, I get it," Teresa broke in. She fidgeted with her purse to avoid his eyes. "I regret my behavior tonight. Even if Lisette did sell her body at some point, it's not like she committed murder. The johns are at least as guilty in those situations. More, in fact. If she did engage in that ... lifestyle, she must have had her reasons. Or she was just young and stupid." When he didn't comment, she added, "I'll tell you what. Next time we all get together, I'm going to give her the full benefit of the doubt, and you should too."

"Me?" Liam gave her the side-eye.

"Yes, you. There was an edge to the way you treated her. Not as bad as me, but bad enough."

He shrugged. "Okay."

He pulled up in front of his house. *Their* house. Teresa couldn't stop thinking of it as his, and the one on Lawrence Street as hers, even though she didn't sleep there. She *could* sleep there if it came to that. Came to what? Weren't they solid now? She rubbed her round belly.

"Is our daughter moving?" He laid his hand on her belly too. "Ah, I think she turned over."

Teresa smiled. "Something's going on in there."

His hand crept lower. "Is something going on here?" He moved his fingers in that expert way of his.

She thought, *If anyone's the pro, it's you. Just because no one paid you* .... Then put those thoughts aside as unworthy. It wasn't Liam's fault that, including him, she'd had exactly three lovers. First, Kilo, her "husband" of a few days—an excellent lover for his eighteen years but just getting started.

Then there was her erstwhile fiancé Paul—educated, rich, and powerful, but in bed, merely competent. According to Ali, until Teresa came along, Liam had chosen disposable lovers. Jealousy of a lover's sexual past was futile. Teresa needed to start thinking like a Buddhist. *Every day is a fresh slate.* There was no question her husband loved her and the baby.

Liam helped her out of the car, eager to rush things along so they could be together upstairs. So far her pregnancy hadn't dampened his desire for her.

She sat on the bed as he undressed her, enjoying every minute of it. She knew better than to help or reach for him. Anticipation was key. He was unwrapping her like one might a precious gift. She closed her eyes as his fingers delved in all the right places.

He paused, leaving her panting in frustration as he kicked off his calfskin boots and shrugged out of his motorcycle jacket, dress shirt, and jeans. They both vibrated with excitement as his blazing blue eyes seared over her. His powerful, beautifully sculpted body, lightly scored on one side with scars from the explosion, defied the imagination. And it was all hers.

It could never be like this with another woman…. Could it?

CHAPTER 11

AFTER THE HAZE OF LUST lifted and Liam could think rationally again, the troubled musings returned. It was so easy to ignore his worries while burrowing into his wife's newly lush body.

Why had he known the precise moment Lisette's life was in danger?

At eleven ten on Friday, he'd been in the living room, puzzling over the new changes in the screenplay of *Kapow*. He was relatively certain David and Jake had no idea that another script doctor had been hired to give it back some of its original oomph. A scene between George and Maddie had been added, and Maddie and he were supposed to exchange a passionate kiss.

Shit.

He wished he could discuss it with Teresa, but she'd gone to bed early.

Then, in a flash, he'd known with certainty that at that very moment, someone was trying to rob Café Lisette, a restaurant he'd never set foot in. Grabbing his coat, he'd jumped on his motorcycle and raced it to Water Street. It might have been the Batpod. He'd come to an abrupt halt at the sight of *Edward* storming in. He decided to wait it out. He had no idea if his brother-in-law had the kind of skills that could thwart a burglar, but if he did, who was Liam to interfere? The man who had been assaulted outside sat up and rubbed his head. Unlike David, Liam couldn't heal, so he saw no point in intervening. He heard no gunshots, thank God. Then the police arrived, and calm prevailed. A policeman came out to talk to the injured man, who accompanied him inside.

Liam breathed through his tension until it dissipated. All was well. No need to explain to Teresa his sudden realization that Lisette was in danger.

He hoped the woman's mysterious past wasn't about to catch up with her. His lips formed a grim smile. She'd better not try to run for public office.

According to Lisette, Edward had felled the would-be burglar with one blow to the neck. That meant he knew some judo, maybe a lot. Liam was a black belt, though he hadn't bothered to pursue the final certifications. What really piqued his curiosity was the timing of Edward's arrival at Café Lisette. The oldest O'Connell brother had not been briefed on the various uncanny "gifts" that ran in his family.

Then there was Saturday night. Liam and Teresa had just enjoyed a quiet evening at home watching *Goldfinger* on television. Sean Connery was definitely the best Bond, at least in the early movies. It was past midnight, and for once they were both too tired to do anything but sleep. It wasn't long before that sleep was interrupted. Liam woke with a start, his heart pounding in his chest. He looked over at Teresa, who was snoring, something she'd started to do since pregnancy had forced her to sleep on her back. *Teresa is fine. Go back to sleep,* he told himself. But now he was wide awake.

They turned off the heat at night, and despite the chilly air, he was sweating. Naked, he padded downstairs. He hadn't told David or Jake about the screenplay changes, and his conscience niggled at him. As he sipped a glass of water, he glanced at the clock in the kitchen. Eleven minutes after two. *Damn.* If it were five, he'd give up on sleep and make coffee. What had woken him, a dream? Not that he could recall. Was Ali okay? Other than Lisette—*God knows why*—and Teresa, Ali was the only other person on his psychic radar. Joe would have called Liam first if his twin sister were ill or in danger. And that wasn't what his Spidey sense was telling him.

It had to be Nancy, their birth mother.

Nancy must have died. Or be in terrible trouble. If so, there was nothing Liam could do about it. She'd been in bad shape when she'd reentered their lives in April—addicted to meth, with liver failure and the beginnings of dementia. David, bless him, had cured her liver failure. They'd cleaned her up and found her a place to live in the interim housing usually reserved for the FOSSP kids. Through her ramblings, Liam had begun to get an idea of the woman she had once been. After abandoning them, she'd become a nomad, traveling in RVs with one man after another, no permanent address, dealing drugs to get by. No wonder she'd been lost to the civilized world.

David hadn't been able to touch her deteriorating brain. Healings had unintended consequences, he'd warned. They should have listened. Just as Liam had begun to hope she might settle down at last, Nancy had withdrawn the entire thousand dollars he'd deposited for her and skipped town.

He shook off the memory, focusing once again on the present. *Shame on you*, he told himself. This evening had been the perfect time to be straight with the family on both these unpleasant subjects—Nancy's fate and the tinkering with the screenplay. Only, Liam could hardly clear the air while Lisette was present. Were she and Edward a couple now? Could Lisette be trusted? This family had too many secrets.

Back in bed, Teresa had rolled onto her side and was breathing easier. He tried to empty his mind so he could fall back to sleep. One thought remained: it was time for this family to clear the air.

* * *

Teresa reached over to confirm that Liam's side of the bed was empty. What was on his mind? Upon hearing the story of the attempted burglary at Café Lisette, she finally understood his behavior the night before. Did he think she could block out the roar of his Harley as he drove away sometime after eleven? That motorcycle was louder than a fighter jet. He'd returned a short time later. She should have asked him about it then rather than feigning sleep. If he were a smoker, she'd have assumed he'd gone off in search of cigarettes. What other explanation could there be?

Other than, he had gone off to rescue Lisette.

Edward's story included no mention of Liam. So her husband had discovered that Lisette already had a rescuer. No wonder he hadn't confessed.

Tears stung her eyes. *Talk to him now*, she told herself. *Something is bothering him. Guilt over his feelings for Lisette? Would he even admit to such a thing?*

After Liam came back to bed, she lay on her side, again feigning sleep. The farce went on for something like a half hour. He wasn't asleep either. His eyes were closed, but his body was tense.

"Liam?"

He opened his eyes.

"Tell me what's wrong."

He pretended to be mystified by her question. She hoped he could summon more acting chops for the movie.

"Tell me about you and Lisette."

Now he appeared genuinely alarmed. "There *is* no me and Lisette."

"I heard your motorcycle Friday night. When the attempted burglary was happening. The timing can't be a coincidence."

He rolled onto his side to face her. "Honest to God. And yet, I did know she was in danger."

He was telling the truth. Teresa sighed with relief.

"There's something else," he said.

She stiffened.

"I think Nancy is dead."

She felt nothing but guilty relief as he related what had happened Saturday night.

"You have to tell Joe and Ali," she said. *Darn*, there was more. She could see it in his face. She heaved another sigh, this one of resignation. "Tell me the rest."

"They've monkeyed around with the screenplay."

"How?" she asked, though she knew the answer. If the changes bothered him, it could only be for one reason.

"The script had strayed too far from the original story. They want Maddie and me to kiss."

She nodded. "Makes sense."

"*Really* kiss."

"And …?"

"They've added a scene between George and Maddie."

"Also not a surprise. Is that what's bothering you?"

"Yes."

She began to thread her fingers through his hair in a soothing motion. "Don't worry, sweetie, we'll get through this. It's just acting. I know you and Maddie of all people aren't going to start anything. You might withhold the specific date you received the new screenplay, but for God's sake, tell Jake and David about the changes as soon as you can. They shouldn't be blindsided. Perhaps they can still argue against them."

"The changes make it better," Liam admitted. He looked like a guilty little boy.

She kissed him lightly on the lips. "Then tell them so."

He rolled onto his back and stared at the ceiling. "Can we trust Lisette, I wonder?"

Her laugh was dry and mirthless. "I don't know. You tell me."

"I don't think she's a bad person," he said. "She might even be the right woman for Edward. Why else would I feel connected to her?"

Liam's words came as a huge relief. He wasn't hung up on her after all.

"Can you sleep now?" she asked him.

His smile melted her, as it always did. If she hadn't been so exhausted, it might have led to something else. But now that her worries were at least temporarily alleviated, she couldn't keep her eyes open.

CHAPTER 12

THE GORGEOUS MAN IN THE other room was waiting for Lisette to rise from the water naked as Venus on a half-shell. Or was he? Was Edward as nervous as she was? He'd been a priest, for pity's sake—had made a sacred vow to remain celibate. Was it possible he was still a virgin? The thought terrified her. He had to know the water would be tepid by now. Her clothing was piled atop the toilet seat. She could simply get dressed. That would send a clear message: *No, no Edward! Nothing is going to happen here tonight.* But if not tonight, when? She wanted him, badly, and this might be her only chance. What was there to fear, really? *She* wasn't a virgin. So what if he were inept, and it ruined everything …. Wasn't there always a chance of that happening, no matter what chemistry you imagined was there between you? With a sigh, she dried herself off, wrapped her body securely in the bulky bathrobe, and tied the sash in a knot.

She knocked. Edward said, "Come out!" in a singsong voice that underscored the situation's absurdity.

She tentatively opened the door and peered around it. He was still lying on the couch, fully dressed, book propped up on his chest. As she slowly emerged, he removed his reading glasses, his lips quivering and eyes dancing in an effort not to laugh. The bed was in stumbling distance of the bathroom. Within arm's reach—if you had long arms. Nowhere to go without leaving the bedroom entirely.

She stood her ground. "*What*?"

"Are we playing wedding night in Regency England?" He indicated her swaddled body with a long sweep of his finger. "If you'd like, I can give you privacy while you position yourself beneath the covers."

She sat on the edge of the bed, nonplussed by his mocking tone. "You're seriously making fun of me?"

Realizing he'd crossed a line, he changed his tune. He knelt behind her and massaged her shoulders through the robe. "What's bothering you?" he said in a soothing voice. "Tell me."

"We haven't even kissed."

"Is that all?" He kissed the nape of her neck, breathing in her fragrance. "I like that scent," he whispered. "What is it?"

She looked at him sideways. "Hotel soap."

"Oh, it's more than that …." His laughter was deep and throaty. Nothing priestlike about him now. Eyes heavy lidded, he sidled up next to her and ran a fingertip along her bare arm, sliding beneath her sleeve until the fabric stopped him. The light touch reverberated downward, and she squirmed.

He stood then, lifting her to her feet so easily, she might have been a toy stuffed with cotton batting—not a tall, solid, muscular woman. Gazing steadily into her eyes, he pressed his parted lips against hers. It was not a novice move. Gradually he teased her lips open, and his tongue began to plunder her mouth. Her anxiety about his inexperience evaporated, and helpless desire filled the void. This man had not only been around the block, but he had also—metaphorically, at least—circumnavigated the earth.

Her breathing shallow, she said, "You've done this before."

He gave that low, throaty laugh again, then squinted in disbelief. "You thought I hadn't?"

"You're a priest…."

"I wasn't always a priest."

"Oh."

"May I?" He tugged at the knot in the sash of her robe, loosening it until it gave. Holding the lapels with both hands, he opened it slowly, drawing out the anticipation. "Your breasts are even more glorious than I imagined," he said in a worshipful whisper. His look asked for permission to go further. She nodded. He began to nibble and suckle as if she were made of sugar. Then his hands joined in the exploration. His touch was exquisite, alternately gentle and firm, nothing like the groping some men mistook for caresses. He was breathing hard, and *oh God*, the way he looked at her…. A woman could drown in those wide blue eyes, dilated with desire.

Her robe was gone, and his diabolical tongue and hands were exploring every inch of her… except where she needed them most. When his fingers skittered away from her clit for the third time, she trapped his hand and placed it firmly on her mound, earning another rumble of devilish laughter. Obeying her command, his fingers pattered and probed until she teetered on the edge. Her orgasm usually eluded her or took too long, and few bothered to persevere. She was used to faking it. Because if foreplay went on too long without results, she just wanted it to end, and a lot of men refused to give up. None of that here. She was falling into the blissful abyss when his fingers retreated, making her gasp with disappointment.

Then his mouth replaced them. If his fingers had known where to go and what to do, his tongue was even defter. It swished and stroked her into a frenzy. She heard moaning. *Damn it*, that was *her*.

In that moment, she snapped back to reality. This behavior was completely out of character. She was *always* in control.

He stood, raking his eyes lazily over her as he pulled off his sweater and T-shirt, his movements so unhurried, he might have been underwater. She reached for his belt. He let her, holding his hands in the air as if submitting to being frisked. After she'd pulled down his trousers, boxer briefs, and socks, he kicked them off and stood there, his beautiful cock springing to life. Holding its base, she ran her tongue down the length of it, determined to do for him what he'd done for her.

In wonder, she observed the unbearably erotic images caught in the surrounding mirrors. Following her gaze, he smiled and said, "Look at how stunningly beautiful you are. And how beautiful we are together."

Then, ever so gently, he touched her forehead as a signal to stop. Was he going to leave it at that? Was he one of those men who believed that if a sexual act didn't involve penetration, it didn't count? She didn't believe a man this sensual could have endured a week of celibacy, much less ten years.

But no, she'd panicked for nothing.

Abracadabra, he produced a condom. "Do you want me … inside you?" he asked in a gravelly voice.

"Yes," was all she could manage. She was panting now.

"Put it on for me?"

Palming the magnum extra-large, she took her sweet time sheathing him. *Now I'm the one in charge*, she thought, viewing their mirror image with a thrill of triumph. His head was thrown back, his eyes closed, his lips parted, his magnificent chest rapidly rising and falling. When the condom was in place, he turned deadly serious, easing her back onto the bed. Kneeling before her, he pulled her legs up and slid inside. He was large enough that the position was too deep. Aware of her discomfort, he let her legs fall back on the bed. After that, he thrust into her slowly while his fingers worked her sweet spot. Sensing the moment she came, he orgasmed with a violent shudder of pleasure.

She simply lay there, shattered, unable to speak. *This* man had been a priest? More like the reincarnation of Casanova. She'd never met anyone so tuned in to her responses. He could have made a fortune as a gigolo.

"You missed your calling," she said to his image in the mirror.

He grinned, also appreciating the triptych of erotic reflections. "Is that right? Thank you, I think."

"I didn't say what calling."

They were lying side by side on the bed now, legs and arms splayed, too languid to move.

She turned to look at him and said, "Confess … you weren't really celibate. I won't judge you."

His smile was bitter. "Sadly, I really was celibate, and happy to remain so. At first. It was my cure for sex addiction. Cold turkey."

Ah, now she understood.

Lying back with his hands behind his head and staring at the ceiling, he went on, "I was twenty-three when Da died—that's what we called our father. It was 1985, and he was only fifty-two. Lung cancer. Young, so young. Such a great guy. From his death bed, he told me how proud he was of my accomplishments. But it was his dying wish that I become a priest. He needed someone to pray for his soul. This man whose only sins, as far as I could tell, were booze and cigarettes. By then I was the only one of us kids who still attended Mass. But when it came to going to confession … that was a horse of a different color. I fully intended to keep sinning. I'm referring to sex, of course. I got an early start, thanks to a counselor at summer camp."

His lips formed tight bands of self-loathing. "I was only fourteen. Somehow we didn't get caught. If we had … well, *she* was the one who would have been in serious trouble." His grin became unsettling. "The kraken had been released. I couldn't get enough. No problem. At fifteen I could pass for eighteen. Willing women were everywhere. I pursued—or let myself be pursued by—older women because that made *them* appear to be the predators. I thought I was in seventh heaven, but I was like a rich celebrity with a coke habit. After a while I was a strung-out mess."

He gave himself a little shake as if only now recalling he wasn't in a confessional. Lisette was amazed at how calmly he spoke as he bared his soul, though he did avoid looking at her. Then, his disconcertingly innocent sky-blue eyes met hers. "Do I shock you?"

He *had* shocked her. Who knew she could be shocked? She lay on her side, not daring to move a muscle. "Not at all."

"Don't deny it," he said, rolling onto his back again.

"It's only that … you have the face of an angel."

He blew out a long breath. "I did a lot of harm. One woman overdosed after I told her it was over. I got her to the hospital, and she survived, barely. At least she was alive when I saw her last. Until then, I had never fully considered the impact of my behavior. It wasn't just me on a binge all by myself. It would have been better to drown myself in alcohol."

"You were young," she said in a soothing voice, "under twenty-five. Lots of men run around like open razors at that age."

"Büchner," he said.

"What?"

"From the play *Woyzeck*. Woyzeck's doctor tells him he tears through life like an open razor."

"Huh. Who did you say wrote it?"

"Georg Büchner, a German Expressionist playwright."

Expressionist, she thought. *I have no idea what that means.*

"You know that painting of the little man on the bridge holding his head, *The Scream*? The dramatic equivalent."

She snorted. "I thought I was quoting Reynard, who compared *me* to an open razor. Of course, with Reynard, it's a pot/kettle thing. I'm paper, you're glue. *He's* the open razor."

"But *you* broke up with him," Edward said.

"After his behavior made it clear he was ready to bolt."

Edward rolled toward her and cupped her cheek, his eyes glistening. "That stupid fool. Anyway, after I left the priesthood, I lost … control for a while. I can hardly blame *that* binge on the folly of youth."

Things had suddenly grown so serious. Clearly Lisette needed some sense slapped into her. She'd known she shouldn't rush things, should have given Edward more time to get to know her. Not that time had ever worked in her favor when it came to men. Perhaps Edward now wondered if *she* was done cutting a swath through the objects of her desire. Was *he*? Edward had been celibate a long time. She wanted reassurances, but one session of lovemaking, even one as mind-blowing as this, didn't entitle her to anything. For him, sex might always be like this. If you wanted to chase that high, didn't you need to keep upping the dose? Did the woman's identity even matter?

He began to stroke her hair, and it felt wonderful. Men *did* like her hair.

She closed her eyes. "I've upset you," he said. "You don't regret this, do you? Did my deep dark secrets scare you away?"

"Of course not," she said. "At this age, we all have deep dark secrets." *Not like yours*, she thought. *I never want this to end*, she wanted to say. *For me, it always does. Why should you of all people be any different?*

"Because …" he began, the word like a caress. She could feel his entire body pulse with desire.

This time he pulled her on top of him and let her adjust the ride. She started slowly but was soon bucking against him. It was over quickly. They were both breathing hard.

He grinned. "You think you're going to wear me out, don't you?"

"I could give it the old college try. Only I didn't go to the college."

Did that matter to Edward? He probably had a raft of advanced degrees from prestigious institutions. Reynard had openly sneered at her lack of higher education.

"You aced the school of life," he said in all seriousness. "And you graduated from an elite cooking school. Who wouldn't be proud of that?"

Not much got past this man.

"If you want shame," he went on, his tone fierce, "I've got enough for both of us. But I'm done beating myself up." He looked at the alarm clock by the bed. "Jeez, it's almost three. Shouldn't we try to sleep?"

"What if I wake up and you're gone?" she said lightly.

"Do I need to remind you that I have no place to go?" he replied in the same light tone. "This is *my* hotel room."

"What if I dreamed you? You could be a chimera."

"In mythology, a chimera is a monster. I'm not a monster … or a saint. For what it's worth, I'm real." He put her hand on his already rigid cock. "Too too solid flesh …."

She chuckled. "Hamlet wasn't talking about his cock."

His eyebrows danced. "How would you know?"

She surrendered to helpless laughter. In the silence that followed, she looked over at Edward, expecting to find him watching her again. Instead his eyes were closed. He snored lightly, lashes fluttering, lips parted. Cupid in the flesh. When Psyche had finally gazed upon her husband's splendor, he had vanished.

What if in the morning everything was different? What if the man she'd imagined into being was gone, replaced by an indifferent stranger? It wouldn't be the first time. What if, now that he had gotten what he wanted, he was ready to move on?

She did sleep, eventually. When she awoke, she saw in his eyes the same wonderment she'd felt while admiring his sleeping form.

"You're still here," he said softly.

"That's my line." She touched a finger to his lips.

"Ready for Round Two?" he asked.

She pretended to pout. "That's not very romantic. Besides, it's more like Round Four or Five."

CHAPTER 13

WHILE LISETTE SHOWERED, EDWARD WENT out to buy them breakfast, settling on large coffees and a couple of scones. Did she even eat breakfast? The minor errand drove home how little he knew about her. What if she preferred tea? She was so slim and fit—did she *ever* splurge on pastries? He should have asked.

By the time he climbed the stairs to the guest rooms, it was ten thirty. Lisette would need to leave for work soon. What if he went there for lunch? Too much? You'd think she was his first ever lover rather than his … what …. At age fifty-five, Wilt Chamberlain claimed in a memoir to have had sex with twenty thousand women—apparently, he liked threesomes. He was quite tall, Edward reflected. Perhaps each woman concentrated on a different body part. *Shame on you*, he told himself. *Look what this night of mind-blowing sex has done? Set you back years.* Or had it? During his worst binges, he might not have given Wilt a run for his money, but he had racked up his own disturbing statistics. Now he couldn't imagine wanting anyone but Lisette, ever again.

He had to take care not to scare her.

He found her sitting on the couch, leaning over to pull on her boots. His breath caught at the supremely erotic sight of silky black hair cascading over toned, denim-clad thighs.

She pointed at the paper bag. "What's for breakfast?"

"Coffee and blueberry scones. Hope that's okay."

"Perfect."

"How do you take your coffee?" he asked, arranging everything on the coffee table.

"No sugar. With or without cream or milk."

"Way to be difficult," he joked, handing her two mini half-and-halfs. "Shall we sit by the window?" They moved to the small dining table on the other side of the room. "Are you always this easy to please?"

"No, you're just a mind-reader"—she grinned—"along with your other skills. I refer to the premonitions, naturally." Something in his expression made her laugh. He smiled, endeavoring to look less like a lovestruck idiot. "For a chef, I'm easygoing when it comes to food. There's no food item I shun so long as it's fresh and decently prepared."

He popped a bite of scone in his mouth and appeared apologetic. "Not the freshest. Day-old was all they had left this late in the morning."

She took another bite. "Tastes fine to me. I'm not as fresh as I once was either." Her green eyes sparkled with mischief. "Don't you know it's rude to stare? Tell me what's on your mind."

What isn't? he thought.

"Ooh … long pause," she said when he didn't answer right away. "Are you breaking up with me already?"

He broke into a foolish smile. "Are we dating, then?"

Her answer was almost shy. "That sounds all right to me."

He recalled how Reynard had asked her to move in with him almost immediately. If Edward were to rush things like that, would that put him in the same category as that controlling jerk? He hated to think of Lisette sleeping on a lumpy sofa bed as the walls closed in, assailed by restaurant smells. *Baby steps,* he told himself. *You don't want to blow this.*

His cell phone rang. The Caller ID told him it was Liam.

"Hello, Liam!" He sounded ridiculously chipper.

"Hey yourself. Teresa and I are headed to lunch at the compound. Come with?"

Hmm. He'd seen them all last night. What was going on? He picked up on the note of urgency in his brother-in-law's voice. "Okay, but I can drive myself. I bought a car."

"What kind?" Liam asked.

"A new Audi A-six."

"No kidding. Year 2000?"

"Hot off the assembly line."

"Color?"

"Black."

"Nice. See you at one."

After Edward ended the call, he noticed Lisette's comically pitiful expression. "I guess that rules out lunch at my place."

He gave her a quick but enthusiastic kiss. Anything else would make her late for work. "Don't you need time to miss me?"

"Miss you already."

"Why don't I meet you at closing and escort you back here?"

"Thought you'd never ask."

* * *

Maddie and David lay together in the master bedroom of the Sea Captain's House. The king-sized bed faced rows of sash windows that made the spectacular view of the Strait of Juan de Fuca look like a landscape painting divided into panels. Puffy clouds scudded across the sky, and two barges were positioned on opposite sides of the tableau amid choppy waters.

"What do you call those multi-paneled oil paintings?" Maddie asked her magnificent husband. If ever a man deserved the description, "handsome hunk," it was David, with his strong features, shock of auburn hair, and face-framing beard. Of the four brothers, he was the most physically imposing—six-foot-five with their father's cleft chin and cheekbones cut from granite. Until David, her "type" had been "sleek, androgynous dancer."

"A polyptych," he said. "You'd prefer one big picture window?"

"No, this is more turn-of-the-century."

"But it's fake. The house is ten years old."

"Hey, we actresses value a good stage set. And just the right fantasy man to go along with it." Her fingers traveled down the smooth muscles of his chest to grasp his impressive erection.

With a groan, he rolled her onto her back and rubbed up against her like an amorous lion. Then he gave her a long, slow, tasting kiss and started to run his hands all over her body. She waited for him to realize she was already panting for him, though perhaps he knew it already. He did like to tease. With a giggle, she gave his cock a little tug and was gratified by his sharp gasp of pleasure. The gasp was followed by a growl as he let her guide him in. She knew he worried that his long, muscular body could crush her. Though she was five-three and petite, they were still a perfect fit.

It didn't take long for her to arrive at the point of no return. Only then did David surrender to his own release. As one, they let loose a long sigh of satisfaction, followed by giddy laughter.

A tentative knock at the door stunned them into guilty silence.

"It sounds like small knuckles," she whispered.

David hopped to his feet and tossed Maddie her robe as he wriggled into his own. They'd had the foresight to lock the door, but they didn't want to keep Lorenzo waiting. The boy was nearly four and a half but crazy smart. He didn't miss much. Once a disturbingly quiet child, he had blossomed under all the love showered upon him at the compound. Chiara still visited most days to tell him stories and keep his Italian fluent. The twins' nanny May Allen and her sister Susan adored him, and vice versa. Joe and Ali treated him like a son, and he was a devoted big brother to their energetic twin girls.

David unlocked the door, lifted Lorenzo into his powerful arms, and whirled him in a circle while the boy squealed in delight. It tugged on Maddie's heart to see them so happy together.

"I already had breakfast," Lorenzo confessed after David set him down. "I tried to wait for you to get up first, but I was too hungry. Susan said to leave you alone while you exercised."

David blanched.

"Susan says you do pushups every morning," Lorenzo elaborated.

A laugh gurgled in Maddie's throat. "Pushups *do* help us wake up," she said. "We were really tired."

"You look awake to me," Lor replied with his usual maddening logic.

Maddie pulled him into a warm hug. "The sight of you energizes us."

"Okay …." He sounded skeptical. "But you're coming down now, right? Susan says it's low tide."

David, fully recovered, smacked himself on the forehead. "Oh, darn! Of course. Be right down. Go tell the others we're on our way. Daddy needs his coffee if he's going to fully appreciate all those sea stars and hermit crabs."

Lor bounced up and down before dashing back downstairs.

Maddie fell back on the bed, laughing, and kicked her legs.

"None of that!" David jumped on top of her and gave her belly button a smacking kiss. "God, you make me crazy. You heard Lor. No time for 'pushups.' Low tide beckons."

Still chuckling, he dressed quickly. "I'll grab coffee and toast on my way out."

After he was gone, Maddie headed for the shower. When was the right time to broach the subject of the revised screenplay? Liam must have read his by now, and if he'd discussed it with Teresa, surely Maddie would have heard. The cowardly producers had kept Jake and David in the dark. They must be counting on Liam and Maddie to break the bad news. Could she pull Liam aside for a private moment? They needed to present a united front.

Liam must see that the revisions were an improvement. You could hardly argue in favor of a less thrilling thriller just to keep peace in the family.

Maddie found Ali alone in the kitchen of the Sea Captain's House. Though the place belonged to David now, Ali and Joe often joined them for breakfast. The rec room in the basement was the ideal children's playroom, and the Log Palace still needed more furniture, rugs, artwork, *something*. Other than Ali's art studio, it might have been a house on the market staged by a minimalist realtor. Log "cabins" were supposed to be cozy.

"Morning!" Maddie chirped, intent on the espresso machine. "Where's Joe?"

Ali's skin had a gray cast, and there were shadows beneath her eyes. Maddie was glad this second pregnancy was almost over. She hated seeing her beautiful sister-in-law looking so peaked. Was she going to be all right? Surely David would intervene in the event of real danger.

Ali perked up when she saw Maddie. "You're a late riser today," she said, the sparkle returning to her otherworldly blue eyes. "What time did you guys go to bed? I thought I heard someone in the hot tub."

Maddie hung her head. "That was us. I'm sorry if we kept you awake."

Ali waved her away. "No worries." She sipped her herbal tea. "I slept in myself. By the way, Edward, Liam, Teresa, and Jake are joining us for lunch. I assume Matthew will be there too. He and Joe are working in the studio this morning."

Hmm, Maddie thought. *That sounds ominous.* "Any particular reason?"

"Liam said he had 'family matters' to discuss—I assume without Lisette present. Chiara has other plans."

No. Her stomach lurched. Was Liam going to meddle in Edward's love life? Or was he going to spill the beans about the screenplay revisions? Either way, it was a shitshow.

When Maddie didn't reply, Ali added, "You don't think he and Teresa are going to try to warn Edward away from Lisette, do you?"

"If so, they're way out of line," Maddie said with more vehemence than she'd intended. What if they'd intervened when she'd blundered into that fling with Kilo during *A Midsummer Night's Dream*? Stuff happened for a reason. David had been too caught up in the drama with Lor's birth mother Sylvia to appreciate Maddie at that point. In the end it had all worked out. But it might not have if she had felt judged. She went on, "If they start bad-mouthing Lisette, I'm going to tell them to butt out." Seeing the curious way Ali observed her, she willed herself to calm down. "Let's not jump to conclusions. Liam might want to discuss the changes in the screenplay of *Kapow*."

Ali's eyes widened with concern. "Changes?"

Maddie raised a placating hand. "Don't worry. It's not *that* bad. But I don't want to say anything more until we're all together. I need to talk to Liam first, get on the same page."

"David and Jake don't know about these changes?" Ali asked with obvious worry.

Maddie shook her head.

"Shit," Ali said under her breath.

"Exactly."

"What's going on, girls?" David said cheerfully as he and Lorenzo burst into the kitchen along with a gust of wind.

Lor was still hopping about like a human pogo stick. "We saw sea stars, and, and, and, crabs, and, and sea enemies—"

David tousled the boy's shock of red hair. "*Anemones*, Lor."

Lor scowled. "That's what I said!" He stopped to give it some thought. "What are they called again?"

"Sea *anemones*."

"A-nem-o-nees," he repeated syllabically. "Aunt Ali, is there a sea a-nem-o-nee in our story?"

Maddie caught Ali's brief look of frustration. Chiara and Ali were struggling with *Salish Sea Stories* far more than they had with *The Way to Moss Manor*. Ali had confessed that Chiara wanted to throw in the towel on the whole project. *The Turkish Towel?* Maddie had joked. Turkish Towel was a type of red seaweed.

With her usual impeccable timing, Susan chose that moment to join them, allowing them to move on from the sticky subject of sea anemones. Lor jumped into her impressively muscled arms, and the two of them, who had a special bond, departed for the rec room.

"Edward, Jake, Liam, and Teresa are joining us for lunch," Maddie told David.

"No Chiara?"

"Not this time."

"That can't be good," David said.

Had Maddie's face given her away? "What makes you say that?"

"We were all together last night. Meeting again so soon means we're discussing a topic not fit for general consumption."

"Your guess is as good as mine."

His "humph" called BS on Maddie's reply, but then he added, "What time?"

Maddie looked at the clock, which said ten thirty. "Ali?"

"One o'clock," she replied. "Joe is grilling salmon patties. Nothing fancy."

Maddie went to the upstairs den to check her email while David headed to the master bedroom to shower. She couldn't shake a feeling of foreboding. They were safe as long as they remained sequestered in their cozy compound, covering their ears, eyes, and mouths like the Three Wise Monkeys. Inevitably, the evils of the outside world found a way to infiltrate.

PART II

CHAPTER 14

———◆———

LUNCH WAS AN ODDLY HUSHED and hurried affair, punctuated by a few brief exchanges, as if it were generally understood that a serious discussion loomed.

They had no history of family meetings. Elephants in the room generally went unaddressed until they charged or backed away. Crises were confronted through a series of one-on-one conversations. A year ago, Teresa never could have pictured such a scene. For what seemed like decades, their mother alone had been in close touch with Jake and Edward. Even with their crazy psychic gifts, no one had foreseen that all the O'Connell siblings would be living in the same small town that time had nearly forgot after the railroad bypassed it a hundred years back.

After lunch, Matthew had fled for the studio, as if taking shelter from the coming storm. The rest of them convened in the reimagined living room of the Sea Captain's House. Teresa grumpily observed the present décor, best described as African colonial. David's idealized Africa. Gone was the elegant Art Deco living room of her design, with its cream-colored furniture, beveled mirrors, Lalique vases, and textured wallpaper. Maybe if she'd opted for a less streamlined concept—more Art Nouveau than Art Deco—everyone would have liked it better. She had to admit that this room was better suited for lounging. Gauzy curtains, wicker furniture, handwoven baskets on the walls. Colorful Kilim throw pillows, a mahogany storage trunk. A potted palm, for Christ's sake. Safari chic. She sank into the heavenly cradle of a couch. Last night's interrupted sleep and the exhaustion of carrying around an unborn human made comfy sofas an invitation to doze.

Joe passed out wine glasses and opened one bottle of white and one of red. A bottle of sparkling cider for Ali and Teresa.

"Are we toasting something?" Edward said in a brightly ironic voice as Joe filled his glass with burgundy. Did he think this was about Lisette? Time to put that suspicion to rest.

Just as Teresa was opening her mouth to speak, Liam sat down beside her and patted her leg in reassurance. "I'm sorry if I spoiled anyone's plans. Edward, no one is going to try to dissuade you from seeing Lisette. Believe it or not, Teresa and I just want you to be happy." Not quite convinced, Edward toasted him and drained half his glass.

Liam continued, "I called this meeting to discuss more pressing concerns. Let's start with Nancy. Edward, I'm referring to Ali's and my birth mother."

Teresa heard Jake's sharp intake of breath. If her brother had been an English Pointer dog, he would have assumed the position. "Jake?" she said.

For a moment, he reminded her of the CEO of yesteryear, never quite comfortable in his body. "Are you sure Edward is ready for this?" Jake asked.

Liam turned to Edward. "I don't think Edward is going to judge us too harshly. I haven't heard him quote the scriptures once, have you?"

Shrugs and smirks all around.

"So, Edward, feel free to write us off as lunatics, but I vote for not censoring ourselves. Besides, I suspect you have your own weirdness to contend with."

Edward's face was suspiciously bland.

"Okay," Liam said, "setting the subject of Nancy aside for a moment, let's start with the attempted robbery at Café Lisette. Edward, I was there. I sensed it happening and raced to the scene, but you arrived before me. I saw you burst in, so I know you weren't helping Lisette close up, as stated in the police log." He waited for Edward to speak, but their eldest brother sat, completely still, as if one small move might set off an avalanche. "It may surprise you to know," Liam went on, "that we are no strangers to weird shit like that. Witness the fact that I knew Lisette was in danger too. I can't explain it." He gestured to David—Exhibit Number One—then Jake. "David can heal with a touch of his hands—a long touch. Jake sees ghosts. Well, mostly *hears* them." He locked eyes with Ali. "My sister and I are psychically connected, which is why she never gave up on me after I had supposedly been blown to smithereens and scattered like so much grisly confetti."

Edward's next words startled them all. "Okay, yes. I have premonitions. Sometimes. When I touch certain people and occasionally their...

possessions." He turned to Ali and then Teresa. "This is a huge relief, actually. Both of you need to head back to Seattle earlier than you think."

The women exchanged looks of alarm.

He waved a hand as if giving his blessing. "You'll be fine, and so will your babies, but there will be complications. You'll need the help of experts."

Teresa looked at David. "Why can't David do something?"

Joe interrupted them. "If he could, don't you think he would have by now? David, can you handle a medical crisis in advance? Besides, he gets those brain-scrambling headaches for hours afterward. I'm worried that they're taking their toll on his general health."

David's face had gone slack. "Edward, can you be more specific?"

Edward nodded. "I assume the term 'mild placental abruption' is familiar to *you*. It wasn't to me. It's not present in Ali yet, but it will be. I'm not seeing it as a problem until after New Year's."

David frowned. "That could be serious. It means the placenta is trying to separate from the wall of the uterus. If you're not nearly at full term and it's truly characterized as 'mild,' they usually recommend bed rest. Ali, have you had any bleeding?"

She shook her head, swaying slightly. In a flash, Joe was behind her chair, hands on her shoulders. Teresa hoped she wouldn't pass out.

"I can't cure something until it actually happens," David explained. "Not everyone bleeds with this condition, which is why it can go undetected." With that, he went over to Ali and knelt at her feet. Joe stepped back, and David laid his large hand on her belly.

No one spoke for a good five minutes. Finally David stood, freckles more prominent than usual in his pale face. "Something's wrong," he said in a shaky voice. "Not with Ali. Not that I know. My hands …." He rubbed them together. "Nothing's happening. I haven't tried anything like this since …" he trailed off.

"Chiara," Jake said, his voice full of dread. "David saved Chiara's life after a car crash."

With a gulp, Teresa turned her attention back to Edward, who said in a soothing voice, "Ter-Ter, don't look so worried. With you it's less serious. You're just going to give birth really, really quickly, so you'll want to be close to the hospital near your due date. But that's strange …. David, are there risks associated with rapid labor?"

"Not usually." Teresa stared him down. "Okay, worst case scenario. It can tear tissue. The body doesn't have time to adjust, and the baby could breathe in amniotic fluid. But lots of people give birth quickly with no complications. You just want to make sure you're in a sterile environment when it happens. When you hear about people giving birth in taxi cabs, that's usually rapid labor."

Liam sprang to his feet. "Should we go back to Seattle now?"

David raised his hand to calm the room. "Ali's due date is the end of January—Teresa's, early February. There's no reason not to stick around for the holidays. Unless you really want to stay with Mom for a month." Liam's grim expression elicited a smile of sympathy from David. "Edward, they're not giving birth prematurely, right?"

"Not if my information is correct," Edward said.

"How often is it wrong?" David asked.

"Well, never … so far."

Ali's warm complexion had assumed an unhealthy pallor, emphasizing the shadows under her eyes and hollows in her cheeks.

David told her, "Ali, I'm so sorry. I'm not sure why, but my hands …." He didn't finish that thought. "I promise to keep an eye on you. And when you return to Seattle, I'll come along. Even if …. Well, whatever happens, I'm still a doctor."

If possible, the atmosphere had grown more funereal. Did that really mean what Teresa thought it did? They'd all believed that they had in David a get-out-of-jail-free card when it came to illness or injury. Had his powers run their course somehow?

"The best thing Ali can do now is take it easy," David went on. "The rest of us can orchestrate Christmas. Let's keep the guests to immediate family and friends."

"Of course," Joe rushed to say, massaging Ali's shoulders.

"Back to Nancy," Liam said. "I don't know how to break this to you gently, so I'm not going to try. Ali, I'm sorry, but I think our birth mother might have … died."

Ali drew in a long breath. "It's not as if the news is unexpected."

Jake raised his hand. "I also believe that … Nancy has … passed."

All eyes were on him.

"She came to me in a dream. The good news is that it appears that *her* mother is still alive. The woman who visited me was young … and beautiful. The resemblance to Ali was uncanny. Her mother's last name is Fitzpatrick."

"But our mother's legal surname was Ryan," Ali said.

Jake gave the matter some thought. "Could be that her mother remarried, or perhaps Nancy changed her name. In any case, her mother—your grandmother—lives in Yakima."

Liam groaned. "A needle in a haystack."

"I'm fairly certain she told me her first name starts with S," Jake said, "or an SH. Then it was as if the connection just… shorted out."

Liam brightened. "My investigator had reached a dead end. This will give him a fresh start."

Joe refilled their glasses and drank half of his. "Damn. I hope that's all for now."

"Not quite," Liam said. Maddie was trying to tell him with her eyes that this wasn't the time or place. He ignored her. "We were sent new screenplays. Maddie, do you want to do the honors?"

Clearly she didn't. *Too late*, Teresa thought. *Cat's out of the bag, and it's got sharp claws.*

Maddie avoided eye contact as she said, "They've added new scenes. Liam and I, uh, kiss, and George and I have a fight … a physical one … that ends with a no-holds-barred make-out session. I hate to say it, but the changes make sense, given Lorelei's character." Shock and discomfort thickened the silence, and she threw up her hands. "It's acting, y'all. We want the film to succeed, right?" She sent Jake and David imploring looks. "Admit it, you altered the screenplay to suit the family's needs. The public would have held their noses at your bowdlerized version. Also, they'd hate how far it's veered away from the source material."

"An improvement, huh?" Jake said, cheered by the news. Teresa bristled. After all, no one was asking Chiara to lock lips with his devastatingly sexy brother-in-law.

David unclenched his jaw enough to say, "I'll reserve judgment." He stood up, stiffly. "Maddie, where's your copy?"

"In the drawer of the bedstand."

"You couldn't have told me sooner?"

"I knew you'd react like this," she said coolly.

In a few long strides, he left the room.

Teresa turned to Maddie. "He'll get over it."

Maddie stared at her, wide-eyed. "You're not upset?"

She shrugged. "I've had time to adjust to the idea. Liam told me last night."

Maddie clamped a hand over her eyes. "Oh, I'm an idiot." She stood. "Angry as David is, he needs me. For other reasons. I'm not sure what happened just now with Ali. This might be the first time since his own accident in Africa that his hands have failed him." She all but ran from the room.

Edward was peering into each face in turn for clues. "What just happened? Will David be okay?"

"*David* will be okay," Joe said. "It's Ali I'm worried about."

Ali tugged on his sleeve. "He *tried*, Joe. It's not his fault it didn't work. It's ours, for becoming so dependent on his … powers."

"I know, I know…." Joe rubbed his temples.

To Edward, Ali said, "David is no longer a doctor because he couldn't resist the temptation to use the skills he picked up in Africa. Well, he didn't 'pick them up,' exactly. These skills have nothing to do with what you learn in med school. And he didn't 'learn' them from shamans. They're the same kind of skills that allow *you* to see into the future. At the end of June, Chiara's husband arrived without warning, and he nearly got her killed by driving recklessly. David saved her life. Perhaps that was one healing too many—the proverbial straw. You may have wondered why Joe has been able to tour again. That's on David."

Joe took up the thread. "Those 'healings' took a heavy toll. Blinding headaches—life-threatening, even. He warned us that messing with fate might cause unintended consequences. I've been pleading with him to intervene with Ali, but he's insisted all along that she'll be fine once the baby is born … that next, we'd be asking him to cure our hangnails. He had—*has*—a point."

It was all too much for Teresa. Helped by Liam, she rose clumsily to her feet and rolled her shoulders to work the kinks out of her back. "I'm bushed. I need to brief Xenia so she can explain the situation to the other FOSSP kids. No big Christmas Eve party for them here. I'd be happy to cover the costs of a blowout in town if we can locate a venue and outside staff. Maybe we'll just make it a New Year's Eve party instead. Or wait until Valentine's Day. Xenia needs to know ASAP that my schedule has to be light for the foreseeable future." She shot Edward a quick smile. "We can 'foresee' *part* of it, thanks to you." To the others, she said, "You know Xenia. She'll be thrilled to do more of the legwork, so long as it's reflected in her paycheck."

"Can I do anything?" Edward asked, surprisingly serene.

"You're still at the Bishop, right?" Joe asked. "Why don't you stay here through Christmas? Take one of the cabins. Frankly, I'm worried about Maddie and David. A few, uh, less familiar faces might put us all on our best behavior." He looked at Jake. "Do you and Chiara want to stay here too? We can pretend we're all on vacation together. Teresa and Liam?"

Liam shook his head a little too fervently. "You can count on us for the parties, but we'll sleep in our own bed, thanks." Teresa instantly breathed easier. Liam could stand only so much intimacy with her family, and if Edward were coming to stay, wouldn't he want to bring along Lisette?

"Chiara would enjoy having more time with Lorenzo," Jake said. "It might help her with her writers' block. Besides, Christmas is better with children. Lor's holidays alone with Chiara and the dour Arnold couldn't have been much fun."

"I would love to stay," Edward said, "under one condition."

Joe didn't need to have it spelled out. "Lisette's welcome to stay too."

Edward smiled. "You read my mind. Is that *your* gift?"

Joe laughed. "Nope, I'm the ungifted member of the family."

"Do you mean to argue," Jake said, "that psychic gifts are the only ones that matter? Some might say that the ability to sing and achieve excellence at playing guitar and composing music are the *real* gifts. Our so-called 'gifts' are just … aberrations."

"What about writing thrillers?" Joe asked.

Jake's smile had a derisive twist. "I suppose there's a certain art to it."

Hands on hips, Joe said, "So… it's all settled?"

CHAPTER 15

TERESA DIDN'T KNOW ABOUT THE rest of them, but she felt like a helium balloon released from its string. For a woman weighed down by a human bowling ball, that was weightless indeed.

In the car going home, she told Liam, "I hope we didn't stir up a hornet's nest for Maddie."

Liam had that determined look that told her his brain was busy coming up with a plan. She supposed he was plotting how best to protect her. "Maddie should have told David about the screenplay earlier," he said.

Teresa snorted. "If you hadn't been tossing and turning, I might not have coaxed the information out of you either."

His eerily blue eyes seared through her with what she hoped was love and not just lust and need. "God knows I don't deserve you."

She smiled. It was about time he realized how lucky he was to have her in his life. Took him long enough.

"Can you drop me at the office?" she asked. "I need to talk to Xenia."

"If it's okay with you, I'll wait in the car. I know it's only a few blocks, but I don't want you walking home by yourself."

This seemed like an excess of caution to Teresa, but she could humor him until the baby was born. "Sure. I'll make it quick."

The front door was locked, and the office was empty. Teresa's call of "Xenia!" echoed through the hallways. She climbed the stairs and knocked on her assistant's bedroom door. She tried the handle and found it unlocked. *Strange.* Xenia wasn't one for housekeeping, so Teresa paid another FOSSP kid, Tom, to clean and change the beds once a week. Xenia did make her bed, usually, but it was always a messy job. This bed had not been slept in since Tom changed the sheets.

She called Xenia on the cell phone she had bought for her.

She answered with a perky, "Hello?"

"Xenia, it's Teresa. Where are you?"

"I'm, um, in town. I thought you weren't coming in today."

Teresa paid Xenia to man the front desk from nine to eleven in the morning and one to three in the afternoon. It was two thirty. Had she been in the office today at all? Not if the blinking message light on the office phone was any indication. Teresa should confront her about it, but she wasn't in the mood after all that had gone down at the compound.

"There have been some complications in, uh, Ali's pregnancy." Teresa saw no need to mention her own. "Minor ones. We can't tire her, so we have to rethink the FOSSP party—maybe reschedule for New Year's Eve or Valentine's Day. I've also promised Liam I wouldn't overtax myself, since my due date is only six weeks away. I'd like you to do more of the legwork. I'll pay you, of course."

Teresa thought they might have been cut off. "Xenia?"

Finally she replied, "Our two current design projects are in the early planning stages, and neither of the clients is clear on what they want—there's nothing that won't wait until after the new year." A long pause. "I hope you're okay."

"I'll be fine. Of course, you're welcome to drop by while the Seattle crew is in town. It's just that we're trying to keep things simple for Ali, which means core family only."

Silence again. *God*, she hated communicating on the phone. Was Xenia offended? Until now they'd been treating *her* like family.

Teresa broke the silence. "How will you celebrate the holidays? I know you were counting on spending Christmas Eve and Day with us at the compound."

To Teresa's relief, Xenia replied in a cheerful voice, "Oh, I'll find something to do. In fact, I might be visiting … friends in … Port Angeles. Don't worry about me."

"All right. I'm glad you have somewhere to go. As I say, we'd love you to drop by. Just give us a heads-up first. If we can't find a venue for the FOSSP party, maybe you can stop by on New Year's Day. After all, January first might be chaos. Y-two-K, you know." Teresa tried to make it sound like a joke. She hoped it was. She didn't really believe the entire digital network was going to go haywire when 1999 ticked over to 2000. But you never knew.

Xenia's laugh sounded forced as she said, "All right. Well, Merry Christmas! Bye now."

Liam gave Teresa a double take as he helped her into the passenger seat. "What's wrong?"

"Xenia wasn't there."

He checked his watch. "But it's not yet three, and you were in there for fifteen minutes."

"I called her cell phone. Everything she said sounded sketchy, as if she were making it up on the spot. Her bed doesn't look slept in. She said she was 'in town.' What does that even mean? Our office is 'in town.' I guess she meant downtown. She didn't offer any excuse for missing office hours. Then she sputtered some BS about visiting friends in Port Angeles over the holidays, 'friends' she's never mentioned before."

"Clearly she could use more supervision," Liam said. Teresa knew his doubts about Xenia. He thought Teresa gave her too much leeway in the job and that Xenia was too much of a flirt. So what if she fudged her office hours? She'd done a nice job with their website. And who could resist Liam?

* * *

Lisette's head was in the clouds. She kept flashing back to erotic memories of last night and this morning. Fortunately, her hosting duties were hardly taxing. All that was required of her was a lot of smiling and a few polite quips. Tallying up the receipts at the end of the evening did prove challenging.

At eleven thirty, Edward knocked on the door, pressing up against the window like a child salivating over a bakery display. Just one glimpse of him was enough to send a thrill of desire zinging straight to her core. She aimed for a leisurely stroll to the entrance but ended up breaking into a run. *Damn it, girl,* she told herself. *Don't leap into his arms like a dog that's been left alone all day.*

But Edward was just as eager. As soon as the door was unlocked, he was on her, walking her backward until they were in the far recesses of the room. He pressed her up against the wall, kissing her with such fervor that he might have been a soldier returning from battle.

She reached for the buttons of his fly and pulled them all free in one tug. *Oh, Lord help me,* she thought, *he's not wearing underwear.* She grasped the hard length of him, but he stilled her hand. "Listen, darlin'," he said in a strangled voice, "it's not like I can hide how much I want you. But maybe not … here."

"I agree," she whispered against his mouth. "The floor is… disgusting. If you keep kissing me like this, I'm going to puddle there like… like a melted snowman."

Their lips were inches away, and both were breathing hard. In a raspy whisper, he said, "I've been reliving last night and this morning all the fucking day long. I could definitely take you right now in any way you choose, but… we'd have to burn all our clothing." Laughter had crept into his voice. "And that would be a shame. You look fucking *amazing* in this hostess outfit. My fingers are itching to just reach through this slit and sneak under your silk panties …." His hand fell away. "I'd better stop there."

She whispered too; no matter that no one was around to overhear. "I can't tell you how difficult it's been to function normally today." She sighed against his mouth.

He gave her another quick kiss, a tad proprietary. "Good. It's a relief to know I'm not in this alone. I was afraid I rushed you."

"Perish the thought," she said. She pulled away and gazed at him with naked desire, lest he doubt her word for a minute. "Let's sit for a moment and decompress. I just want to feast my eyes on you."

"God, *yes*."

She fetched them two glasses of wine, and they sipped, gazing into each other's eyes with such intensity that they both started giggling. "And how was *your* day, honey?" she asked.

"It just took a definite turn for the better." Then his smile faded. "To be totally frank, my day was weird as hell."

Uh-oh. He had turned deadly serious. She waited.

"I have a proposal for you."

"A proposal?" She fought a wave of vertigo.

He pretended to tweak her nose. "Not a *marriage* proposal, you goofball. We had a family meeting at the compound. I wish you'd been there. To think I believed *my* life was the height of surreal."

She couldn't believe her ears. "You told them about the pregnancy complications, didn't you?"

"How did you guess? Yes, I did."

"And they believed you, just like that?" She snapped her fingers.

"They had their reasons."

She whistled. "You *did* have a weird day."

"They invited me to come stay at the compound through the holidays."

Her heart sank. Seeing each other had just become way more complicated.

"I want you to stay there with me. When you're not working, that is."

Though flattered by his request, she didn't believe he'd thought it through. "Come on. They can't be okay with that."

Grasping both her hands, he insisted, "They *are*. Jake and Chiara will take one of the cabins too. Teresa and Liam want to remain in town. I can tell that Liam would like to avoid being, um, *nestled* in the family bosom." He gave a dry little laugh.

She breathed easier. As long as Teresa and Liam wouldn't be underfoot …. "Is there a special reason they want you there?"

He paused as if unsure of the answer himself, then said simply, "I need a place to stay. Living at a hotel is getting old. It'll be fun, you'll see. There's a hot tub …." He seemed to hold his breath while he waited for her to answer.

In truth, there was nothing to consider. The prospect of spending Christmas alone in the cramped apartment was simply too grim to contemplate.

"Say yes," he whispered.

She threw her arms around his neck and whispered, "Yes, yes, *yes*."

CHAPTER 16

MADDIE LAY NEXT TO DAVID in the darkened bedroom. He wasn't asleep. Was he in shock? The ability to heal had been a curse of sorts, but to have it taken away…. The day had been an all-around shitshow. David believed he had let Joe down. The very idea made her want to throw one of those ubiquitous handwoven baskets across the room—nothing that would actually break, Maddie not being the destructive sort. Really, she had no one to blame but herself. First, who could fault Joe for relying on David's magic hands in situations that weren't matters of life and death? She had done it herself. As for the screenplay, she should have forced Jake and David to reconsider the changes from the start rather than let them believe they could manipulate the plot to suit themselves. And not confiding in David immediately about the latest rewrites was a ham-fisted move on her part.

Hearing a gentle knock on the door, she opened it a crack to find Joe. Has she summoned him with her thoughts? He appeared thoroughly chastened. *Good*, she thought. *He knows it's not David's fault he couldn't help Ali.*

She joined him in the hallway, shutting the door behind her.

"How is he?" Joe whispered.

She didn't reply immediately, weighing her words. "I'm not sure. He blames himself, which is ridiculous. The Lord giveth, the Lord taketh away." She paused. "However we define 'Lord.' Could be the Lord of Darkness. Or the Lord of the Dance."

Joe's half smile acknowledged her attempt to lighten the mood. "Can I bring you anything? A plate of food?"

She waved him away. "I'll be down in a bit. Whatever David is going through, he has to do it on his own. I'm not sure he even wants *me* here."

"The screenplay—" Joe began.

"He'll get used to the idea," she broke in. "He must have known there was a good chance Jake's and his revisions would get nixed. Happens in Hollywood all the time. Most screenplays have multiple writers." She gave his shoulder a gentle shove. "Go back downstairs. Ali needs you."

After Joe left, Maddie again lay down next to David. She must have dozed because she dreamed George Reed Masters stood by the bed. "Are you a real actress or not?" he said. "Or are you just another traditional woman who lets her husband call the shots? Isn't that exactly what you swore up and down to avoid?"

Great. As if *George* could ever be the voice of reason. She had a sneaking suspicion that having sex with Maddie had risen to the top of the actor's bucket list. No one said no to George. Although she would never let that happen, she couldn't stop him from getting his jollies while they were filming as long as the screenplay called for it. Sex was sex, even if the act was incomplete. Arguing otherwise didn't let President Clinton off the hook.

She awoke to David holding her in his arms.

"How are you feeling?" she whispered.

"Hungry. What time is it, anyway?" He sat up so he could see the clock radio. "Ten after eleven. Guess we slept through dinner."

They went downstairs to see what they could scrounge from the refrigerator. They were alone in the house.

When they were seated with plates of food, he asked in a bone-weary voice, "Okay, hit me. Tell me what they did to the screenplay."

She avoided his eyes as she said, "They didn't reduce Troy Benz's part. The additions that matter most to us are … a passionate kiss between me and Liam and a fight scene with George that turns sexual."

With an air of resignation, David popped a green bean in his mouth and chewed slowly. "That doesn't sound too bad … as long as they're done making changes."

She looked down at her mostly full plate, appetite gone. "One can only hope."

David gave a small huff of exasperation. "I knew we should have taken over as producers. But I was promised…." He didn't bother to finish. He knew the value of promises in the movie industry.

Humoring him at this point was bound to bite them in the ass later on.

So Maddie said, "Don't you want what's best for the movie? If Liam and I weren't the actors in question, would you have made the changes you did?"

Eyes narrowed, he asked in turn, "Would you argue that the movies they made in the forties, after the code, were worse because the sex had to be limited to inuendo?"

"No." She took her plate over to the sink. "But this is a nineties audience we're talking about. Whatever you want to call it. An 'aughts' audience, the year 2000 being mere weeks away. They have different expectations. Much as you and I love those old classics, most of the current generation doesn't appreciate their subtlety."

I don't know, she wanted to tell him. *I can't predict the future. I doubt even Edward could predict the fallout of this movie.* They'd all been thrilled when David first altered the screenplay to calm their insecurities.

She kissed him then with all the love in her heart.

If only that is enough, she thought.

* * *

Edward had just checked out of the motel, and he and Lisette were caravaning to the compound. Every few seconds he glanced at Lisette's black Miata, reflected in his rearview mirror. He couldn't believe his luck. He kept expecting to wake up back in his single bed at the parish, with only his faltering faith for company.

Despite his reassurances, Lisette was bound to feel like she was on probation with his family. Surely by now, a woman so beautiful would be used to defusing jealousy. Men with Edward's impressive physical gifts also needed to work hard to put others at ease. Though in general, men weren't threatened by priests. Women automatically assumed Lisette was up to no good.

He didn't know his family well anymore—did he ever?—but he believed them to be basically kind people who would give Lisette the benefit of the doubt. Even his mother. Or so he hoped. He'd worry about her later.

He knew next to nothing about Lisette's past, other than those few stories from her childhood. He hadn't shared much with her, either. He'd mentioned his stint as a satyr, which some might see as bragging. Most people preferred the company of sinners to saints. He'd never been a candidate for sainthood, even at his most righteous.

He punched the code into the pad at the outer gate. Almost there. As he bumped along the gravel road, he wondered if Lisette would consider taking time off instead of leaving in the morning and returning at midnight. Couldn't

Ali and Joe recommend a FOSSP kid who could act as a hostess at Café Lisette? Lisette's bartender could handle the money part.

A code was also required at the main gate. Joe, flanked by dogs, greeted them at the open part of the parking area on the crest of the hill, next to Maddie's Vespa scooter and Joe's ancient pickup truck. All the sons had learned to get their hands dirty from their father and considered manual labor to be a form of relaxation.

Joe reintroduced them to the dogs, who sniffed their hands and wagged their tails tentatively, then looked at Joe, as if requesting permission to take further liberties.

"Do you like dogs?" Joe asked Lisette.

"Not all dogs," she said in a silly voice suitable for dogs or babies, "but I like these friendly boys." She knelt down to give them her full attention. They gazed at her with soulful adoration, ignoring Edward entirely.

"You must have the magic touch," Joe said. "They're your slaves."

You have no idea, Edward thought.

As Joe walked them to the cabin farthest from the compound, he said to Lisette, "I hear you have a punishing schedule. Have you considered taking time off for the holidays? It's pretty relaxing here."

Lisette gave him her most dazzling smile. "That's kind of you. As of this weekend, Sid's wife will act as hostess; then we'll be closed until after New Year's. I'm overdue for a vacation."

"Can you afford that?" Edward asked, fearing that her desire to please him trumped her need to keep the restaurant solvent.

"I can," she assured him. "My employees want the holidays off too, and they'll get a bonus."

Once they were alone at the cabin, Edward asked again, "Are you sure? I assume Port Townsend is hopping with tourists at Christmas."

She patted his cheek. "You worry too much. After tonight—Karaoke Night, remember?—I'm going to leave the restaurant at nine instead of eleven so I don't wake up the entire compound."

He wanted to summon Joe back and crow about how considerate she was. Though Joe had been perfectly nice, Edward feared they'd be tolerating Lisette for his sake, and she deserved better. *Patience*, he told himself. *You're hardly neutral. They'll grow to love her too.*

Edward took a look around. This cabin had received an Ali makeover. *Whimsical* was the word that described it. The one he'd stayed in earlier had little character beyond cheap rustic. He didn't care as long as the bolt was working. He fiddled with the lock. *Yep*, this mechanism worked fine.

"What are you doing?" Lisette asked.

"Just checking. During that winter storm, I stayed in a different cabin, and there was no way to lock the door. Even the chain was broken." Not wishing to explain further, he asked, "What do you think of the décor?" He indicated the warm orange walls and the African prints of the runners, duvet cover, and rugs. The rattan chair with lemon-yellow seat cushions. "David is a fan of African colonial."

"Now that you mention it," Lisette said as she filled two dresser drawers with clothing, "it reminds me of the living room of the Sea Captain's House. What did Maddie call it, 'safari chic'?"

"As a child," Edward went on, "David loved H. Rider Haggard's *King Solomon's Mines*."

"Hmm," Lisette said. "Haven't read it."

"Don't bother, although it's the best of something like fourteen books featuring big game hunter Allan Quatermain—who was sort of an ur-Indiana Jones. They're hardcore adventure tales for boys—although the ideal audience is probably British boys who grew up a century ago."

"Good, that's one I can skip. I've tried to read books that might have been assigned if I'd gone to college, but I get overwhelmed. I even started *The Rise and Fall of the Third Reich*. Then I discovered the 'Dummies' and 'Idiots' books. Not for literature. For stuff like philosophy."

He instantly regretted his reflexive laugh, but she didn't blush or backpedal. "They're way better than the titles imply. The franchises choose experts to write them, people who can explain things clearly and concisely, even with humor." She smiled. "But mostly I'm trying to read literary classics. I get them out of the library, or I buy used paperbacks I don't mind parting with. I try to travel light."

The word "travel" struck him. "Were you contemplating a trip somewhere?" He came up behind her and wrapped his arms around her, as if to keep her in one place. *If only you could*, he thought.

She leaned against him, and they melted together. "I meant 'travel' in the metaphorical sense. I don't collect things, especially not books."

"What are you reading now?"

"*Lorna Doone*. Don't laugh. I doubt it's on any of the 'Great Books' lists, but it's entertaining."

"I think you'd enjoy *Kapow*," Edward said. "Jake may not be John le Carré, but he spins a good yarn. I look forward to getting to know him at this current phase of his life. He and I have more in common than he probably realizes."

"The broken lock…" Lisette prompted. *Damn*. He thought he'd successfully dodged that bullet. "Why would you need a working lock here? At dinner the other night, they went on and on about security at the compound. Why bother to lock doors?"

He had to come clean. "Xenia," he said with a sigh. "Teresa's intern. At dinner, she barreled down on me like an amorous freight train. The wine flowed freely, which meant no brakes. I was seated between her and Ali. Ali kept disappearing to the kitchen, as hostesses do, though the dinner was in capable hands and she shouldn't have stressed herself …." He was rambling. He paused, tried to organize his thoughts. "I had a hunch that Xenia would attempt a booty call."

Lisette looked more concerned than troubled. And unsurprised, even though he'd skipped this part while telling her how Reynard had contrived to meet Xenia. "Premonition?" she asked.

"No, common sense. A vibe I picked up at dinner."

"But nothing happened, right?"

He grimaced. "Not for lack of effort on her part. It wasn't pretty." He cleared his throat. "She is quite… confident. I hate to say it—because I suspect she is one of those toxic people—but I'm rooting for Reynard to take her on."

Lisette's laugh had a bitter edge. "Reynard is also one of those toxic people. They might deserve each other."

Edward's first Karaoke Night had been exhilarating. This one had the added advantage of Lisette as a full partner. They might have been co-hosting an award show. She kept lobbing little quips and questions at him, keeping him on his toes but mostly conveying a not-so-subtle message of "hands off" to anyone with ideas of picking him up. They opened with the duet "Baby it's cold outside" and encouraged others to concentrate on the holiday repertoire too, especially the secular kind.

One pretty, very short young woman he thought he recognized from the FOSSP crew who worked at the compound made a valiant pass at a song called "All I Want for Christmas Is You," and the boy she was with, a scruffy young man not much taller than her with shifty eyes, took a stab at "Last Christmas." While he was a priest, Edward had actively ignored pop culture. Judging from the uneven results, it seemed foolhardy to take on repertoire made famous by these singers, identified by Lisette as Mariah Carey and George Michael.

For him, the highlight of the evening was Lisette's one solo, "Have

Yourself a Merry Little Christmas." Sad as the song was, her rendition offered hope for the future. As he sang "White Christmas," it occurred to him that it wasn't a feel-good romp either.

CHAPTER 17

———◆———

JAKE HAD A WEIRD DÉJÀ-VU moment as he and Chiara pulled into the carport at the compound Thursday morning. Only six months had passed since David's wedding, when he'd thrown caution to the wind and driven right into the lion's den, egged on by Rory's snarky spirit. Joe and Ali could so easily have turned him away. Annoying as Rory's ghost had been, without him, none of this would have been possible: the introduction to the love of his life, the success of his thrillers, the détente with his family. *Thanks, Rory*, he thought, grateful that his friend's ghost wasn't around to reply.

Jake had become so attached to the gaudy old Victorian with its drafty rooms and ghostly presence that he wondered if he could write anywhere else. *It's not as if the compound is in Forks*, he reminded himself. *You could go hang out there for a few hours anytime you like.*

The advantages of a temporary stay at the compound were clear. Chiara could spend more time with Lorenzo, giving Ali and the nannies one fewer small human to watch over, and Chiara and Ali's children's book would progress more quickly. *The Way to Moss Manor* had practically written itself while Chiara resided here. Brainstorming would be easier, and for Chiara, the need to invent details on the spot for Lorenzo would keep those improvisational skills honed. Inventing how Lor might react to a particular plot development was a lot harder than simply recording the response from the horse's mouth.

As for Jake, he wanted to see if David was truly at peace with whatever remained of his *Kapow* screenplay once the dust had settled. Maybe Jake could even ferret out why Edward had left the priesthood.

"Jake?" Chiara laid a gentle hand on his thigh. "We've been sitting here a while now. Can't you hear Coogan and Harry's mournful howls? They believe something terrible has happened to us. Are you having second thoughts about this visit?"

He shook himself back to the here and now. "Of course not. Sorry. I was recalling the day I arrived here."

"You were brave. You had no idea what to expect. They might have treated you with hostility."

Jake opened the car door to reassure Coogan and Harry. As he hauled the suitcases out of the trunk, he waved to Ali, standing at the window of her office on the second floor of the Log Palace. Having fulfilled their duties as the welcoming committee, the dogs trotted off together toward the house.

"I knew they would, at the very least, put on a show of hospitality," Jake said.

Chiara gave him an odd look. "The dogs?"

"Ali and Joe. It was Maddie and David's wedding, after all. As long as I didn't do something blatantly rude, like get rip-roaring drunk and raise objections to the marriage or strip and run naked around the compound, they weren't going to treat me like a wedding crasher. They're too well-mannered for that. What I didn't expect was a warm welcome. It kind of blew my mind." He noted her mischievous grin. "You're imagining me naked and running around the compound," he said, smiling back at her.

"I'm also remembering the box of clothes and shoes, the things you'd given to Ali when you were dating."

He blew out a disgusted puff of air. "*Dating*. As if. I just couldn't give anything so beautiful away."

"Most men wouldn't have had the guts. That's the expression, yes?"

"If you mean that returning the clothing was brave, I don't agree. Ali might have believed I was throwing them back in her face."

"Even if Ali *had* thought as much—and I'm sure that wasn't the case—your siblings know you too well for that."

He opened the door to their cabin. A sign identified it as "The Country Cottage." It featured burlap curtains, a crazy-quilt comforter, and a folk-art rug with primitive trees and cabins woven in. Not *his* taste, but not tasteless.

Chiara was still dwelling on "the box." "If you hadn't brought those clothes back, I would not have worn that beautiful dress, and you would never have noticed me."

"Oh, ye of little faith. From the minute I first saw you, I was a goner." She certainly looked glorious now in her Calvin Klein jeans, Dansko boots, cashmere sweater, and puffy parka. Chosen for quality, fit, and comfort. "You were so clearly a diamond in the rough."

"Diamond 'in the rough,' " she repeated with a delighted clap of her hands. "We say a 'raw' diamond, *un diamante grezzo*. To them, I was just Lorenzo's babysitter."

"They never treated you like that."

"I *felt* like that."

"You were an outsider, like me. That's what brought us together. How about I bring us together right now?" He walked her backward toward the bed.

"What do you call that?"

"Stalking. I'm stalking you, like a hunter."

She giggled. "I meant the bed covering. It isn't really a pattern."

"It's a crazy quilt. Women used to make them from random pieces of fabric left over from other projects."

"*Caro*," she laid a hand on his chest, "it's almost noon. They expect us for lunch. Don't you want to be a good houseguest?"

"If we don't show up, they'll understand." He kissed her neck.

She pushed him away. "That's what I'm afraid of. Also, I'm hungry. There's always *piacere pomeridiano*. You call it 'afternoon delight.' No?"

"Yes. Definitely yes."

She pouted adorably. "Lorenzo will want the whole afternoon."

He gave her an affectionate nudge. "There's always *late* afternoon."

Jake and Chiara found the granite kitchen island of the Sea Captain's House brimming with a spread of cold cuts, bread, and fruit. Most of the family was already comfortably seated in the living room, looking as if their greatest concern was whether afternoon tea would keep them satisfied until dinner. For once, Ali let the interns Jake privately referred to as Foxface Steve and Cutiepie Angie take care of everything.

Despite David's failure to intervene, Ali appeared healthier. Even more beautiful than the coltish young woman who had caught his eye that fateful evening at La Fête Sauvage. Maddie and David seemed … fine, though it was almost as if the collective worries of Ali and Joe had been transferred to them. Maddie was thinner than he recalled, almost frail, as if she were made of fine china like one of his Victorian figurines. In contrast, David appeared to be carved from granite. How did he manage not to roll onto Maddie in the night and break her? Edward and Lisette made you want to croon the chorus of "I Only Have Eyes For You." They made a formidable couple, as if the forces of light and darkness had merged. Edward—lucky devil—had their father's rugged solidity *and* their mother's aristocratic beauty. Lisette's athletic build might have graced a package of Wheaties. Make that the *Sports Illustrated* swimsuit issue.

The O'Connells were, by anyone's reckoning, an unusually good-looking family. At six feet, Jake was the shortest and smallest, favoring his mother rather than his larger-than-life father. Not that Jake wasn't handsome enough by more reasonable standards, just not by the ones set by these denizens of Mount Olympus on the Peninsula. His eyes rested on his own radiant love, Chiara. A soft brown curl fell across her sweet face as she spoke with Lorenzo. Jake had no complaints. For him at least, all was right with the world.

The conversation was mostly logistical—what guests were coming and when, where they would stay, which of the FOSSP kids had agreed to help out. Becca and Jean-Louis would be in town as of Saturday, and Carrie and her man-of-all-trades Rostand would arrive on Christmas Eve. Lisette would preside at her restaurant through Sunday night, though today, Edward had convinced her to let others take over so she could join them for lunch.

"Xenia's plans are a mystery," Ali said. "Teresa told me there was something not quite right there, that she hadn't shown up for work at all Tuesday and was vague about where she'd spend the holidays."

A knowing look passed between Edward and Lisette.

Curious. "Edward," Jake said, "care to speculate?"

"Nothing that doesn't qualify as gossip," Edward said with a wry smile. "I'll tell you later." His head bobbed in the direction of the FOSSP kids, who were clearing the last of the dishes. "Excuse me, Steve and Angie, didn't Lisette and I see you at Karaoke Night? I believe you gave George Michael and Mariah Carey a run for their money."

Lisette snapped her fingers. "I knew I recognized you two from somewhere. I have trouble placing people out of context. Nicely done, by the way."

Angie was blushing furiously. "We love Karaoke Night."

"Thank you for all your help today," Ali told them. "We'll see you at dinner." To the others, she said, "Tiger's cooking again. I made him promise to skip the dessert."

"Edward … you'll tell us what you know later?" Ali said in a low voice when they were gone. "About Xenia?"

Edward raised his palm to stop her. "You should ask Teresa. All I did was put two and two together."

"*Which* two is the question?" Joe said with a smile.

Lisette was twisting a long black curl around her finger. "I'd say Xenia and Reynard."

Joe's brow furrowed. "Hmm."

Personally, Jake didn't worry about Xenia's ability to handle Reynard. He wouldn't be the first to state the obvious—that Teresa's faith in her protégée might be misplaced. He hoped the woman didn't have access to her bank account. "Are Teresa and Liam coming to dinner?" he asked to break the awkward silence.

Joe replied, "They'll be here Saturday. Jean-Louis's helping Tiger plan an even more ambitious spread."

"Who's cooking Monday night?" Lisette asked Joe.

"Leftovers okay? You know Jean-Louis—every meal is basically a potlatch, and Ali and I hate waste. Tiger also produces quantities that could feed a football team."

Lisette waved her hand, as if to get the teacher's attention. "If you don't mind, I'd like to do the honors. My café is closed Mondays, and I'm going to let Sid and Margie handle things the week following so I can"—her eyes met Edward's—"take some time off."

Jake was fascinated by Lisette. She seemed nice, despite the naughty implications of her appearance. He'd bet she was a talented chef too. Now he wished he'd given Café Lisette a shot rather than following Liam's lead and always patronizing Kelpies.

After lunch, Lisette headed back into town and Chiara and Ali joined the children in the rec room. All that remained were the three brothers. Would they agree to an outing if Jake suggested it? It was blustery, and an icy ocean mist made it feel colder than the forty degrees on the thermometer. Still, no rain or snow was in the forecast, and they were a hearty lot. That described David and Joe, anyway. Jake was less fond of roughing it, more inclined to seek out creature comforts. Face it, he was a sensualist. But he wasn't a complete bust as an outdoorsman. Since Rory's death, backpacking trips were out, but he still liked a challenging day hike, and he'd mastered the special throwing knives Liam had given him. Now, if only he could learn to throw a hunting knife.... Too bad that required years of practice. Jake had climbed enough mountains and no longer had anything to prove there. Edward, like all of them, was athletic, and if Jake was a sensualist, Edward was a voluptuary. Or a sybarite. Whatever was worse. Had been, anyway. Way back when, their oldest brother had gobsmacked them all by foreswearing the libertine's life. Now, Lord Byron was back. If you were going to fall off the wagon, you couldn't land in the hay with anyone more suitable for a good roll than Lisette.

"I don't know about you," Jake said to the godlike crew that remained, "but I could use a brisk walk on the beach. You guys want to head over to Fort Worden with me?" He produced a flask from his pocket. "I have provisions to ward off hypothermia."

Joe agreed enthusiastically. Edward, though warier, said, "Why not?"

Ever the practical one, Joe filled a backpack with water bottles.

David offered to drive them in his Nissan Pathfinder.

The Four Musketeers themselves (if you counted d'Artagnan) could not be more daunting.

CHAPTER 18

EN ROUTE TO FORT WORDEN, David reflected that this was the first time the brothers had been alone together in … forever. That made the outing far from casual. As the driver, he'd stick to water and let the others down the truth serum, otherwise known as whiskey.

To break the silence, he remarked, "I know Liam used to go to Fort Worden regularly to help some guy out—Peter, I think his name is. The one in charge of maintenance. Liam's got so much on his plate now, I wonder if he has time to stop by anymore. I hope Peter managed to hang onto his job without his help."

"Knowing Liam," Jake said from the passenger seat, "he still drops by when he can."

"I confess, I don't want to like Liam," Edward leaned forward to say. "I get the feeling he purposely keeps Teresa off balance. He's the furthest thing from the husband I'd have imagined for our sister."

David pulled into the parking lot and zipped up his parka. "Because the entirety of his higher education is an unimpressive two years of community college?"

David's snarky question seemed to startle Edward. They locked the car and headed toward the beach, where supercharged waves crashed against the shore.

"Yes, that," Edward admitted. "We were all raised to be intellectual snobs—you too, by the way. But also, she's always fetishized 'creative' types. I figured she'd end up with someone like Reynard." He made a disgusted sound. "Not that you'd wish that jerk on your worst enemy, much less your sister. He's a cold-blooded SOB."

David gave him a playful punch in the arm. "Even Xenia?" He hadn't told the others about the intern's failed attempt to seduce his older brother. Here was a chance for Edward to come clean. He wanted Joe to know her true colors too.

Edward pulled his wool cap down over his ears. "That wind has a bite to it." He gave David a pointed look. "I don't know. Reynard may have met his match. I'd wager Xenia would come out ahead on that one. I see her as a user. Probably figures she's gotten a raw deal her whole life, so it's payback time."

Joe and Jake had fallen behind and missed that part of their exchange. The relentless wind and screaming seagulls compelled David to stand close to Edward in order to be heard. "Joe needs to be informed what went down," he said. "I know Xenia told Teresa she'd be in Port Angeles over the holidays, but what if she has second thoughts and turns up at the compound—like the bad penny she is? What if she lies about what happened?"

Edward, hands in the pockets of his peacoat, gave an exaggerated shrug. "I've already told Lisette that Xenia made a play for me."

David wondered exactly how much he'd told her but didn't pursue the topic. "So … Lisette's cooking for us Monday. I hear she's a trained chef."

"Yes," Edward said, and added with obvious pride, "at the Cordon Bleu in Paris."

David gave him a thumbs up. "One of the most prestigious but also expensive cooking schools in the world. Jean-Louis was trained there too—that gives them something in common. Does she come from money?"

"No," Edward said. "Her parents run a restaurant in Cape May."

"A high-end place?"

"More like a diner. Plain ol' American cooking."

"Not much profit there."

Edward stopped walking and stared him down. "What are you implying?"

Too late, David regretted his heavy-handedness. "Nothing, Bro. Liam had this idea—"

"I know what Liam thinks," Edward interrupted him. His tone had turned glacial.

"You know that once Mom realizes you're serious about Lisette, she'll have her investigated, right? She does things like that. No one can stop her. Her investigator told her Liam was trained as an assassin and mercenary after he survived that terrorist attack in Israel."

Edward's eyes widened. "No kidding."

"It was partly true. Liam acquired major combat skills in Israel, and he did go on a mission for his adopted mother, to rescue her daughter. I'm just saying that it would be better to hear the details from Lisette rather than wait for Mom's investigator's skewed take on her past. If she funded her cooking-school tuition legitimately, then great. Though I don't imagine they give scholarships to women. Then there would be getting the dough to cover travel, accommodations, food, and incidental expenses. Plus, she dresses really well."

"Can we change the subject?" Edward ground out.

"What subject?" Jake asked, slightly breathless. He and Joe had rushed to catch up. David was impressed that the formerly hostile twin brothers were getting on so well. He'd heard something about their mending fences—literally. Jake had helped Joe repair the fence that surrounded the vegetable garden. Their rapport seemed to be much improved.

"Nothing," Edward grumbled. "Liam's not here, so let's talk about him instead. Teresa told me that guy she eloped with is contributing to their current tensions—Kilo, her teenage crush."

"Kilo," David spat out, as if the name were the obscene kind of four-letter word. "What a troublemaker. Thank God he's moved on."

"He still owns the yoga studio," Joe said, "though he's hired someone to run it. I won't rest easy until he's got no more unfinished business here."

"Weren't he and Maddie involved for a while?" Edward asked.

It was David's turn to gnash his teeth. He did *not* want to discuss Kilo. If their love triangle had been a fairytale, Maddie would be Snow White, Kilo the prince, and David the Huntsman. Snow White did *not* choose the Huntsman. When Maddie had gone for him over Kilo, David couldn't believe his luck. But he couldn't stop fretting that the rules of happily-ever-after would compel her to realize her mistake eventually and go back to the prince. He replied with a terse "Yes," hoping that would be the end of it. If Kilo did return, it would be because of Maddie. She was his real unfinished business, the one who got away.

Fortunately for David, Edward seemed to understand that he'd struck a nerve and needed to let that one alone.

Jake passed the flask around again. In the brief silence that followed, he said, "Edward, feel free to shut us down, but we're all curious about your, uh, break with the Church."

A gust of wind had them wiping sand from their eyes, and Joe had to yell to be heard. "Let's get out of the wind, shall we? We can shelter in one of these old… what are they, batteries?" They all stared at the cement shell of a building.

"Or bunkers," David said as he ducked inside.

With the volume lowered on the howling wind, they stood in a circle in the dark, dank interior, passing the flask around. David drank from his bottle of water.

"What's Kilo up to now?" Edward asked.

Jake replied, "I believe he's on location in Hawaii, filming new episodes of the reboot of that old detective series, *Hawaiian Eye*. Anyone seen it?"

They all shook their heads. David wondered darkly if Maddie had watched the pilot. They had satellite TV at the compound.

Edward slumped down against the wall and hugged his knees. "I don't remember the original."

"You weren't watching TV then," David said, crouching down beside him. "You must have been about two when it was canceled. Joe and I hadn't been born yet. Kilo is cast as Tom Lopaka, Robert Conrad's role. Tom is supposed to be mixed race, and unlike Conrad, Kilo is part Asian."

Edward was rubbing his hands together and blowing on them. "Wish I had some gloves. Come on… you really think Kilo is still a threat to your marriage? Maddie's made her choice."

"I hope you never meet the guy," Joe said. "He's a force to be reckoned with. Even Liam is still intimidated by him. Kilo's not only gorgeous in that androgynous way some women can't resist, but he's also got this Zen thing going on, being a yoga teacher and all. He's a smooth talker who dances like Paul Taylor. He once toured with Groban Phillips."

"The dance troupe?" Edward asked.

"Yep. Pretty much the top of the heap in the modern dance world. On a par with the Merce Cunningham company. He's also a trained Shakespearean actor. In *A Midsummer Night's Dream*, he set every heart racing, including some of the men's. Reynard has the creds, but if you scratch the surface, you'll find a controlling asshole with a considerable dark side. Kilo is, ostensibly, all sweetness and light—charm and more charm. If he weren't such a natural lothario, he'd be fun to hang out with. Liam and he were friends for a while, believe it or not. Can't say the same of Reynard, though Matthew defends him. Maybe Reynard can only befriend gay men."

"Kilo and George Reed Masters would probably hit it off," Jake said. "Unless they can't handle the competition. Sorry, David. I know George is a sore subject."

"Lots of sore subjects here," David grumbled. "Are we going to address any of them? I'd really like to put that smarmy matinee idol George out of my mind until filming starts in April." He was fresh out of patience. If they were going to discuss unpleasant topics, at least they could do it someplace warm. The air in the bunker was frigid.

"I hate to say it," Jake said, "but I like George. Then again, he never made a play for Chiara. Like Kilo, he's got that hard to define thing they call star quality. I can't believe our luck that he agreed to take the part of Troy Benz in *Kapow*. With his reputation, he could have insisted on playing Damon Morehouse."

Considering his own and Maddie's stake in the movie's success, David knew it was unreasonable to write George off. "His participation might just make that movie, much as it kills me to admit it. If you saw him in person, you'd go, '*This* guy?' He's kind of short and weaselly. But those sharp features look fantastic on film, and his presence just leaps off the screen."

Edward's head was in his hands. Was he crying? No, the bastard was laughing. "Listen, you guys," Edward said, "you have nothing to fear. Look at you! It's like an elephant being terrified of a mouse. Totally irrational."

They all stared at him. David hoped Edward never had the misfortune to witness either man in action with Lisette as their goal. "I believe elephants are afraid of the mice crawling up their trunks," he said. "That's what these guys are to us—minor irritants. Only in this case, females seem to welcome them crawling up…." He stopped himself. Not the point he'd intended to make.

The others were wiping away tears of laughter. Giving in to the moment, he laughed too. Edward was right: they were being ridiculous. The flask made the rounds again as the wind howled like a banshee. David thought longingly of the hot tub and realized he could have suggested a communal soak instead. Still, he wasn't going to waste this opportunity to delve into Edward's past. Once again, he zeroed in on his eldest brother, a master at diverting attention from himself. "Back to you, Edward. We're all dying to know why you left the Church."

Edward's smile was smug. "I kinda figured that was what this walk was all about." He paused for a long moment before continuing, "First, you have to understand why I sought out the Church."

"Celibacy," Joe said with no hesitation. "Something had to stop you. None of us could. If death by sex were an option, you'd have achieved it."

Edward leaned back against the cement wall, his tone and attitude so casual and detached, he might have been discussing a distant acquaintance.

"Death by sex *was* an option. AIDs was rampant by then. Only I always used condoms."

Jake covered his eyes with one hand. "Please don't tell us you're a pedophile."

Edward didn't appear to be offended, just disgusted. "Believe it or not, my exit had nothing to do with sex. And don't think for a moment most priests keep those vows. Not that I observed. If you want to understand what beautiful women endure getting hit on all the time, become a priest. I can't tell you the number of times a superior—a fellow priest, bishop, even an archbishop—took me to some ceremony that required an overnight stay and expected me to share the only bed."

"Shit," Joe said. "What did you do?"

"Slept elsewhere," he said. "The couch. The floor, if necessary. Lots of priests believe their good deeds outweigh their sexual indiscretions, as long as they're consensual, and from what I saw, 'consensual' was loosely defined. If you could convince someone to fuck you or get you off for whatever reason, it was 'consensual.' A lot of what goes on sexually is between priests. Fun fact … in the early Church, no one demanded celibacy. The Apostle Peter was married. Most of us kept thinking, given the shortage of good priests, that a pope would eventually come along who would allow them to marry. In the meantime, they believe God is okay with the half-measures they take to get by. A little mutual masturbation—what they used to call heavy petting—with men or women. You could go as far as your own conscience would permit. The more you see others break the rules, the more you think, 'If he can do it, so can I. I'm only human.' No one wants to be a snitch unless children are involved." He paused. "But that wasn't me. So, yeah, not about sex. You already know I have these … *premonitions*, we'll call them for lack of a better word." He waved the flask Jake offered away. "I'd love some water."

They all held their breaths as Edward drank, the whistling of the wind adding texture to the rapt silence.

"Admittedly, sex was never far from my mind. Not that I did anything about it while I was an active priest. I had plenty of opportunities—so many curious nuns and bored wives. Men hit on me too, of course. One of our earlier deacons was particularly persistent…. He ended up getting transferred. I hope his tastes ran exclusively to men and not boys or teenagers. One never knows.

"Anyway, about three years ago, I started to wonder about the newest deacon, Patrick. Not about his sexuality. I suspected him of being a thief. The congregation had remained more or less the same size—frankly, my appearance and sermons were a big draw—but I was fairly certain not all the cash in the collection plates was making it to the bank. The thief was skimming off maybe two hundred dollars a week, as if that would keep him or her under the radar. Deacon Patrick was the obvious suspect, though it could have been others in the chain of responsibility, even a parishioner passing the plates.

"We didn't have a lot of physical contact with others, but I knew that my first order of business was ruling out Deacon Patrick. So I rested a hand on his shoulder. It was awkward as hell—he assumed I was testing the waters sexually. I hadn't thought it through. I had no plausible excuse for touching him. It didn't help that this almost electric current passed between us that he definitely misinterpreted.

"That charged moment was when I 'saw' the whole thing. Deacon Patrick was having an affair with one of the unsatisfied wives I'd rejected—we'll call her Mary. The two had decided to feather their nests. The plan was to pin the theft on me, with Mary claiming I had raped her if I denied it—a kind of insurance. But in that instant Patrick had a new plan. Now he'd be saying I'd come on to *him*. I saw the denouement, the moment a large amount of cash was found among my possessions and I was handed over to the bishop to be dealt with. They would leave town before the mess could be straightened out. Fortunately, they weren't ready to act. Not enough cash had accumulated in their coffers. That gave me time to come up with a plan of my own. So much was—and is—covered up by the Church. Chances are, I'd simply have been transferred."

"But you had no incentive to steal," Joe said. "You were already rich by then, thanks to Grandma. Like the rest of us."

Edward shrugged. "No one knew about that inheritance. I never touched it while I was a priest except to make anonymous donations. I had another secret weapon: my mentor, Bishop Paul, who had been a priest in my parish for several years before being promoted to bishop in a cathedral in Upstate New York. He was well respected and in line for more advancement, and I'd told him about my premonitions. Knowing me as he did, he had no trouble believing my story. He had a spy planted in the church, and Deacon Patrick and Mary were caught red-handed and arrested. They were later released and charged a hefty fine, which neither could afford. They were allowed to skip town. Bishop Paul tried to convince me the entire incident was an aberration, but I'd had enough."

Joe raised his hand. "I have a question." They'd all switched to water now that the levity had been leached from their gathering. "Why did you cut *us* off?"

Edward wiped his brow, sweating despite the cold. David felt bad about putting him in the hot seat. "Do you know how hard it is to renounce the world?" Edward asked. "If you hold onto your attachments, you are constantly reminded of what you're missing. You see your brothers and sister living rich lives, finding love, enjoying earthly pleasures. From what Mom relayed during our short visits, you were all *too* happy—or at least successful—and steeped in the worldly life. If I had any hope of staying the course, I needed to put on blinders."

Jake was scratching his head. "What did you get out of it all, other than relief from your sexual demons?"

Edward regarded him thoughtfully. "As long as I truly believed in what I was doing, I found peace. Peace in the sacraments, emotional distance from the human condition, the satisfaction of helping others. I stopped fearing death. I thought my premonitions were proof of a spiritual world. I believed in God and the Holy Ghost and … the whole shebang. Now I just … don't." With a grand shrug, he finished off his bottle of water.

"Will you be okay without all that?" David couldn't help but ask.

"Do you mean, will I return to being a sexual deviant?" His laugh was bitter. "I did, for a while. I don't think it will be a problem now."

"What got you on that path, do you think?" Joe asked. "Were you molested? I'm not sure you knew that I had a run-in with a priest when I was an altar boy. Nothing happened," he added quickly after noting David's bug-eyed stare. "I fled the room and told our parents."

"Good for you," Edward told Joe. To the rest of them, he said, "I can see you want all my secrets at once. Listen, as you know, it's bad news to be too good looking as a kid. Predators are everywhere. And physically, we're game if the temptation is right. Let's leave it at that, shall we?"

What happens if things don't work out with Lisette? David thought, though he didn't say it aloud. Then came the inevitable question, this one relating to himself: *What if things with Maddie don't work out? As long as she's acting in movies, there will always be another Kilo, or George, or God forbid, Brad Pitt or Hugh Grant.*

"I'm happy," Edward went on in the silence, though no one had asked, "and I'm calm. I don't need any of it anymore. I believe in spirits, just not holy ones, necessarily." To Jake, he said, "The scriptures aren't clear on the subject of ghosts. According to Luke twenty-four thirty-nine, after his resurrection, Jesus said, 'A ghost does not have flesh and bones as you can see I have.' Some point to that as confirmation ghosts exist. I'm more than willing to acknowledge the possibility, unless what you are experiencing,

Jake, is a type of premonition embodied in a being you conjured in your imagination." He smiled. "Having read your books, I'd say your imagination is impressively active."

They all laughed.

Jake appeared thoughtful. "Could be."

"I'm still a priest," Edward said with an acidity David felt in the pit of his stomach, "a priest who's broken his vows. If I wanted to marry in the Roman Catholic Church, I'd need a dispensation from Pope John Paul the Second himself. Those dispensations are rare, and they are never given to men under forty. To my mind, there's no point in trying."

"Bummer," Joe said in a heartfelt voice.

That released the tension. Even Edward had a good laugh.

CHAPTER 19

———◆———

AT NINE SATURDAY NIGHT, LISETTE sat at the small round table in the corner of her café poring over her to-do list, which included reviewing the food inventory and delivery schedule and doublechecking the receipts from previous nights. Everything seemed to be in order. The party was still in full swing at Café Lisette, with everyone in a holiday mood. The background music was '50s Christmas classics sung by the usual suspects—Elvis, Frank Sinatra, Bing Crosby, and Tony Bennett.

A few days ago, Edward had given her a hardcover copy of *A Christmas Carol*, with the original illustrations. She'd felt particularly bad for Jacob Marley, forced to "witness what he could not share." There it was—the hospitality business in a nutshell. Why couldn't Dickens have let poor Jacob shed a few chains as a reward for his role in inspiring Scrooge to repent? Lisette didn't personally believe in heaven and hell, except as they manifested themselves on Earth.

Tonight even she was caught up in the festive atmosphere. Two skinny Christmas trees glittered with white lights, and colored lights shone from every other available surface. They sparkled along the ornate ceiling moldings, dangled from the garlands draped along brass wall sconces and chandeliers, and rimmed the frames of photographs and prints. The walls of Café Lisette were filled with photographs featuring historic Port Townsend. Most were from the 1890s, its heyday before the railroad chose another route and shut the town out of the new wave of prosperity. They depicted Victorian landmark buildings, ships in the harbor, the old sawmill, the docks, and groups of working men bellying up to the bar.

After Sunday night, Lisette would hand the reins over to Sid and Margie and enjoy the holidays like everyone else, maybe for the first time since Paris.

She climbed the stairs to her office to pack a duffle bag with a few more outfits. She had just grabbed her coat when there was a knock on the door leading to her office and connected bedroom. *Weird.* She could have sworn she'd locked the door to the first-floor landing. Troy, Sid, and Bobby usually phoned her if they needed anything. She opened the door to find Bobby shuffling his feet.

"There's a man here to see you," he said. "I told him you were busy, but he won't take no for an answer. He looks familiar."

"It's not Reynard, is it?" Reynard had mostly avoided Café Lisette, so it was possible Bobby wouldn't recognize him.

"No, not Reynard."

Lisette followed him down the stairs. A man loitered there next to the wall, head bent, upper face concealed by a wide-brimmed cowboy hat. His thick mustache, which curled up at the edges, was patently fake. Unlike Bobby, he appeared totally relaxed.

"Can I help you?" she asked in her formal hostess voice.

A dry laugh. "You don't recognize me?" He removed his hat. When he leaned in to kiss her on the cheek, she recoiled.

"Kilo? What the hell are you doing here?" she said in a harsh whisper. "If you're recognized, there's going to be pandemonium." She turned to her headwaiter. "Thanks, Bobby. We'll be upstairs." She crooked a tense finger at Kilo and mounted the stairs as quickly as her high-heeled pumps and slim skirt would allow.

Once they were in her office area with the door shut behind them, she took a deep breath before asking, "Are you in town for good or *not* for good?"

Though smiling at her sarcastic take on Mae West's famous quip, Kilo said in all seriousness, "I'm in town for the holidays. There's no filming in December. I may sell the yoga studio. Come on, Leslie, relax. Take a load off."

"*Lisette*, damn you."

"Whoa." He gestured for her to dial it down. *As if.* "Business is good, I see." He pointed to the floor, which only slightly muted the noise of the crowd.

She continued to stand behind her desk, glad for the barrier between them. Without invitation, he pulled a chair opposite her and sat as if for an interview. He was so loose-limbed, she half expected him to prop up his cowboy boots on her desk.

"What were you aiming for with this… *ensemble*"—she painted a finger in the air from his hat to his boots—"Yosemite Sam?"

He laughed good-naturedly. What was it with TV actors? His skin appeared poreless, his black hair was glossy, and his teeth would probably glow in the dark. No expense spared, obviously.

"You're looking good," she said in a flat voice.

"You too," he said with a waggle of eyebrows.

She rolled her eyes. "Kilo, save it for someone who cares. Why are you here? Cut to the chase already."

He leaned forward, zeroing in on her face and letting his eyes dip briefly to her cleavage. "Look, I know we didn't part on the best of terms, but that was hardly my fault. *You* broke up with *me*."

"After I walked in on you playing hide the sausage with an anonymous blonde."

He frowned. "You didn't let me explain."

"Ah," she nodded sagely, "you were doing naked yoga. I should have realized it was something innocent like that."

"She was ancient history—someone I'd known in Seattle who was in town for a visit. It was nothing. An old times' sake thing." From his tone, he might have been discussing a faux pas he'd committed with her maiden aunt.

She huffed out a breath. "Obviously, you and I don't agree on what constitutes 'ancient history.' " He opened his mouth as if to offer another excuse, so she added, "Please, don't bother. Apology accepted. Now, if that's all—"

His hand shot out. "Hold your horses. I'm not here to dredge up the past. Although I have to wonder how much Edward knows about yours."

"How the *hell* do you know about Edward?"

His grin was positively feral, and she could swear one of his whiter-than-white teeth winked at her. Was it a diamond stud? "It's Port Townsend, darling. Grapevine. Guess things didn't work out with Reynard. Did he cheat on you too?"

With a sigh, she sat down at her desk and folded her legs primly. "That wasn't the problem. As far as I know."

"Ah, you met Edward and decided he was the better bet"—he paused to smirk at her—"especially after he made like a superhero and stopped that robber in his tracks."

"Kilo…." She gave him a warning glance. "Don't imply anything ugly when it comes to Edward. I was done with Reynard. We were done with each other."

He curled his lip. "I'm not sure he would agree."

"He's already seeing someone else."

"To make you mad."

Jesus, how did Kilo know all this stuff?

"I taught a yoga class," Kilo continued, "unannounced, of course—for a laugh. The women were just dying to update me on all the latest gossip."

"How would they even know you and I are … acquainted?"

"I mentioned you, specifically. They didn't ask why. Guess who else is in town?"

She didn't bother to guess. No one she'd be pleased to hear about—of that she was sure.

"George Reed Masters."

"The movie star." She knew all about *Kapow* and its complications, George being one of them.

"Yeah, we're friends now," Kilo said with pride. "He sought me out, actually. He'll be stopping by the compound any day now; my sources tell me you're spending a lot of time there. I'm not sure how much longer he can keep his presence in town a secret." He twirled his mustache and winked. "He's bad at the disguise thing."

She didn't speak, so he went on, "I doubt he'll be much more welcome than I would be, but they're going to have to pretend he is. For the sake of the movie. He has the latest version of the screenplay with him."

What was he getting at? "Wait a minute … why aren't *you* welcome at the compound?"

"Ah, I forget you and the priest are only a few weeks old," he said with a hint of bitterness. "That means you're not well informed." He wasn't smiling now. "Teresa and I used to be married."

"*What*? In all the time you and I … knew each other, you never mentioned an ex-wife."

"It was a short-lived deal, thanks to Edward. Mayflies have lasted longer."

"*Edward*?"

"We eloped right out of high school. Edward caught up with us at a motel in Redding, California. You'd think I was some vaudeville villain who'd tied Teresa to the train tracks. Not a fond memory for me."

No, she could see it wasn't. A nasty memory he'd kept fresh, in fact. She recalled how Edward had dispatched the would-be burglar. Had he beaten Kilo up? She didn't want to give him the satisfaction of asking for details.

"They had the marriage annulled." Another smirk. "And then there's Maddie."

She was beginning to see why Kilo wasn't welcome at the compound.

"Okay, I'll bite. What happened with Maddie?"

"We were in *A Midsummer Night's Dream* together."

"Didn't see it," Lisette said.

"You know, when you fold your arms across your chest like that, you make your cleavage more pronounced. Not that I mind."

Annoyed, she unfolded her arms. She didn't need to broadcast how tense she was.

Kilo continued, "You know how it is when you're in a show together."

Yes, she knew. Kilo had left on his tour with Groban Phillips at the same time she departed for Paris. He'd told her some lurid stories. She hadn't been one to judge, given her own freewheeling behavior. When all the traveling had left him burned out, they'd decided to go west together and start fresh. He'd promised to behave. But Kilo couldn't help himself.

None of this needed to be dredged up now. Uncomfortable with the silence, Kilo confessed, "You know, you were the closest I ever found to a soul mate. You and I both had to do the bootstrap thing. We came from nothing, and now look at us." Was he congratulating himself for leaving her in his dust? Or was that the little devil of self-doubt whispering in her ear? She didn't think her situation was much to write home about.

After all, she had financed it on her back.

"This new screenplay …" she began. Then came the light-bulb moment: Kilo wanted a role. Was that what this was all about? He couldn't possibly think *she* could help. "Kilo, I have no influence with this family, zero." She had not intended to sound so pitiful.

"Just speak kindly of me," he said softly. "If so, I'll return the favor."

She was starting to understand, God help her. "If I don't scratch your back, you'll scratch out my eyes," she interpreted.

"When George and I show up at the compound…"

No, no, no. She wanted no part of this.

"…argue in my favor. It's not like I *want* to bring up Doctor Dan the Boob Man."

"But you will, if it comes to that."

"So you haven't told them—not even Edward?"

She threw up her hands. "Does *anyone* bring up stories like that when a relationship is this new? It wasn't as if I was renting my body by the hour. I had *one* lover."

"One generous, married lover who put a contract out on his wife."

"That was never proven. The woman is still alive, and he was acquitted."

"Thanks to his expensive legal team. Carrie O'Connell is the worst. She investigates everybody. It's just a matter of time before she digs up all your dirty laundry and hangs it from the rafters for all to see."

Lisette wanted to die. She'd hoped to bury Leslie Guzinski forever. The O'Connells might forgive her for being poorly educated, for being qualified for nothing but the restaurant business, but she doubted they could ever get over that part of her past. The part where she'd used the spoils of her stint as the mistress of a married boyfriend to finance her year in Paris. Kilo and she had been friends, not lovers—then—and had crossed paths many times on catering jobs for Caviar Tastes. With all their shared history, she couldn't believe he'd throw her under the bus now. Didn't a man who cheated on you in your shared bed secretly long for his freedom?

She checked her watch. *Damn it, how did it get to be ten thirty?* Edward had expected her at the compound an hour ago. She had a pounding headache.

She rose unsteadily to her feet. "Kilo, go away, *now*. I promise not to say anything bad about you, but you've totally overestimated my pull with this family. If you feel you must destroy my reputation here, then that's on you and your conscience, if you have one."

"Spare me the martyred act," he said lightly. "I've never gotten over you. I was weak, but you were ruthless."

It was no use arguing. She held open the door for him.

"Lisette!" He grabbed her hand and held it to his heart. She felt the rush of energy between them and knew that, at least at this particular moment, he wanted her badly, if only to salve his bruised ego. "We could try again. A fresh start. Hollywood would love your beauty and style. We could have children. You're still young enough."

This reminder that she was four years older was like a bucket of ice water in the face. For a second there, she'd almost felt sorry for him. But she hadn't been tempted. No, she was done with Kilo and his ilk, even if Edward rejected her. She wasn't afraid of being alone.

He tugged gently at her hand to reel her in, but she pulled free and took a step back. "No, Kilo," she said with all the calm she could muster. "You have the world by the tail. You don't need my tail too."

She hadn't meant to be funny, but they both smiled in spite of themselves.

"You don't need to hurt me to gain your ends," she went on, the smile gone. "I know it's a big leap from TV to the movies, but give it time. There will be more opportunities for you, I'm sure of it." He didn't speak. She sighed. "Do what you must."

He went over to the wall mirror to adjust his mustache. "See you around, ma'am," he said, leaning in for a kiss on the mouth. She turned away in time. Then he put on his hat, bounded down the stairs, and slammed the door to the first-floor landing behind him.

For a while, she stood stock-still, her mind racing. What if she didn't go back to the compound tonight? She needed time to think, to plan, to decide what to do next.

She heard heavy footsteps on the stairs. What now? Had Kilo returned to add a few more threats?

Edward stepped into the room, slightly out of breath. "Everything okay?"

She burst into tears.

CHAPTER 20

Edward hadn't known what to expect. Not this. He'd left Lisette a voicemail when she didn't show up. Her lack of response had him imagining all sorts of terrible things. A carjacking, a deer in the road ….

He helped her into the other room, and together they flopped down on the sagging sofa. The piece of furniture was a sorry excuse for a couch and had to be hopeless as a bed. Slowly extracting himself, he handed her a box of tissues, not knowing what else to do. Women's tears were his kryptonite. He couldn't remember the last time he himself had indulged in a good cry, though many occasions had warranted it.

"Lisette, sweetheart … I'm going to get us something to drink." He hurried down the stairs and fetched a bottle of chardonnay and two glasses.

By the time he'd returned, Lisette was sitting, dry-eyed, mascara staining her cheeks. She still looked impossibly beautiful. He filled their glasses and placed them on the side table. Then he went to the bathroom and found a washcloth. She let him gently bathe her cheeks, closing her eyes and heaving a deep sigh.

"Want to tell me what happened?" he said in a soothing voice as he handed her a glass of wine.

"No." Her laugh was brittle. "But I will."

He waited.

"I had a visit from Kilo."

Kilo. How did *she* know the actor? If his brothers were to be believed, the guy really got around.

"Kilo is the man I came to the Olympic Peninsula with. We lived together in Port Angeles for about a year before I found him in our bed with someone else and broke it off."

"Damn, that's rough," was all he said, wanting to sympathize but not interrupt.

"We met in New York. After high school, I moved from New Jersey to the city and got a waitressing job at a seedy Irish pub. Then a friend turned me on to Caviar Tastes, the most exclusive catering company in the city. They'd lost a lot of waiters to AIDS and were hiring women to take up the slack. I wasn't Lisette Manegold then; my given name was … Leslie Guzinski."

The way she quailed told him the name was supposed to ring a bell. It didn't. What had Leslie Guzinski done? Nothing good, it seemed.

"I met Kilo in the fall of 1989. I was four years older, so I thought of him as a little brother. We flirted, I guess, but he flirted with everyone. He was notorious. Then, at a big fundraiser at the Temple of Dendur—the room where they exhibit the Egyptian artifacts at the Metropolitan Museum—I met Dr. Walfred Dahlstrom."

Again, she expected him to recognize the name. He shook his head.

"I was stuck at a buffet table where my job was to open champagne. He told me he was a plastic surgeon, and that my face was perfectly symmetrical. It was such an odd compliment. I told him that if he wanted an *amuse-bouche*, he should get it from one of the waiters offering trays of hors d'oeuvres. I was used to being hit on at these things. Far from put off, he was amused by my response. He asked for my number. I told him no. That should have been the end of it."

She squirmed in discomfort. "He got my number from someone else, paid them for it in fact—or so he told me later. Several of the waiters had it because I assembled crews for jobs with other catering companies. Few worked exclusively for Caviar Tastes. He started calling me, leaving messages on my answering machine. Then he figured out where I lived—I shared a two-bedroom apartment in Washington Heights with two other women—and started sending flowers and other gifts. Finally I agreed to have coffee with him."

She blinked a few times. "I'll get to the point. It's bad, but not as bad as you seem to think, judging from your expression."

Edward took her hand but didn't comment. Didn't she realize he was the last person to throw stones?

"Walfred Dahlstrom was fifteen years older—thirty-eight—handsome in a fancy-pants way. Expensive clothes, nails, haircut, teeth. On the short side, maybe five-eight. I never dated older men. Why would I? I liked men who were my equals." She stopped suddenly, as if just now realizing that Edward himself was precisely thirty-eight years old. And she didn't seem to think she was his equal. He saw all these thoughts flit across her face.

"It's okay," he said, playing with her hair. "I'm not going anywhere, no matter how this story turns out."

She didn't look convinced, more like someone confessing to the police, throwing herself at their mercy.

"I didn't know he was married but could easily have found out. I should have guessed. His wife was a surgeon too, but she traveled quite a bit and did a lot of charity work. No children. He had oodles of money, not just from his job, but inherited from his family. There was a Roman numeral after his name."

"A suffix?" Edward said.

"Yes, Walfred Dahlstrom the Third. Old American family, came over on some famous boat or other, possibly the Mayflower. I wasn't particularly impressed with that sort of thing."

Painful as this conversation was for Edward, he didn't want to rush her. It didn't escape his notice that he also came from a "fancy-pants" family with inherited wealth, even if West Coast royalty didn't quite measure up to the East Coast kind.

"I resisted his advances for a long time, especially after he confessed to being married. But then he offered to move me into this apartment in Chelsea where he stayed during the week. He gave me an allowance. I knew he expected me to spend that money on clothing, hair, and makeup so I'd look nice for him. Most of it I socked away in the bank. I kept catering on weekends—when he wasn't there. After eight months, I had saved enough to go to Paris and attend Le Cordon Bleu." She paused. "Then Walfred was arrested."

She turned her keen, forest-green gaze on him, expecting disapproval. "He was accused of hiring someone to kill his wife. They couldn't make it stick. The situation was messy. His wife had a married lover too. They questioned me endlessly to find out if I was involved in the plot, but I was way too clueless. They also satisfied themselves that I did not envision a future with the doctor." Reading his thoughts, she added, "No one died. Well, their marriage … it died. I changed my name and went to Paris, where I lived as cheaply as possible with roommates until the new term began at Le Cordon Bleu."

* * *

Lisette didn't want to tell Edward the rest. How the New York *Post's* Page 6 had found out about her and printed ugly insinuations, day after day. How the headlines in the tabloids wrote themselves: "The Gold Digger," "The Love Nest," "The Boob Doctor and his Babe."

After Walfred was arrested and released on bail, he told her she had to move out. The money would stop—at least until the dust settled. He wanted their arrangement to continue, though she'd already decided it was over. She moved into Kilo's rent-stabilized apartment in the Forest Hills neighborhood of Queens. The little-brother thing evaporated in such close proximity. Kilo was way too seductive to put off for long, and by then she had no moral high ground to climb onto. He was helping her, and she owed him. Besides, as a lover, he was far superior to Dr. Dahlstrom. And he was fun. It was with genuine regret that they parted ways: he, to tour with Groban Phillips and she, to board a plane to Paris. He'd even found her a pair of gay male dancers on the outskirts of Paris who needed a roommate. By then she'd legally changed her name, sold what she could, and ditched her few remaining possessions.

What not even Kilo knew was that Walfred hadn't wanted to let her go. He'd proposed all sorts of foolish scenarios. They could move to Uruguay or Argentina. When he found she couldn't be persuaded, he reacted badly. She'd made the mistake of initiating the ultimate breakup at his place. He'd raped her, leaving her bruised and humiliated. Not that she put up much of a fight. Part of her thought she deserved this final humiliation.

Since then, traumatized in a way she didn't want to admit, she'd always feared he'd resurface in her life and try to force a reunion. Though surely he'd found a new, much younger plaything.

"Lisette?"

She'd lapsed into silence, so of course Edward would read into it. She rested her head on his shoulder, staring into space with a sinking heart as she contemplated the end of their all-too-brief idyll.

"None of what you're telling me matters," he whispered against her hair. "Not even the stuff you're *not* telling me."

She looked up into his kind, beautiful face, and saw the sincerity there. He was too good to be true. *It does*, she thought. *Just you wait.*

"What was Kilo really doing here?" Edward asked.

"He wants a part in the movie. He thinks I owe him, but he didn't hesitate to back up his 'request' with a little blackmail."

"Blackmail?"

"It's not what you think," she said. What did he think? That she really had plotted to kill Walfred's wife? *Lord, help me.* "His only ammunition is the story I just told you. He wants a role in *Kapow*. Any part, no matter how minor, would help him make the leap to the big screen. He thinks I can orchestrate that somehow. If not, all he has to do is let slip my real name. Then anyone who knows how to Google will have access to the whole story. The whole story according to the tabloids. Not the real one." She gave him a pleading look. "It's not as if I believed I could keep it silent forever. But your family hardly knows me, and what they think they know isn't good."

Edward stroked the nape of her neck as he considered the situation. Finally he said, "Actually, I think the movie would benefit from Kilo being in it. He's a good actor, right?"

"So I hear."

"Joe told me he brought down the house in *A Midsummer Night's Dream*. I think … if you weren't threatened by him, as my family clearly is, he'd be a logical addition to the cast." He focused his warm gaze on her. "Let me be the voice of reason. I assume he's going to show up at the compound soon. Only … how would that work? He's on their shit list."

"He'll come in the company of George Reed Masters, who has the new screenplays."

Edward gave a low whistle. "*New* screenplays? You mean they're still revising? Damn. Kilo's right: they can't turn George away. They might even feel compelled to invite him to stay. Where is he now?"

"With Kilo, I gather. Kilo owns the building where his yoga studio is located. There must be a guestroom somewhere."

Edward nodded. "He'll definitely angle for an invitation to the compound. For the added security, if nothing else. Even though the guy's been a real burr under my brothers' saddles, they need him in their movie. I think that, if not for what's at stake for Jake, Liam, and Maddie, David would gladly see *Kapow* go up in smoke."

Suddenly Lisette couldn't keep her eyes open. All the drama and confession had zapped the last of her energy. The next thing she knew, daylight shone through the window. Her head was in Edward's lap.

"Oh no," she groaned, "I fell asleep."

Edward smiled down at her in that angelic way of his.

"Is it dead then?" she asked in a small voice.

He touched the back of his head experimentally. "Not dead, but my neck might be on life support."

"I meant our relationship. Or whatever it is."

"I hope not," he said with a broad smile. "It's just getting interesting."

"You don't think I'm the Whore of Babylon?"

He responded with full-throated laughter. "The Whore of Babylon wasn't really a person—more a symbol of idolatry. The Mormons, Jehovah's Witnesses, and Fundamentalists think the Catholic Church is the Whore of Babylon."

"Oh great, more proof of my ignorance."

"If you were *that* knowledgeable about the Church, that would make you highly unusual—or a nun. I find you totally enchanting. And … if you had described any other woman enduring what you did, I guarantee you'd view her with a lot more compassion. Give yourself a break. You were young, and you were feeling stuck. You saw a way out, and you took it. You weren't the first person to embark on a foolish journey that took you into unexpectedly dangerous territory."

She gave him a curious look. "Are we talking about you now?"

He kissed her lightly on the lips. "I'm going to find us some breakfast. But first I'll phone Ali to let her know we're okay." He looked at his watch. "It's ten after eight. Do you have a change of clothing here, or shall we go back to the compound?"

"I have other work clothing. This is my last day before I let Sid and Margie take over. I want to discuss deliveries and specials with Chef Marky before lunch, so I'd better stick around until tonight."

He stood and stretched, and she heard some pops and creaks as he unfurled his long body. Her own neck was sore, her clothing was rumpled, and her bra straps dug into her shoulders.

"Do you want to shower?" she asked.

He hesitated. "Your shower has had some negative reviews."

She shrugged. "It gets the job done. Unfortunately, it's too small for a big man and a tall woman."

"Okay, a quickie. A quickie shower, that is." He grinned as he stripped off his clothing, watching her watch him. Ten minutes later, he was clean and dressed.

"I'll need much longer," she said as she strolled, naked, to the shower.

"I'll need a lifetime," he said, intercepting her with a long, heartfelt kiss. Before she could respond, he was out the door. From the staircase she heard, "Coffee and scones, right?"

CHAPTER 21

LATE MONDAY MORNING, MADDIE WAS returning from a low-tide beach walk with Lorenzo when she saw Lisette gazing out to sea. She looked so melancholy that Maddie could picture her as the disconsolate girlfriend of a drowned sailor. Or the tragic fallen woman at the center of John Fowles' novel, *The French Lieutenant's Woman*. Maddie had been listening to the audiobook while she worked out. When Lisette turned to wave at her, all smiles, the illusion vanished. Now Maddie was more curious than ever to hear this elegant woman's sure-to-be-juicy story. She was glad for a new distraction at the compound, especially in the form of Lisette, a potential confidante, someone who might have closet skeletons that clacked as noisily as her own. Much as she loved them, the rest of the women in their orbit had lived sheltered lives, their sexual experience limited, their paths made easier by money and influence. Even former foster child Ali had been able to rely on her twin brother Liam for protection, and Joe had come along in the nick of time, before she could be "collected" by some jerk—like in that creepy earlier John Fowles novel, *The Collector*, Maddie's Recorded Books rental last month.

People not gifted with beauty believed it opened all doors. But Maddie knew its dark side: that beautiful women born into poverty or abusive families were the most likely to be preyed upon. She sensed that Lisette, like her, had climbed some rickety ladders to get where she was and had stumbled badly more than once along the way.

Or… her imagination was running wild. With no project other than

Kapow, still months away, Maddie had too much time on her hands. David was no help. He'd been in a foul mood lately.

"*Zia* Maddie, you're not listening!" Lorenzo tugged at the sleeve of her parka. He'd been recounting the latest Salish Sea story, which could not possibly be as convoluted as he made it sound, unless Chiara had run out of ideas and was simply throwing stuff at the walls—or at Lorenzo, in this case—to see if it stuck. Something about an octopus with three hearts and nine brains. Could that be true? Oxana Octopus was planning a special Christmas celebration for the community. A sea star, a ratfish, and a crab were inventing a dance in her honor and counting on Polly Plankton and her friends to provide the lighting. According to Lor, they were "bayou loamy Nestle." After wondering if in this fantasy world the plankton were made of chocolate, she realized that he must mean "bioluminescent." Choreographing the dance number had proved to be unexpectedly challenging. The crab could only move sideways. The sea star had thousands of little tube feet but wasn't quick or graceful. That meant the ratfish had to take the lead. She didn't envy Chiara and Ali this project, though she imagined any distraction would be welcome. Chiara was still waiting for her divorce to be final, and Ali tended to worry about everything and everyone, though the complications of her pregnancy were surely enough cause for distress.

"Hey, Lisette, what's up?" Maddie asked, having reached the spot where Edward's girlfriend stood. "Enjoying the view?"

She'd just left Susan a message asking if she could come outside to fetch Lorenzo.

"Always," Lisette said. "Gotta love the ocean." In her cloth barn jacket, calfskin boots, and tight jeans, Lisette was a living, breathing Patagonia ad. It was the legs, so long and muscular. Maddie knew her own hourglass figure was part of her appeal as a movie actress, but she'd have preferred to have a long, lean, athletic body like Lisette's.

"Edward and David are having lunch at my café," Lisette said. "I was just about to head to the market to buy supplies for tonight's dinner."

Ooh, Maddie definitely wanted in on this errand. She hoped Lisette would welcome her company. Lorenzo was still tugging at her sleeve and whining, so she crouched down to bring them eye to eye. "Lor, Susan was counting on playing a boardgame with you before lunch. Doesn't that sound like fun?" His pout told her he wasn't fooled. "Thanks for catching me up on the latest chapter of Salish Sea Stories. I can't wait to find out how the Christmas party turns out. That sounds like one wild dance number. I'm sure

Silas will steal the show. Let me know when *Zia* Chiara is ready for another episode. David and I will definitely be there."

Susan was running toward them, arms spread to receive Lorenzo. He gave her a huge hug, and she lifted him above her head before setting him gently on his feet. Maddie relaxed. Susan winked at her before she and Lor skipped up the hill toward the house.

"That is one strong woman," Lisette remarked.

"Yes, she's an amateur body builder, senior class. By the way, did you know the compound has a gym?"

"Really? That's great! I usually run, but that might not be so easy here."

"Yes … I mean no, not easy," Maddie said. "The little beach doesn't extend very far, and even at low tide, you wouldn't want to run on seaweed-slimed rocks. The gravel drive is boring, and all there is beyond that is the main road where everyone drives too fast. The gym is really nice. Come on, I'll show you."

Like the recording studio, the gym was a freestanding building, with a TV and sound system. It had two treadmills, two elliptical trainers, two stationary bikes, and a vintage NordicTrack.

Lisette observed the space with wide eyes. "This is totally cool. The windows all face the ocean. Do you watch TV while you work out?"

"There's a satellite dish, but I don't usually watch regular TV. Sometimes I pop in a video. Mostly I listen to audiobooks or music."

"As a rule, I avoid public gyms," Lisette said.

"Me too," Maddie admitted, thinking of all the annoying male attention there. "Your errands today … need company?" She tried not to sound too eager.

Lisette didn't hesitate. "Of course. I spend far too much time by myself."

"How can David and Edward go to Café Lisette without you there?" Maddie asked.

"My bartender Sid's wife Margie is covering for me as hostess this week, and Chef Marky doesn't mind picking up the fresh seafood and ordering other supplies. It's only for a few days. The place will be closed from Christmas Eve through New Year's. I know Edward is looking forward to catching up with David. Apparently the boys had quite the bonding session last Tuesday afternoon."

"Really? David didn't get into specifics."

"Then I'll tell you," Lisette said with a sly smile. "Edward is the least secretive man I've ever met. And the stuff he shared with me about his years as a priest needs to be common knowledge."

When they reached the black Miata, Lisette prompted, "Silas?"

It took Maddie a moment. "Oh," she laughed. "Silas is a spotted ratfish."

Lisette's brow knit in confusion. "*He's* the featured dancer?"

"Apparently. The others don't have the moves. Crabs can only go sideways. Sea stars have all these tiny suction-cup feet that make dancing awkward. Lorenzo is happy as a clam—sorry, the cliché seems apt—about the Salish Sea Christmas party, so Chiara must be on the right track. Better her than me. I don't know how you write a children's book about fish and crustaceans." After they'd fastened their seatbelts, she added, "Ali told me that in real life, they'd all be eating each other. She's not sure what Oxana's going to serve at the Christmas feast."

"Oxana?"

"The octopus. Having three hearts, she's best qualified to be the mother figure."

"Three hearts, huh? Maybe she can whip up a big bowl of plankton."

Maddie shook her head. "Then who's going to provide the lighting?"

Lisette took her eyes off the road long enough to express interest in the punchline.

"The plankton is bioluminescent, or as Lor put it, 'bayou loamy Nestle.' At first I thought they were serving chocolate for dinner."

"Maybe they should. It sounds as if everything else is off limits." Lisette bit her lip. "Does anyone at the compound have any restrictions, foodwise? I was going to make jambalaya."

"Nope. Weird, right? If this were a group of actors, you'd have a long list of no-nos."

"I hope Lorenzo's story doesn't include Shelby Shrimp," Lisette said, "because otherwise, he's going to be horrified when he views tonight's meal."

"Not yet. But it's a great idea. Mention it to Ali. I assume she's going to need a diverse group for the actual holiday party, and it sounds as if Shelby could boogie down. But no worries. Lorenzo doesn't usually eat with us when we have company. He has a typical child's palate, though we do encourage him to sample everything."

"So, how do you like being a stepmom?" Lisette asked.

Maddie almost said, "Great," but instead blurted out the truth. "Luckily Lorenzo has a bunch of mommy figures. Chiara, Ali, and Susan are all better at it than I am. I love him, of course, but he's a handful. Spending significant time with him is exhausting. And little children aren't easily fooled. I think he knows I'm uncomfortable. David knows it too."

Lisette shot her a look of sympathy. "That's rough. From what I saw, however, you're selling yourself short. He knows you love him. I have to say, I never pictured myself as a mother. Technically, I could still have children, I suppose."

"Does Edward want children, do you think?" Maddie asked.

Lisette's laugh was brittle. "We haven't discussed it."

"Not to rush you," Maddie said, "but you were going to tell me about Edward…."

Lisette nodded, keeping her eyes on the road as she gave Maddie the condensed version. Maddie listened in rapt silence, astonished by what she was hearing. "I had no idea. Poor Edward! David must be relieved. He was afraid Edward had gotten caught up in some sex scandal."

First stop was Café Lisette, so Lisette could gather the cooking utensils she required. They didn't want to interrupt David and Edward's intense conversation. Maddie gave them a cheery wave, which was halfheartedly returned.

"Let's go to Kelpies," Lisette said. "Believe it or not, I've never been there. Pub food wasn't Reynard's thing, only high-end cuisine with first-class wine lists."

Kelpies being crowded, they sat against the back wall with no view of the bay. The location did give them more privacy. After they ordered cups of clam chowder and agreed to split a Caesar salad, Maddie said, "You're not afraid the grocery will run out of prawns?"

"Shrimp," Lisette said. "Prawns are the freshwater version. They know me at Key City Fish Company and have put aside what I need. I'm also serving a green salad, cornbread, and baguettes. What about dessert? Maybe bread pudding with bourbon sauce?"

"I was going to say, don't bother, but that does sound fantastic," Maddie said. After the waitress served their food, she added, "Did they warn you that Jean-Louis and Becca will be there?"

Lisette paled but recovered quickly. "That does add an element of daunting, but I can handle it." In the silence that followed, her expression turned grim, and she averted her compelling forest-green eyes. "There's something I need to tell you," she said.

The statement filled Maddie with dread. Hadn't Lisette already told her everything about what went down at Fort Worden?

"I believe I know why David appeared so serious at the restaurant."

Maddie nodded in encouragement. "I'm afraid that's his usual expression lately."

"You're about to get some unwelcome visitors at the compound. In fact,

I'm surprised they haven't shown up already. Thank God they didn't descend upon you last night."

Feeling her stomach roil, Maddie shoved her plate aside. "*They*? Who are we talking about?"

"Kilo Mahelona and George Reed Masters."

Maddie aspirated a sip of water and started coughing. When she'd recovered, she said in a raspy voice, "*Both* of them? I didn't realize they'd even met." Then something else occurred to her. "How do *you* know Kilo?"

Lisette signaled the waitress. "Could we have two chardonnays?" She told Maddie, "If you don't want yours, I'll drink it."

"No, that's great! You read my mind."

"Kilo and I moved from New York to Port Angeles together. I opened the first Café Lisette, and he taught yoga. After we broke up, he bought the studio in Port Townsend. He'd saved a nice nest egg from his Groban Phillips days. It was Reynard who urged me to move the restaurant here. So I did. Silly me. After Kilo, I should've known better than to follow a man anywhere. Reynard has deep pockets, of course. In the early days of our relationship, he made a show of being generous. I suppose he was infatuated. We both were. The relocation suited him so he financed it. I let him, though I could have managed it on my own. I don't think he realizes that I still own the building that housed Café Lisette in Port Angeles."

"No need to explain about Kilo," Maddie said. "He's the Pied Piper. Most women would follow him over a cliff. I've only met Reynard once, at Matthew's cocktail party, but I imagine he can also be quite… compelling."

CHAPTER 22

Over wine, Lisette told Maddie her story, including meeting Kilo while working for the catering company, the affair with the plastic surgeon, the pre-trial hearings, and her eventual name change. The move to Paris to attend cooking school, all financed by Dr. Dahlstrom's allowance and her savings from caterwaitering.

They ordered more wine. "I thought we might have common ground," Maddie said. "Someday I'll tell you about acting school and my first theater roles. But we'll leave that for later. Like you, I haven't been feeling 'merry' about Christmas." She sighed. "If only the movie were filming in January so we could get it behind us. As it is, I'm worried it will be the final nail in the coffin of my relationship with David. We've only been married since the end of May."

She was surprised to see Lisette's eyes brim with sympathetic tears, quickly wiped away.

"Christmas has never been a time of romance or warm, fuzzy memories for me," Maddie continued. "My happiest holidays involved being in shows."

"Let me guess," Lisette said, "*A Christmas Carol*? I recently read the book for the first time."

"Really? My mother used to read it to me every Christmas. Yes. I played either Belle or The Ghost of Christmas Past. But sometimes I was cast in an original holiday show not destined to become a classic. I still had fun. The camaraderie made it worthwhile. Most of the actors I've known are emotionally needy and from broken homes—entertaining and cheerfully amoral. I could almost always count on finding a lover within the cast or crew for the run of the show. If I were the lead, then it was my love interest, unless he was gay or married. I assume some of my lovers were bisexual. If they started talking about sexuality having a 'spectrum,' I pretty much knew where they stood, or how they lay." She chuckled. "Needless to say, we always used condoms."

Maddie was definitely feeling the wine. Spurred on by Lisette's confession, she continued to speak too freely. "My dad, who was never better than a half-assed father, left me and my mom for one of my mom's friends when I was fourteen. A year later, I saw him one last time. By then he was dying of liver failure in hospice. I'm still close to my mom—too close. She's kind of hyperactive. You'll see what I mean when she and Duncan arrive at Christmas. You do *not* want all that nervous energy focused on you alone, kindly meant as it is."

"My parents were more the hands-off variety," Lisette said as if it didn't matter. "They loved me and my brother, but they weren't very affectionate. They believed in keeping a stiff upper lip."

Maddie went on, "So, yeah, Christmas. Last Christmas David was engaged to Sylvia, Lorenzo's mother and Chiara's sister. I was a guest at the compound, thanks to Mom's status as the girlfriend of Ali and Liam's birth father, Duncan. So, not great for me. In defense of the holiday, the O'Connells really know how to celebrate." Recalling the pending visit, she said, "Back to George and Kilo ...."

Lisette ordered them coffees. "I never drink at lunch," she said. "My head gets all muddled. I need to sober up so I don't blow it tonight."

"Thanks," Maddie said, "coffee sounds good. It's about the movie, of course."

Lisette nodded. "Kilo wants in, and George is the bearer of the latest screenplay."

Maddie scowled. "The version I just read was bad enough. The producers aren't idiots. The audience is keen to see me as scantily dressed as possible, and they want the 'action' to extend to the bedroom. You know, my character used to be a gloriously catty villainess. In David's version of the screenplay, I was declawed and spayed. I didn't even have much of a meow left." Lisette's eyes were dancing, and Maddie saw the humor in it too and laughed. "So it doesn't surprise me that each new version of the screenplay regains more of those elements. I just hope David can get over it." She paused. "Okay, say George and Kilo stop by ... why do they need to be houseguests? Why can't they stay at Kilo's?"

"Kilo made a surprise appearance at a yoga class," Lisette explained.

"The locals are cool, but mark my words, at any moment, the Forks, Port Angeles, and Quilcene teenyboppers will get word that both men are in town and swarm Port Townsend."

"What an idiot Kilo is," Maddie mumbled to herself.

"It's brilliant, actually," Lisette said. "How can your family turn them away? The success of the movie basically rides on George's shoulders. Oh, one last thing: Kilo said that if I don't put in a plug for him—a successful one, mind you—he'll let my real name slip. From there, you're just a few clicks away from the whole sordid story."

Maddie scowled. "What an *asshole*. I didn't realize he would stoop so low. Every time I've seen him since we broke up, he insists I'm his soul mate and urges me to run away with him."

Lisette surprised her with a merry peal of laughter. "You too? We should call him on his bluff and show up together."

"Don't forget Teresa," Maddie said. "She got the same 'come away with me' line when he was leaving to shoot the pilot episode of *Hawaiian Eye*."

Lisette rolled her eyes. "Not that I'm surprised. He'd keep us all in a harem if he could. He needs to check in every so often to make sure he still has a little piece of your heart."

As they finished off their refills of coffee, Lisette checked her watch. "Oops, better get a move on. It's already two thirty."

On the car ride home, she said, "Would it be so bad if Kilo were in the movie? He's a hot commodity right now. If you're already putting up with George, what's one more fly in the ointment? I'm not trying to protect my own privacy here—though that would be nice—I'm just pointing out the obvious."

Maddie made a face. "They've estimated three months of filming. I've been missing my profession, but this movie is going to be about as fun as … oh, three months of dental work." Noting Lisette's impish expression, she said, "What?"

"It doesn't have to be that way. Make it a game. Torture them both. Keep David at your side. I know you can do it. I have faith in you."

Her advice made perfect sense. Why should Maddie be the victim? Hadn't every show she'd done presented some kind of intrigue? She thought of *A Midsummer Night's Dream*, how the rest of the cast had resented her for getting one of the only three union salaries, meager as it was. The ever-shifting sexual alliances. She could rise above this situation too.

* * *

Knowing dinner would be jambalaya, David and Edward both ordered shrimp étouffée. David had to admit what they'd been missing by giving all their business to Kelpies.

"It's the atmosphere, right?" Edward said. "The historic pub thing. It's like you stopped by for a beer and suddenly it's a hundred years ago."

"Well, not quite," David said. "Most of the waitresses have a lot of piercings and tattoos. In those days, only the sailors had tattoos."

Edward introduced David to Bobby, the headwaiter, who acted as if Edward were visiting royalty, as did Sid the bartender. He was their hero after he'd intervened during the robbery and "did a Captain Kirk move on that scumbag." He was pretty sure that their orders contained unusually generous helpings of shrimp. Their beers would have been bottomless too if Edward hadn't pointed out that he was driving.

David pushed Edward for details about his latest trip to Paris, and Edward asked David about his honeymoon. Neither had inherited their father's zeal for storytelling, and they soon ran out of small talk. Finally Edward said, "Great as it is spending time with you, I have an ulterior motive for inviting you to lunch."

David laughed. "Do tell."

"I'm not about to ask a favor."

"Thank God. I thought you were going to confess to having a bad rash that needed healing."

Edward looked apologetic. "It's lucky you managed to keep that gift a secret."

"No kidding. Although it seems secrecy will no longer be required."

"Damn," Edward said. "That must be some adjustment."

"It's for the best," David said. He was by no means okay with the loss of his healing powers. The next time a loved one was injured or deathly ill, he would be forced to let nature take its course. Unless the skills he'd learned in medical school sufficed.

Edward blurted out, "Lisette had a surprise visit from Kilo."

David's body went rigid. "That scumbag," he said.

Kilo? he thought. *Why would he visit Lisette?*

Edward kept talking as if David hadn't turned to stone. "That's not all. George Reed Masters is in town."

David let loose a long stream of oaths.

"Shhh," Edward cautioned him, looking around for outraged patrons. Fortunately, the loud New Orleans jazz had drowned him out. "Drink your beer. It gets worse. I expect they'll both be angling for an invitation to stay at the compound."

"Bloody hell," David growled. "They'd better well not."

"Take a deep breath," Edward suggested, taking one himself. "A long, deep breath. I'm telling you now because the worst thing you can do when you see them is to overreact. I know I haven't been here long, but you have nothing to fear from either of them when it comes to Maddie."

David ground out, "We may have to tolerate George on the film set, but I sure as hell don't have to put up with him and Maddie's conniving ex as house guests."

"I'm afraid you do," Edward said. He put down his fork and crossed his arms. "The tabloids and the superfans are going to besiege them if they don't move to the compound, Kilo has made sure of that. He taught a yoga class. Surprise!" In a smarmy voice, he said, " 'Hiya, girls! The great Kilo is here to teach your class. This is just between us, right?' "

David gave a snort of derisive laughter. "You make him sound like an idiot. He's as devious as any supervillain." He recalled George's inept attempts at disguise on his last visit. "And I know from personal experience that George is bad at traveling incognito."

Edward went on, "George brought new screenplays with him, and Kilo wants in." Seeing that David was about to blow a gasket, he held up a hand. "Hold on. Kilo is hot right now, and I'm guessing we're talking about a minor role. If you're already putting up with George, you can handle Kilo too. And maybe, if they're both staying at the compound, they'll keep each other entertained. If you and Jake and Maddie want this movie to succeed, you'll have to kiss up to them both, and they know it. The question is, do you let them get under your skin, or do you find a way to make it work? You don't have to let them ruin the holidays for you."

David's prior question came back to him. "Uh, Edward, how does Lisette know Kilo?"

Edward uttered a bitter little "hah." "I could tell you the whole sordid story … but I'd rather do that back at the compound, where there's no chance of being overheard. For now, suffice it to say that Kilo gets around. They met in New York and moved to Port Angeles together."

David just stared at him, thinking maybe he'd had more Guinness than he realized. "Here I was thinking it was easy for you to be neutral and say we should put up with Kilo …. Now I see we're in this together. What did Kilo want from Lisette? Why contact her now?"

"He thinks she might have some influence with you and Jake."

"Uh, doesn't he realize you guys just met? I mean, in the general scheme of things. No offense intended."

"None taken. Kilo sounds a little desperate, right? Maybe he thinks an opportunity like this won't come around again anytime soon. He's raring to graduate to movie stardom."

Realizing his hands had balled into fists, David willed his fingers to relax. "He's used to getting his way through charm and good looks." Then he realized who he was talking to, Prince Charming himself. Charm and good looks could make you your own worst enemy. Edward didn't comment, handing Bobby a wad of cash and refusing change.

"I'm sorry how things ended up for you," David said, "in the Church, I mean."

Edward nodded. "As I told you before, at the onset and for a few years, I experienced a profound peace. My mentor Bishop Paul was a true inspiration. I know I gave you all an earful about corruption, but there are plenty of people in the Church with true callings. It's just that my circle didn't include many of them. I have not found life outside the Church to be peaceful." He grinned, and for a moment David might have been looking at their father. "That is, until I came here."

"Port Townsend did the same for me, at first. After Maddie and I got together, anyway. Then this movie business …."

Edward put on his coat and scarf. "Let's go. This 'movie business,' as you call it, is just a speed bump on an otherwise smooth road. We don't have to let these two snakes spoil paradise."

CHAPTER 23

LISETTE REGRETTED HER TWO GLASSES of wine at lunch, though she could probably make jambalaya in her sleep. She wasn't worried about driving drunk because the tipsiness had mostly worn off by the time they'd finished their coffee.

She and Maddie had talked a blue streak at lunch. During the drive back, they were lost in thought. In her certainty that George and Kilo had already infiltrated her refuge, Lisette was wondering how to proceed. Act like the coolest of customers? Turn up the dial on charm and enthusiasm until their heads began to spin? The problem was, Lisette was not an actor or even a calculating person. Her only choice was to play it by ear.

Poor Maddie. Lisette's love affair with Kilo was ancient history, and she had Edward in her court. Maddie's run-ins with George and fling with Kilo were recent, and David was jealous of them both. She suspected Maddie had held a lot back, because how could you come clean about such things? Recalling the details of a romance with Kilo was like trying to remember an acid trip. He turned your brain to mush.

Sure enough, an unfamiliar dark-gray Mercedes that looked like a rental was parked next to the carport. She and Maddie exchanged mournful looks then dissolved into nervous laughter. "We're going to act as if nothing's unusual, right?" Lisette said. "No indications of surprise."

"No enthusiasm either," Maddie said. "I'm going to treat them both like the pesky little brothers I never had."

"I *do* have a pesky little brother," Lisette said, "and if he showed up uninvited, I wouldn't be any happier."

Maddie filled her arms with groceries. "Ah, a subject for another day."

"Don't worry," Lisette said, "we'll laugh about this someday."

She picked up the remaining bags and they made their way toward the Sea Captain's House, which blazed with light. All the outdoor Christmas lights were turned on as well, though the sun was just going down. In the kitchen, Ali and Teresa stepped forward to warn them, but Maddie waved a dismissive hand. "We know," she said in a low voice. "I just hope Edward and David were able to give you a heads-up."

Lisette noticed that the doors to the kitchen were closed.

No longer whispering, Maddie said, "When is dinner? Lisette, how much time do you need?"

"An hour and a half at the most."

"We'd love to help," Ali said. Teresa nodded eagerly.

"I just bet you would," Lisette said. "But someone needs to entertain our visitors." She pointed toward the living room. "It's not fair that the men shoulder the burden alone. Will the guys be sleeping over?"

With a heavy sigh, Teresa said, "Once they explained the situation, how could we refuse? I wish it were for just one night. But we may be stuck with them until Christmas Eve, when Mom and Rostand and Duncan and Laurie arrive. That's when we'll have a full house."

Lisette wondered if George and Kilo realized how transparent their ruse was. They were no doubt slapping each other's backs in triumph. *It's cunning versus intelligence*, she thought. *They are talented and sneaky but not smart. That* should *make them easy to manipulate.* Her next thought was, *Don't underestimate them.* Maddie had said most of the actors she'd known were cheerfully amoral. Contrary to the schoolyard taunt, cheaters often prospered.

She opened the kitchen door and strolled into the parlor, where the Boys from Hollywood were acting as if *they* were the hosts. She hadn't expected all the men to be there: Jake, Joe, Liam, Edward, and David. Like an audition for an aftershave commercial. Had Edward and David called for a united front? Oh, for a transcript of *that* discussion.

As if it were all a lark, Lisette said, "Well, hello! If it isn't a meeting of the He-Man Woman-Haters Club." At their puzzled expressions, she explained, "Uh, The Little Rascals? At the very least, REO Speedwagon. It's a joke, guys. I gather we have two more for dinner."

"Is that okay?" Joe asked.

Lisette was taken aback by his question. Was he giving her an opening to say no? She was tempted.

"Of course," she replied, with a barely perceptible soupçon of distaste.

"Becca and Jean-Louis will be here too, right?" Not waiting for confirmation, she turned to George, who had risen, along with Kilo, to introduce himself. "You must be George Reed Masters." Rather than extend her hand, she inclined her head and put on her warmest smile. "I'm a big fan of your work." The clichéd compliment went down like honey. George acted as if Pauline Kael herself had just pronounced him the greatest actor of his generation. She could swear he blushed.

When Kilo attempted to introduce himself, she said, "Hello, Kilo. No need for that. Everyone here knows about our … past connection." She spoke gently, as if breaking difficult news. "Isn't that right, gentlemen?" At their bemused nods, she added, "They know everything, actually." Kilo paled a little. *Gotcha, you lowlife*, her eyes told him. "I hear you'll be staying for a few days," she went on as if she'd been elected their social director. "Wouldn't you like to freshen up?" They didn't move. "Unpack. Change for dinner." Her laugh sounded stagy, even to her. "You knew dinner is formal dress, right?" They exchanged confused looks. "Just kidding," she added.

Joe rose to his feet. "We've made some recent additions to the compound. Shall I take you on a tour? With all the Christmas lights, everything is illuminated after dark. I can show you the recording studio and Ali's and my house, which we affectionately call the Log Mansion. As long as it's okay with Ali. Sweetie, can I show them our house?" he called out so she could hear him in the kitchen.

"Yes," she called back, "it's fine!"

Jake stepped forward. "I'll tag along," he said. "I've never seen your recording studio."

The unwelcome visitors had shed some of their cockiness, as if Lisette's intervention had knocked the wind out of them. *Good*, she thought. *Score one for me*. Joe, Jake, George, and Kilo threw on their coats and scarves and exited through the kitchen. Maddie, who Lisette didn't blame one iota for making herself scarce until now, opened the door and stuck her head out. "All clear?"

With obvious irritation, David said, "You're not going to hide the entire time they're here, are you?"

"No, but I'd sure like to try," Maddie said.

Teresa and Chiara joined them, having come from the rec room. "Try what?" Teresa asked.

"To make myself scarce while George and Kilo are here," Maddie replied.

"That's not a good idea," Teresa said. "This is your chance to normalize things with them. Otherwise, how will you survive the movie?"

Maddie was standing in a tense, folded-up posture. David touched her shoulder, and she relaxed. "Sweetie, let's go read this verkakte screenplay. I'm tired of imagining just how bad it might be."

"How many copies are there?" Teresa asked.

"Three. One for Maddie, one for Jake, and one for Liam."

Liam held his at arm's length as if it reeked of some foul odor. To Teresa, he said, "Come on, darlin', might as well see what we're dealing with."

Jake's copy lay on the glass-topped rattan coffee table, so Edward picked it up. "I'll take a quick look while Jake is otherwise occupied."

Chiara went back to rejoin Lorenzo in the rec room, leaving Edward and Lisette alone to come together in a long kiss. "What time do you need to prepare dinner?" he whispered in a husky voice.

"I'd better start now."

"How much concentration is required?" he asked.

"Not much, not for me. I made the crab dip and combined most of the dry ingredients for the cornbread and dessert this morning. I still need to sauté the vegetables and meat for the jambalaya. I've already mixed the seasonings and cut up the chicken and sausage."

"Why don't I skim the screenplay while you work? I'll give you the condensed version. Unless you could use an extra hand."

"No extra hands required." She grinned. "Not for this, anyway. What, no dramatic reading?"

"Nah, I couldn't do it justice." He flipped through the single-sided script bound with two brass brads. "It's a thriller, after all—a lot of action scenes with minimal dialogue. The action will lose something in the telling."

He settled in at the granite island and started to read silently. "Okay, it opens at the Chatuchak Weekend Market in Bangkok. Damon and Mickey are fleeing a group of assassins led by Ailani." He looked up. "That's the character Kilo wants to play."

Lisette chopped the green onions, bell pepper, and celery with excessive gusto. "I hope his character gets killed off quickly." After slicing the okra, she added, "Damn. He already confessed that's what he wants?"

"George mentioned it, not Kilo. And he doesn't die in this scene. Sorry."

"Who is Damon, anyway?" Lisette asked.

"He's undercover CIA. So is Mickey."

"And Maddie's character?"

"Lorelei? An undercover agent for the Soviets."

"Naturally." Lisette dumped the sausage slices in the hot oil, where they landed with a satisfying sizzle.

"Action, action, action. Miraculous escape by helicopter."

Lisette rolled her eyes.

"Next scene, Lorelei seduces Mickey. Hoo-boy, David is *not* going to like that. I was told that in *his* rewrite, there were no sex scenes between Lorelei and Mickey."

"That's George's part?" Lisette clarified, and Edward nodded. "Does Mickey know Lorelei's true identity?"

"No, he thinks she's an American tourist. She drugs him and steals some blueprints from his briefcase. Blueprints he just retrieved from Damon and is supposed to take back to D.C. the following day. Some kind of ultra-precision weapon." He skimmed the next few pages and grunted. "Worse and worse. There's a scene between Ailani and Lorelei, who are lovers. Their sex is of the S and M variety." He kept skimming as Lisette worked. "Damon screws a beautiful spy who doesn't realize he's already handed the blueprints over to Mickey, who has lost them to Lorelei. He catches her going through his suitcase and shoots her dead. Okay, Damon and Mickey …. Mickey confesses to having lost the blueprints. Damon's sources tell him Lorelei is in Paris."

Lisette set the browned sausage aside and began to sauté the chicken. After putting the jalapeño cornbread in the oven, she said, "At least the actors get to go somewhere nice."

"Bangkok is nice," Edward said, "especially in early April. Then it can get wet."

"You've been there?"

He nodded. "During my various travels."

She'd heard that Bangkok was a good place to go for casual sex. She hoped he never gave her the details. "So, Paris …" she prompted as she set the chicken aside and started in on the vegetables.

He skimmed several more pages. "Damon hunts down Lorelei, who has heard of Damon but doesn't realize that he and the charming American businessman are one and the same. There are some sexual hijinks before Ailani blows his cover to Lorelei."

"How do they deal with the scars?" Lisette asked. "Surely Lorelei knows about those."

"I have no idea," Edward said. "This screenwriter might not know about Liam's shrapnel scars. Damon could hide them with makeup, but even if they had sex in the dark, she'd still feel them." He looked back down at the screenplay. "The CIA has sent a third agent named Folker Persson, described as a 'godlike blond.' With Folker's help, Damon gets the blueprints back." He paused, then asked, "Do you need to concentrate? That looks complicated."

"Maybe for a moment." As Edward continued to skim the screenplay in silence, she stirred in the okra slices and seasonings along with the sausage and chicken. After pouring the chicken broth and rice into the large pot, she put on the lid and turned up the heat. When it began to boil, she turned the heat down to low.

She looked up to find him watching her in wide-eyed wonder as if she were performing a miracle. She laughed. "You are really good for my ego," she said. "The secret to my recipe is in the combination of spices. Unless you overcook the shrimp at the end, this dish is hard to ruin." She reached for the pineapple.

Now he appeared concerned. "Are you going to add that to the jambalaya?"

She chuckled. "You probably don't like pineapple on your pizza either."

"No, not especially," he admitted.

"You can rest easy. The pineapple goes in the dessert. She brandished the chef's knife with a few extra flourishes for his benefit as she cut off the skin and stem, cored it, chopped it up, and put the chunks in the food processor. When the noise stopped, she explained, "Cajun cake. I was going to make bread pudding with bourbon sauce, but this seemed more festive."

"Yum." He was looking at her, not the pineapple.

She laughed. "No time for that. Get to the good part—where Ailani dies. Horribly."

Lisette took the cornbread out of the oven and replaced it with the cake while Edward read on in silence. She was chopping pecans for the Cajun cake's icing when he said, "Ailani is jealous of Damon, and they fight it out with various weapons. You'll love this part: Ailani gets shot by his own gun."

Lisette raised her fist in the air. "Hurrah! Although he deserves a grislier demise."

Edward smiled and shook his head. "Hmm. Is he really dead? It's not clear. Naturally Lorelei is pissed off. Of course now she knows Damon's identity. She wants those plans back, but it's too late. This time Mickey has managed to get them to D.C."

Lisette slapped the counter. "Oh, come on. He gets a second chance after he lost them the first time? That makes no sense."

"He gets a second chance because he's George Reed Masters and he needs more scenes. Mission accomplished," Edward went on. "Damon relaxes in Hawaii with a fellow CIA agent, who is, it won't surprise you to hear, quite beautiful. Folker is there too, with his very own CIA lovely. But wait … don't celebrate yet, Damon …. Lorelei has riled up Ailani's relatives, and they all attack at once in an impressive show of martial arts. Lorelei is injured, Damon believes fatally. The end."

"The end?"

"I skipped some stuff—two or three more eye-candy women for Mickey, Damon, and Folker. Do you remember Bambi and Thumper in *Diamonds are Forever*? Something like that, women in Lorelei's employ. Several female bodyguards and assassins have a go at our CIA studs. Some meet a bad end. Of course, Lorelei isn't really dead."

"Of course. Sounds like a rip-off of James Bond."

"James Bond doesn't have a sidekick. So, maybe James Bond and *Lethal Weapon*. I thought the book was better … more original. Too bad movie producers never trust the material that made the story a success to begin with."

Lisette sighed. "Even if Ailani really is dead, I'm sure Kilo's career will be properly launched. He's like a taller Bruce Lee. I hope David doesn't raise a stink and piss everyone off. It does sound entertaining."

Edward pulled her against his chest. "Our family doesn't always get its way. At some point they'll have to accept that."

CHAPTER 24

After the tour, Jake decided he still had time to skim the screenplay before dinner. As he was about to enter the kitchen of the Sea Captain's House, he saw Becca and Jean-Louis arrive. They looked up from lavishing affection on the canine welcoming committee.

"Jake!" Jean-Louis called out with his usual air of joviality. "Ali told us you and Chiara were staying at the compound."

Born and raised in Quebec, Jean-Louis Lapointe was a handsome barrel-chested bear of a man who spoke crisply enunciated, Québécois-accented English in a loud voice as if acting in a theatre-of-the-absurd play. Ali's best friend Becca was a flamboyantly beautiful hothouse flower of Russian-Jewish heritage whose family moved from New York to Seattle when she was in the tenth grade. Jean-Louis owned three restaurants—in North Bend, Bellevue, and more recently, Port Townsend—that featured wild game and fish. All were called La Fête Sauvage—The Savage Feast. The restaurant had been one of Jake's hangouts when he was the CEO of the O'Connell family business, Big Paul's Outfitters.

After they shook hands, Jake said, "You should know that we have unexpected guests for dinner."

With her usual perceptiveness, Becca said, "*Merde*. What now? Reynard?"

"That *would* be bad," Jake said, "but no. George Reed Masters and Kilo Mahelona."

"Kilo?!" Becca put her hands on her hips. "What the hell. What does that skunk want now?" Trust Becca to say it like it is. Jake found her quite refreshing. She expressed all the outrage the rest of them did their best to suppress. "He came with George? How do they even know each other?"

Jake gave a broad shrug. "I don't know. They met at a big Hollywood party, maybe. Serendipity… whatever. George has the latest revised screenplays for *Kapow.* He argued that, outside the compound, they were both in danger of being besieged by fans and paparazzi. Joe and Ali had no choice but to invite them to stay."

"Because of that accursed movie," Becca said. Then, as if realizing who she was talking to, she went on, "Sorry, Jake, but so far *Kapow* has been a giant pain in the tuchas for this family."

"You're telling me," Jake said. "Becca, Ali's in her studio, if you want to grab a private moment. Jean-Louis, I'll let you introduce yourself to Lisette. She's a little intimidated to be cooking for you."

"For me?" He threw up his hands and laughed. "*Mais c'est ridicule.* I'm easy to please. I so rarely get to relax and allow a fellow chef to do the work. As long as she isn't serving wild game, I promise to be a pussycat."

"Have you ever eaten at Café Lisette?" Jake asked. "David and Edward were bowled over."

Jean-Louis's smile had an air of mischief. "*Là là*, I'll be the judge of that. But"—he raised an index finger—"if I am not impressed, I promise not to state that out loud."

" 'State,' " Becca repeated with a snicker, not needing to add that everything Jean-Louis said sounded like a statement. For the first time, Jake wondered about the health of their marriage. Perhaps all married couples did a little sniping after a while. At least those with strong personalities.

In the living room, the cocktail hour was in full swing. Jean-Louis immediately helped himself to crab dip on a toast point and raised his eyebrows in approval. Then he wandered into the kitchen to hobnob with Lisette. You could hear him from the living room. Jake couldn't help but smile. Obviously they were getting on like a house on fire. He'd have to remember to use that idiom around Chiara. He seemed to recall that the French version had something to do with thieves. Thieves on fire? That couldn't be right. Thick as thieves? No, it was "*larrons en foire*," or "thieves at the fair." That made more sense. He couldn't wait to hear the Italian version.

Seeing that George and Kilo hadn't made their grand entrance yet, he went down to the basement in search of his sweetheart. She was sitting on the floor next to Lorenzo, working on a puzzle composed of characters from *The Way to Moss Manor.* The network of trails all led to the enormous moss-covered stump where Beverly Bigfoot lived. Beverly stood at the door wearing a welcoming grin, her fur black and glossy and her eyes sapphire blue like her frilly apron. The other characters also stood by their various dwellings. He recognized Willy the Leather Bear next to his cave, Slinky the Mouse next to a hole in a tree, and Otto the River Otter poking his head out of the river. River otters didn't *sleep* in the river, did they? More like took over other creatures' hidey holes after they vacated. Artistic license, he supposed. He thought it might make an interesting boardgame.

Chiara gave him one of her devastating shy smiles. As he kissed her neck, she giggled. "What's the Italian idiom for 'getting along great,' " he asked. "In English, one might say, 'They get along like a house on fire.' "

"It is similar in Italian. *Una casa in fiamme.* A house in flames."

"Well, that's Jean-Louis and Lisette."

She smiled. "What a relief! Have George and Kilo joined them yet?"

"Nope, just our core group."

By the time they went upstairs, George and Kilo had arrived. They both wore jeans, black T-shirts, and flannel shirts as if in imitation of—or homage to—Liam. Which was amusing, because tonight his brother-in-law was dressed like the guy in the Irish Spring commercial, with a thick Irish-wool turtleneck and beige corduroys. Everyone was laughing too much, though they couldn't have consumed much alcohol yet. In fact, they were frighteningly jolly, trying too hard to pretend nothing was amiss.

Becca, bless her, was unintimidated and up to her usual tricks, grilling George about the changes in the screenplay. "Is it back to an R-rating?" she said, deceptively pleasant.

"Don't blame me," David said. "In *my* revised version, you could take your grandmother."

"Not *my* grandmother," Becca said. "She has a bad habit of talking to the screen and ruining it for everyone. Although … her outrageous comments have been known to provide comic relief when things get too tense."

"Lots of humor in this movie," David said. "At least there was…."

"It's still a hoot," George said. "The new Hawaiian character has some real zingers. Kilo would totally nail them."

Kilo squirmed a bit at George's heavy-handed approach. This was the first time Jake had met the infamous Kilo. David and Liam had led him to believe that "devious" was more the actor's style.

As Jake made himself a gin and tonic, he asked with apparently casual interest, "I haven't had a chance to read the latest version. Anyone care to brief me on the changes? Maddie, David?" When neither of them stepped up to the plate, he said, "Anyone else?"

Edward raised his hand. "I skimmed it. Lorelei has sex with everyone. All the men, anyway. Even Ailani. Theirs includes some bondage."

In spite of himself, Jake was shocked. It was surreal to hear "Father Edward" discuss sadomasochism so matter-of-factly.

" 'Sex scenes,' " George repeated, legs crossed and hands folded in an oddly prim pose. "Hardly *that*. You know this kind of movie. There's nothing explicit. You got your kissing, racy outfits, bare male chests, lots of cleavage, some bare butts. The S and M stuff is mild. There's no, you know, uh"—he looked around the room, reluctant to go there—"banging, for lack of a better word. No actual nudity. Ya know, people expect Lorelei to be naughty."

"I get that," David said, a dangerous glitter in his eyes. "Do you think they're done making changes?"

Silence.

"So, Kilo," Liam said with the jokey affability of a talk-show host, "I hear you're selling the yoga studio."

Kilo avoided Liam's eyes. "Yes, I'm selling the building. With any luck, it will be to someone who'll keep the business going. They've ordered another season of *Hawaiian Eye*, and I've got other, er, prospects, so it seems clear I won't be teaching again anytime soon. Maybe in retirement." He looked out the window. "I miss Port Townsend and my life here, but you can't beat the money and excitement of starring in a TV series."

"They'll miss you at Theatre by the Marina," Ali said. "I hear they've been counting on you to fill the house."

"Jeremy will fit the bill for now," Kilo said. "He's been cast in the Cary Grant role in the February show, *Arsenic and Old Lace*. How *is* Jeremy?" he asked Maddie, addressing her directly for the first time. Jake didn't think he misread the longing in Kilo's eyes. Perhaps Maddie really had meant more to him than a fling. If so, that made his panting for a role in the movie even more troubling.

Maddie was drumming her fingers on the arm of the easy chair. "Did anyone else notice the role for Jeremy in the new screenplay? He would be the *perfect* Folker Persson."

"Would they consider him, do you think?" David said. "I thought you told me he burned his bridges."

"It wouldn't hurt to propose him," Maddie said. "Although I'd hate to screw over Theatre by the Marina."

Lisette announced dinner. Ali didn't do the name card thing, leaving everyone to find their own places. There was a predictable scramble to sit next to Maddie, but Jake noted that the eagerest beaver was Kilo, not George.

Maddie tensed but seemed to understand that moving to another seat wasn't an option.

George sat next to Lisette, Edward grabbing the chair on the other side of her. George's obvious interest in Edward's new flame surprised the hell out of Jake. He wondered how much the movie star knew about her. Had Kilo spilled the beans about Leslie Guzinski? It seemed so. Clearly George was intrigued by the idea of a bona fide femme fatale. Edward dominated the three-way conversation. Jake couldn't hear their words from his position at the other end of the table. Their body language alone was fascinating. Edward, with his casual touching, was laying claim. George was as flirtatious as a man could be without touching. The guy oozed sex appeal, but Edward was no slouch in that department either. A regular *pas de trois* with Lisette as the principal dancer.

The meal was superb, and the compliments were plentiful and sincere. The side conversations ceased as Lisette became the center of attention, allowing Jake to hear her clearly. At first she glowed, answering questions about Le Cordon Bleu and her parents' restaurant in Cape May, but then George had the gall to ask about her time in New York, and she clammed up. Was it possible Kilo *hadn't* told him the whole story?

"I was a caterwaiter," she said. "Not much of interest there. Unless you want to hear my celebrity-encounter stories, and frankly, they're too insignificant to be of interest. Everyone's an a-hole sometimes, and it's not fair when one incident of assholery gets trumpeted far and wide like that." Then, as if suddenly recalling that she was surrounded by celebrities, she gulped. "Um, excuse me, I'll just… get the dessert." She fled to the kitchen.

Seated next to Teresa, he felt his sister's cell phone vibrate. She checked the caller ID and went to the other room to answer. When she returned, she was a little green around the gills. "Uh, Xenia is at the front gate. She says she's leaving town tomorrow and wants to drop off a present for me. I invited her in for dessert. I hope no one minds."

Jake saw Edward's jaw clench, though he didn't protest. The rest of them went suddenly still, as if playing a game of Statues. Except Kilo and George, of course, who exchanged a secret look, practically rubbing their hands together in anticipation of meeting this new, clearly unwelcome player.

Hoo boy, Jake thought when he saw Xenia wasn't alone. Reynard—was that a gleam of triumph in his eye?—trailed along behind her.

"Merry Christmas, everyone!" she chirped, as if oblivious to the impact of her surprise visit. Her pupils were dilated. Was she drunk or high? She carried a gift bag that held a bottle of wine. *Ice to the Eskimos*, Jake thought.

"Reynard and I leave for Paris tomorrow," she sang out. Then she noticed George and Kilo and lost a degree of her chutzpa. "You have company." She turned to the men, who stood and introduced themselves. Recognizing them, finally, she turned beet red and started to simper. "Oh, my! This is a fun group. I'm so honored to meet you, Mr. Masters, Mr. Mahelona." While she eagerly shook their hands, Reynard was the very picture of cool. He acknowledged the rest of them one at a time, including Lisette, with marked formality.

Ever the peacemaker, Ali suggested they move to the living room for dessert and sauterne. Reynard wasted no time lamenting the loss of Teresa's Art Deco living room, while Maddie and David gritted their teeth.

Upon opening the gift bag, Teresa looked like she was going to be sick. Reynard was a difficult man to read. He had one of those mouths that, at rest, turned down at the corners, giving him a perpetually disdainful aspect.

"I knew you liked this wine," he told Teresa. "When I served it to you at my house, you were quite effusive in your praise."

Liam's face started to twitch. He might have been a bull fuming at a red flag rather than a bottle of red wine. At least he didn't start pawing the ground. Reynard didn't appear to notice.

"How long will you be in Paris?" Ali asked.

"Three weeks," Xenia said. "It's so exciting. We have reservations at three restaurants with stars!"

"Which ones?" Jean-Louis asked with genuine curiosity.

Not surprisingly, Reynard answered. "Two have three stars—L'Ambroisie and Arpège. And there is one I've never been to before. It earned its two stars in the 1999 *Guide Michelin*, Le Violon d'Ingres."

"*Ça c'est malade!*" Jean-Louis exclaimed with enthusiasm. "Getting reservations must be a bitch."

Reynard preened a little. "I have my connections. Well, we won't impinge on you further. Teresa, enjoy your present. I don't recommend sharing it with Lisette." He paused. "She does like her wine."

Teresa rubbed her baby bump. "I'm sure I will enjoy it at some point in the future. Wine isn't the most thoughtful present for a pregnant woman, after all."

Boo-yah! Jake thought. *Gotcha, Reynard.* His malice now obvious to everyone, the man turned an unflattering shade of red. Xenia seemed genuinely puzzled by the exchange, as if unaware that the Christmas gift had been meant as an insult.

After they left, Edward said, "Xenia cleans up well. I do believe she was wearing Givenchy boots. May I see the bottle?"

In a daze, Teresa handed it to him.

He read the label aloud, "E. Guigal Côte-Rôtie La Mouline 1990."

Her expression unreadable, Teresa said in a flat voice, "It was the number-one red wine of the year at some point."

Liam asked through clenched teeth, "Okay, Teresa, what is the not-so-subtle message here?"

She met his eyes. "He served a bottle of that wine on our first date."

"Ooh, that's cold," George said, vastly entertained.

"Xenia seems happy," Edward remarked with more than a hint of irony.

The house phone rang, and nearly everyone checked their watches. Ten o'clock—too late for good news. No one dared break the silence as Joe left the room to answer it. When he returned, he looked grim. To Liam, he said, "It's Nancy. They think they've found her body. It's in a hospital morgue in Forks."

"How are we going to handle this?" Liam asked.

"I told the officer I'd drive there tomorrow to identify the body. Liam, I think just you and I—"

"No," Edward interrupted them. "I want to be there to support you."

"Me too," Jake was quick to add.

Joe asked David, "Do you mind staying here? If there are any issues with Teresa or Ali—"

"No problem," he rushed to say. "Teresa, why don't you and Liam stay in a guest cabin tonight? Everyone will want to get an early start tomorrow."

The group dispersed with terse farewells. Maddie, Chiara, and Ali left to check on Lorenzo and the twins, and Becca and Jean-Louis followed after Ali—though Jean-Louis did pause long enough to give Lisette a warm hug and a *"Chapeau!"* of congratulations, doffing an imaginary hat.

"Who is Nancy?" George asked when only he, Kilo, and Jake remained in the living room.

"Liam and Ali's birth mother," Jake replied. "She was, uh, an addict. We suspected she was dead." Looking at Kilo, he added, "It's a long story."

George didn't probe further. Six months earlier, while staying first with Jake and later at the compound, he had stumbled upon the truth regarding their psychic gifts. Jake hoped he understood that Kilo must be kept in the dark.

"We'll leave around five in the morning," Jake told the actors. "The door to this kitchen will be left unlocked. Help yourselves to espresso and anything you can forage."

The path to the cabins was well lit. That and the outdoor Christmas lighting meant the two actors would have had no trouble finding their accommodations. Jake escorted them anyway, waiting until each man was safely inside before going in search of Chiara.

"What a fiasco," he murmured to himself. "At least Lisette's dinner was a hit."

CHAPTER 25

LISETTE WOKE AT THE SOUNDS of Edward dressing in the dark the next morning. Hearing her small groan, he gave her a kiss of reassurance. The night before, when they'd fallen into an exhausted sleep, had been the first time they'd spent the night together without making love.

Reynard had infiltrated the compound Trojan Horse style. Or like a flea hitching a ride on a dog. With one Christmas present, he'd managed to remind Teresa of the bad blood between them and accuse Lisette of being an alcoholic. As he left, he shot her a slitty-eyed look that didn't bode well. Why the grudge? She'd thought him classier than that. Then again, in order to reach the top of his profession, he'd had to rise above his festering pit of a childhood. Some wounds never healed.

At six o'clock, she gave up on sleep and wandered down to the house to make herself a double latte and two fried eggs, grateful that no one else was about. As she lingered over coffee, she heard a car enter the compound. It was still dark, but in the well-lighted parking area, she observed a woman who looked like an older version of Teresa and a younger, dark-skinned man, possibly Arabic. Knowing this could be none other than Carrie O'Connell, she raced back to the cabin, following a circuitous route to stay out of their sightlines.

* * *

Teresa heard a car roll in, and from the cabin window, verified that it was her mother's brand-new white Escalade. She'd been told Carrie and her factotum Rostand would arrive Christmas Eve. Why not give them a heads up that their plans had changed? And why the early hour? She couldn't even begin to come to grips with what had happened last night. What had Reynard been thinking? What had the O'Connells done to him that they deserved such treatment? She and Reynard had dated a few times, and it hadn't worked out. Had that one rejection been enough to crush his fragile ego? Did Xenia have any idea what havoc they had reeked with that visit, or was she Reynard's dupe? She had seriously misjudged the younger woman, and that hurt. All that time spent teaching her about antiques and design styles …. And poor Lisette! She and Reynard had lived together for over a year, which had to be unusual for him. Obviously he still smarted from Lisette's rejection as well. His film scores had won numerous awards, and he was a masterful pianist. Why did the approval of two women matter at all?

As she headed down the path toward the Sea Captain's House, Teresa saw George waylay her mother and accompany her into the kitchen. Fearing what he'd say or do, she hurried to join them. She and her mother hugged—gingerly, like porcupines—and Carrie went back to gushing over George. Who knew she could be starstruck?

"Rostand and I are staying at Manresa Castle while we're here," her mother was saying. "So you see, there's no need to vacate your cabin for our sakes."

Where was Kilo? If her mother had known he was part of the deal, she would have dropped the beneficent act. Didn't Carrie understand that it wasn't her place to invite George to extend his stay?

So much for getting rid of those two vipers before Christmas.

Her reaction to the news of the death of Ali and Liam's birth mother was predictably hard-hearted. "It must be a relief to you all," she declared. "What a sorry excuse for a human being. Darling, Rostand and I are headed into town for breakfast. We'll be by after the boys return from their errand."

They didn't ask Teresa to join them, which struck her as odd.

* * *

There would be no better time for Lisette to use the gym. The last time she'd checked, George was schmoozing with Carrie, whose excited body language showed that even she was thrown into a tizzy by movie stars. Maybe it was all the catering for fancy companies, but Lisette reserved her admiration for people who had earned it. Most of the movie stars she'd met had acted entitled and imperious.

It was now around eight, and the sun was rising. If a view could heal, this was the one. The shimmery water, the gray and coral clouds. She popped Joni

Mitchell's *Court and Spark* into her CD Walkman and turned up the speed on the treadmill.

Sometime later, she heard the door open, and her heartrate increased for all the wrong reasons. George sauntered in, wearing sweats and a T-shirt that advertised some craft beer she'd never heard of. She was glad to be clad in sweats and a T-shirt, not her usual spandex. She nodded in his direction, but otherwise kept up her pace, too rapid for talking. She didn't lower the volume on her Walkman, even though he was waving his arms to get her attention. Pointing to the headphones, she mouthed, "I can't hear you."

She managed to ignore George while Joni serenaded her two times with her *pièce de resistance*—an hour and fifteen minutes. Finally she realized he wasn't going anywhere and slowed her pace for a cooldown. Having sampled every other piece of equipment, he'd settled on the NordicTrack. The volume on the TV news show was turned way up. Was he deaf?

She took off her Walkman and propped it on the shelf of the treadmill, looking pointedly at George. She wasn't about to encourage him. If he didn't speak, she'd finish her cooldown and leave with a simple "goodbye." She was a sweaty mess and makeup free. If that didn't deter him, she wasn't sure what would.

"Am I bothering you?" he asked with a decorous smile. He knew damn well he was bothering her, was actively trying to bother her.

"Not at all," she said coolly. The treadmill came to a stop and she started to stretch.

He turned off the TV. "That was some dinner last night," he said.

"Thanks."

"Does the entire family exercise here?" he asked.

"No. Both houses have home gyms. They wanted the guests to feel comfortable using this place." She didn't add that Maddie preferred this gym … usually.

"You're not much of a talker," he said, finally.

"How would you know?" she said. She kept her tone even, no undercurrent of annoyance.

"Actually, I know quite a bit. Kilo likes to talk, and he loves to talk about you. I think he's obsessed, actually."

Lisette did not appreciate hearing this. Kilo was a mischief maker on an epic scale.

"I've upset you," George said, unapologetic.

"Kilo needs to learn to shut his trap," she snapped. *Easy*, she told herself. *Don't let him get under your skin.*

"I don't know … the more I hear, the more I like," George purred.

Her look called him on his BS. "George…" she began, wondering how to shut him down. Finally she said, "Save it for someone who cares. You seem like a nice enough guy, but honestly, I'm not interested."

"You don't even know what I'm proposing," he said.

"The answer is still no."

"Hear me out."

The man was relentless. She sighed, waiting for him to continue. She was doing sit-ups, and if he wanted to keep talking, she wouldn't stop him.

"I know you think you have a future with Sexy Priest, there. But let's get real. It's the O'Connells we're talking about. They may act all aw-shucks and down to earth, but they are one elitist little clan. Edward is on the rebound. He's not ready to settle down, especially with a Jersey girl with no higher education and a doozie of a past."

Her baleful look had no effect whatsoever.

"By all means, see it out. But when it ends—when your cover is blown—you have options." He switched to a stationary bike with barely a pause to breathe. "Start a restaurant in L.A.; I'll back you. So what if they find out about Leslie Guzinski? They love a good scandal. Better yet, I'll help you pitch the story. It would make a great movie."

Her continued lack of interest didn't deter him.

"Come live with me and be my chef. I'd be the envy of all my friends."

" 'Come live with me and be my chef,' " she repeated. Did he really not see the similarity to Christopher Marlowe's poem? *Come live with me and be my love, and we will all the pleasures prove.*

"You're smiling," he said, "but it's not a happy smile."

"It's a great offer for a girl like me," she said, thinking that now she was perilously close to quoting Julia Roberts' prostitute character in *Pretty Woman*. "Believe it or not, I don't need your charity."

He gave her a card with nothing but his initials, GRM, and a phone number engraved in gold lettering.

"My cell phone," he explained. "The offer is open-ended. I just bought a new place in Beverly Hills, and I could really use a chef. And that's all you'd be expected to do, I promise. I'm gone a lot of the time anyway. Your duties would be light. Mostly you'd make sure the staff were fed. Keep the freezer stocked with dishes they can microwave, and they can serve themselves. When I'm around, there'll be dinner parties, and I'll hire you lots of help. It'll be a pretty great life. I have a pool, an exercise studio, a movie theater, a separate casita in the back where you can live for free…. I'll be the envy of all my friends. I'll pay you top dollar."

He spoke like it was a done deal. She had to wonder what "top dollar" meant but wasn't about to ask. Because, even if everything here did fall apart, she would *not* consider his proposal. Basically, he wanted a live-in lover who could cook and didn't require a commitment. Another "mistress" position.

"That's all I'd be expected to do," she repeated with obvious sarcasm.

"Okay, I admit it, I'm attracted to you," he said. "So, yeah, I'd *want* more. That doesn't mean you'd have to give it to me."

That's because you're certain you can win me over, she thought.

"That Reynard clown … really? And Edward, of all people? I know you think you're in love with him, but come on, that family doesn't get people like us. My dad owned a motel, a modest one at that. In Seaview, Washington— hardly Cape Cod. Your parents owned a diner. We did what we had to do to succeed. See how much we have in common?"

He had her there.

"Get real. Sooner or later, you're going to be unmasked. Maybe by that Xenia woman, who has her knives out for you. She's a piece of work. Your thing with Edward is brand-new. Do you think it will survive you being exposed as Leslie Guzinski in this image-conscious family?"

"Unless you or Kilo blow the whistle on me, I'm safe enough," she said. "Edward doesn't care, and in the end, his family won't either."

His laughter sounded genuine. "Keep telling yourself that, kiddo." He got off the bike. "Jesus, I'm beat. I think I need a nap. Come with me? Showering together saves water."

She laughed, as she was meant to. "That line may work in California, but there are no water shortages here. Besides, it's a myth."

"True," he said, raising his distinctive eyebrows suggestively, "because I promise, if you showered with me, a lot of water would get used before you were … *wet* enough to suit me."

There was so much passion in that corny line that she had to remind herself he was a consummate actor. "George, stop it!" she demanded in the tone you'd use to discipline a dog.

He tried—and failed—to appear chastened.

She was desperate to change the subject. "Where's Kilo?"

"He went into town. He might have an offer on the yoga studio."

"Kind of puts the lie to his 'I'm a celebrity and they'll mob me' excuse for staying here."

George shrugged. "They're used to him in this town. He was already a celebrity of sorts. The O'Connells tolerate him because they need to make nice with me."

"Why do you want the part in *Kapow*, really? I'd have thought it would be Damon or nothing."

He appeared thoughtful. "Good question. At first it was because …" he trailed off, thinking better of giving her an explanation.

"Rory," she said. "Edward told me about the family 'gifts' in some detail." Lisette also suspected George had hoped to score with Maddie. He was the kind of guy who would always need a fantasy woman and never be satisfied with the real thing. Apparently, Lisette was now the object of his crush. Men did tend to fixate on her, but those fixations never lasted. Why was she so certain Edward would be different? Had he ever had a real girlfriend? He'd confessed to being a "satyr," but his one real commitment had been to the Church.

Meanwhile, George's expression could only be described as slack jawed. The "Rory" remark had genuinely thrown him. *Aha*, she thought, *you really believe Edward isn't serious about me. If it were nothing but a fling, would he have shared that secret?*

"Rory's gone," George said. "Sometimes I wonder if he was ever there to begin with." He resumed his cocky air. "My cabin is the third one over. I'll leave the door unlocked. Edward will be gone all day …." He raised his sweatshirt slowly to give her an eyeful of washboard abs.

"Dream on," she said, laughing.

His parting words were, "I'm serious about that offer. All my offers." He blew her a kiss.

Back at the cabin, Lisette worried more than ever about Xenia and Reynard's nasty little drive-by attack. Recalling Edward's story about Xenia, she locked the cabin door before turning on the shower.

* * *

Ali and Teresa were holed up in Ali's attic studio as if angry hordes were storming the gate.

"I can't believe Mom invited George to stay through Christmas." Teresa lay on the couch, propped up on pillows.

Ali sat at her desk, sketching. "Can things get any weirder?" she mused, then gave a dismissive wave. "Don't answer that. Did you have any idea Xenia would turn out to be…. What's up with her, anyway? Gullible, oblivious, or evil?"

Teresa threw up her hands. "I thought I was a better judge of character.

Not evil, I think, just mean-spirited. I believe she resented us all along. I'm not that much older than she is. Was I being condescending? Did I lord my design business, fancy family, and social connections over her?"

"Don't ask me," Ali said. "I don't know how her brain works. It's possible. I believe her childhood was way more nightmarish than mine. That does things to a person."

Teresa nodded. "Or … some people are more resilient than others. You and Liam rose above your scorched-earth origins like phoenixes, wanting to do good. Xenia would rather spread the misery around."

Teresa ran a hand back and forth over her bowling-ball tummy. Still holding her sketchpad, Ali joined her on the couch after Teresa lifted her legs to accommodate her. "Just look at us. I am *so* glad this pregnancy is almost over."

"Ditto," Teresa said. "I'm exhausted all the time. Just climbing the stairs to your studio did me in."

"I almost asked Joe to set up a temporary office for me on the first floor, but I need the exercise."

"Can I see what you're working on?"

Ali handed her the sketchbook.

"Sasha Shrimp?" She regarded the sketch for a long moment. "Cute. I'm glad you didn't show me this before last night's dinner. They're delicate, almost pretty."

Ali laughed. "My drawings are all about cute. The real thing isn't that cute, and it certainly is delicious."

"The way Lisette prepares it, anyway," Teresa said. "She's an excellent chef. Even Jean-Louis was impressed. Are you sure it's not a prawn?"

"Prawns are the fresh-water version," Ali said. "They do look similar. They use their fanned tails to dart backward when they're in danger. It's called 'lobstering.' They have a special set of legs for swimming called 'swimmerets.' "

"Sounds like an all-girl rock band," Teresa said. " 'Sasha and the Swimmerets.' Hey, why not? They could entertain at Oxana's Christmas party. Are you finally warming to this project?"

Ali smiled. "Yeah. Chiara is such a great collaborator. She can make anything work." She regarded her pensive sister-in-law. "So … Reynard. What was *that* all about?"

Teresa held her forehead and closed her eyes, as if praying for strength. "I think he's gone around the bend. Giving me that special bottle of wine just to goad me—to let me know he hadn't forgiven my rejection. And telling me to keep it away from Lisette. Buying those expensive boots for Xenia when he hardly knows her."

"Oh, Xenia …" Ali broke in, tossing the sketchpad aside. "She's the ultimate 'fuck you, Teresa.' It's like he's angrier at you than he is at Lisette."

"Of all the women to pursue …" Teresa said. "He knows she's been my protégée. She's also a lot younger than Lisette, so there's that."

Ali nodded. "I doubt the relationship will survive Paris. The truth is, you were Reynard's ultimate prize. Lisette didn't have a hoity-toity background, though she did have the beauty and sheen of sophistication. You're the real thing. Xenia is beautiful and smart, but not sophisticated or classy. He's going to start ragging on her in record time."

Teresa blew out a long breath. "Hopefully they're safely on the plane by now and out of our hair." She paused. "I wonder what happened to Nancy?" Laying a hand on Ali's arm, she asked, "Did the news upset you?"

"The entire subject of Nancy upsets me. I always felt as if her sole reason for contacting us was to get money."

Teresa shook her head. "I don't know. There may have been an element of that. I like to think she also wanted your forgiveness."

Ali hoisted herself up using the arm of the couch. "If that's what she wanted, she has it. I bear her no ill will."

"I have one bit of encouraging news," Teresa said, hopping to her feet with enviable ease. "Liam says he's pretty sure her mother's name is Sheila."

"Why didn't he tell me? Who figured it out, the investigator?"

Teresa bent over to pick up the discarded sketchpad and lay it carefully on Ali's drafting table. "He woke this morning with the name on his lips. You know how he is. He's connected to all his women somehow. Now that Nancy is dead, Sheila must be one of them."

"What about Lisette. Why not Chiara and Maddie?"

Teresa's brow furrowed. "Good question. Who knows how his psyche works? Perhaps it got mixed up after that initial encounter in Port Angeles." Checking her watch, she said, "Shall we see what we can scare up for lunch? David and George must be getting hungry."

Ali stretched, trying to work out the kinks in her back. "I made bacon this morning and no one but David ate it. How does turkey club sandwiches sound? And there are leftovers from last night."

As they made their way carefully downstairs, Ali wondered how Joe and Liam were doing with their depressing errand. She was glad they had the support of Jake and Edward. Who would have guessed that those two errant brothers would turn out to be such steadying influences?

Back at the Sea Captain's House, Ali went downstairs to check on the twins. *The Nutcracker Suite* played in the background. Under May's watchful eye, the twins were sitting together, picking up blocks and trying to stack them, for once working together in perfect harmony. Had she and Liam played together at that age? With what, their mother's crack pipe? Now they'd never know.

She settled in on the couch, and the girls toddled over. She helped them up so they could snuggle on either side of her. Upstairs, she heard David say in his booming voice, "Take a load off. I'll make lunch."

CHAPTER 26

———◦———

At half past four in the afternoon, Teresa sat in the Sea Captain's living room enjoying the latest Stephanie Plum novel, a light read that required little concentration. At the sound of tires on gravel, she perked up, thinking it might be the men, unlikely as that was. They'd left at around 5:30 this morning, but the drive to Forks was two-plus hours. It would take time to ID the body, make burial arrangements, and eat lunch. Even if everything went like clockwork, she didn't expect them until 7 at the earliest. That left two possibilities: Kilo or her mother. Neither prospect thrilled her.

"Teresa?"

Her mother, then. Did she plan to eat dinner with them? How would she react to Kilo's presence? Surely she wouldn't leave Rostand to his own devices. What was Rostand doing here, anyway? His help wasn't needed now that they had so many interns eager to work for the overly generous O'Connells.

"In here!" she called out, not wanting to leave the comfortable couch for what was bound to be an uncomfortable conversation.

"In a minute," her mother said. "I need to make a stop first."

That was her mother's discreet way of saying she needed to pee. Teresa put down her book, awaiting the pending interrogation with growing dread. Maddie, Chiara, and Lorenzo had just joined Ali, the twins, and May Allen in the rec room, which left Teresa a sitting duck. Maddie had kept Lorenzo company all day, first taking him down to see low tide—an activity he usually did with David, who was working on a screenplay—then playing ball with the dogs over by the safari tent. As long as Lorenzo was around,

George couldn't get up to any funny business. Teresa wondered how he was occupying himself, since Kilo had the rental car they'd arrived in. He'd joined Lorenzo and Maddie outside, briefly. What had he done the rest of the day? Napped? Soaked in the hot tub? Read a book? Strolled around the compound? Maybe he'd worked out in the gym.

As soon as her mother joined her in the living room, Teresa noted how tense she was.

After one or two obligatory questions about Teresa's health, Carrie got straight to the point. "What do you know about this woman who's living with your eldest brother?"

"She's not *living* with him, Mom; she's staying here with him over the holidays. She has her own place. At the moment, he doesn't."

"Edward has spent his entire adult life married to the Church. He hasn't had one serious girlfriend I know of. He is ripe to be exploited by some … adventuress."

Teresa couldn't believe her ears. "Moooomm," she moaned, "don't turn Edward against you. Leave him alone."

"You were the one who told me she'd made a big play for Liam. That he thought she was a call girl."

"That was before we got to know her. She's really nice. And she's a talented chef."

"But what do you *really* know about her?"

Carrie was bristling like a hedgehog. Teresa wished she wouldn't work herself into such a state.

"We know she's owned a few successful restaurants and has investments of her own. She doesn't need Edward's money."

"You don't have to *need* more money to *want* more money," her mother said. "I doubt she's in *our* ballpark. Who are her people? What is her education?"

"She has a degree from Le Cordon Bleu. That's nothing to sneeze at. As for her 'people' and designs on Edward's money, you thought the same of Liam."

Her mother stared her down. The fact that her views on her husband hadn't changed was confirmed by her silence. At least now that Teresa was about to have a child, her mother had the decency to leave that one alone.

Carrie took a moment to smooth her skirt and uncross her legs. Without looking up, she said, "Edward is vulnerable right now. The last thing he needs is for some vamp to suck him dry."

Teresa wanted to scream. "*Please*, wait till you meet her. She's great. Give her a chance."

Her mother's pursed lips quivered a little before she finally said, "Edward's known her for a matter of *weeks*. It can't be anything but a fling. My investigator has done some preliminary poking around. Lisette followed a lover to Port Angeles—*Kilo*, of all people. Did you know that? Then she got involved with some local celebrity musician and followed him to Port Townsend. Now that he's tired of her, she's looking for someone else to latch onto and follow around."

"Mom, you're being super unfair. Lisette left Reynard. And we all know about her relationship with Kilo. She was the one to break that off too."

"That just makes her fickle. And what about her life prior to moving to Port Angeles? What if there's something truly scandalous there? If she genuinely cared about Edward, she wouldn't risk bringing further scandal to this family. You know how the tabloids hound Joe and Ali. And now Maddie."

Don't forget Liam, Teresa thought, but her mother wouldn't care about that.

"Oh, Mom…" she began but had no idea how to win her mother over. In her mother's mind, *she* was the only one who counted. It was her *own* reputation that worried her. She'd always been able to brag about her children. The country music star, the priest, the CEO, the doctor, her daughter the socialite …. Now none of them were on paths Carrie deemed respectable. If Lisette's past did become common knowledge, her mother would be mortified, but the rest of them would weather the storm. They always did. Of course the scandal involving Liam had been different. The tabloids had portrayed him as a dashing figure. The stories of his past as a soldier for hire in Israel and his attack on the man who had stalked her had only enhanced his reputation—one of the reasons the public wanted to see him as Damon Morehouse. That same kind of scrutiny could well ruin Lisette's life. Customers were drawn to Café Lisette partly because the owner was so charming and gracious. What would they do if she were revealed to be a gold digger and possible femme fatale? Women never got a break. The silence was beginning to vibrate like glass about to shatter, so she said, "If you're so sure Lisette is just a temporary fling for Edward, why worry? I know you have too much class to ruin Christmas for the rest of us. If you want to remain in your son's good graces, leave them alone. Let the relationship play itself out."

Privately, she believed Edward and Lisette were perfect for each other. Her mother wasn't prepared to hear it.

Much to Teresa's relief, Carrie was done arguing for now. She asked a few logistical questions about their holiday plans, and Teresa told her that both she and Ali would be heading to Seattle soon after the new year and planned to stay until they gave birth.

"That sounds fine," her mother said in a clipped voice. "Rostand and I will come to dinner tomorrow night when all the family is assembled."

Teresa had not mentioned Kilo.

Please, God, let him go back to his own apartment.

* * *

Lisette had driven into town to buy groceries, having planned a meal of comfort food for the men when they returned. Carrying the ingredients for beef stew and biscuits, she had just entered the kitchen, intending to lay them out on the counter, when she became aware of the raised voices in the living room. At the mention of her own name, she froze.

Carrie was grilling Teresa about *her*. The woman knew about Lisette's history with Kilo and Reynard and believed she was after Edward's money. She was convinced their "fling" would damage the reputation of the entire family.

She must have been holding her breath, because when George touched her shoulder, she almost passed out. *Oh, come on*, she thought. How long had George been standing there, and why hadn't she heard him come in? Realizing that the disturbing conversation was winding down, she panicked, turned tail, and ran, George right on her heels. She moved as quietly and as quickly as possible, breaking into a full run once she was outside the door and not stopping until she was inside her cabin. Unfortunately, George was right behind her.

She leaned against the wall, trembling and breathing hard.

"You okay?" He touched her arm, but when she flinched away, backed off. He was just itching to take her in his arms, ostensibly to comfort her. *God knows I could use a hug ... just not from him.*

"Do I *look* okay?"

"No. Jeez Louise. And here I thought my ex-wife's mother was Queen Bitch. Carrie's got her beat by a mile. Not that I'm surprised. Kilo told me about his quickie marriage to Teresa and how brutally the family treated him. Like he was a dog that needed to be whipped and then put down. You really wanna be a member of that club? Hell, might as well join the He-Man Woman-Haters Club."

She laughed at the reference in spite of herself.

She was feeling a little calmer, thanks partly to George. "Listen... I

189

appreciate your support. I'm a big girl, and it's not like I haven't encountered this kind of disrespect before." She pointed toward the house. "I'm going to go back into that kitchen and cook dinner. If Carrie's still there, I'll say hello and pretend everything's cool. But maybe I'll luck out and she'll be gone." She looked out into the festive, colored-light-speckled darkness. "Will you do me a favor? Don't follow me right away. The last thing I need is for someone to see you coming out of this cabin."

George was grinning in that irresistibly cheeky way of his, reminding her why he was a star. "Jeez, I'm impressed! You *are* courageous. Misguided, but courageous."

She had to ask, "If they're so awful, why do *you* want to be here?"

His shrug expressed supreme nonchalance. "There's something about this place …. Talk about wanting to join a club that doesn't want you. They *really* don't want me here, and everywhere else I go, I'm treated like Elvis reincarnated. For some reason I crave the famous O'Connell stamp of approval."

Try as she might, she couldn't help but like George. You had to hand it to him: he could still laugh at himself.

"Edward is his own person," Lisette insisted. She couldn't deny wanting to be one of the O'Connell insiders, hopeless as that prospect seemed.

"Listen, babe, when you're with someone like Edward, his family is part of the deal. I know this from bitter experience. My ex-wife is Hollywood royalty, and she has a degree from Princeton. Even with all my acting awards, I would never be anything to them but scum."

Wait a minute … hadn't he cheated on his wife? No point in bringing that up. She turned to go, but he grabbed her hand.

"Offer still stands," he said, the last word pitched like a little song. "You would *love* my house. It's really a villa—a Spanish villa. Like something out of the Alhambra. The kitchen is state-of-the-art. I would *totally* appreciate you."

She gently withdrew her hand. It might be fun to hide in George's ivory tower for a while. But she figured that when it came to women, he had the attention span of a flea. They'd probably have a brief but torrid affair; then she'd step out again into cold reality, where the loneliness would be even harder to face.

Besides, she thought, *I'd just be proving that awful woman right. That I'm "looking for someone else to latch onto and follow around." Better to stand on my own two feet, even if that means embracing celibacy for the rest of my life. If Edward could do it, so can I.*

* * *

As Teresa followed her mother to her car, she noticed the bag of groceries on the kitchen counter. *Oh no*, she thought. *Lisette. Did she overhear any part of that conversation?* She hoped against hope that David had been the one planning dinner. But her brother would have joined them in the living room.

At the parking area, she kissed her mother on the cheek and told her she'd see her tomorrow. As she watched the Escalade drive away, her heart was filled with dread. Did Carrie have any idea how thoroughly she was pushing her children away?

As she headed down the hill, Teresa caught movement out of the corner of her eye, and thinking it might be the dogs, turned just as George left the cabin Edward shared with Lisette. *No*, it couldn't be. Were they really messing around while Edward was away?

But then, back in the kitchen, Lisette was chopping carrots as if she didn't have a care in the world. She must have returned from shopping and left her groceries on the counter, then returned to the cabin when she heard the voices in the parlor. Her smoothly braided hair, lip gloss, jeans, boots, and sweater were all in order. She didn't have the rumpled and mussed appearance of a woman who'd been messing around, certainly not with ten minutes to do it. So what had George been doing in her cabin? Lisette couldn't have overheard Teresa and her mother. She looked too cheerful. There had to be another explanation.

"You're cooking dinner?" Teresa asked, stating the obvious. "That's so nice."

Was Lisette's smile a little strained?

"I thought the guys would appreciate comfort food, tonight of all nights. Stew can sit until they get here. Any news?"

"No," Teresa said, reevaluating. Lisette appeared *too* cheerful. *Oh God*, she *had* overheard. The question was, how much? "I expected Liam to check in by now," she went on. "I'll see if Ali's heard from Joe. She's downstairs with the children. Need any help?"

"No," Lisette insisted, "but thank you! Feel free to join them."

Downstairs, everyone was crowded onto the couch watching the old Disney classic, *The Sword and the Stone*. The girls were asleep on either side of Ali, who looked drowsy herself. Only Lorenzo, cuddled up between Maddie and Chiara, was wholly absorbed in the movie.

"Any news from Joe or Jake?" Teresa whispered as she sank into one of the easy chairs.

Ali and Chiara shook their heads.

Not wanting to wake the twins, Teresa sighed and tried to concentrate on the movie, which she'd never seen. Knowing how children liked to watch the same videos over and over, she figured she'd catch the beginning next time. She was desperate to tell the other women about her conversation with her mother, but not with Lorenzo in the room. For a four-year-old, the boy didn't miss much.

CHAPTER 27

WHEN THE MEN RETURNED AT seven fifteen that evening, they looked wrung out. The stew had thirty minutes to go, so everyone retreated to their rooms to shower and change, convening in the Log Palace dining room at eight. Lisette stayed in the kitchen to oversee the last-minute prep.

To give the others privacy, Kilo and George had opted to dine separately in the Sea Captain's House. *Surprisingly considerate*, Lisette thought.

"It was a grueling day," Joe said at dinner. With some satisfaction, Lisette noted that everyone was eating heartily, especially the men. As usual, the wine was superb. Reynard's catty comment had made Lisette self-conscious about her own drinking. Tonight, she let that go. The rest of them—other than the two pregnant women—were drinking her under the table.

The men had met with the forensic pathologist in the Forks Community Hospital morgue, there being no independent morgues in Clallam County. Nancy had died of exposure, with drugs in her system consistent with addiction.

As Liam put it, "She got high, wandered into the woods, and passed out face first in a stream. They found her a week ago. We'd reported her missing, which is why they knew to contact us. Not to be indelicate, but she was in bad shape. She was wearing the Big Paul's boots and parka we gave her. Even without the clothing or, uh, recognizable features, I knew who she was. I just *knew*." None of them questioned his certainty. "If it were up to me, we'd cremate her. Joe is hesitant to go that route. Catholics don't get cremated, I gather."

Joe asked, "Did she ever mention religion? You and Ali seem to think you were supposed to be raised Catholic."

"I asked her if we were baptized," Liam said. "All she said was, 'It's possible.' As you know, her brain was already scrambled by the time she stumbled back into our lives."

"So we've tentatively decided to bury her," Joe said. "We found a funeral home in Port Angeles that will prepare the body as best it can. No open coffin, obviously. No memorial service. We'll do a simple family burial when I locate a crypt."

Patently annoyed, Ali said, "I hate to be the naysayer, Joe, but reading between the lines, her body is badly decomposed. Please, let's cremate her and scatter the ashes. I know money is no object, but why just throw it away? Crypts are expensive, and she was a poor excuse for a mother."

Liam raised a hand to call for silence. "Let's tell the funeral home to keep her in cold storage for now." He paused, as if absorbing his own words, then added, "I didn't mean to sound callous, but Ali's right. It's hard to be sentimental about the woman, considering what she put us through. The good news is, the investigator believes he's located Nancy's mother, and if the Sheila Fitzgerald he found turns out to be the right one, we can ask *her* if she thinks a burial is necessary."

Lisette and Maddie turned to him in shock. The rest were unsurprised.

"Another bit of 'intuition,' " Liam explained. "The name just came into my head. I plan to travel to Yakima to meet her."

Hands flying to her belly, Teresa asked with obvious distress, "Even if it means missing Christmas?"

Liam replied in a soothing voice, "It should be a one-day trip. Whatever happens, I promise to be back by Christmas Eve."

"Don't worry, Ter-Ter," Joe said from across the table. "Liam and George will fly on the same charter plane to Seattle on December twenty-third, then Liam will take a puddle jumper to Yakima. The pilot will spend the day in Seattle and fly Liam home that evening, no matter how late he gets in."

Liam was grinning from ear to ear.

"What could you possibly have to smile about?" David remarked with obvious irritation.

"I think George and I are overdue for a talk," Liam said. "Of shoes and ships and ceiling wax, of movie stars and sex."

Now Joe was smiling too. "Not the Walrus's exact words."

"The walrus?" Lisette asked.

Their evident surprise told her most people would get the reference. *Oh well, that's me*, she thought. *The ignoramus.*

Edward took her hand. "It's from *Through the Looking Glass*, the sequel to *Alice in Wonderland*. 'The Walrus and the Carpenter'? You're in for a treat. I can't wait to read it to you. Lorenzo can sit in. He will love it."

Chiara spoke for the first time that evening. "Those books will be right up his alley. What a nice Christmas treat." She glanced at Jake. "Did I use that idiom correctly?"

"*Perfetto*," he said with a smile.

Lisette's heart thumped harder at the reassuring squeeze of Edward's hand. She would be *so* sorry to part with this man. She'd never met anyone as sweet, kind, or sexy.

She planned to leave town the day after Christmas. If she told Edward her decision to his face, he would certainly talk her out of it. That couldn't happen. She was more certain than ever that she was poison to him and his family. Therefore, true to her cowardly nature, she'd leave a note.

She didn't know what came next. It was time to start fresh, and this go-around, she'd do it on her own. She wouldn't prove Carrie right by chasing after some new man. What should she choose for her new name? She wasn't particularly attached to "Lisette." Maybe "Louisa," who sounded like a sensible, "mature" woman. She'd sell the building in Port Angeles and try to find someone to take over the restaurant here. Perhaps Marky would be interested. He and Sid could run it together. She'd like to be done with the restaurant business. Only, what else was she good at? She was too young to retire from the one profession she'd ever mastered.

"Edward's a wonderful narrator," Teresa was saying. "He read to me when I was a child. He did all the voices." Lisette wondered what it might have been like to be read to by a parent or brother.

"Edward, would you be upset if we cremated Nancy?" Ali asked in a small voice.

"Church doctrine doesn't forbid cremation," Edward said. "I'd feel a lot better if I knew Nancy's wishes. The worst sin is to go against the deceased's religious convictions. Catholics believe that the entire body, even if there's not much left of it, is resurrected at the Second Coming of Christ. Not as it was, but in its 'glorified' form—healthy, strong, and powerful. But if she held onto any of her Catholic beliefs, don't scatter her ashes. They'd need to lie in sacred ground." After a moment of silence, as they absorbed this information, he added, "Whatever you do, I won't disapprove. I don't believe in any of this anymore. It's for your own peace of mind that I don't advise going against Nancy's or her mother's beliefs."

"Of course," Joe said in a firm voice.

The conversation turned to praise of Lisette's stew and biscuits. She imagined they were all sick of serious, depressing subjects. She certainly was.

For once there were no FOSSP kids present, so David and Jake loaded the dishwasher and handwashed the pots and pans, letting Lisette off the hook. Ali even suggested she and Edward enjoy the hot tub. The others could soak after they were done. Not Teresa and herself, of course. Being pregnant ruled that out.

Before they dispersed, they discussed the next few days. "How are we going to deal with your mom being here at the same time as Kilo," David asked, "now that she has explicitly invited George to stay?"

"Easy," Jake said. "While we were on the road, I phoned William, my agent. Kilo has been offered the role of Ailani, which gives him no more reason to be here. He leaves tomorrow. And like Joe said, George will fly out of Port Angeles with Liam on the twenty-third."

"At least he'll be gone by Christmas Eve," Ali said. "Now we can try to salvage Christmas."

Lisette and Edward wasted no time in climbing into the hot tub—naked, since they were by themselves. Though weary of sticky subjects, Lisette said, "Your mother will be here tomorrow. What will you do if she objects to my presence?"

He was holding her against him, sliding his hand up and down her body. Cupping her cheek, he looked deep into her eyes. "Did something happen while I was gone?"

What didn't happen? she thought. *Your mom is dead-set against me and George wants me to be his live-in cook-slash-mistress.*

"No," she said, too firmly. "It's just that I have an awful feeling Reynard's revenge isn't complete."

"Did you ever tell him about Leslie Guzinski?"

"No. Perhaps I should have. If he found out now, he'd figure I deserved exposure all the more for keeping that secret from him."

He gave her a long, lingering kiss, floating her toward him until she wrapped her legs around his waist. "I've told you I don't care, and I mean it. Even if it all comes out, I'm not going anywhere."

They both spoke in soft, impassioned voices.

"You say that now, but we've known each other such a short while."

He nuzzled her neck. "Look, I've been infatuated before. It's true that I've had a lot of brief encounters, but I've also had actual girlfriends my family doesn't know about. Before I took my vows. One lasted six months. This is different. Besides, my own misbegotten past is no less shocking than yours."

Her laugh was bitter. "Mine is *far* more shocking. Even if your deacon's scheme had played out, the scandal would have been minor. In the end you would have been believed, no matter what your premonition told you. All that foresight did was prevent you from having to deal with a few weeks of uncertainty and unpleasantness. If word gets out about *my* past, I will be seen as, at best, a money-grubbing kept-woman, and at worst, an aspiring murderess. As for your wild oats, there is no one to attest to sowing those except you, and most women would just admire your virility."

"I left the Church and broke my vows. To my mother, that's the ultimate shame, and if she knew my reasons for leaving, she wouldn't think they were valid."

"Lots of priests leave the Catholic Church," Lisette insisted. "It's a wonder anyone stays. Sooner or later, they'll have to allow for married priests."

His fingers traced her cheek, stopping just short of her breast. "I haven't seen any signs of that happening. There have got to be others like my mentor Bishop Paul—priests with genuine vocations—and they provide a lot of comfort to their congregations. I'm done with the Church, but I would never judge those who keep the faith."

Back at the cabin, Edward made love to Lisette with an intensity that was both exhilarating and frightening. It reminded her of those early days with Reynard when it seemed their hunger for each other could never be sated. *You see?* her conscience told her. *It's no different. In a few months, the euphoria fades, and after it's gone, all that remains is regret. Better to end it before that happens, and certainly before the shit hits the fan.*

Then the voice of reason intruded. *You're being paranoid. Unlike Edward, you don't have premonitions. You simply don't trust happiness.*

She ignored it.

CHAPTER 28

BACK AT HER OFFICE, TERESA sat at her desk, staring into space. Upstairs, Tom was doing a thorough cleaning. Xenia had moved out before she left for Paris, and Teresa assumed the young woman's few boxes of possessions were at Reynard's. As far as she could tell, nothing was amiss; that is, her erstwhile assistant hadn't embezzled money or taken souvenirs. *There was no need*, Teresa thought bitterly. *She has a man buying her thousand-dollar boots.*

What did Teresa really know about Xenia's background, other than her humble beginnings as an abandoned baby with only a first name? She'd turned up in Port Townsend at the former boarding house they'd renamed FOSSP Place asking about jobs, and Ali had taken a liking to her. At first Xenia helped with the children. Then she expressed interest in interior design, and Teresa became her mentor. Even though Xenia was objectively beautiful and flirted with every man who crossed her path, her flirting had a playful aspect and she never pushed. Not that Teresa had observed. It was her way of being friendly, or so Teresa assumed. She acted more or less the same way with women.

Then came Edward, and for the first time, Teresa wondered if Xenia were unbalanced. David had told Liam about the night of the snowstorm— when Xenia entered his cabin uninvited. Edward had rejected her, and she stole his underwear. Too bad it took so long for David to pass the story on to Liam—only after Xenia and Reynard's surprise visit. Not wanting to make trouble for Xenia, Edward had sworn him to secrecy.

Tom, done with the cleaning, appeared at her door. He was a quiet young man with a do-it-yourself haircut and thick glasses, and he was dressed in baggy jeans, a long-sleeved T-shirt, and tennis shoes. Now she wondered what his deal was. *Still waters run deep*, she thought. *That's supposed to be a good thing. But what if we're talking about the Black Lagoon? What kind of creatures lurk in Xenia's psyche?*

"Tom, do you have Christmas plans?" she asked. "I'm sorry we couldn't go forward with the party at the compound."

Tom smiled and straightened his glasses. "Everyone understands. Ali and Joe gave us big cash bonuses for Christmas. Joe also designated a generous sum for a party at FOSSP Place. Don't worry about us. See you next week?"

"Sure," she said. "You know I'll be closing the office until after the baby is born, right? Ali and Joe will find other work for you in the new year. Until you go off to college."

"Yeah, I've applied to several places. Joe and Ali have promised to pay my tuition. But the academic year doesn't start until September."

"What is it you want to do?"

"Be a veterinarian," he replied promptly, "maybe for exotic animals. I've always loved going to the Woodland Park Zoo in Seattle."

"That's cool," she said. "Merry Christmas!"

"You too," he said with a cheery salute.

After he left, she berated herself for not asking earlier. Did these young people want to talk about themselves, or did they prefer to keep their private lives private? If only she'd thought to draw out Xenia a bit more. *You tried*, she thought, *but she always evaded your questions.*

The wall clock read eleven thirty. There was nothing more to do here, and she should go home. She was sitting here brooding, hands folded on the desk, literally twiddling her thumbs. She might have been waiting for her boss to come in and give her a performance review. Funny—she'd never had to put up with anything like that. What was normal for most people, she only experienced by watching TV and reading books. What a sheltered life she'd led!

A knock on the door. Had Liam come for her early? She didn't expect him until twelve thirty.

"Who is it?" she called out.

"Kilo," came the voice.

Her heart began to race. She did *not* want to talk to Kilo. She stood up, suspended in time, afraid to move. Here was a rude reminder of her first futile attempt to break free from the overprotective bosom of her family. What if she'd been willing to drop everything for Kilo? She had not rebelled again until Liam came into her life.

"Uh, Teresa?" he went on from behind the door. "I just came to say goodbye. I'll make it quick, I promise." Another minute passed. "I'm not going away." The note of amusement in his voice raised her hackles.

Bracing herself, she opened the door with the same impersonal formality she might have used with a tax auditor. He, however, kissed her limp hand and sauntered in as if she'd greeted him with open arms.

"We didn't have a chance to catch up at the compound," he remarked, shrugging out of his cashmere coat and straddling the chair across from her. He seemed to glow with health and beauty, enhanced by all the pampering money could buy. She felt like a total frump.

When she didn't speak, he said with surprising candor, "I'm sorry about the strong-arm tactics. I'm perfect for this role, and I was afraid your family had so soured on me that they might act against their own best interests."

"As I recall," she said in a clipped voice, "you've done your best to cause trouble for me and Maddie. You can't blame Liam and David for holding that against you."

"I suppose not," he said, deflated in a way that surprised Teresa. She observed his work boots, jeans, tight T-shirt, and flannel shirt with some amusement. Other than the fact that the jeans were obviously a designer cut, he seemed to be emulating Liam. She knew he missed the friendship.

"You look comfortable," she said. "Going for a hike?"

He laughed. "Nope. Just trying to blend in."

"I doubt that's possible anymore. I'm surprised you're not being mobbed."

"I've been mobbed a few times," he admitted sheepishly. "Today I've managed to elude them. That aspect of fame I could do without." He paused and said, as if talking to himself, "Funny, I thought I would enjoy it more. It was a lot more fun to be a yoga teacher and act in the occasional play."

"Are you still hung up on Maddie?" she surprised herself by blurting out.

He looked up, startled. There was her answer. What he said was, "I leave a little bit of my heart with every woman I make love to. Part of me has never gotten over you, for instance."

"Or the way Edward treated you." In spite of herself, she pitied him.

"Edward," he muttered. "I will *never* forget that. Now he's totally changed his tune. You'd think he was the Dalai Lama."

"He's suffered, too," Teresa said gently. "Maybe not enough to satisfy you. But I guess you're not done."

"With what?"

"Seeking revenge on our family. Now you'll have a chance to kiss and fondle Maddie again, even if it's all make-believe. Too bad *she's* not married to Edward, then you could really stick it to him."

"I love Maddie," he said simply and with no trace of irony, "and I think she loves me too."

Teresa bristled. "You know, if it weren't for Sylvia, she'd have chosen David over you to begin with." She watched the jab hit its mark—a few blinks, a flinch. "Why can't you enjoy this fame you've wanted so badly and leave Maddie alone? The tabloids are full of your exploits."

He grinned. "You pay attention."

"So does Maddie. She's not immune to you. She's probably still attracted to you. You're pretty irresistible. However, she *adores* David." She didn't add her private view that Kilo was too shallow for anything but a fling, and David had depths a woman could spend a lifetime exploring. She was all too aware of the harm her family had inflicted on Kilo. Even she had toyed with his heart when they'd met again ten years later. If not for Liam …. *Thank God for Liam.*

She stood. "Unless you'd like to run into my husband, you might want to say your goodbyes now. I wish you well, and I hope this role makes you a superstar." She opened the door, waiting for him to leave.

"Goodbye, Teresa," he said. "We'll meet again during filming, I'm sure."

She nodded, thinking that if they did meet again, it would be in some public situation where she could pretend not to know him.

Five minutes after he left, Liam arrived, visibly harried.

"You saw Kilo leave."

"Yes." He raked a hand through his straight black hair, which stood up in tufts, as if he'd been through a windstorm.

"He wanted to say goodbye. Did you know he's still into Maddie? Apparently, he loves her."

"So he says." Liam pulled her into his arms and rocked her back and forth, as if they were dancing. "Of course he'd tell you that, to make you jealous. But if he really does believe he's *in love* with Maddie, that will make for a tricky situation during filming."

"Poor Maddie," Teresa said, closing her eyes and breathing in his fresh scent of soap and leather and forest. "She's going to have to deal with George *and* Kilo. She'll worry that if she makes the scenes with you look too real—"

"We'll make it work," he cut her off. "I'm more concerned about George, and not for the reasons you think. I believe he's obsessed with Lisette now. He's waiting for her life to fall apart so he can swoop in and save the day."

"Still feeling protective of Lisette, I see," she said, ashamed of the pangs of jealousy.

"Only in a brotherly way." He stared into her eyes. "I don't trust Kilo or George as far as I can throw them, which is farther than most men could. I wish they'd find some other sandbox to foul up."

"No kidding."

"I love you," he said, "more than life itself. You don't ever have to worry about me."

Her only response was a long sigh. She *did* believe him, finally. After all, even after seeing Kilo leave her office, he had trusted her. Now she could face her fears about the coming birth of their daughter. Also the dread she felt at the prospect of sitting on the sidelines of a movie that featured her impossibly sexy husband making love to one beautiful woman after another, including her own sister-in-law.

* * *

Edward had just left the cabin and was heading over to the house to see about breakfast. Drying her hair with a towel, Lisette heard knocking. Lisette had asked Maddie if she could join her and Lorenzo to view high tide, and it was just about time. She opened the door. Luckily, she was fully dressed.

"George," she said warily, "why are you here?"

"Listen …." He paused to take a deep breath, then continued in a rush, "I leave tomorrow morning, and I might not get another chance to catch you alone. I just wanted to repeat my offer about the chef's job. The more I think about it, the more I'm convinced it's a great idea. Ask for any salary you like—an outrageous one, even. You'd have a beautiful bedroom in the casita and a relaxed schedule with lots of free time. Your own workout room. You'd hardly see me while I'm filming *Kapow*."

Yes, she thought, *but that still gives you several months, maybe just enough time to get me out of your system.* Whatever he claimed, she knew his offer included her willingness to sleep with him whenever he felt like it. If not for Edward, that might have been a pleasant perk.

"Thanks, George," she said, knowing he'd argue if she refused him outright. "I'll keep it in mind. Just don't force my hand, okay?"

"Huh?"

"By notifying the tabloids yourself."

He was the very picture of wide-eyed innocence. Because she'd guessed his plan or because he would never do such a thing?

"Tsk, tsk. What you must think of me …."

He *seemed* sincere.

"I don't know what I think of you. I hardly know you."

"I'm a heck of a nice guy," he insisted, slapping his chest a few times for emphasis. "I'm just trying to help out, make you aware of your options … your very delightful options."

"Okaaay …." He was still standing outside the door. "Listen, I have to dry my hair, and Edward is waiting for me. Have a nice trip."

"We'll be in touch?"

No, she thought. "Anything's possible."

He understood the futility of pushing his luck. Before she could pull away, he leaned over and kissed her cheek.

"George," she said in a warning voice, pushing him away. As if burned, she tore her hand away from his hard chest.

He grabbed that hand and kissed it. "We would have had a blast," he said in a sultry voice, then disappeared so quickly she expected to see a puff of smoke where he'd been standing.

Edward was sitting with David in the kitchen when Lisette came in.

"Where are Lorenzo and Maddie?" she asked. "I'm sorry it took me so long to get ready."

Edward handed her a to-go cup. "I made you coffee. When you guys get back, I'm going to start reading *Alice in Wonderland* aloud. After lunch, Joe wants a quick meeting about Christmas Eve. At Lorenzo's request, we're staging a little variety show. Maddie will explain more." Her qualms must have been obvious, because he added, "At the very least, you have to sing 'Have Yourself a Merry Little Christmas.' "

He made it sound like a modest request, though she'd be displaying her meager talent in front of Joe Bob Blade himself. *Oh well*. Expectations would be low.

* * *

Once Lisette was gone, David said, "You really want to put her on the spot in front of Joe and Matthew?"

Edward wasn't the slightest bit worried. He knew what Lisette was capable of. "She has a great voice," he said. "You'll see."

David laughed. "You and I could do a duet. Too bad we're both basses."

" 'White Christmas' isn't too challenging, range-wise," Edward said, "as long as we transpose it down a few notes. I'll tell you what: we'll go back and forth and sing the last phrase in unison."

David looked appalled. "That sounds ridiculous."

"It's a *variety* show. We'll ham it up. Add light choreography."

David rolled his eyes and then concentrated on his breakfast, finishing off his second espresso and fourth piece of bacon. "You know, if you read Lorenzo *Alice in Wonderland*, the kid's going to be quoting it back to us from now until Doomsday."

Edward slapped him lightly on the back. "Better that than *The Cat in the Hat*. I never get tired of 'You are old, Father William.' "

"Lorenzo is so smart," David said, "that he probably outgrew 'The Cat in the Hat' when he was two."

It was clear David regretted missing Lorenzo's early years. "The kid is here now," Edward said, "and he adores you and all his aunts."

Edward wondered if David wanted more children. Maddie wouldn't be eager to pause her career once it heated up again, and she'd be justified in worrying about spoiling her beautiful figure. But then David turned the tables on *him*.

"Do you think you'll want children someday?"

Edward burst into incredulous laughter. "If so, I'd have to get busy. I don't want to be chasing a toddler around in ten years." It occurred to him that Lisette and he had never discussed children. Somehow she didn't seem like the maternal type, even though she was great with Lorenzo and the twins. When it came right down to it, how well did he know her? Was he truly in love with her or simply infatuated?

"You don't need Mom's approval," David said. "None of us followed the paths she would have paved for us. Jake is shacked up with a married woman."

He hadn't read Edward so well after all. Edward looked him in the eye. "If it were up to me," he said, "no problem. But I have an awful feeling Lisette is getting ready to bolt."

David raised his eyebrows. "Premonition?"

Edward shook his head. "Common sense. And she's been skittish. Almost as if Mom warned her off. She doesn't want to force her way into a family that doesn't want her."

"You know," David said, "according to Teresa, that was the objection Liam kept waving in her face—that her family would never accept him."

Edward grimaced. "And by 'family,' they both mean Mom. I have half a mind to give her an ultimatum: join the twenty-first century or else."

"Good luck with that," David said. "Joe has had more than a few come-to-Jesus talks with her, and she never changes her tune. Sorry, you know what I mean. Not *literally* come to Jesus."

Edward sighed. Could any of them forget for one minute that he'd been a priest? *You are still a priest, technically*, he reminded himself. *That's the problem. David can't forget that Kilo and Maddie were lovers. Liam can't forget that Teresa and Kilo were once married. None of that stuff can be truly forgotten, even Lisette's ill-conceived affair with Dr. Dahlstrom. All you can ask of them—and all they can ask of you—is that they put those past relationships behind them once and for all. Forgive, even if they can't forget.*

What was that famous Mister Rogers quote? Something like "It's hardest of all to forgive the ones we love."

As a priest, he knew all too well that it was even harder to forgive oneself.

* * *

After cooking two dinners in a row, Lisette was glad to let someone else do the honors. That night, Tiger treated them to another of his gut-busting feasts—pork chops stuffed with mozzarella, sun-dried tomatoes and spinach, garlic mashed potatoes, and green beans sprinkled with roasted almonds. The kid showed promise.

Despite her fears, Lisette hadn't had the occasion to exchange more than a nod of greeting with Carrie all evening. Ali's birth father Duncan and his fiancée Laurie, who was Maddie's mother but resembled her hardly at all, had also arrived earlier than planned, providing a welcome breath of fresh air. They were on the opposite end of the pretensions scale from Carrie. Carrie's manservant—why must she travel with a manservant?—had come as well, though they seated him at the opposite end of the table. They called him a "factotum," a term no one used anymore—an all-purpose servant. Laurie did like to keep the conversation rolling, but not in a way Lisette minded. She filled in the blank spots, never running out of questions or some fun fact from current events.

Then there was Carrie and George. A brilliant move on Ali's part to seat them together. George had Carrie giggling like a schoolgirl, lavishing her with attention as if she was the most attractive and fascinating woman in the room. In no time he was calling her "Carrie" and questioning her about her charities and travels. Only once did he catch Lisette's eye, actually daring to wink. She looked away quickly, worried that the others would notice and realize how full of BS George was. But then, everyone but Carrie knew that already. Laurie looked downright jealous.

As Carrie's pale cheeks grew flushed with wine, she started to touch George's arm and lean in. He continued to play along. That was when Lisette noticed something very interesting indeed: the supposed manservant was glowering. Funny. He was a lot younger than Carrie—at least twenty years—and one might have thought a little too dark-skinned to interest such a woman. If there was funny business going on between them, that would make Carrie a prize hypocrite.

Or perhaps the longing was all on Rostand's side.

CHAPTER 29

As Liam drove George to Port Angeles, neither spoke much. The sky was dense with clouds, and the temperature hovered around forty degrees. Eastern Washington was much colder in the winter. Yakima was forecasting a low of twenty-five with zero chance of precipitation. Thank God. The long day ahead included a drive through unfamiliar territory, and the last thing Liam needed was icy roads. Sheila lived on the east side, which according to his investigator wasn't the safest neighborhood. Liam carried his smallest hunting knife. It had a blade three inches long, one inch shy of the limit the airlines allowed in a carry-on. He didn't want to check his small bag, and you never knew when you might need protection. He was beginning to imagine his rental car being hijacked when George broke the silence. His normally lighthearted traveling companion obviously had some heavy stuff on his mind as he stared out the car window at the ocean.

"Man, how do you deal with having Carrie as a mother-in-law?"

Liam gave him a sidelong look. "What? The way you were 'carrying' on—sorry—I assumed you were her number one fan."

Chuckling, George pointed as they passed a collection of chainsaw art for sale. "That's exactly what I need in the front yard of my villa in Beverly Hills—a giant chainsaw-art salmon." He took another minute to savor the image before answering Liam's question. "I enjoyed tweaking Rostand's nose. That man really knows how to give a person the evil eye."

His words earned him a double take from Liam. "Rostand?"

"I'd swear up and down those two are more than employer and butler, or whatever the hell he is."

"I've never been completely clear on that," Liam admitted. "Joe calls him a 'factotum,' which covers just about everything. It just never occurred to me that they'd, uh, get involved." He frowned. "I can't picture it."

"That's what Teresa will look like in thirty years, ya know," George said.

"Teresa and Carrie may resemble each other physically, but that's where it stops."

"If you say so." George was quiet for a long moment before continuing, "Carrie's still a beautiful woman, even though it costs a lot to maintain beauty like that when you're in your sixties. Her plastic surgeon must be top notch. They're always coming up with new procedures to sell to actresses, even when they're young. You can't be too perfect for the camera."

"What about male actors?" Liam asked.

"Oh yeah, no one's exempt. The audience wants us to be pretty too."

Liam thought of his scars. No one had suggested he deal with them. If he stuck with this acting business, he might have to go there. He rarely gave his looks a second thought and didn't want to start now. He'd rather play bad guys anyway.

"Back to Rostand," Liam said. "I hardly think he's Carrie's type."

"Yeah, I know. He's kind of, uh, exotic, for the likes of Carrie. Where's he from?"

"Algeria," Liam replied. "I think they're mostly Berbers. North African."

"He's a great-looking guy," George said.

Come to think of it, Rostand *was* a good-looking guy. Liam pictured the dark-haired, dark-eyed, dusky-skinned man, often a fixture at family gatherings but usually disappearing into the kitchen to help out. He was the quiet, observant type. But he was so much younger than Carrie. Were they really having an affair? Since when? A mind-blowing possibility.

The conversation shifted toward Hollywood and its obsession with beauty, and Liam got an earful about who had had plastic surgery and who was just pretending not to have had plastic surgery. Then they talked about George's new villa in Beverly Hills and his plans for renovation. The light chitchat was a welcome distraction.

It wasn't until they were on the plane that Liam broached the subject of Lisette. "George, I wanted to ask you something."

George looked up from his *Men's Health* magazine. "Yeah?"

"What were you doing in Lisette and Edward's cabin?"

George's face went blank. Finally he said, "Oh. You mean that one time? I followed Lisette in. Not her fault. She had overheard Carrie giving Teresa the third degree about Lisette's relationship with Edward. She was upset."

"It was your job to comfort her?" Liam couldn't hide his annoyance.

George gave him a big, shit-eating grin and waggled his distinctive dark eyebrows. "I'd like it to be my job. But seriously, that relationship is doomed. All I did was offer a safety net. You know, when she gets ejected from paradise. A place to lick her wounds. I need a chef in my new home."

Liam cocked his head. "How did she react?"

"She didn't exactly jump for joy, but give her time …."

"There's more to Lisette than you might guess," Liam said.

George nodded. "I know that. If she accepted my offer, I'd be over the moon. She's special, all right. I'd be the envy of the neighborhood."

Liam laughed, wondering what it would be like to consider Beverly Hills your neighborhood. He wanted to stay mad at George, but he was a hard guy to dislike. Why shouldn't he offer himself as an alternative if Edward got cold feet? Liam hardly knew his oldest brother-in-law. Edward had been through a hell of a life change. Maybe he was too screwed up right now to handle a woman as complicated as Lisette.

"You think I'm a jerk?"

"In general," Liam said, "but not in this case. I'm worried about Lisette." George might be exactly what Lisette needed to get back on her feet if the past came crashing in. She'd never fall hard for a lightweight like George. For her, it would be nothing but a casual fling as she tried to get over Edward, her one true love. George was the one who would need to guard his heart.

Now George looked suspicious. "Why do you care? You want her for yourself?"

Liam laughed. "Nothing like that. But there's something about her that makes me wish her well." He didn't add that he felt weirdly protective of her, as if keeping her safe and happy mattered. "Does this mean you've given up on Maddie?"

Ah, he'd surprised George. Did the guy really think his crush on Maddie had gone unnoticed?

"Well, yeah," George said, reluctantly. "In fact, I'm thinking of bowing out of the movie entirely. I've had a better offer—a serious project. Best-Actor-Award-type stuff. I'll have to see if I can break the contract."

Even though they'd counted on George's casting to ensure the success of *Kapow*, Liam breathed easier. "I'll see if I can help you make a graceful exit. For the sake of family peace, I'm not sorry. Still, it might have been fun doing a movie with you, and without you, it might be a big ol' turkey."

George punched his shoulder—more like a tap with his fist—and grinned.

"There'll be other movies, bro. *Kapow's* gonna fly like an eagle. It'll be a big hit. I can feel it in my bones. *Your* hit, not mine."

By the time they'd arrived at SeaTac Airport, George had donned his wool cap and floppy mustache disguise. Shaking Liam's hand, he said, "I'm sorry about your birth mom, bro. I hope the visit with Grandma goes well."

"Thanks," Liam said. "At least we can stop wondering what happened to her. I just hope her mother isn't a basket case too."

It was a less than ten-minute drive from Yakima Air Terminal to Sheila's house. Liam had rented a car, which now seemed ridiculous. A taxi would have worked fine. The route was just as straightforward as the map suggested. Naturally the less desirable areas would be near the airport.

He arrived just before dark. The investigator had told him Sheila cleaned houses for a living and was typically home by four. He'd paved the way for Liam by telling the woman to expect a visit from a colleague bearing news of Nancy. He was also saving the police from one of their least favorite duties.

Sheila lived in a modest manufactured home that had seen better days, located on a street with little visual interest. The only landscaping was grass and a few bare trees. The neighborhood reminded Liam of the one where he and Ali had lived along with their foster parents, Emily and George. That period of their lives was a step up from what had come before, but that wasn't saying much.

He rang the doorbell and waited, rang it again. Then he knocked. After several minutes, he heard a woman's voice say, "Yes?"

"Mrs. Fitzpatrick," he called out through the door, "I'm the man the investigator told you to expect."

It took her a minute to unlock the door.

When she stuck her head out, Liam blinked several times, absorbing the reality of what he was seeing. Sheila Fitzpatrick was a light-skinned black woman. It made perfect sense. As he flashed her his warmest smile, he thought, *Carrie will freak out.*

"Young man?"

He held out his hand, and she shook it tentatively.

"Pleased to meet you, ma'am. I'm Liam Ryan."

"Ryan," she repeated. A huge smile lit up her sweet face. She was a pretty woman, despite the baggy housedress. In her early seventies, was his best guess. You could tell she must have been quite a looker in her youth.

"Mercy's sake," she said, "is it possible Nancy had a son? You've got my husband's blue-blue eyes." Liam wanted to give her a giant hug. "Come in, come in." She made a broad gesture of welcome. "I'd make us some coffee, but it's almost four thirty. How about decaf with a drop of brandy?"

"That's not necessary," Liam said.

"No trouble at all," she said. He followed her into the kitchen.

She looked so joyful that Liam dreaded even more the task ahead. She sang to herself as she bustled about. It sounded like a hymn, not that he knew many of those. She had a strong, true singing voice that he and Ali had most definitely *not* inherited.

"'His eye is on the sparrow, and I know He watches over me....'"

One of the walls was plastered with photos and drawings. As a teenager, Nancy had looked like an American Indian princess, tall and lithe. Sheila's husband was a red-haired Irishman. In their wedding photo, he stood a head taller than his bride. The polaroid was too faded for Liam to make out the color of his eyes. Nancy had inherited his stature and her mother's oval face and symmetrical features.

"Wasn't she a beauty?" Sheila beamed. "It's the Navajo blood on my mother's side." Shyly, she touched his hair. "That's where you got that beautiful head of hair." She ran a finger over the scars, and her smile vanished. "How did *this* happen."

"That's a long story," he said, wanting to keep her focused on the present. He was remembering the Navajo medicine bag his drama teacher had given him. Where was it now? "Wait ..." he began, suddenly realizing Sheila had spoken in the past tense. "You know she's dead?"

"Yes," the woman said softly. "I sensed it. But also, I'm surprised she lasted this long. She got in with a bad crowd in high school, left home at sixteen. I'd heard she changed her name to Ryan, was doing some modeling, not the respectable kind. But Ryan is such a common name. I know she wanted to pass as white and am sure she had no trouble doing that. It's clear I'm black, so she couldn't risk associating with me anymore." She sighed. "She asked me for money a few times, and I sent her what I could via Western Union. But then Conor died in a construction accident, and I had to support myself. Finally she disappeared for good. I knew she had problems with addiction, and I kept trying to find her." She shook her head mournfully. "She didn't want to be found. I had no idea she had a child."

He took her hand and gave it a squeeze. "Children. Ali and I are twins."

Sheila let loose a squeal of delight. "A daughter!" Then she shivered. "Is she all right?"

"Oh, yes," Liam reassured her. "Better than all right. Happily married, pregnant with a son. She and Joe already have identical twin daughters. My wife Teresa is also pregnant. We going to have a daughter."

Sheila looked fit to burst with happiness. "I feel as if I've died and gone to heaven!"

Liam's cell phone rang, and he saw that it was Teresa. "Sweetie, I'm talking with Sheila right now. Would you be up for an extra guest at Christmas?" He smiled at his grandmother. "I'd like to bring Mrs. Fitzpatrick home to meet everyone. She's lovely."

"Of course!" Teresa said. "How exciting. Tell her to bring as many photos as possible."

"Hang on." To Sheila, he said, "Are you free to join us for Christmas?"

She nodded vigorously. Fifty years seemed to fall away.

"She'd love to come," Liam said. "I'll have to see about a reservation for you," he told Sheila. "My flight leaves at seven. A charter plane will take us to Port Angeles."

"Port Angeles? Where's that?"

"On the Olympic Peninsula, north of Seattle. We live in Port Townsend."

After Liam made the reservation, he saw that Sheila had become more subdued.

"Do they know I'm black? You'd better warn them. Looking at you, they might guess American Indian blood, but with those blue eyes…."

"It won't matter," he said, "but if you'd like…."

She gave a curt nod. "I insist."

Ali answered immediately. "Liam?"

"I'm talking to Sheila. She's great, fantastic. You will adore her. I'm bringing her home for Christmas. She can stay with Teresa and me."

"Don't you think she'd be more comfortable here? She'll enjoy the children, and everyone will want to meet her."

"She asked me to tell you that she's black." He feared he'd relayed the information too casually, as if telling his sister their guest didn't eat meat.

Ali didn't disappoint him, responding after the briefest of pauses. "It's not as if the possibility hadn't occurred to us. I'll make sure everyone—and by 'everyone,' I mean our mother-in-law—is prepared. Tell Sheila we can't wait to meet her."

He ended the call. "Ali says everyone looks forward to meeting you." He stood and pulled Sheila into a warm hug. "I've been wanting to do that ever since I got here."

"She was a wild girl," Sheila said when he released her. "Nancy, I mean. I'm afraid she wasn't much interested in others, besides good-looking men, that is. She was too pretty for her own good, I think. She just never matured into a caring human being." She smiled again. "I can see you're nothing like her."

"Well, not now, anyway, or so I hope," Liam said uncomfortably, "and Ali is a peach. You'll adore her."

"What did you do with Nancy's body?" Sheila asked, her tone no-nonsense.

"It's in … cold storage." He saw her flinch. He didn't know how to mince words in this case. "We were waiting to hear if you're okay with cremation."

Her look told him she wasn't.

"It's all right," he went on, "we have a spot picked out in hallowed ground, not far from Forks."

Her smile returned, he noted with relief. His watch told him it was five forty-five. "We'll need to leave soon or change the airline reservation. Do you have any pets?"

"Tinsel, my sweet little tabby cat, died last month. I was afraid to replace her. Didn't want a cat to outlive me and end up a stray."

Sheila looked as if she might easily live to a hundred, but Liam was glad she hadn't rushed out to get another cat. Trying to look sufficiently sympathetic, he said, "I'm sorry about Tinsel. As soon as you pack, I'll drive us to the airport."

He glanced again at the wall. "Can you bring some of those photographs? Who did the artwork, you?" There were watercolor landscapes, sketches of horses, and a portrait in pastels that had to be Sheila as a younger woman.

"Oh, that was Nancy. She was *such* a talented artist as a girl. I wanted to pay for art classes, but she was too frivolous. Given a purpose in life, she might not have frittered it all away."

* * *

Ali and Joe had been dozing on the giant couch in front of the fire in the Log Mansion when Ali awoke to the sound of tires on gravel. The rest of the compound was asleep, but they'd wanted to stay up to greet Liam and Sheila.

She switched on the light and whispered, "Joe, honey, wake up."

"Wha—?" He opened his eyes and blinked a few times, adjusting to the light. "Are they here?"

"Either that or a burglar has breached our security."

He caressed her cheek. "Are you nervous?"

"Excited, more like it."

They put on their coats and walked to the parking area, where Sheila and Liam were chatting as if they'd known each other for years. Liam hefted a large bag from the trunk, and Ali immediately wondered if Sheila was planning to move in.

The woman surprised her with an enormous hug, and Ali's heart instantly melted. "Oh, my lands," she exclaimed, gazing about her in wide-eyed wonder. "So many lights! It's all so lovely." She clapped a hand over her mouth. "Oh, sorry. I don't want to wake anyone. Don't mind the bag. I couldn't resist bringing some of Nancy's toys I saved, though they've probably been loved to death. I promise not to overstay my welcome."

"She also brought a bunch of photos," Liam said, "and drawings. Just wait till you see them."

"I'm afraid the rest of the household is asleep," Ali said. "Liam, Teresa is in the third cabin down. I'll show Sheila to her room."

Liam kissed his new grandmother on the cheek and told her he would see her in the morning. After he left, Ali said, "We're putting you next to the twins' nursery. I hope their babbling doesn't wake you too early."

"I can't think of a nicer way to wake up," Sheila replied happily.

CHAPTER 30

———•———

At two in the afternoon, a turkey was roasting in the oven, a puzzle of Sol Duc Falls was in progress, and *Scrooge*, the 1951 version of *A Christmas Carol* starring Alastair Sim, was playing on the TV in the rec room. Teresa loved that she could laze the day away on the couch next to the seven-foot Christmas tree and let Christmas Eve unspool without her help or input. A program of song, dance, and Christmas carols was planned for after dinner. They would eat at four so that Lorenzo could fully participate. The "talent" had set aside several hours yesterday and this morning to rehearse in Joe's studio. Normally Teresa would play the piano, but her advanced pregnancy had given her an out. She hadn't practiced for several days. There would be time for that after the baby was born.

Even though she could have summoned enough energy to accompany a few pieces, Teresa had felt tired lately, mildly depressed over her poor judgment with regard to Xenia and the feelings of regret Kilo's bitter departure had engendered. And yet, she had so many reasons to rejoice. This morning, Liam had bubbled over as he related the details of his trip—from George's decision to turn down the role in *Kapow* to the pleasure he took in his newly discovered grandmother's company. All the hustle and bustle of the evening's preparations and Lorenzo's excitement were welcome distractions. After hearing Edward narrate the first chapter of *Alice's Adventures in Wonderland*, Lor ran around the house driving them nuts with his recitation of "How doth the little crocodile," fully memorized.

Edward plopped down on the couch next to Teresa with an "Oof!" and gave her a long, assessing look. "You okay, Ter-Ter? You seem a little down."

"I might try to take a little snooze before dinner," she said. "All this activity is exhausting. Where's Lisette?"

"She's over at the Log Mansion with Ali, Joe, and the twins—Liam, Sheila, and Becca. Sheila is showing them photographs and Nancy's artwork and Ali and Liam are catching her up on the lost years."

Edward looked down at Chiara, Jake, and Lorenzo, who were working on the puzzle. "Is anyone watching the movie?"

"I am. Sort of. I've seen it so many times, I could recite the lines along with the actors. We watched it every Christmas when we were growing up, remember?"

"Sure," he said with a smile. "What's up next, *It's a Wonderful Life*?"

Teresa shrugged. "Why not? If I doze off, go ahead and pop in the video." They watched in silence until Mr. Fezzywig's Christmas ball.

Edward said, "I missed the action this morning because Lisette and I went Christmas shopping. How is Carrie handling things?"

Teresa laughed. "Oh, you mean the fact that so far all but one of her grandchildren are or will be mixed race? Surprisingly well. It has to be a major adjustment, but she's putting up a good front. Liam says George believes she and Rostand are a couple."

"No, really?" He grinned. "How do we get them to go public?"

"I'll leave that up to you."

"All in good time," Edward said. "Where are Duncan and Laurie?"

"Christmas shopping, separately from Carrie and Rostand. Is Jean-Louis still in the kitchen? I'm surprised he rejected our offer of help. Joe had Tiger lined up."

"He insists he doesn't want any help," Edward said. "As energetic as that guy is, I think he's secretly an introvert and needs alone-time to regenerate."

Teresa gave him the hairy eyeball. "If anyone is an extrovert, it's Jean-Louis."

"You may be skeptical, but there are different degrees of extroversion and introversion. No one is purely one or the other. You know, the Myers and Briggs thing."

She laughed. "Whatever you say."

Lorenzo came over and climbed up on the couch next to Edward. "Uncle Eddy, could you read some more *Alice*?" he pleaded.

"As soon as the movie is over," he said.

Seeing Teresa struggle to rise, Edward helped her up.

"I'm off for a nap. No need to finish the movie for my sake."

* * *

Lisette basked in the warmth of the little group that had gathered in the living room of the Log Palace, the gas fire blazing merrily. Ali explained that they'd just added two new recliners, a glass-topped coffee table, and a loveseat. Now all that was needed to lessen the echo in the cavernous room was something on the walls. Lisette could picture long tapestries of moss-covered trees and craggy, snow-capped mountain ranges.

She sat riveted as Ali related the story of her and Liam's upbringing, followed by Ali and Joe's meeting in the woods and the gap between that meeting and their unlikely romance. If only her own story could end so happily. Sheila had a wonderfully expressive face and seemed to cry in one breath and laugh in the next. The old photographs revealed Liam and Ali's birth mother as the spitting image of Ali—a willowy woman with long, straight black hair and classic features. It was so sad that drugs had made her lose her children and then utterly consumed her. And yet, somehow, Ali and Liam had matured into the strong, compassionate adults they were today.

The cozy session ended when Ali became visibly tired. Lisette went back to the cabin, intending to sneak in a workout. She was debating exercise versus a nap when Edward came in and decided the issue for her. Sitting next to her on the bed, he lifted her braid to his lips then wrapped it around his hand and pulled her in close for a kiss. Soon he was nuzzling her neck and unbuttoning her cardigan. She closed her eyes and gave in to the delicious rush of heat. "I was going to work out," she protested weakly.

"This is a kind of workout," he argued, giving up on the buttons and pulling the sweater over her head.

She laughed and surrendered to the moment. They undressed each other as she wriggled out of her jeans. "This is nice," he said, appreciating her lacey hot-pink bra and pantie set. "Maybe you can put on some thigh-high stockings for me."

"I don't think we have time for that," she said with a laugh, sliding her hand down his long erection. "This situation seems to require some urgency."

"Don't mind my impatient friend."

"I have an impatient friend too," she cooed, rolling him onto his back and grinding her pelvis against him.

"You convinced me." He deftly reversed their positions. "Can I rip these off?" He pulled at the elastic on her panties.

"No," she said, helpless with laughter. "You'll hurt yourself." She took them off.

"What about this?" He pulled on her bra strap, as if testing its strength.

"If you want to rip off my clothing, let me choose something more fragile and a lot less expensive," she said, but he was already unhooking her bra.

She wrapped her legs around him as he slid into her with a low moan of pleasure. "Like liquid silk," he whispered. Then he stopped talking and lost himself in her, and she in him. Their hands roamed each other's bodies as if memorizing every dip and curve. Then her climax rushed up to meet her.

Afterward, Edward continued to nuzzle her neck and rub his body against hers, his warm, sweet breath bathing her neck. "I love you," he said in a low, husky voice.

She held her breath, unsure if she'd heard right. *He's just caught up in the moment*, she told herself. What if she declared her love, and circumstances forced her to leave tomorrow? But he fixed her with his hot gaze, his long-lashed bedroom eyes scorching her, and the words came out unbidden.

"I love you too," she whispered.

CHAPTER 31

WITH TWENTY-TWO GUESTS, DINNER WAS held in the Log Mansion dining room, all three leaves completing the custom-made Amish trestle table. Even then, it was a tight fit. Ali knew she was supposed to leave everything to the others, but she couldn't help but worry. Joe had offered Steve and Angie, their usual kitchen crew, double their already generous wages. It had been such a smart move to buy the relatively modest house down the road and turn it into a dormitory for staff. Now whoever was working the parties could simply walk home when their work was done. Steve and Angie were the only permanent residents. They would be going to college next fall, but that was eons away. May Allen and her sister Susan ate separately in the kitchen of the Sea Captain's House as they watched the twins, while Lorenzo dined with the adults.

Jean-Louis had reluctantly agreed to prepare commercially bred turkeys—three in all, there being an extra oven in the utility kitchen. Too many skinny wild turkeys would be needed to feed the hordes. He'd included all the traditional—to him, boring—trappings. Oyster and sage stuffing, asparagus with Hollandaise sauce, mashed sweet potatoes, gravy, cranberry sauce, and homemade dinner rolls. The meal was served buffet style.

Ali felt like a mother hen with all her chicks gathered round. Was this what motherhood did to you, turn you into everyone's mother? She hoped not. She didn't want that responsibility. The boy she was carrying—they were going to name him Brian, after Joe's father—was doing a jig, as if desperate to participate.

Teresa, seated next to her, laid a hand on her shoulder. "How are you doing?" She'd had to speak up to be heard above the loud conversations that were, as usual, dominated by Jean-Louis and Laurie. Jean-Louis was pontificating in a wine-amplified voice to Lisette about the difference between wild and domesticated turkeys, and Laurie was grilling Jake and David about the latest twists and turns in the road to *Kapow*, the movie.

"I'm doing well," Ali told Teresa. "I'm so relieved that George lost interest in *Kapow*."

"No kidding," Teresa said. "The question is, did he lose interest in the movie or Maddie? I thought he was so obsessed with her that he'd have taken just about any role."

"Don't forget," Ali said, "he was the one who convinced them to expand the Troy Benz part. That might make the part more attractive to another A-list actor. Anyhow, it's one less thing for Maddie and David to worry about."

"Until they replace him with Tom Cruise," Teresa said, taking a large bite of turkey and chewing with her eyes blissfully closed. "Yum. This doesn't even taste like turkey. How does he do that? Must be some secret ingredient in the gravy. But back to the movie …. There's still Kilo. He had the gall to come by my office to say goodbye. And get this … he told me he *loves* Maddie."

Ali was taken aback. "Oh no. Have you told David?"

They gazed furtively around them, but no one was paying attention to their low-key conversation.

"Leave it up to fate," Teresa said. "Whatever happens, Maddie's done with Kilo. At least she won't be fending off *both* him and George."

"Good point."

Becca came over and took the seat next to Ali. It had been occupied by Rostand, but the man had taken off soon into the meal, ostensibly to supervise the kitchen help. Ali figured he was desperate for any excuse to leave the table early.

"What's with Rostand?" Becca immediately asked. Something in Teresa's face made her say, "Spill, girl."

"Let's just say, I believe he's become very, uh, *special* to my mom," Teresa said in a low voice.

Ali couldn't believe her ears. Or had she known all along? It made perfect sense. Was Rostand Carrie's boy toy or something more serious? It wasn't cool to have an affair with your servant. "I think that's a conversation for another time," she said, afraid that Carrie would overhear.

Jean-Louis's laughter culminated in a giant guffaw, and Becca shuddered a little.

"Becca?" Ali asked. "Everything okay?"

"I admit I don't like it when he gets like this, but it's part of the deal. I thought *my* family was outrageous. He's used to letting loose at the holidays."

"There's no one here who minds," Teresa said.

Becca blew out a sigh. "I know. Don't look so concerned. We're fine, really. He gets a little too, uh, spirited in public sometimes. No biggie." She pointed her chin at Jeremy, seated next to Matthew. "*That* must make Maddie happy."

"Yeah," Teresa said, "Jeremy's moved in with Matthew, at least till the end of February, when *Arsenic and Old Lace* closes. But the biggest news is that he's going to play Folker Persson in the movie. They don't need him until March. "

"Oh my God!" Becca said.

"After George bowed out, David met with the director to float some ideas for other changes."

Becca brightened. "George bowed out? That simplifies things!"

"A better part came along," Teresa explained.

Becca tapped her cheek. "Wasn't the original plan to make Troy black? What about Eddie Murphy?"

"He turned it down," Teresa said. "They're talking to that dreamy R&B singer, Rosey Cleveland."

"Oh man! He is *so* charismatic. That would be wild."

Cheeks ruddy, Jean-Louis rose, arms spread, with a magician's fanfare. All he needed was a cape. "*Attention*! Please make your way to the Sea Captain's Parlor for our evening's entertainment, which will be followed by plum pudding and a selection of dessert wines."

It was a cold, crisp night with almost no wind, so they didn't require coats for the short walk between the houses. The Sea Captain's parlor had been arranged with all the seating on the perimeter of the room, forming a theater in the round. It was a small stage, but Ali's understanding was that there would never be more than a few performers at a time.

The program opened with Lorenzo's interpretive dance, inspired by the Christmas chapter in *Salish Sea Stories*. His costume consisted of three aprons, each decorated with sketches of characters from Ali's Salish Sea collection: Sammy the Sea Star, Duncan the Dungeness Crab, and Silas the Spotted Ratfish. "The three of us dedicate this performance to Oxana Octopus," he piped up. "Aunt Maddie is setting the scene." Maddie circled Lorenzo with a string of white lights. "I would like to introduce Aunt Maddie in the role of Polly Plankton. She is bio-lumin-escent," he explained, his demeanor hilariously serious. With his bright red hair and long face, you could almost imagine David at his age.

"Don't look at me," Maddie explained quickly, shielding her eyes with her hands and tiptoeing off to the side. "I'm invisible. I'm the stage hand and costume mistress. The lights represent Polly."

Lorenzo began the dance in his Duncan the Crab apron, zigzagging in a jerky motion from one side to the other, arms extended, opening and closing his index finger and thumb, like pincers. He then raised his arms, and Maddie helped him exchange the crab apron for the sea star. Lorenzo tiptoed about in dainty movements, waving his arms around. Ali, fighting tears of laughter, was glad he was wearing the apron, because otherwise no one would have guessed he was a sea star. Lorenzo last role was as Silas the Spotted Ratfish, twirling about until he lost his balance and fell on the floor. The unchoreographed fall didn't seem to faze him. He quickly hopped to his feet and struck a pose. The audience oohed and aahed, their eyes bulging and faces reddening as they tried not to lose all semblance of control. No one knew how Lor would react to laughter, since he clearly took this performance so seriously.

"And now," he said grandly, "the three of us—Duncan, Silas, and Sammy—have composed a special song for Oxana." He cleared his throat as if ready to hawk up a hairball and signaled to Matthew at the piano. Matthew played a zippy introduction, but when Lor began to sing, he appeared to be improvising. It wasn't clear if the boy could carry a tune. Or maybe it was just a really elaborate melody using the twelve-tone scale. Ali could see that he probably hadn't inherited the O'Connell music genes, but he might have a future in comedy. She wiped her eyes, reaching for another tissue.

> We love you, 'Xana! Leggy girl,
> For you we sway and dip and whirl.
> You are all heart, three hearts in fact,
> Eight brains, and that is truth exact.
> Oxana dear, our wisest mama,
> Without you there would be no drama.

When he finally folded at the waist in a classic bow, one stiff arm in front, the other in back, the audience erupted in thunderous applause, but also raucous laughter. Lorenzo took it well, never assuming they were mocking him—which, of course, they really weren't. Perhaps he'd meant to be funny. After several more bows, he ran to Chiara and gave her an enormous hug, then followed that up by doing the same for Maddie. Finally he jumped into his father's lap, ears perked, ready to be entertained.

Becca was close to hysterical. "Oh my God," she said, "that kid's a tough act to follow. I hope no one has a comedy sketch planned. It doesn't get any funnier than that."

Chiara came over and took the chair next to Ali.

"Did he really write that himself?" Ali asked.

Chiara gave her a broad wink. "Let's just say it was a collaboration."

"I can't wait to illustrate that."

Matthew continued to accompany them as David and Edward did a goofy bass-baritone version of "White Christmas," trading lines back and forth. As one sang, the other performed some basic dance steps, along with a few shimmies. Maddie opted for serious as she sang a moving version of "What Are You Doing New Year's Eve?" directly to David. The performance that surprised Ali the most was Lisette's plaintively sung, "Have Yourself a Merry Little Christmas." Her voice wasn't as strong as Maddie's, and it was breathier, but if Lisette had wanted a career as a popular singer, Ali believed she could have succeeded. Jeremy and Maddie brought down the house with a heart-stopping duet of "Oh Holy Night," accompanied by Joe on the guitar.

The final number was Joe singing one of his songs that his manager Linc believed would be nominated for a Grammy, "Love's Death Rattle." He played guitar and Matthew bass, with Jeremy on drums. The chorus went,

> I was crazy with lust,
> damned sick of the battle,
> Now the thing is a bust,
> It's just love's death rattle.

The rest of the lyrics involved all the crazy antics of this woman, so off the wall they bordered on absurd—that's what made the song so funny. With the addition of some impressive guitar riffs and a catchy bridge, she could understand why it was such a hit. She suspected the lyrics had been inspired by Joe's on-again off-again affair with fellow country star Rina Bakersfield, but Ali was done worrying about other women. Joe had never given her cause for jealousy and went to great lengths to let her know how much she was loved and valued.

Joe passed out caroling booklets, and for another hour, they sang Christmas carols, including all the unfamiliar weird verses. Lorenzo had fallen asleep in David's arms. "I don't think plum pudding is his thing anyway," he told the group as he and Maddie took him off to bed. "Save us some, though. We'll be back soon."

Joe came over and kissed the top of Ali's head, then her belly, and she too began to long for her bed. Everyone apparently felt the same, for the party broke up soon after. She couldn't recall a more contented gathering of happy couples.

CHAPTER 32

LISETTE PEERED FROM BEHIND THE curtains of the cabin at the thick blanket of snow that covered the compound. Lorenzo would be delighted. The rest of them, not so much. Maybe it would melt by dinnertime so they could all reconvene for turkey leftovers. Jake and Chiara were staying at the compound, and Liam would have no trouble transporting the non-resident family members unless the streets iced over.

Edward ran his warm hand down her bare back, startling her.

"Oh!" She gave him a quick kiss. "I didn't know you were awake."

He looked out the window. "A white Christmas. David and I must have summoned it. It's Irving Berlin's revenge for butchering his masterpiece."

"You didn't butcher it. It was fun. And I think the snow is beautiful. After breakfast, we can all make snow people. Lorenzo would love that." She looked at the wall clock, which read ten after eight. "What time are we expected for breakfast?"

He went back to the bed and propped himself up on the pillows. They'd both been tipsy when they came in the night before and had thrown themselves into a sloppy bout of lovemaking no less satisfying than the sober kind. "I'm guessing Lorenzo is already opening presents. Kids can never sleep in on Christmas morning, and the rest of us decided that our own gift giving would be private. Speaking of which …." He pulled out the bottom drawer of the nightstand and reached for a small package.

Lisette held her breath, worrying it might be a ring; instead, it was a pair of emerald earrings that must have cost the earth. She gasped. "It's too much."

He pretended to pout. "You don't like them?"

"It's not that. They're exquisite. It's just that … I got you socks."

He started to laugh, and she smiled too.

"Not socks, actually, but sock puppets. I thought they would enhance your popularity with Lorenzo." She pulled a box out from under the bed. "I've only made two so far—Alice and the White Rabbit."

"When did you have time for this?" he marveled, examining the yarn details of Alice's hair, the rabbit's little silk waistcoat and felt ears.

"I have Ali to thank for that. She had all the art supplies on hand, and yesterday, when she and Sheila were telling their stories, I worked while I listened." She gave them a critical once-over. "They don't look finished. Do you mind if I keep working on them?"

Half-assed, she thought, *like all your so-called creative endeavors*.

"They're minimalist," he said. "I love them." He put a puppet on each hand and said in the White Rabbit's voice, "Oh, my ears and whiskers!" and in Alice's, "Curiouser and curiouser!"

She laughed and pulled out another box. "Liam said you'd like them."

That box contained three knives with no handles. "Throwing-knives!" he said with obvious delight. "Jake has a target at his house too. I can't wait to try." He examined one of them more closely. "It's engraved." He read the inscription aloud, "XOXO, Lisette." She'd carefully avoided the word "love," which hadn't yet been spoken when they'd visited the jewelers to have the knives engraved. She still thought she'd done the right thing.

She picked up the earrings and jiggled them in the light so that they flashed. "You know I can't wear these in front of your family." *Maybe never*, she added silently. "You really shouldn't have. They're too expensive."

"Put them on," he urged. "You can wear them when we go out on the town."

"Seriously? In Port Townsend?" But she was already putting them on.

"You look … amazing," he whispered before moving in for a kiss.

Lisette couldn't recall another day like this one, imbued as it was in dreamlike perfection. Lorenzo was camped under the Christmas tree in the Sea Captain's House's parlor when they wandered in at around ten and helped themselves to lattes, bacon, and coffee cake. Then everyone bundled up and headed for the area next to the safari tent to make snowmen—or rather, snow dogs—the real dogs running happily among them as if to provide inspiration and supervision. Lunch was turkey sandwiches, then they worked on the puzzle as the video of *The Shop Around the Corner* played, followed by *A*

Christmas Story and another dramatic reading from *Alice's Adventures in Wonderland.*

By dinnertime, the streets were clear, and the same crowd gathered for leftovers—skipping the formal setting for plates on laps in the Sea Captain's parlor and kitchen. After dinner they dispersed, some reading, some lingering over tea, but most retiring to their rooms or cabins.

Edward asked her to put on her earrings as soon as they returned to their cabin, and she laughingly agreed, thinking, *What if this is the only chance I have to wear them?*

Nonsense, she reassured herself.

Then she thought, *Surely happiness like this can't last.*

The day after Christmas, Lisette loaded her overnight bag into the back of her Miata and headed toward the restaurant. After so much socializing, she looked forward to a morning on her own. She could listen to her messages and do her laundry and still be back at the compound by lunchtime. Edward, his brothers, and Liam had left early to spend the day snowshoeing on Hurricane Ridge, and although the outing sounded like fun, she didn't want to crash the otherwise all-male party.

The snow had mostly melted, and brilliant sunlight bathed the streets. It was Sunday, so hardly anyone was about, and a rare feeling of peace stole over her. Was it time to move on from the claustrophobic lifestyle of the restaurant business? She thought of *Kapow* and all the locations the actors would visit. All she knew other than Cape May, New York, and the Peninsula was Paris. How wonderful it would be to travel with Edward to exotic locales like Bangkok. Why stop there? Egypt, Africa, go on safari, swim with the dolphins. Do a wine tour of Tuscany. There was a whole world out there she wanted to experience with Edward.

She pushed "play" on the café's answering machine. A few people enquired about reservations, even though the outgoing message clearly stated that Café Lisette was closed until Tuesday, January fourth. Then she heard a man say, "Lisette, it's Reynard." Why did that voice fill her with dread? Because she heard the sympathy in it. Her legs wobbled, and she had to sit down. "I wanted to tell you that I'm sorry. I should not have brought Xenia to the O'Connells. I assure you I was not the one to divulge your secrets. Although I suppose I am partially responsible. Despite everything, I wish you well."

She couldn't move, though every instinct told her to flee. Flee from what and to where? If only she could jump down a hole, like Alice, and escape into an imaginary world.

That was when she noticed the package—the one with no return address, just a PO box. This couldn't be good. Inside, she found a pair of boxer briefs and a note. "I think Edward may be missing these. Tell him thanks for me?" It was signed with only an X. X, as in Xenia. She recalled Edward's story of the snowy night he'd been stranded at the compound. He hadn't mentioned Xenia taking his underwear. Why not? Had he had sex with her that night? She was certainly a beautiful woman, a *young* woman, a temptation to any man with working parts. How well did she really know Edward? They'd met a scant month ago.

She turned on her computer to check her email. Sure enough, Marky had sent a link to the website of a gossip magazine she'd seen sold in grocery stores, *Latest Greatest*. His note read, "Hate to be the bearer of bad news. I doubt this will affect our business, but I thought you should be aware of it. There are different versions in other tabloids and country music gossip magazines, but this was the first to break. Call me if you want to talk. It's not like this includes anything you haven't told me already. It's a shame someone felt the need to dredge it up now and put the worst possible spin on it."

With a sinking heart, Lisette opened the link. The headline read THE HOT PRIEST AND THE DOCTOR'S DOXY.

> Country music idol Joe Bob Blade, whose touring career has been sidelined by fatherhood and vocal issues, has a new family scandal to contend with.
>
> Joe's given name is Joe O'Connell. He and his wife Ali have built a family compound just outside the quaint Victorian town of Port Townsend, Washington. Joe's brothers Jake and David and their wives now reside in town as well. Ditto their sister Teresa, married to Liam Ryan, no stranger to scandal himself. Liam's star may eclipse his brother-in-law's once his brother Jake's bestselling thriller *Kapow* hits the big screen. The movie also stars David's wife, Madeleine Leftwood, who recently made a splash as an ill-fated sex kitten in *Insanity*.
>
> And now… ta da! The juiciest scandal yet: Joe's oldest brother Edward has left the Catholic priesthood and shacked up with the former Leslie Guzinski, a gorgeous femme fatale who made her own splash in the tabloids ten years back. The dishy ex-priest is handsome

enough to have inspired Father Ralph de Bricassart in *The Thorn Birds*—the 1977 best-selling novel by Colleen McCullough. No one knows why Edward left the Church, but rumors abound. Some kind of impropriety involving sex or money, no doubt. The black-haired, green-eyed beauty Leslie Guzinski reinvented herself as Lisette Manegold, owner and manager of Café Lisette in Port Townsend. Lisette found notoriety in 1990 as the mistress of plastic surgeon Dr. Walfred Dahlstrom, whose clients were among the crème de la crème of New York society. The famous doctor plucked young Leslie out of the aspiring actor/model staff of the catering company Caviar Tastes for his own private amusement.

Now the kicker: Dr. Dahlstrom was accused of hiring a hitman to kill his equally famous heart surgeon wife, Dr. Esme Dahlstrom. Dahlstrom allegedly wanted his wife dead to clear the way for Leslie.

To be fair, no evidence linked Leslie to the scheme, which was nipped in the bud by an undercover police officer. Dahlstrom himself was acquitted after evidence surfaced that the hit was ordered by a jealous colleague. However, the formerly penniless Leslie Guzinski had socked away enough moolah to finance the most expensive chef's training program in the world: Le Cordon Bleu in Paris. After she legally changed her name to Lisette Manegold, the transformation was complete.

Still a tall drink of water in her early thirties, the lovely Lisette might tempt any man to risk his reputation, and now she's nabbed herself a fallen priest whose wealth equals if not exceeds Dr. Dahlstrom's. Edward O'Connell might even be the best-looking of a truly eye-popping group of siblings.

Lisette's former lovers include acclaimed film composer Reynard Silvestre and Kilo Mahelona, the star of *Hawaiian Eye*, a reboot of early '60s TV show. Will the hot priest and the doctor's doxy stay together? Don't count on it. The last thing the lofty O'Connells of Seattle need is more negative publicity.

As a sidenote, fans have been anxiously awaiting Joe Bob Blade's next album. The time is ripe for a comeback. Covers of Joe's songs recorded by Billy Bob Camden ("Love's Death Rattle") and Tootie Belle Sweeten ("Last Gasp Romance") have been big hits, and one or both are expected to receive Grammy nominations for

Best Country Song. Their success has renewed interest in Joe, whose devastating everyman handsomeness still sets hearts aflutter.

Here's hoping this latest scandal doesn't prove too much of a distraction.

CHAPTER 33

Lisette thought of the opening of *Alice in Wonderland*. "Down, down, down. Would the fall *never* come to an end?"

The article was accompanied by several photos, two dating back to when the original scandal had broken. In the first, Leslie/Lisette, looking impossibly young and dewy, was trying and failing to shield her face. In another she was dressed in her catering tux, a photo originally taken by Caviar Tastes for an advertising pamphlet to show they also hired women. *As few as they could get away with,* she thought wryly. Walfred's professional headshot. A photo of Edward in liturgical garments. Her stomach lurched as the reality of his life change hit home. A shot of Liam and Teresa walking down Water Street. A staged photo of Joe, Ali, and the infant twins that had run in *People* magazine.

When had Reynard uncovered her past? After she left? Clearly, he'd told Xenia all about it. Or had George alerted the tabloids? She didn't think so. He was basically a good guy. Hounded by the paparazzi himself, he wouldn't sic them on his worst enemy.

She'd been wrong to believe she could fit in with such a respectable family. Edward would swear up and down that he didn't care, but hadn't he come to Port Townsend seeking refuge? Instead she'd landed him in the lion's den. Fortunately she had her overnight bag with her, and the earrings still sat on her nightstand at the cabin. Nothing to stop her from leaving. She'd get in her car and keep on driving.

She called Marky, who answered right away. "Damn, Lisette, I'm so sorry. Hey, I've been thinking… your customers won't care. And it'll blow over. You know, today's news wraps tomorrow's fish, or news and fish stink after three days. Something like that."

You couldn't find a nicer guy than Marky. They'd been through so much together. Still, no one who hadn't survived something similar could possibly understand the despair and anguish Lisette had endured during those terrible months after Walfred was arrested. The endless questioning by investigators and the siege of reporters. Whenever she crossed the street, she hadn't much cared if she made it to the other side. She had never felt so alone. In her zeal to sock money away, she hadn't taken the time to cultivate close friendships with anyone other than Kilo. He had been her rock. Hard to believe he had joined the Dark Side.

"To be honest," she told Marky, "I'm too upset to think long term. All I know is that I need to leave the Peninsula *now*. I feel cornered here. I can either close up for a month and cover your wages or you and the crew can keep the café open and see what happens. Your call."

"Shit, Lisette, that Edward guy is crazy about you. Don't leave without talking to him."

"I can't, Marky. Not right now. His entire family is in town. It's too humiliating." She tried to sound neutral, but she couldn't hide the distress in her voice.

"Okay, sweetie, don't worry about the café. I'll keep it open. Sid's wife has been doing a good job managing the day-to-day stuff. Let's wait and see. There might be zero impact on business. The publicity might even attract new customers."

Lisette wanted to scream. "I can do without that kind of customer," she said. "I've had enough of feeling like a freak show to last a lifetime. I should have known not to hang out with people who live in the spotlight. I was just begging to be exposed."

"Nah," Marky said. "If you take a step back, you'll see it differently. Stay in touch. You gonna ditch your cell phone?"

She hadn't thought that far ahead. "I'll have to change my number. I'll call you with the new one."

After she ended the call, Lisette retrieved her laundry and packed her carry-on bag with essential clothing and a stash of cash she kept on hand. As she drove toward Hood Canal Bridge, she debated where to catch the ferry—Kingston or Bainbridge Island. Where the hell was she going? When she got to the turnoff, she followed an impulse and went left toward Kingston. From Edmonds, it was a faster drive north on I5 to Bellingham, a city where no one would think to look for her. She would need to change her name again. Was she really going with Louisa? How about Louise? Neither name appealed. Maybe having a plain name would inspire her to be less reckless. Not a hooker's name. Louise Smith. Perfect. There had to be a million of them. She told herself she was doing this for Edward, who didn't understand what a jinx she was. But deep down, she knew she was a coward. Exposed like this, she couldn't face him or his family. She was a fraud, her carefully constructed persona of sophisticated businesswoman ripped away to reveal a common opportunist who lived by her wits.

She thought of her parents, whom she'd last spoken to on Christmas Day for all of ten minutes. True to form, they were hard at work and didn't have much time to chat. They had urged her, as they always did, to make a trip East when she could. They were proud of her success as a restaurateur. She wondered how they would react to this latest debacle. She never discussed the men in her life.

Facing an hour's wait for the ferry at Kingston, she used the payphone to call her mother at the restaurant. She needed a decent connection, and cell service here was still too spotty.

"Leslie, are you all right?"

Her mother sounded panicked. Of course she would think it strange that she was calling so soon after one of their infrequent phone calls.

"Mom ...." A sob escaped.

"Leslie ... sweetie .... Tell me what happened."

And Leslie, now Lisette, soon to be Louise, told her. The whole sordid story, starting with Reynard. Aware that she was making a spectacle of herself, she struggled for control. Her voice grew steadier, though tears still rolled down her cheeks.

Against all expectations, her mother remained calm and sympathetic. "Oh, honey. You've worked so hard to put all that behind you. Why don't you come home? You can stay with us for a while, help out at the restaurant if you want to stay busy or make some extra money."

"That's a nice offer, Mom. I'll definitely consider it. I'm doing fine financially—for now, at least. Until I figure out what comes next, I'd like to relocate someplace not too far away."

"Why don't you try Yakima? Do you remember my mentioning an uncle who the family disowned when he married a black woman?"

Lisette's tears dried and she sat up straighter. "Great-Uncle Conor."

"He and his wife settled in Yakima. It's in Eastern Washington—not quite so wet. He liked it there. Unfortunately, he died in a construction accident."

Conor Fitzgerald. Her mother's maiden name was Fitzgerald. When

Edward had told her that Liam and Ali's grandmother was named Sheila Fitzgerald, she'd thought nothing of it. Her mother hadn't spoken of Conor in years. Fitzgerald was such a common name. Lisette hadn't known where Conor had gone after his family stopped talking to him. That meant Liam, Ali, and she were related, though distantly. What a weird coincidence. How she longed to call Teresa or Ali and let them know. But of course she couldn't.

As she sat in a booth on the ferry, staring morosely out to sea, she heard her name called out. Startled, she pivoted, primed for a confrontation. But it was only Becca, arm in arm with Jean-Louis, looking calm and normal. Of course. They didn't understand that her world had ended. Maybe no one in their tightknit group knew about the tabloid stories yet. *Good*, she had a head start. The men wouldn't be home till after dark. Who had alerted Marky to the article? She should have asked. He didn't normally read those gossip rags, did he? She guessed a reporter had tried to reach her at the restaurant and talked to Marky instead.

Becca slid in next to her. "I'm surprised to see you here." Not getting an answer fast enough, she asked, "Lisette, what's up? You seem upset."

Her lips trembled, and her eyes stung. She saw no reason not to share the sorry story with Becca and Jean-Louis. Close as they were to the O'Connells, they weren't related by blood. She took the crumpled printout from her purse and handed it silently to Becca.

Becca uttered a disgusted "Hmph" and passed the story on to Jean-Louis.

"Listen, Lisette, the O'Connells are *so* over this type of thing. It won't faze 'em."

With an outraged *Pfft*, Jean-Louis said, "I agree. There is no reason to run."

"You don't get it: I could only be Lisette as long as she wasn't associated with Leslie. Back then, everyone believed I wanted Walfred's wife dead. That's what they'll believe now too. At the very least, I'm a person who got by because of sex and her wits, not her talent."

"*Ben voyons donc,*" Jean-Louis exclaimed. "That's ridiculous. But let's not argue. The important question now is, where will you go?"

"I don't know. Bellingham, I thought. Or maybe I'll fly south for the rest of the winter. Phoenix or Tucson."

"Can you afford that?" Becca asked.

"Yes. Contrary to popular belief, I don't need Edward's money."

"Damn." Becca scrunched up her nose in disgust. "Neither does Ali. Who even *wants* that much money? It's bound to turn you into a monster.

Jean-Louis and I prefer to put our money into more restaurants rather than enjoy it."

"*Becca…*" Jean-Louis growled.

Becca brightened. "Baby, didn't you just tell me you were short a cook?"

Jean-Louis nodded vigorously. "We are short a sous-chef in Bellevue, and you could occasionally fill in for our *chef de cuisine* in Bellevue or North Bend once you familiarize yourself with the menu."

Lisette sniffed back tears. "You're both so kind. I'm not sure I want to work that hard. I need to think and plan. Maybe I don't even want to stay in the business."

"*C'est de valeur*," Jean-Louis said. "So much talent, wasted."

"Story of my life," Lisette quipped, instantly regretting her flippant tone.

Becca ignored the remark. "At the very least, come stay at our house in North Bend. We have lots of room, and North Bend has an ambiance similar to the Peninsula—you know, mossy trees, mountain views, natural beauty. A lot more rain, unfortunately. But what's a little rain? You shouldn't be alone."

It was on the tip of her tongue to turn them down, but … the offer felt like a life line. "You all are too nice. I feel bad accepting your generosity."

"*Ben là*," Jean-Louis protested. "You jest! Becca is in sore need of a shopping companion."

"In all seriousness, I don't have any real friends in North Bend," Becca said. "I'd welcome having another city girl around."

"All right. I accept. But only if you promise not to tell Edward or any of the O'Connells where I am."

"They are about to be fully occupied with childbirth," Becca said. "Edward—I'm sure you realize—will be frantic."

Lisette averted her eyes. "Edward is better off without me."

Becca, though unconvinced, said, "No blabbing. Cross my heart." She did just that. "Right, Jean-Louis?"

He gave a broad "what can you do?" shrug.

"Thank you, then. Just until I get on my feet."

* * *

Edward had resisted the invitation to go snowshoeing on Hurricane Ridge with the guys. In the middle of the night, he'd had a sinking feeling he couldn't shake. When he woke up to the alarm, Lisette looked so vulnerable and beautiful in the dawn light—her glossy black hair spilling across the pillow and sooty lashes contrasting so nicely with the cream of her smooth cheeks—that he almost decided not to go. But she had her own business to attend to, and his brothers wanted his company. Staying behind would make him look paranoid and possessive.

And now, high in the mountains—the fresh powder crunching beneath his feet and covering the evergreens and mountains in glistening drifts, the bracing freshness of the air, the peaceful silence—he was reminded why his family was so attached to this part of the country. He almost managed to put aside his earlier dread. But then Liam pulled him aside and said, "Something's up with Lisette." *Ah,* he'd forgotten that for some reason his brother-in-law was also mysteriously in tune with Lisette. They were about halfway along their route, so there was no point in turning back. Not wanting to share the burden of their anxiety, they kept their worries from the others.

When they reached the end of the road and the entrance to Port Angeles, Joe was able to get cell service. As he listened to his messages, his expression grew grim. "My agent Linc left me a message," he told them. "On Christmas Eve, a series of articles came out online about Edward's relationship with Lisette and the scandal with Dr. Dahlstrom. The longest one was especially nasty. He read me the juicier bits before the message timed out." Seeing that neither Liam nor Edward appeared surprised, he said, "You two knew something was up?"

"At least her life isn't in danger," Liam said. "But Edward, don't be surprised if she's gone by the time we return."

Suffocating in a cloud of dread, Edward immediately tried her cell phone, which went straight to voicemail. "Lisette? Please, sweetie, call me. Whatever's happened, we can face it together. I love you."

When he hung up, the others—except for Liam at the wheel—were staring at him.

"What?"

"You've only known her a month," David said.

Edward was having none of it. "You wanted to marry Maddie from the first moment you saw her," he told David. "And Jake, tell me the one about how you didn't know right away that Chiara was the love of your life. It took Joe only a few days to fall so hard for Ali that he moved heaven and earth to find her again. And last but not least, Liam. Confess … you knew Teresa was the one when you were still in Israel."

Liam was the first to speak again. "Give her time, Edward. She loves you too. Obviously she's important to this family, or I wouldn't have this weird connection to her. But heading off on a wild goose chase is going to end with your goose getting cooked."

"If Jean-Louis is the chef, anyway," Jake said in a lame attempt at humor. "You know, wild goose…. Never mind."

Edward knew he was right. No point in embarking on a search with no leads. But he couldn't help but think that if she really was gone forever, his goose was definitely cooked. He could see no future without her.

CHAPTER 34

BACK IN THE VICTORIAN MANSION that was their home, Jake held Chiara in his arms as they reclined on the parlor couch, enjoying the crackling fire.

"Jean-Louis says he can accommodate us for Valentine's Day." He kissed the top of Chiara's head. His own happiness weighed him down. Edward must dread February 14th. Ali, Joe, Teresa, and Liam were still in Seattle. As predicted, they'd both had a hard time, but everything had all come out right in the end. He chuckled to himself. *So to speak.*

Chiara turned to look at him. "What? Tell me what amuses you so much."

"Just the expression 'everything came out all right.' I was thinking of Ali, Teresa, and their babies. The babies literally came out right."

"In Italian, we say, '*a posto*,' which means 'in its place.' Everything came out in its place."

He tugged on a loose curl of hair. "Good to know."

She sat up. "I wish one of the movie locations was in Italy."

The plan was to travel with David, Maddie, Teresa, Liam, and baby Claire to help Teresa out with childcare and distract David from Maddie's screen encounters with other men. Liam and Maddie were currently in L.A. doing hair and makeup tests and costume fittings. Maddie was taking a crash course in martial arts. Liam, who needed only a refresher course, was commuting back to Seattle as often as possible.

"Do you miss your family in Florence?"

She gave a brisk wave of denial. "Hardly. But I'd like to see other parts of Italy with you. We didn't travel when I was a child."

"How about when the movie is over, we tour the Lake Region."

She clapped her hands. "Oh! I'd love to visit *Lago* Maggiore."

He nodded. "And Lake Como. I'll figure it out. We'll have to plan now if we want to reserve rooms at the most desirable hotels."

"I wish we could cheer Edward up. He is so down in the dumps," Chiara said, savoring the recently acquired idiom.

Jake kissed her neck. "What makes it worse is that the rest of us are so happy. What great luck that Nancy's mother turned out to be this totally lovable sweetheart who was willing to drop everything and move here to help with childcare. And then, after George left the film for another project, Rosey Cleveland agreed to do the movie."

"Isn't he just as much of a threat as George? He's a beautiful man, even prettier than Denzel Washington."

"According to Jeremy, he's gay. Can you believe it? I never would have guessed. No need for jealousy there."

"Did George tell you what movie he's doing in place of *Kapow*?"

"As a matter of fact, he called this morning. It's a period piece, turn of the century. The story of a landscape painter who dies young. Many of his works end up in major museums, only they are attributed to several different people, some of whom never existed. No one realizes they were all painted by one tubercular shut-in. Until a ghost whisperer finds a way to set the record straight."

Chiara clapped a hand over her mouth. "Simon Elliot!"

Jake laughed. "Can you believe it? Somehow *he* found a way into George's head. Not that George minds. He says Rory was an entertaining companion, but Simon is helping him expand his horizons in ways he never dreamed possible. Plus, our ghost gets to live vicariously through George. Knowing George, Simon is getting quite the sentimental education."

Chiara giggled. "I hope he has more fun than Flaubert's characters."

"Simon is finally getting the recognition that eluded him in life," Jake said, "ever since Teresa and I managed to get those art experts to investigate the painting in the Musée d'Orsay attributed to P. Day Moray."

"Do you know if Reynard agreed to include his pieces in the special exhibit at the Frye?" Chiara asked.

"Why wouldn't he? He must have been thrilled to find out they're worth more than he realized."

Chiara rubbed her hands together. "It's so neat that David convinced the director it's better for the plot of *Kapow* if Ailani's desire for Lorelei is unrequited. Now David doesn't have so much to fret over."

"Only Liam, and we know he would never betray Teresa."

Chiara squeezed his hand. "And then there's Joe. Not only does he have a beautiful new son, but everyone believes that his brain child, 'Love's Death Rattle,' will win Best Country Song on February twenty-third. Even if that doesn't happen …."

Jake made a face. "It means he'll be touring again."

"There is a downside to every high," Chiara said.

He laughed at her use of the idiom. "You mean '*un aspetto negativo*'?" "*Certo.*"

"I see no downside to you and Ali finishing *Salish Sea Stories*."

She smirked. "Tell that to Lorenzo. He's already clamoring for more. We'd rather do a sequel to *The Way to Moss Manor*."

"Especially now that it's reached the *New York Times* best-seller list."

She scowled. "Meaning that the publisher wants Ali and me to do a book-signing tour."

He touched her frown lines. "Always a downside. No matter, they can't guilt Ali into a tour as long as baby Brian is breastfeeding. And you know us, we'll find a way to make it fun."

With a sly smile, she unbuttoned his shirt. "We always do."

* * *

For the past month and a half, given that Edward was the only human knocking around the compound, his best friends had been the dogs, Harry and Coogan. Not that they weren't grateful for his attention. With everyone off having babies and preparing to make movies, he was living like a hermit—a hermit with a really fabulous cave. Jake and Chiara, back to living in the shockingly violet Italianate Victorian mansion that now belonged to them, included him in their activities whenever possible. Mostly day hikes and dinners at their place. Jake was paying Tiger to teach him what he'd learned from Jean-Louis, though Jake confessed that he'd have enjoyed Jean-Louis's company more. Other than cooking, Tiger had one obsession—videogames.

Edward was cooking and cleaning for himself, as he had most of his adult life, not really caring what he ate. He tended to make large vats of soup or stew or chili and then eat the same dinner every night until they were gone. He spent too much time exercising in the freestanding gym and watching movies, often both at the same time. Liam had stocked the library with Ian Fleming novels, and they passed the time, sexist and improbable as they were. Jake would never have overlooked so many glaring plot holes, and the female characters were utterly forgettable.

After the initial shitstorm of salacious tabloid articles ran out of excrement, another front came in, fed by revelations that the O'Connell matriarch was involved with her Algerian manservant. Ali and Liam's heritage had also made the news, though with Sheila now part of the family, it was hardly a secret. Word had spread around the FOSSP crew, the source being, apparently, Angie. Angie had confessed to being friends with Xenia, who had been keeping her up to date on her travels. Unaware of her friend's agenda, Angie had reciprocated. Enough said.

The original tone of the articles was smug and self-righteous, as if the O'Connells somehow deserved this egregious violation of their privacy. Edward now understood that his mother's fears of scandal centered on the need to guard her own secrets. After all, Edward's fall from grace attested to his own high standards, Lisette's sins were those of youth, and Ali and Liam could hardly be accused of hiding a heritage they knew nothing about. By February first, the gossip rags found new targets, and in the end, none of their worst fears had been realized. Carrie and Rostand decided to marry and dedicate themselves to a charity for refugees fleeing Algeria's long, painful civil war.

The rest of them were flying high, though Edward still waded through a gray miasma of pain and loss. That was when he received the call from Joe that changed everything. An editor from a major publishing house had contacted Linc, who had asked Joe to set up a meeting with Edward. Having nothing better to do, Edward agreed. The editor was an attractive East-Indian woman of roughly forty whose empathy immediately endeared her to Edward.

"What we've heard of your and Lisette's ordeals is fascinating," Lakshmi told him when they met at Kelpies for lunch. "Of course, it didn't hurt that you and she are so beautiful and publicity shy. The more we looked into it, the more we were convinced that you could write a compelling memoir of your journey. You and Lisette, together. It would be a joint effort, culminating in the most recent tabloid stories."

"I'm afraid there is no 'me and Lisette,' " Edward admitted. "Those stories effectively destroyed our relationship."

Lakshmi leaned forward to look him straight in the eye. As if sensing his suspicions, she flashed a wedding ring. "Mr. O'Connell, you are one of the handsomest men I've ever met, but rest assured, I'm a professional and happily married. Whether or not Lisette collaborates on this project, we are interested. And when it is published, you would have a platform to advocate for Church reform."

Though tempted to refuse her outright, Edward said he'd think about it.

He had no wish to make further waves in the Church. Still, writing it all down might help him come to terms with the last several years.

"If you want to embark on this project," she continued, "you would need to resist the urge to censor yourself. There's little point in writing a memoir if you keep the most painful parts to yourself. Would that be too difficult, given your family's reputation?"

That eked a laugh out of him. "What reputation? It's safe to say that is pretty much in shreds."

"Not at all," she said without cracking a smile. "What has anyone done that's so terrible? Nothing, when it comes right down to it. Your mother is perhaps the worst sinner in the eyes of the public, but by marrying her, uh, butler and devoting herself to charities benefiting his country of origin, she has more than redeemed herself."

Since then, Edward had begun to write, finding comfort in the process. "Next, you'll be going to therapy," he said aloud, causing Coogan and Harry to look up. They'd been stretched out at his feet as he sat on the couch in the Sea Captain's House parlor. "Not you," he told them. "*You* don't need therapy. You are therapeutic."

They wagged their tails joyfully.

Edward had no idea why he had agreed to accompany Jake and Chiara to Valentine's Day dinner at La Fête Sauvage. Not a holiday he wished to celebrate. Never had been, come to think of it. Jake and Chiara were celebrating her divorce being finalized and trying to convince him to come along on the great adventure tour that was *Kapow*.

"We are going to be camp followers," Chiara said happily.

"I think you mean part of their entourage," Jake said with a chuckle. "The term 'camp followers' has some other, uh, darker connotations. As in women of ill repute following the army to battle."

Chiara rolled her eyes. "You don't always have to correct me." To Edward, she said, "After the cast and crew return to the United States, Jake and I will travel to Italy's Lake Region. We would love it if you came along. Bring a friend if you like."

"Who do you suggest?" Edward asked. "My only friends at the moment are of the canine variety."

The two of them peered over his shoulder, their smiles smug.

When he turned to look, his face went slack. It was Lisette, dressed in chef's whites. She appeared as startled as he, and both stood frozen in place for a long moment.

"Uh, Edward, people are staring," Jake said. "Why don't you and Lisette move to that 'reserved' table over in the corner?"

Edward wanted to strangle his brother. Also to kiss him. Jean-Louis himself emerged from the kitchen to seat Lisette. "I am sorry, 'Louise,' for bringing you here under false pretenses. *Faque là*, I will take over for you." He winked at Edward before returning to the kitchen.

Edward wanted to announce, "Nothing to see here, folks!" There was a lot of whispering. Clearly some people knew the story. Lisette was chalk white.

He leaned over and said in a low voice, "If we try to carry on a natural conversation, they will forget we're here."

The waiter, one of the FOSSP crew, put a bottle of red wine on the table. Edward examined the label. "Jean-Louis, you shouldn't have," he said in a soft voice.

The waiter uncorked the bottle and filled their glasses. They had both already had dinner and neither was interested in dessert. The wine was treat enough.

"They aren't going to forget we're here," she said, stealing surreptitious glances at their fellow diners. "But if I keep drinking this, *I* will forget. That they're here, I mean."

"Good. Carry on. If we don't finish this bottle off, Jean-Louis will take it personally. Why did he call you 'Louise'?"

"That's what I've been calling myself. Louise Smith."

He tried it out. "Louise. Nope. You're definitely a Lisette."

She laughed. "I'm with you. Louise sounds like a timid little mouse. She definitely doesn't have a sex life."

"Where have you been?" he asked as if they were old friends catching up after a vacation.

"Living with Becca and Jean-Louis in North Bend. Don't be angry. I swore them to secrecy. After I left Port Townsend, I ran into them on the ferry, and I was in no fit state to make rational decisions. I've been subbing at the Bellevue and North Bend locations of La Fête Sauvage because I didn't want to work full-time. Other than that, I would go running and hang out with Becca whenever she was free. We'd walk, shop, and go to the movies. They've both been wonderful." She cleared her throat. "How have you been?"

"Miserable." They both laughed. "But I've been writing. You know, *Memoirs of a Randy Priest*."

She grimaced. "You can't be serious."

"Not that title, obviously." He told her about the meeting with the editor.

"She wants *me* to collaborate with you?" she said, disbelieving.

"Don't you think it's time the public heard your side of the story?" Seeing her consternation, he was quick to add, "Don't decide right now."

Her expression turned bleak. "Nothing has changed."

He raised an eyebrow. "I'd say the opposite. Everything has changed."

"What about your mother?"

"Come on …. Carrie and Rostand are getting married and devoting themselves to an Algerian charity. All her concerns about scandal were about covering her own ass. She knew that having a secret affair with Rostand was shameful."

Lisette just stared at him.

"Chiara is officially divorced, and Jake bought the Victorian he'd been renting. I'm sure Becca told you that the babies, Claire and Brian, are thriving, as are their mothers. David's latest rewrite of *Kapow* includes no sex scenes for Kilo and Maddie. And after George bowed out, Rosey Cleveland agreed to play Troy Benz. Once he read the interview with Liam—a touching account of finding his black grandmother—he was all in."

Lisette looked alarmed. "He's a major heartthrob. Isn't David worried about those scenes with Maddie?"

Edward chuckled. "We have it on good authority that he's gay. Jeremy, you know. *He* has a juicy part in the movie too. He couldn't be more thrilled."

"So, Sheila is living with Joe and Ali?"

"They're all staying at the house on Capitol Hill while Carrie and Rostand are on their honeymoon."

"They're awfully trusting. Nancy was a lost soul. How do they know Sheila isn't the reason for that?"

Edward finished off his glass. "Trust me, they know. My damn family investigates everyone. She is sorely missed by her friends, neighbors, and church. Everyone loves her." Seeing the smile return to her face, he asked, "What?"

"Conor Fitzgerald was my great-uncle."

"Huh?" She couldn't be talking about Sheila's dead husband.

"My mother's uncle, disowned by the family because he married a black woman. That makes Liam and Ali first cousins, once removed."

Edward couldn't believe his ears. That explained Liam's connection with Lisette. He couldn't wait to tell him. Well, he *could* wait. Because right now he had only one thing on his mind.

"I'm alone at the compound," he said.

"You expect me to follow you, just like that?" She snapped her fingers.

"I expect you to marry me. To marry me and come on the *Kapow* tour, starting with Bangkok. After filming is finished, we'll go where the wind takes us."

"What about the memoir?"

"We can write that anywhere."

Her fingers touched his across the table. "We'll have to take your car. Mine is in North Bend."

EPILOGUE

Joe was basking in the sun in a mesh chaise longue while Ali sat in one of the Adirondack chairs, nursing Brian. *It doesn't get much better than this,* he thought. They were hanging out in the courtyard of his childhood home, a half-timbered Tudor mansion on Capitol Hill, enjoying an unusually mild and sunny March day. In normally gray Seattle, it was sixty-five degrees, with only a few puffy clouds on the horizon. By his side was the beautiful mother of his beautiful children. He loved her to distraction.

"When can we go home?" Ali asked, gazing fondly at baby Brian, who suckled contentedly at her breast.

"You're not enjoying Seattle without Carrie? This place is pretty darn luxurious when our scolding mother isn't in residence."

"I miss Port Townsend. The ocean. The mossy forests. And of course, the dogs."

With the twelve-foot-high privacy hedge, they were safely enclosed, and the rest of the world was shut out—in this case, the residents of the other mansions, many of which remained unoccupied while their owners were away in their winter homes in the desert, tropics, or ski resorts.

The garden was coming to life, with crocuses and daffodils and a Japanese cherry tree covered with candy-like hot-pink blossoms. The fountain, with its Romanesque cherubs and fish, almost made Joe regret that they'd be missing the *Kapow* tour.

"The twins are looking more and more like Carrie's stone cherubs," Ali remarked.

"Only ten times more mischievous. Their little brother is going to have a hard time keeping up." He reached over and touched the tiny hand with his finger, which the baby grabbed. Then he smiled up at his daddy and gurgled.

That gummy smile robbed Joe of fifty points of IQ. "Who do you look like?" he said in his silliest baby voice.

"Like you, you goofball," Ali said. "Look at those hazel eyes and curly brown hair." She handed him to Joe, who cradled the baby against his broad chest, where he appeared impossibly small.

"All babies look like their fathers at first," Joe said. "Even the ones who aren't related. It's a survival mechanism."

Ali laughed. "There you go, getting all gooey and sentimental again."

The twins had picked up steam and were running wild, emitting high-pitched screams of excitement as they collided like human bumper cars, tumbled to the soft green grass, and rolled to their feet to do it again. *Or tumbleweeds*, Joe thought. They were closely monitored by May, Susan, and Sheila, who were all needed to keep them corralled.

He watched Teresa cross the lawn with baby Claire in her arms. With her sooty black hair and dark-blue eyes, Claire resembled Ali more than his sister. The twins, who weren't yet two, were still fixated on the concept of "mine." As if to echo his thoughts, Caryn plopped down on her bottom and started to cry, Josie having grabbed her favorite stuffed giraffe. "Mine!" she cried out, wailing at the injustice in the world.

Sheila scooped her up and rocked her, muttering soothing endearments. It did his heart good to see that sweet woman pour her love into this child. You couldn't ask for a more doting grandmother.

"That will be Claire in a couple of years," Ali told Teresa, whose brow was furrowed in dismay. The baby girl appeared unruffled by her cousin's temper tantrum.

"My child is a little angel," Teresa said as Claire nuzzled her breast in search of a nipple.

"Satan was an angel once. Just sayin'," Joe said.

Teresa stared him down with mock reproof.

"When do you all leave for Bangkok?" Ali asked. "Have they given Liam a date to be on set?"

"Filming is slated to begin on April tenth, but we'll see. Liam and I will fly separately because he doesn't know his schedule from day to day."

Sheila had volunteered to accompany Teresa and Liam on the trip so that they wouldn't have to look for additional childcare with everything else going on. They'd paid off the mortgage on her house in Yakima but told her she was welcome to stay with them indefinitely.

Joe surrendered to a jaw-cracking yawn. On top of helping with childcare, he'd been assembling a crew of Seattle musicians—along with Matthew—in anticipation of a late-summer tour to promote his new album, *No-No Love*.

"What are the *exact* dates of the tour?" Ali asked.

He heard the weariness in her voice and wished life weren't so complicated. "The last one wasn't so bad, right? It's like that again, Thursday through Sunday over a five-week period from late July till the end of August. So … starting July twenty-third and ending August thirtieth." When Ali didn't comment, he pleaded, "Why don't you join me for the whole tour this time? We can all go—the kids, May and Susan, Sheila too, if she likes. It'll be exciting."

Eyes on her sleeping son, Ali said, "It would be a shame to miss the peak weather in Port Townsend. But I do *so* love seeing you perform."

Brian began to squirm and fuss. "Hungry again," Joe said, putting the baby back in her arms.

The boy immediately latched onto her breast. Joe loved seeing her like this. Was it normal to get a hard-on from watching your wife breastfeed?

"I'll tell you what," Ali said. "You choose two weekends, not consecutive ones. I don't want to tire you out when you need all your energy for performing and keeping your voice in shape. Six weeks isn't so long."

She's thinking about the next tour, and the next one after that, he thought.

"This is my last tour," he assured her.

Teresa snorted in disbelief and Ali kicked him with her tennis shoe. "Don't make promises you can't keep," his sweet wife told him. "Besides, I *do* want to be part of your entourage when the children are older." Kissing Brian's head, she said, "Look, he's asleep again. Shall we put him down together? Teresa, do you think anyone would mind?"

"We'll hold down the fort," Teresa said in the low, twangy voice of a Texas lawman.

Joe gave her a doubletake as Ali carried the baby toward the bedroom. "Liam's been forcing you to watch those Clint Eastwood Westerns again, I gather."

"I reckon so."

"Great, another actor in the family."

"I'll keep my day job," Teresa stared down at Claire, "which, for the moment, seems to involve raising a miniature Ali. I see nothing of myself in this child."

Joe had to admit that right now the resemblance to Ali was striking. He stood and touched Teresa's shoulder. "Patience. I agree with you as to the hair and maybe the eyes, but other than that, it's impossible to know what she will look like at this early stage."

Teresa fluttered her fingers in the direction of the sliding French doors. "You're wasting precious alone-time with your wife. Git along little dogies!"

"And a 'whoopie ti yi yo' to you too," Joe said as he headed to the house. At the back door, he called out, "Claire could do worse than look like Ali."

As soon as Ali had set Brian down in the crib, Joe gathered her in his arms. She was such a sensual woman, his wife, still as eager for him as he was for her. Knowing the baby could wake any moment, he whispered, "Do you mind if I skip a few preliminaries?"

She whispered back, "Have at it, you sweet talker, you."

Afterward, as they spooned on the bed, he said, "It's a good thing Brian is a sound sleeper. I'm sorry about the quickie."

She rolled onto her back and folded her arms behind her head, her dress still hiked up to provide a tantalizing view of a long, shapely leg. "You'll get no complaints from me."

"The first time I saw you," he said in his most seductive voice, "I couldn't believe my luck. I thought I'd conjured you up. You were sweet and vulnerable and so goddamned beautiful." His fingers crept up her thigh. "Do you know how hard … how difficult it was to keep my hands off you?"

She took the wandering hand and placed it on her breast. "Was I worth the wait?"

He grinned. "No other woman could do *this* to me." He put her hand where he wanted it.

She gave a theatrical gasp. "*Already*? I thought old married men—"

"Hey!"

"Someone has to keep your ego in check." She ran a finger along his lower lip. "These are the lips that launched a thousand ships," she said, making him smile, "and the smile that sets millions of hearts aflutter."

"It was a face that launched ships. And there's only one heart I'm interested in."

"It's definitely fluttering. See?"

He obliged her by feeling for her heartbeat.

"What if we'd never met?" she said.

"I'd be a lost and lonely guy, his life a tragic lie."

It was a lyric from one of his songs in progress, but he meant every word. He was still tinkering with it. "A run of bad luck, you're sure it won't end, but it might not suck, if you know how to bend." Or "With one good fuck, love is just 'round the bend"? With country music, no f-words. "Climb out of the muck, and you'll be on the mend"? *Yuck*. Back to the drawing board.

She rolled on top of him. "That's a funny smile. What are you thinking?"

"Oh, you know me, a few lyrics just came into my head."

"Inspired by me?"

"Always. The happy ones, anyway."

* * *

Liam sighed involuntarily as he let himself into the hotel suite. *Home is where the heart is*, he reflected. Love and marriage had turned him into a cliché-spouting, sentimental fool. *God knows my heart is with Teresa, wherever she is*, he thought.

He'd spent the last few days racing back and forth along the same section of the Chatuchak Weekend Market, sweating buckets, feeling like a poached salmon. They'd cordoned off a narrow portion and enlisted as extras the people who ran the sales booths along with their friends and families. Most of them understood not to treat the actors and crew as celebrities. That didn't stop the gawkers and tourists from trying to breach the boundaries.

They homed in on Kilo, who had quite a following in Thailand. Liam laughed as he saw the man's dismay at being treated like a prize they'd rather squash than share. After his T-shirt was torn off, he'd been assigned two bodyguards. Liam didn't have much call to interact with Kilo, but he had already decided to bury the hatchet. Kilo had wasted no time hooking up with one of "Damon's Girls." Like "Bond Women" in that franchise. Teresa mostly remained behind in their luxury hotel, which had a pool and spacious courtyard with a formal garden of topiary animals. Teresa and Sheila had become close, and so far Claire had been an easy baby, though both parents fought the usual sleep deprivation that came with night feedings. Teresa bore the brunt of that, but sometimes Liam couldn't get back to sleep. He caught cat naps on the set, but mostly sheer adrenaline kept him bright-eyed and raring to go.

So far, movie making had been a blast, at least the action scenes. The one sex scene so far had been enlightening, though he'd never admit that to Teresa. Only he could know how little the encounter meant, but his body's response to the beautiful woman was automatic. The scene consisted of nothing but light foreplay and brief nudity, unlike what Maddie had dealt with in her first movie. No wonder George had fallen so hard for her. It was a testament to Maddie's bond with David that she hadn't gone with the flow. Unmonitored and unattached, Liam could easily have fallen into his old ways. Knowing that Teresa—the most beautiful, intriguing woman he had ever met and now the mother of his daughter—waited for him at the end of the day kept him on the straight and narrow.

They would be moving on to Paris soon, where it would be much cooler. How he missed the briny sea breezes and fresh forest smells of damp moss, live evergreens, and rotting stumps.

Teresa stirred in her sleep when she felt the bed sag with his weight. Liam pressed against her until the length of him conformed to her body, a sheen of sweat forming between them in the tropical heat that never abated, even at night. The ceiling fan rotated in a lazy rhythm above.

"It's too hot for cuddling," she complained.

"You're too hot for *just* cuddling," he replied, rubbing against her like a cat.

She giggled and relaxed into his kisses, allowing him to have his wicked way with her delicious new curves and riding the wave with him to a sweaty climax.

At the start, he'd been so determined not to give in to their mutual lust. Her family was too grand for him, made him feel like a big, ignorant oaf. His skills would have been worshipped in a clan of survivalists or a frontier family traveling by stagecoach in 1870. But her mother had fixated on his lack of formal education and humble origins. Even after they married, he'd wondered if their differences would eventually tear them apart. Until Claire arrived, and his last defenses fell away. He was convinced she would end up looking like Teresa, only with his and Ali's eyes, hair, and coloring.

"Liam?"

"Yes."

"How did it go today?"

"I think summer camp would have been like this … if I'd been allowed to go. It was a blast and a half."

"Kilo?" she whispered, her voice heartbreakingly vulnerable.

"What about him?" Liam said.

"Are you getting along?"

"We don't talk much. We have that one choreographed fight scene, and this was the first time we went through the motions with each other rather than the fight masters. It would have been so easy to accidentally mess up that pretty face." Liam chuckled, remembering the flash of fear he'd detected when the fight got too real. "Don't worry. I'm too much of a professional for that. Besides, if I damage him, that just prolongs our time here. Did you know he's screwing Serena?"

"Who's that?"

"One of 'Damon's Girls.' That will last a minute or two. She's about as deep as a spill of milk."

"What's she like?"

He hesitated. Should he lie? "Very photogenic." *Particularly her body*, he added silently. "Petite. A little vapid. She's Thai and has family here along with a huge fan club. Between her fans and Kilo's, it's a wonder we get anything done." He smoothed back the strawberry-blonde locks from her face, massaging her scalp with his fingers. "Poor Kilo."

She made a derisive sound.

"What's he gonna do?" Liam went on. "He has to console himself somehow. Try as he might, he'll never find another woman like you."

"Maddie's the one he wants now."

He thought of Lisette, who he now knew was his first cousin, once removed. He'd been so relieved to have that connection explained. Perhaps he'd recognized in her a kindred spirit, but not the romantic kind, which is why he'd resisted her advances. He remembered thinking she was like a photographic negative of Teresa, with her black hair and black Miata. He and Lisette were too much alike. Teresa was his perfect complement. *Vive la différence.*

"You think it's Maddie he wants? I don't. Deep down, you're the only one he ever really wanted, the one he married. Trust me, he looks for you in every woman who crosses his path."

"Is that what you would do?" He could tell she still didn't trust him completely. He'd have to remedy that.

He cupped her face between his hands and stared into her eyes. "Absolutely. But I'd never find her."

* * *

Oahu in May was the closest thing to heaven, David thought. That is, if you were a tropical plant … or Lorenzo. Must be his son's Italian blood. Unlike his father, Lor loved the heat. David was more a rain-forest plant, a sword fern, maybe—he liked the sword idea, anyway.

They were, at long last, in the final stretch of *Kapow*. The filming hadn't been entirely without mishaps, but damn close. They'd arrived mid-month to avoid the Japanese tourists that flocked here to take advantage of Golden Week and the Americans who swarmed the beaches Memorial Day Weekend.

Lorelei didn't appear during the Bangkok portion of the film, so they'd begun their adventure in Paris. Initially, David wanted to be on the set as much as possible. After a week of too much waiting around, he let Jake, Chiara, and especially Lorenzo, convince him to take advantage of the museums, walking tours, and cafés. Liam had requested that he keep off the set during his sex scene with Maddie. Later she insisted that their biggest issue had been fighting the giggles.

"It was just as you wrote it," Maddie told David. "Lorelei stages a little striptease for Damon while he reclines on the bed in his underwear. They filmed me from behind. Liam was told to ogle my breasts, where I'd pasted two icky faces over the nipples …. I swear, it took him ten takes before he could do it with a straight face."

David summoned an anemic "hah-hah," regretting that he'd asked for total honesty.

They'd gotten around Liam's scars by making it clear that Damon's identity was a closely guarded secret. None of the Russian spies knew what he looked like. But in future movies, he wouldn't be able to go undercover if his quarry knew anything about Damon Morehouse. Not without a lot of concealer.

Mercifully, no more sex scenes were on the schedule for Damon and Lorelei. "At least that's over with," David grumbled.

It was easy to keep busy in Oahu while Maddie was on set. David, Lorenzo, and Maddie shared a rental house with Chiara and Jake, and while Maddie was away, the four of them hung out at Kailua Beach Park, within easy walking distance and surprisingly tourist free. Lorenzo loved to snorkel and body surf.

Today was a rare day off for Maddie as the director and crew assessed what needed to be accomplished on the final two days of filming. After a morning spent on the beach, they drove ten miles to the ResortQuest Waikiki Beach Hotel for lunch.

"I've been so envious of you all," Maddie told them as they sat in the shade of an umbrella on the terrace. "I can't just run into the surf for a half hour because I might get tanned. Plus, my makeup and hair have to stay perfect." They'd given her those silly hair extensions again, which meant she'd be rocking the "Jean Seberg as Joan of Arc" look when they returned home. David noted how she only picked at her Greek salad. They probably weighed her every day to make sure she kept that starved waif look.

"Any problems with Kilo?" Jake asked. Like the rest of them, he'd ordered a burger and fries. David caught Maddie's look of longing—for the burgers, not him.

She rolled her eyes. "Now he's sleeping with Lotus. Rosey and I had a good laugh over that one. This is his third Damon Girl—unless there's one he screwed under the radar."

"Why is he sleeping with Lotus?" Lor asked. "Doesn't she get her own bed?"

They all stared at him, dismayed at having let down their guard. "Sometimes the actors get tired and take naps," David rushed to say. "Lotus doesn't mind sharing her bed."

"I think there's more to it than that," Lor insisted, wiping the grins off their faces. "I bet he buys things for her, like, like"—they held their breaths while he paused to consider—"ice cream."

Lorenzo, now five years old, was definitely going to keep them on their toes.

"If Kilo is so nice to Lotus," the boy persisted, "why don't *you* like him?"

Jake noisily cleared his throat in an effort not to laugh. "So, Lorenzo, you still enjoying *Alice's Adventures in Wonderland*?"

Lorenzo screwed up his face in concentration. "Uncle Edward is a *really* good reader. Maddie and David are quite 'competent' too." The way Lor pronounced the word showed it was new in his vocabulary, so David tried not to take the slight too much to heart. Edward and Lisette had opted to stay on in Paris rather than accompany them to Oahu.

"Maddie is an excellent Alice," David admitted. "I, on the other hand, am not quite up to snuff. I think Maddie should ask her agent about doing animated films, or maybe something with Disney."

Chiara laughed. "You mean so she won't be required to—" She abruptly cut herself off.

"Be required to do what, *Zia* Chiara?" Lorenzo asked as he snatched a French fry from her plate, having finished his own.

"Uh, do so much flying," Chiara improvised. "Flying all over the world is exhausting. Disney movies are filmed in one place. The animated ones. *Recorded* in one place, that is."

Maddie stifled a yawn. "Sorry, folks. I'm beat. We were shooting until the wee hours. I'd love a nap."

Jake and Chiara exchanged significant looks. "Why don't the two of you go to the house for a rest?" Jake said. "Chiara and I will buy Lorenzo ice cream then take him back to the beach. How does that sound, Lorenzo?"

The boy nodded enthusiastically.

Maddie had stumbled in at four in the morning and fallen into an exhausted sleep. Lor roused them only four hours later so they could join the others for breakfast.

On the short drive back, Maddie dozed, but when they arrived, she seemed to rally. The beach house, which dated back to the '20s, was large enough that Edward and Lisette could have joined them as well. The yard was dense with tropical foliage and palm trees; it even had a coconut grove. There was a large, enclosed yard. David, with his love of colonial style, appreciated all the dark-wood details, the Hawaiian koa-wood cabinets, marble, and crown molding.

Once they were inside, Maddie grabbed the front of his Hawaiian shirt and started dragging him into the bedroom. As eager as he was, his conscience bothered him. "Sweetie, you're dead tired," he protested.

"Are you kidding?" she said. While fighting another yawn, she stripped off her white jeans and T-shirt. "When will we get this chance to be completely alone again?"

"You're so tiny," he said as she urged him on top. "It's like Captain Hook ravishing Tinkerbell. I might break you."

She laughed. "Hasn't happened yet."

When it was over, more quickly than David would have liked, she closed her eyes and sighed. "Oh, how I've missed this."

It had been only a week since they'd indulged in a bout of passion, but to David too it felt like months.

"What comes next?" he said as they lay side by side.

"I thought you were going to—"

"I don't mean in the next few hours," he said.

She giggled. "I don't think I can keep this up for hours."

"Please be serious." He cupped her chin in his large paw and made her look at him. Clearly she didn't want to discuss the future.

"All right." She started absentmindedly twirling the wiry red hair on his chest. "My agent has been talking to Disney about my doing a musical live-action movie."

At least it would be G-rated, he thought, though it would keep her away from Port Townsend. He hoped they'd film it somewhere other than L.A. He really disliked that city.

"You could get more work as a script doctor if we were in Los Angeles," she said, clearly not reading his thoughts. "But we don't have to move there. It isn't so far from the Peninsula. They're on the same coast. We'll divide our time. It won't be so bad."

"Anything for you, sweetheart," he said with a subtly sarcastic edge.

She settled in next to him on the bed and sighed. "I know you'd rather reside full-time in Port Townsend. It would be better for Lorenzo, too."

No matter what challenges they faced with balancing her career with their family life, she was worth the trouble. "That's the great thing about being rich," he said. "We'll make it work." He lay on his side, facing her. "By the way, how is it having fake sex with Rosey?"

"Oh, he's great," she said. "With straight actors, there's always this weirdness, as in, he's afraid you'll freak if he gets an erection, or he doesn't want you to think he's genuinely interested in you. Rosey throws himself into it, although he told me my breasts kind of freak him out. We had a good laugh over that. With Rosey, I know it's one hundred percent make-believe, so I don't have to worry either." In her pause, David heard the unspoken words, *the way I did with George*. She went on, "I bet those will be the most convincing scenes in the movie."

No comment, David thought. He figured Maddie could make anyone at least consider bisexuality. But he let it drop while he worried over Maddie's almost ethereal fragility, which she insisted was necessary so she didn't look heavy onscreen.

"I adore you," she told him, making his heart lurch. "You will always be my magic man."

"You're the magical one," he said.

You'll make the perfect Disney princess, he thought as he watched her sleep. He was no prince. Score one for Huntsman!

* * *

Lisette sat on the terrace of Les Deux Magots, sipping her espresso and watching the world go by. It was a sunny but cool day in May, and the tourists hadn't yet descended en masse. It was such a strange feeling to have no worries. Chef Marky and his wife had taken over Café Lisette while keeping the name. They insisted the publicity hadn't hurt them one iota. Quite the opposite. In fact, if she ever chose to come back, a fan club awaited.

The waiter asked if she'd like another espresso. "Thanks but not yet," she told him in French. "My fiancé will arrive momentarily."

"But of course, madam," he said in English.

Stubbornly sticking to French, she said, "It's a pity, *monsieur*, that you won't indulge me by speaking in your own language. Am I so difficult to understand?"

He seemed at a loss as to how to respond, and she scolded herself for ruffling his feathers. "*Pas de tout, madame*," he said, blushing, and made a swift retreat. Was there a secret pact among all Parisians in the hospitality industry to discourage Americans from speaking French? It seemed so.

Lisette watched a smartly dressed older man with slicked-back gray hair pass by, his dog trotting by his side as if tethered by an invisible leash. The dog paused to do its business and the man made no effort to clean it up. You had to watch your step when strolling in Paris.

Her heart leapt at the sight of Edward, who strode confidently down the sidewalk, waving when he saw her too. A head taller than any of the men around him and twice as handsome, he was impossible to miss. His passionate kiss, which included an old-Hollywood-style dip, drew the amused attention and twitters of the other diners, who didn't even pretend to avert their eyes. They might be snobs when it came to their language, but the French appreciated an enthusiastic public display of affection.

"We're America's best emissaries," she said after they took their seats.

He looked up from the menu. "Oh?"

"The French think Americans are lousy lovers. But that kiss …." She fanned herself with her menu. "I'm the envy of the café—make that the entire *arrondissement*."

"We could do it again." He lunged as if to grab her, but she giggled and held up the menu as a shield.

"Let's wait until we're alone, shall we?"

"Oh, all right," he said in mock exasperation, as if she'd spoiled his fun. He signaled the waiter and ordered a carafe of white house wine and a Croque-Monsieur. "I'm starving. Did you eat already?"

"No. I'll have the steak tartare," she told the waiter in French.

"*Oui, madame.*"

Edward raised his eyebrows. "You see? Not every Parisian refuses to speak French with you."

"I had to shame him into it."

"Oh, damn."

They laughed as the waiter poured the wine, glad he wasn't aware the joke was on him.

After the food was served and they began to eat, Edward leaned forward and said, "You'll never guess who I ran into."

She put a bite of meat in her mouth and chewed slowly, murmuring her appreciation. "I can't guess. Tell me."

"Xenia."

The bite went down wrong, and she started to cough. After she'd recovered enough to speak, she said, "No! She must have ditched Reynard when he brought her here at Christmas. No wonder he was so apologetic."

"*What*?"

She cringed. "I guess I never told you that story."

"You've seen him? When?"

Hearing the jealousy in his voice, she rushed to explain, "No, no. I didn't *see* him. He left a message on the café's answering machine saying he regretted the tabloid stories and had nothing to do with them. That was all."

Edward breathed easier. "I can't tell you how sorry I am for that. If I'd handled Xenia better, she might not have turned on us so viciously."

Lisette took a long sip of wine. "Mailing me your underwear was a truly low blow."

"She *what*?"

"I guess I didn't mention that part, either. Of course, later, when I wasn't feeling quite so insecure, I realized that her having them in her possession didn't prove anything."

He groaned and smacked his forehead in frustration. "They were sitting on the chair, and she surreptitiously grabbed them as she left the cabin. Fagin and his crew of pickpockets would have been impressed. I told David about the underwear the day after the incident. I was afraid she planned to make mischief. I can assure you—"

She waved him away. "No need. I believe you. So, Xenia …. How did she look? Does she appear to be thriving?"

"She appears to be acclimating, and she still has the Givenchy boots, meaning she hasn't had to sell them. If I didn't know better, I might mistake her for a Parisian. She wore a miniskirt, tights, and a low-necked T-shirt, and her hair was styled in elaborate ringlets pinned back with butterfly barrettes. Perhaps she's modeling for art classes or shacking up with an artist or musician. She has that look. Aggressively original and happy-go-lucky. As if she envisions herself as starring in the remake of *An American in Paris*. Until she saw me, that is."

Lisette frowned. "I'm not enjoying this story."

"We locked eyes, that's all. There was recognition but no greeting. Her expression could only be described as 'thunderous.' I pity the man who's taken up with her."

"Me too."

After they finished their meals and Edward paid the check, she asked, "Where to? Shall we jog in the Botanical Gardens? It's a gorgeous day. *Pas un nuage*."

"Yes, let's."

"Were you able to reach David or Jake in Oahu?" she asked.

"Yep. Kilo is involved with yet another Damon Girl. His third—that they know of. His flings seem to keep him occupied and out of Maddie's hair. Maddie and Rosey are best buds."

Lisette giggled. "Rosey … buds …."

Edward waggled his eyebrows. "Speaking of rosy buds, we might have to postpone that jog." He helped her to her feet and swung her in a circle, making the skirt of her polka-dot A-line dress twirl. "I love that outfit. You look so … Julia Roberts in that polo match in *Pretty Woman*."

Her eyes widened. "*Pretty Woman*. Weren't you a priest when that movie came out?"

"I was in divinity school, but I didn't see it in the theater. After you left, I watched nearly every videocassette in the library. And I helped myself to a good portion of Joe's wine cellar. It wasn't pretty."

As they walked back to their hotel, holding hands, she touched the emerald earrings to confirm they were still there. She understood that sometimes he touched her for the same reason. She wasn't going anywhere. She had an engagement ring to match the earrings.

"I have other news," Edward said, solemn enough that she pulled him out of the foot traffic to wait for an explanation. "The pope has given his okay for me to make love to you."

She wanted to punch him for scaring her like that. She wiped her brow with the back of her hand. "Phew! That's a relief." She wondered where he was going with this. He couldn't be serious.

"No, I mean it. I've been granted dispensation from my vow of celibacy."

She could see how much this news meant to him, even though she, personally, hadn't lost any sleep over his celibacy vow. She supposed that despite his protestations, a part of him wanted approval from the Church to move on with his life. To leave the priesthood in the most final sense.

"Darling!" She gave him a huge hug. "I thought that never happened."

"What with all the sex scandals, these dispensations aren't as rare as they once were … and my friend and mentor, Bishop Paul, pulled some strings." He moved in for a tender kiss. "We could get married in the Church now, if that's what you want. After all, 'seasoned' as we are, neither of us has ever been married."

She laughed. "Ah, that's the Church for you. Only the people courageous enough to marry are punished for it when it doesn't work out. But no thanks. I'd hate to disappoint Jean-Louis."

Edward rolled his eyes. "Okay, he can officiate. I believe in the Universal

Life Church as much as I do the Catholic Church at this point. Perhaps we can have a double wedding with Carrie and Rostand."

"I hope you're kidding."

"Yes, definitely. How about Las Vegas?"

"You *are* in a hurry."

"Not enough to brave Las Vegas. Although they probably have a version of Paris there. It's a weird city that way."

He indicated the cobblestoned, ivy-draped courtyard of their boutique hotel, the Relais Christine, where they now stood, their admiring gaze taking in the elegant exterior. The stately mansion had been built in the sixteenth century. Inside, vaulted ceilings and stone walls hearkened back to its origins as a thirteenth-century monastery.

"*My* Paris was never like this," Lisette said as they passed through the lobby, with its white bas-relief walls and plush velvet and damask furniture.

The arm encircling her waist drew her in tighter. "Darling, this is your Paris now. From now on, the sky's the limit."

He spoke in French. What better way to tell her he would do anything to make her happy?

"Are you willing to fight for my right to speak French in Paris?" she asked, also in French, nuzzling his chest.

"As long as you don't mind bailing me out of jail from time to time."

"Awww," she said in English. "You say the sweetest things."

AUTHOR'S NOTE

I was raised Episcopalian, which I understood to be "Catholic Lite," though the version my father favored was high church, with all the bells and smells and a desperate attachment to the old traditions. (King James version of the Bible only, please!) As an adult, I would never have attended church, except that I was hired as the alto section leader in an Episcopalian choir for a time. The services were too long, but I liked the meditative aspect of sitting through the ritual, and I loved the music. Someone I knew converted to Catholicism, and my understanding was that only the vow of celibacy kept him from becoming a priest.

I am hard on religion in this series, especially Catholicism. At times, religion brought me comfort, and I haven't totally let go of the hope that there is a being up there and some type of existence after death. My motto is, "Whatever brings you comfort."

Like everyone else my age, I devoured Colleen McCullough's *The Thorn Birds* and watched the miniseries. But, spoiler alert, it does not end happily, as I gather it doesn't for most Catholic priests. When I wrote *The Silent Woodsman*, I intended it to be a standalone. But as I described Liam and the O'Connell family, their fates began to unfold before me, and they kept on unfolding.

There is no end of online research into the scandals of the Catholic Church, both financial and sexual. But my main source was Paul E. Dinter's excellent memoir, *The Other Side of the Altar: One Man's Life in the Catholic Priesthood*. Though Mr. Dinter is about ten years older than Edward, he leaves the Church about the same time. After finishing it, I couldn't help shaking my head at the politics that would prevent an intelligent, compassionate, and hardworking man like Mr. Dinter from rising in the ranks. Also the many sexual and financial shenanigans and abominations he observes among his fellow priests in his long career. He makes a compelling case for allowing priests to marry.

If this book is your introduction to the series, please know that my version of Port Townsend is not strictly accurate, especially the O'Connell Compound. With its size, view, and beach access, it could only exist in Sequim. And, I believe, there are no Italianate Victorians in Port Townsend.

I hope you've enjoyed the books in this series as much as I've enjoyed writing them. Maybe someday you'll find out how the next generation of O'Connells fares. And perhaps George, Reynard, or even Kilo will get a chance to redeem themselves. I'm kind of fond of those rascals, even if guys like that usually dedicate their lives to making women miserable.

I would be so grateful if you'd help me get the word out by taking a moment to leave reviews on Amazon, Goodreads, and Barnes and Noble.

To learn more, go to my website, www.CatTreadgold.com.

Photo by Claudia Meyer-Newman

CAT TREADGOLD HAS BEEN A publisher and editor, a classical singer, an Equity actress, a coordinator in Newsweek's External Relations Department, a secretary at Siemens AG, a voice teacher at Shoreline Community College, a receptionist at a major recording studio, a cater-waiter with Glorious Foods, a restaurant hostess, and a coat-check girl at a fancy New York nightclub.

Cat has an AB *cum laude* in German Literature from Princeton University, a Master of Music in Vocal Performance from the University of Washington, and a certificate in Technical Writing and Editing from the University of Washington.

She was once semi-fluent in French, German, and Italian and occasionally attempts to revive those languages.

Thank goodness she's good with computers (for a digital immigrant) and learned to touch type in high school.

Two of her unpublished novels made it to the finals in their categories (mystery and romance) in the Pacific Northwest Writers Association Annual Contest.

Three of her one-hour adaptations of operas (original translations and dialogue) were performed by Shoreline students while she was a teacher there.

She and her husband Jeff reside in Washington during its drier months and Arizona during its cooler ones.

Cat loves to hike and walk, ride her bike, hula hoop, golf, listen to audiobooks, cook dishes with lots of leftovers, play piano (she used to be good at it), and play accordion (she will never be good at it). She sings in the occasional concert with Ladies Musical Club, but never in the shower. Her favorite classical composers are Ravel, Debussy, and Brahms. She prefers pop music from the '60s and '70s, particularly Steely Dan and the Rolling Stones.

One hot, humid summer in Ohio, while playing a Shawnee Indian in an outdoor drama during the week and Anne in the musical *Shenandoah* on the weekends, she became certified in stage fighting. That skill later helped her win the role of a broadsword-wielding Maid Marian in a Theater for Young Audiences musical titled *Maid Marian (and Robin Too)*. She always wanted to sing the role of *Carmen*, but only did it in Seattle Opera previews. She has played Edwin Drood in *The Mystery of Edwin Drood*, Maria in *The Sound of Music*, Julie Jordan in *Carousel*, Cherubino in *The Marriage of Figaro*, Prince Orlofsky in *Die Fledermaus*, Maddalena in *Rigoletto*, Julius Caesar in *Julius Caesar in Egypt*, and Rosina in *The Barber of Seville*. Along with other fun gigs (a few at Port Townsend's UpStage), her opera quartet, the Operatic Four Players, performed most Friday nights for about a year at an Italian restaurant. For three years, she toured with NOISE (Northwest Opera in Schools Etcetera).

Videos of her vocal performances can be found on the Cattread Channel on YouTube. Go to the CatTreadgold Channel for Trailers and videos.